Lost in the Arctic

Explorations On the Edge

Lost in The Arctic

Explorations On the Edge

Lawrence Millman

Series Editor, Clint Willis

Thunder's Mouth Press
New York

adrenaline classics ®

Published by
Thunder's Mouth Press
An Imprint of Avalon Publishing Group Incorporated
161 William Street, 16th Floor
New York, NY 10038

Library of Congress Cataloging-in-Publication Data is available.

ISBN: 1-56025-411-4

Book design: Michael Walters and Sue Canavan

Printed in the United States of America

Distributed by Publishers Group West

Contents

Introduction

Lawrence Millman has said that a writer's first responsibility is to be the loser's advocate; to celebrate the outcast, the forlorn, the forgotten. I prefer to say that a writer's first responsibility is to engage his experience and try to tell the truth about it. We're probably both wrong. Maybe a writer's first responsibility is to be amusing—no, make that wildly entertaining.

It doesn't matter: Millman fills the bill on all counts. He is compassionate, interested and honest; at moments he is flat-out hilarious.

Anyone with the courage and interest to look the world in the face is bound to find it engaging and sad and funny. Not everyone can manage to pull off this trick of clarity on a consistent basis. That's because it's not a trick, really; it's hard work.

Millman's hard work often involves traveling to ridiculously remote places (Utshimassits, Labrador; Micronesia's Yap islands; Iceland's East Fjords) or investigating extraordinarily eccentric people (forgotten explorers, Inuit storytellers, mushroom hunters, Irish tinkers). His subjects are the kinds of places and people that somehow (often as a matter of sheer neglect) have managed to remain authentically themselves—have evaded the steamrollers of commerce.

Some of those people can be described as ignored or forgotten, and some are indeed forlorn. But what matters most is that they are interesting—often precisely because they have been overlooked by the world of growth, of packaging, which so far has neglected to buy or sell them. Thus, Millman's Yap islanders, Ecuadorian peasants, Arctic murderers and drunken self-appointed bards have at least a chance to remain whatever they have always been: ugly, beautiful, failed, violent, glorious or any of those things.

Like many rebels, Millman admires behavior that many people might find offensive. His interest in the marginal, which informs his essays, travel writing, criticism and stories, stems from the simple but profound fact that he doesn't want to be bored—with the result that he does not bore his readers.

Millman does not engage in self-indulgent literary experiments; his experiments are so restrained or so successful as to be invisible. The collection's three works of fiction ("The Great Winter", "Mingulay" and "The Preserved Woman") are populated by characters who are quirky, eccentric and downright strange; in all of this, however, the characters are as authentic as the people he encounters in his travels in the world's farthest reaches—or hanging around Walden Pond, for that matter.

Millman rarely idealizes a person or place (least of all when the person under scrutiny is Millman). When he does, he is delighted to be brought up short. Waiting out difficult weather in a cove on the northern part of the Canadian Arctic's remote Melville Peninsula, Millman and his guides (Qungujuq and Zacharias) encounter walrus hunters from Iglulik; one of these worthies informs Millman that the wind will die during the night. Millman, impressed, wonders from what signs this Child of Nature has derived his forecast; turns out the guy heard it on the radio.

Millman in fact often is brought up short by his experience, his expectations falling short of the reality he encounters. Meanwhile, his encounters also remind us that life may be nothing but a series of disappointments—but that these misadventures, if we live them fully, are far more interesting than anything we could have arranged or even expected ourselves.

All of which helps to explain why reading Millman is such a treat; why Annie Dilliard once called him one of America's best-kept literary secrets; why Paul Theroux is a fan; why Larry McMurtry refers to his writing as "finer than anything one has a right to expect", and why Millman's fans constitute the kind of club any reasonable reader would wish to join. Millman dodges the familiar and the tedious; he courts the odd, the difficult and even the frightening. Cannibals interest him; excessive drinking interests him; failure fascinates him; poverty interests him; violence interests him; fear interests him; death interests him.

And yet his sensibility is not perverse. Courtesy interests him; so do kindness and generosity, beauty and courage—all qualities he cultivates in his work. The courtesy and sincerity of his writing is evident in the clarity of his prose; he works hard to convey his experience and his understanding, and he succeeds.

And did I mention that he's funny?

—CLINT WILLIS
SERIES EDITOR, ADRENALINE BOOKS

Lost in the Arctic

In the Canadian Arctic, ice is the final arbiter of human affairs. From Sanirajak on Melville Peninsula, I'd planned to travel by boat across Foxe Basin to Prince Charles Island, an uninhabited, virtually unknown chunk of land almost as large as the state of Connecticut. But Foxe Basin turned out to be choked with sea-ice, so I was stuck in Sanirajak, an Inuit hunting community, until a gale came along and whisked the ice away.

Sanirajak isn't the sort of place where most people would want to spend more than a few hours, maybe not even more than a few minutes. Imagine Appalachia crossbred with a gypsy encampment, then struck by an earthquake. Likewise imagine residential landscaping that consists of discarded snow-machine treads, ragged fuel drums, cast-off Pampers, beer bottles, slops, and the bones of animals. The town's chief attraction, or perhaps its chief distraction, is a several-hundred-year-old whale carcass whose odor is still pungent enough to upset the nostrils.

But at least it hadn't been Wal-marted, Taco Belled, Gapped, Star-bucked, or CNN'd. And at least it didn't have an armada of Urban Assault Vehicles (a.k.a., SUVs) piloted by somewhat human beings with cell phones surgically attached to their heads. This, for me, automatically made Sanirajak more civilized than almost every other town in North America. Still, I couldn't wait to exchange it for the wilds of Foxe Basin.

Each morning my guide Qungujuq would study the ice with the seriousness of a scholar gazing at a palimpsest, then come to my tent and say, "*Nagga.* Not today." After that, he'd join me for coffee. He got his caffeine fix by sticking the grounds directly into his mouth like a wad of tobacco, thus avoiding the bland intercession of water. When I tried to imitate him, I accidentally swallowed the grounds and ended up with very bad heartburn.

Sometimes Qungujuq would bring along his father, a barrel-chested elder whose face resembled the contour lines on a topo map. Like a number of other people I'd met in Sanirajak, the old man, Sivulliq, knew only one expression in English: "You're a better man than I am, Gunga Din." Some years ago the town's Hudson Bay Company trader would perform the occasional interment and, instead of reciting the proper burial service, he'd solemnly intone Kipling's "Gunga Din." The poem's famous line entered the local ver-nacular as a sort of vaguely reverential sentiment, although no one had the slightest idea what it meant.

Sivulliq said there were Tunit on Prince Charles Island, and he warned me to be careful of them. They would attempt to unravel my intestines—a popular Tunit form of entertainment—if I gave them the opportunity.

The Tunit, otherwise known as the Dorset People, were early Eski-moans who, according to most archaeologists, died out before 1200 A.D. Yet if there was one place in the Arctic where a small band of them might have survived, that place would be Prince Charles Island. It was discovered as recently as 1948, when a Royal Canadian Air Force pilot was taking a series of aerial photographs of Foxe Basin and a large unknown island showed up in one of the pictures. Being low-lying as well as surrounded by ice for most of the year, the island had escaped detection ever since the first European explorers came this way en route to not finding the Northwest Passage. And even though it's now been detected, it's never been fully mapped.

One other thing: the old man told me: that the weather on Prince Charles Island is awful, and thus it's very easy to get marooned there.

Then came the morning when Qungujuq woke me up by shouting "*Tuavi!* Ice blown away by big wind." Groggily, I lifted the tent flap and at once saw open water where the evening before I'd seen only an uncompromising sheet of ice.

Within an hour, we'd piled our supplies into his 24-foot motorized freighter canoe and were heading east across Foxe Basin. Rather, we were trying to head east, but the wind that had blown away the ice kept shoving us in a more northerly direction. Finally, we decided to wait out the wind, so we put ashore in a cove on the northern part of Melville Peninsula. Here we encountered some walrus hunters from Iglulik, one of whom told me that the wind would die down during the night. I asked him how he knew this. Was he observing the flight patterns of certain birds, or perhaps using some time-honored Native technique to read the weather?

"No," he said, "I heard it on the radio."

The following day the wind did die down, but it left in its wake a strong lateral swell. Qungujuq and his brother-in-law Zacharias, the other member of our expedition, took turns trying to keep the boat from being bashed by waves, and despite both of them being expert helmsmen, we still got wet. At one point a wave rushed our gunwales and dumped a jellyfish into the boat. Zacharias found this vastly amusing, even though Arctic jellyfish can deliver a very nasty sting. But he seemed to find everything vastly amusing, even the albino walrus whoofling at us from an ice pan. An albino walrus, he informed me, means death.

"Death to whom?" I asked.

"Us," he grinned.

Zacharias also happened to be his own grandfather. Here's how this highly unusual phenomenon occurred:

His actual grandfather died when an avalanche came tumbling down on his snowhouse. Evidently, the poor fellow had tried to claw his way out, because when he was found, his right arm was protruding from the snow, gnawed to the bone by foxes and ravens. When Zacharias was born several months later, he had a birthmark that extended all the way from his fingers to his shoulder, exactly where his grandfather had been gnawed upon. There was only one explanation for this—the grandfather's *isuma* (soul) had migrated to the boy's body.

Zacharias rolled up his sleeve and showed me the birthmark. It was so much bigger than an ordinary birthmark that I did in fact wonder if something other than the vagaries of capillary action might have been responsible for it.

In spite of the swell, we were making good progress. We spent the night on Rowley Island, pitching our tent not far from an abandoned Distant Early Warning radar site—strange to think of a Soviet nuclear attack being monitored from a place so remote that it wasn't even thought to exist until shortly before the so-called Cold War began.

Earlier in the day, Qungujuq had shot a ringed seal, and after caching most of the meat for our return trip, we cooked the flippers and liver. I couldn't help remembering the first time I'd eaten seal liver, in Greenland. It was not only raw but still steaming, having been plucked from a recently killed animal. Whatever hesitation I might have felt about eating it was quickly dispelled by a tangy, iron-rich flavor compared to which the equivalent organ from cows tastes like it's been manufactured in a generic foods laboratory.

"*Nattiup tingua mamarijara,*" I said. (I like seal liver.)

"*Uvanga ijingit mamarniqsaujakka,*" Qungujuq told me. (Myself, I prefer the eyes.) Later he dissected one of the seal's eyes and showed me how the inner clear spheroid can be used as a magnifying glass—a useful tidbit of information if you happen to have a seal eye handy.

The next day the sea was as smooth as blue glass. By early afternoon, I estimated we were no more than twenty-five miles northwest of Prince Charles Island. I was, to put it mildly, excited, since I knew of only one other non-Inuk—the English explorer Tom Manning—who'd ever set foot on the island.

All morning the boat's motor had been making curious burbling noises, as if there was a newborn trapped somewhere inside it. I hadn't thought anything of this, probably because I was engrossed in conversation with my companions. We'd been talking about, of all things, blow jobs. The concept was unknown to the Inuit, and Zacharias wanted to know what possible pleasure could be derived from a woman blowing on a man's penis. I tried to convince him that it was only a figure of speech, but he'd already made up his mind—*qallunaat* (white people) had very peculiar ways of getting their kicks.

Then the motor did what it had shown every intention of doing for the past few hours: it died. Qungujuq and Zacharias bent over it, trying to figure out what was wrong. Meanwhile, we started drifting in a more or less southeasterly direction. But it wouldn't have mattered what direction we were drifting in, since my map did not indicate any landfall in this part of Foxe Basin except for Prince Charles Island itself.

"Motor very kaput," Qungujug announced, as if this weren't already obvious. "Must take it apart." It was also obvious that there wasn't any room on the overloaded boat to take apart a wristwatch, much less a 85 horsepower Yamaha motor.

We continued to drift for the next few hours, as Qungujuq examined various parts of the motor. I confess I wasn't in a particularly jovial frame of mind, since I knew how unforgiving the Arctic can be in situations like this. The Inuit have many stories of people going off in boats and disappearing, and years later their bones turn up on some distant beach.

"*Ela!*" Zacharias exclaimed.

He pointed to a small island maybe five miles away, then grabbed our one oar (we'd somehow managed to leave the other one on Rowley Island) and began paddling toward it. After a while, Qunjuguq took over from him, and then I took over from Qunjuguq. I paddled until my arm was ready to fall off, then I passed the oar to Zacharias, who was at least five years older than me but much stronger. He paddled the rest of the way, neatly parrying the ice floes that surrounded the island like guardian sentinels. At last a wave thrust the boat onto the gravelly shore with a resounding crunch.

The Arctic had granted us a reprieve, of sorts.

The island on which we now found ourselves looked to be about two miles long and half a mile wide. It didn't appear on my Canadian Geological Survey map, and what was even more significant, neither Qungujuq or Zacharias had known about its existence even though they'd both traveled this way once or twice before. We were lost. *Very* lost.

"Maybe we've died and gone to Heaven," quipped Zacharias.

If this really was Heaven, then a lot of clean-living people are going to be very disappointed. From the shore, the island looked bare with the absolute bareness of the stillborn. There didn't seem to be any pearly gates, only scoured limestone intersected by the occasional quartzite dyke. Nor was there any sign of Saint Peter or, for that matter, anybody else. The closest thing I saw to an angel was an ivory gull hovering in the air above us, its stiff wings bright against a high overcast.

The only other winged entity was positively unangelic: mosquitoes. From the instant we landed, they attacked us so aggressively and in such Biblical proportions that I figured they hadn't dined on any warm-blooded life for a very long time.

Soon Qungujuq had scattered pieces of the motor on the beach. It was 10:00 p.m., but there was still enough light for him to work on our stricken motor. Enough light, too, for me to see a screw that had rolled away and retrieve it for him. But that's almost all I could do: I know less about machines than a not necessarily bright three year old. But I do know that I hate them, and they seem to hate me too, because they promptly malfunction whenever I come within a few paces of them.

The Inuit, on the other hand, seem to have a knack for machines. In East Greenland, I once saw an elderly Inuk take apart and repair a helicopter engine, much to the surprise of the chopper's Danish pilot, who'd been unable to repair it himself. When I asked the old man where he'd learned about such things, he just pointed to his head and tapped it. He'd been born in the Stone Age (literally, the Stone Age—the East Greenlandic word for stone, *ujaraq*, is the same as the word for earth), a realm where, if you don't how to improvise, you don't survive.

Qungujuq was still working on the motor at midnight when Zacharias and I turned in. I woke up during the night to answer Nature's call, and there was Qungujuq beside me in the tent, snoring mightily. Zacharias was now down on the beach, working in the semi-darkness. In his hand was a tangle of wires that looked like a cat's cradle.

"Think you can fix it?" I said.

"*Immaqa,*" Zacharias replied. This is by far the most popular word in Inuktitut, the Inuit language. It means "perhaps," with an intimation of "probably not." If you're someone who needs straight answers to your questions, you can easily find yourself immaqa'd to a state of gibbering idiocy by the Inuit.

When I woke up the next morning, both Qungujuq and Zacharias were down on the beach, alternately staring at pieces of the motor and swatting at mosquitoes. I tried to gauge from their expressions whether they'd made any headway, and I noticed that neither man looked particularly pleased.

"We need a part for the gas line," Qungujuq told me.

"And it will be very hard to order it from here," added Zacharias.

We hadn't brought along a radio or locator beacon (stupid, I know: but in our haste to leave Sanirajak, we'd also forgotten flotation jackets), so I had a hunch we'd be stuck on the island until someone rescued us. Already knowing what he would tell me, I asked

Qungujuq whether he thought another boat might pass this way in the not too distant future. He didn't say immaqa; he said *aakka* (no).

"Maybe an airplane will see us," I said.

Another aakka. We were nowhere near a flight corridor. Also, our lone paddle had cracked when Zacharias was beaching the boat and it now consisted of two wholly useless pieces. So we were not only lost, but marooned, too. I'd been marooned once before, in Scotland's Outer Hebrides, and while I hadn't exactly enjoyed that experience, at least I knew I'd eventually be picked up by a passing fisherman.

Maybe I was taking my cue from my companions, who weren't at all panicky, or maybe the true nature of our predicament hadn't sunk in yet, but I wasn't overly worried. I told myself: You're not dead until you're dead, and besides, you were the one who had the bright idea to go to a place that's not on the map. Now you've fetched up at just such a place—for God's sakes, go out and explore it . . .

"You don't need me for anything?" I asked.

Both Qungujuq and Zacharias shook their heads vigorously, as if whatever I could do to help would only make a sorry situation even worse. So I wandered off, accompanied by a full escort of mosquitoes. Qungujuq called me back and gave me his .30-06 rifle, uttering a single word: "*Nanuq.*" He was not suggesting that I shoot the hero of the Robert Flaherty film, but that I protect myself against a possible attack from the animal for whom Flaherty's hero was named, the polar bear.

Thus armed, I climbed the hogback behind our camp. Several minutes later I was standing on another hogback, probably the highest point on the island, and staring out in every direction over the expanse of Foxe Basin. There was no other land in sight. Indeed, there was nothing at all in sight, since even the ice-floes had disappeared during the night. If I'd been standing on the moon, I might have felt a greater sense of solitude than I felt at that moment, but I doubt it.

Now I turned my attention to the island itself. In the sunlight, it looked a lot more colorful than it'd looked the previous evening. Here and there I noticed delicate Arctic wildflowers—purple saxifrage, Lapland rosebay, moss-campion, Arctic cinquefoil, dwarf hawksbeard, mouse-ear chickweed, and buttercups—rising bravely from, it would appear, solid bedrock. Gossamer tufts of arctic cotton swayed to an imperceptible breeze. A brilliant patch of Yellow Lichen (*Cetraria tilesii*) exploded from its dour limestone host, and an equally bright yellow butterfly was flitting busily from flower to flower.

It was so quiet that my steps sounded downright raucous on the gravelly ground. I got the feeling that nothing had changed or even moved on the island since its soil was swept away ten thousand years ago. In every respect, it was a harsh place; not nice, not comfortable, not by a long shot (to invoke the contemporary cliche) user-friendly. Even so, its forlorn beauty took my breath away.

And then I came upon the cairns. There were half a dozen of these beehive-shaped structures piled along a gently sloping ridge in the northwestern part of the island. Peering through the chinks of one of them, I saw a human skull and several bone fragments; in another, there was a brownish occiput, a jawbone with very worn teeth, and a scattering of vertebral arches; in a third, a lone skull.

My first thought was: here's what happened to the last group of people who washed up here when their motor conked out.

But then I noticed in one of the cairns a more or less intact skeleton curled into a fetal position. This suggested that the skeleton's owner was an Inuk from the so-called Thule Period (the Thule Inuit, immediate successors to the Tunit, believed your journey to the Afterlife would be a lot less perilous if you left the world in the same posture as you entered it). I felt somewhat relieved, for the Thule Period ended approximately two hundred years before the invention of marine engines.

Still, the graves reminded me of my predicament. There was the possibility that this bare speck of land might turn out to be my own final resting place, too. I imagined my last fragile thoughts drifting away, and then I imagined some archaeologist discovering my bones and wondering what the blazes a middle-aged Caucasian male was doing so far from his native habitat. For almost the first time since I'd left Sanirajak, I found myself wondering the same thing.

Meanwhile, I was being sucked dry by the mosquitoes, whose persistent probing had located the holes in my bug net. Not relishing the prospect of death by acupuncture, I began quickening my pace. Now only the most aerobically inclined of the little bastards could keep up with me. But the gods of the Paleozoic had not set up the island as a race course, and I tripped over some glacial till and went flying through the air. *Don't land on the rifle*, I told myself. I didn't land on the rifle. Instead, I landed on my compass, which made a gouge in my chest—possibly the first compass-related injury in human medical history.

I also landed in a literal boneyard. There were hundreds of floating ribs, clavicles, vertebrae, scapulas, and coccyges scattered around me. They were all from walruses, and they indicated why the occupants of the cairns had inhabited such an apparently unbountiful place—it was only a short distance from the floe-edge, home to the paunchy, hulking *aivik*. For the Thule Inuit, bounty was determined not by the soil or lack thereof, but by the object at the end of a harpoon.

When I returned to our camp, I saw Qungujuq and Zacharias hunched over a checkerboard. They were so intent on their game that neither of them noticed me until I was standing right next to them. Then Zacharias smiled up at me and said, "We were hoping you would kill a nice big nanuq for our dinner."

"Maybe you were hoping that a nice big nanuq would kill me," I told him, "and then you'd have one less mouth to feed."

In fact, I was a little concerned about our food supply. We hadn't expected this misadventure, so we'd brought only enough food for a few weeks. Likewise, we'd planned to supplement our diet with meat from seals or a walrus, but we couldn't get within shooting distance of either animal without a properly functioning motor.

That food supply, which now seemed to me incredibly meager, included the following medley of items:

A box of expedition-standard oatmeal ("bloatmeal"); five boxes of rice; a bag of dried prunes; a pound of raisins; two bags of pilot biscuits (hardtack); two dozen Snickers bars; eleven packets of freeze-dried fettucine alfredo; six packets of freeze-dried chicken cacciatore; four packets of macaroni; a half empty jar of Cheez Whiz; a small bag of flour; several slabs of *pipsik* (dried fish); a few rubbery pieces of *maqtaq* (narwhal skin); and one slightly mouldy apple.

After my companions had finished their game, I asked Zacharias what would happen if we ran out of food.

"We eat each other," he said. He was grinning in his usual fashion, but he was also studying me with, I thought, the appreciative gaze of a chef.

That night the wind accelerated, first baying, then howling, and then shrieking at the top of its lungs, until it reached a higher decibel level than any wind I'd ever heard. Every hour or so, we would go outside and gather a new batch of rocks to pile along the tent's guylines. Were it not for these rocks, I'm convinced the wind would have picked up the tent—poles, occupants, and all—and deposited it somewhere in the middle of Foxe Basin.

The next day the wind continued to blow and, except for the occasional rock-collecting mission, we stayed hunkered down inside the tent. Even so, the wind found us, pushing grit under the tent's fly and into our sleeping bags, our clothes, our food, our hair, our Primus stove, everything.

I didn't like being trapped like this. It made me even more aware of the degree to which we were trapped on the island. But Qungujuq and Zacharias were as composed as a pair of Zen Buddhist monks on a retreat, except when they were playing checkers, and then Zacharias—a less accomplished player than Qungujuq—would occasionally shout "*Tuqulirama! Tuqulirama!*" ("I'm being murdered! I'm being murdered!").

"I'm the best murderer in Sanirajak," Qungujuq told me, referring, of course, to his skill at checkers.

Ajurnamaat: this is doubtless the second most popular word in Inuktitut. It means something like "Why worry?" or "Hey, what can you do?" In our time together, I came to regard my companions as living, walking, checker-playing embodiments of ajurnamaat. I envied them this attitude, not to mention their ability to remain unruffled in the face of what I felt was a pretty dire situation.

At one point they burst into riotous laughter. They were talking about a certain Anglican minister, a member of the Bible Churchman's Missionary Society, who'd come to Sanirajak fifteen years ago. The man had learned just enough Inuktitut to confuse one word with another. One Sunday morning he confused *ijjujut* (Bible) with *igujut* (testicles) and told his congregation that they should pay more attention to their testicles.

Later Zacharias recounted a story about a man who'd run out of food on a sledging trip in Baffin Island. The man was starving, and he prayed for God's help. All at once he noticed a big slab of meat on the floor of his tent—God had provided! He quickly flensed this meat, chopped it up, and threw it into his cooking pot. But he died before he could eat it, since he'd flensed and chopped up his own thigh . . .

My companions thought this story was quite funny. I suspect Zacharias may have told it for my benefit, as a way of saying, Come on, man, take it easy, or you might end up doing something rash yourself, like, for example, eating *your* thigh.

The wind, which I guessed was blowing at sixty-five or seventy knots, showed no sign of relenting. Once, when I ventured outside to pee, an especially strong gust caught me in the face and made my teeth ache. Back in the tent I scribbled these words in my journal: *This damn wind's blowing away what's left of my sanity. Also, I'm bored, worried, and tired. Plus I'd love a big greasy cheeseburger right now.* Instead of a cheeseburger, though, I had to be satisfied with a packet of fettucine alfredo. It tasted like sawdust, probably because it was sawdust.

Inside the tent, we inhabited a world whose boundaries were dictated not by day or night, light or dark, but by our own bodily functions. Oddly enough, our appetites seemed to be inspired by our relative immobility, or maybe we just ate a lot because there wasn't much else to do. Qungujuq and Zacharias could take naps without any difficulty, but I remained awake—how could I sleep with the meteorological equivalent of a pneumatic drill only inches from my ears? So I occupied myself with my journal. *If I ever get out of this mess*, I wrote, *I'm going to adopt a more sedentary lifestyle.*

"You are missing your home now?" Qungujuq asked me. "What you call it in English, your 'roots?' "

Lack of sleep was making me testy. "Human beings don't have roots," I snapped at him. "They have feet."

Three days later the wind moderated to a mere breeze with astonishing abruptness, as if it had suddenly grown tired after such a prolonged display of its muscle power. We could now go outside without being pummeled to jelly and, as it turned out, without being bitten by mosquitoes, who were nowhere in sight (had they been pummeled to jelly themselves?). It was early evening, and a sort of ethereal hush had fallen on the world. There was a soft pink marbling in the clouds—solar iridescence. On the island itself, the light had that tentative quality so typical of the Arctic, where every last sunbeam feels like it's been snatched from the perpetually imminent winter.

Soon Qungujuq and Zacharias were disassembling and reassembling the motor for, it seemed, the hundredth time. They had expressions of tundralike patience on their faces, as if they really thought they could repair this defunct piece of machinery.

After being imprisoned in a cramped tent for so long, I needed to stretch my legs, so I began wandering along the shore. The storm had washed up all kinds of oceanic booty—a golden plover's wing tangled in a matting of seaweed, a dismembered starfish, strands of kelp, fish, and a dead seal. Initially, I thought the seal might be salvageable as food, but upon closer inspection I saw that it was scarcely more than a husk, its flesh and organs having already been consumed by crabs, isopods, and other gluttonous creatures of the sea.

Now I began scavenging the beach for something that might bolster our rapidly diminishing larder. I wouldn't have turned up my nose at a newly dead fish or bird, but I only found very dead fish and a bundle of feathers so mangled that it was impossible to tell whether it was a bird or stuffing from a mattress. Then I saw a fruiting of *Lycoperdon* puffballs on the mossy ground near the shore. I knew neither Qungujuq or Zacharias would eat them (the Inuit believe mushrooms are the shit of shooting stars), but I certainly would; they'd be a welcome respite from all the freeze-dried quasi-food I'd been eating.

My foraging was interrupted by the sound of a gunshot. At first I thought one of my companions might have accidentally shot himself, then I wondered if one of them had shot a polar bear. I began running back along the beach, not knowing what I would discover. I soon saw Qungujuq waving at me, and when I got closer, I noticed Zacharias had a bigger than usual grin on his face.

"All fix now," Qungujuq said, pointing to the motor, which was back on the boat and roaring with life.

At that lovely moment all I could think of to say was this: "You're a better man than I am, Gunga Din . . ." A religious oath from a devoutly unreligious person.

Apparently, the motor's O-ring had been badly chewed up, with the result that the fuel line wasn't getting any gas. Qungujug had replaced the grungy remnant of the O-ring with some kelp, and that had done the trick. If the storm hadn't washed up the kelp, Zacharias said they would have tried to use a piece of my Gore-Tex anorak, about whose myriad virtues I had spoken perhaps a bit too fulsomely.

So now the question was, did I want to continue on to Prince Charles Island? We had enough fuel, Qungujuq told me. Well, maybe enough fuel. And we probably had enough food. If not, we could always shoot a seal or two. The gas might eat through our improvised O-ring, but if that happened, no problem, we'd just use another piece of kelp. Or a section of my $450 anorak.

I couldn't tell whether he was speaking in ajurnamaat mode ("Whatever will be, will be, and let's not worry about it now"), or whether he was trying to talk me out of a trip he considered risky. But it didn't matter. I'd already decided it was time to head back to the scuzzy charms of Sanirajak. For I'd satisfied my desire to explore an island in the Back of Beyond; an island that turned out to be even farther off the map than Prince Charles Island. Also, I didn't want to risk being marooned again, perhaps for a longer period, perhaps forever. In the Arctic, Fate doesn't like to be tempted, much less seduced.

And yet I felt a curious sadness as we pulled away from the island. Maybe I'd left a part of myself on its obdurate shores, or maybe I just felt sad because I was surrendering a rare privilege— the privilege of solitude. As the island receded in the distance, I thought to myself, There are a lot worse places to which you could bequeath your bones.

The trip back across Foxe Basin went without incident. We spent another night on Rowley Island and gorged ourselves on the seal meat we'd cached there. We didn't encounter another albino walrus, a fact which seemed to disappoint Zacharias. Nor did we encounter any ice except for a few vagrant floes. And most surprising of all, there was hardly any wind other than a light breeze from the south, a compass point I hadn't thought about in a long, long time.

At last we came in sight of Sanirajak. Even at sea, I could detect the smell of the dead whale, and it seemed to me the sweetest smell in all the world.

Beauty and the Beast

Eagerly voluble, the man at the bar identified himself as an old-time ("Most guys my age are dead") bear guide, then proceeded to regale me with the following story:

Back in the 1940's he was leading some hunters through dense bush in the heights above Olga Bay. All of a sudden a bear rose up from behind a clump of salmonberries and gave him a mighty swat. This swat knocked out all the teeth in his head, every last one of them. Considerably upset, he shot the bear on the spot and then made himself a quite serviceable set of false teeth from the bear's own teeth.

Needless to say, I didn't believe this story, so I asked the man to open his mouth. When he did, I saw an empty cavern graced neither by human or ursine teeth. Graced, in fact, by almost no teeth at all.

"So where are these improvised dentures now?" I inquired.

"Back home in a glass," the man shrugged.

The tales grow unusually tall on Alaska's Kodiak Island. But everything else in Kodiak would seem to be either oversized or somewhat improbable, too. Strands of kelp can grow two feet in a single day; streams turn literally red with spawning salmon; and eagles appear big enough to carry off small children. As for Kodiak's bears, their size is legendary—an adult, even when it's not standing fully upright, would dwarf an NBA center, and it might outweigh an NFL fullback by as much as 1,200 pounds.

A few years before my trip, I'd met a Kodiak Native man named Sven Haakonson at, improbably, a sheep roast in Cambridge, Massachusetts. One thing I remember him telling me: that his people, the Alutiiq, sometimes used a particular bracket fungus called "bear's bread" as chewing tobacco.

To use a fungus as tobacco suggests a certain desperation. Because of this, or perhaps because the Alutiiq were Pacific Yup'ik, an Eskimoan people, I figured Kodiak would be more or less similar to other hardscrabble high latitude places I've visited over the years. So you can imagine my surprise when the place I encountered on occasion made me think of the Amazon (is there anywhere else in the North where you need a machete to hack your way through the bush?). You can also imagine my surprise when I saw people riding the surf at Pasagshak: had they climbed aboard an especially errant wave at Waikiki and somehow ended up at Latitude 57'25'N?

At times, too, Kodiak put me in mind of a Marineland on steroids. Thanks to the gentling effects of the Japanese Current, its waters are extraordinarily bountiful. "Just try to fish me out," these waters seem to say, and local fishermen have taken up the challenge. In doing so, they're displaying a not atypical Alaskan attitude: Hey, our resources are *ours*, and we have the right to exhaust them if we so desire . . .

But Kodiak is not the Costa del Sol. Consider the weather. Rain does not fall so much as throw itself at you like shrapnel; fogs creep in not "on little cat's feet," as fogs often creep in poetry, but on the robust paws of a lion or tiger; and the wind can feel like a malevolent force. Early in my trip, I found myself in a single engine plane knocked about so vehemently by williwaw winds that I almost longed for a crash: at least then my stomach would be *in situ*.

Then there was the time I was getting ready to take off in another small plane. "You're flying with Ernie," I was told. "A remarkable guy. He's the only pilot in Kodiak who can drink a bottle of Southern Comfort and at the same time negotiate his way through a whiteout."

"And when did he last accomplish this feat?" I asked.

"Earlier today . . ."

This turned out to be another tall tale. Ernie was completely sober, my stomach was fine, and the flight was a lot better than fine: we didn't encounter a breath of wind during the entire trip, and the air was so clear that I could see three three distant brownish specks—bears—lolling on a hillside greener than any green Ireland could imagine.

Kodiak City (pop. 10,000), the only sizable community, is not a town so much as a gallimaufry of buildings aspiring to be a town. Here's the blue dome of the Holy Resurrection Russian Orthodox Church, and there squats the Golden Arches of a McDonald's; here's an upscale restaurant whose waiters all seem to be Southern Californians named Kevin, and here's a down-and-dirty fisherman's bar whose walls are decorated with fading *Playboy* centerfolds. Appropriately, everyone seems to come from somewhere else; I even met a *cordon bleu* French chef working the counter at a local coffee shop.

But I hadn't traveled to Kodiak to have an urban experience, even an idiosyncratic one, so a day or two after my arrival I decided to drive south to Cape Chiniak, a distance of forty-five miles. Cape Chiniak was the end of the road, or at least the end of Kodiak's road system; for me, this was an attraction in itself, but I'd also heard that I might see bears there.

A few miles after I passed the largest Coast Guard station in the U.S. (its bailiwick includes the Bering Sea as well as the tumultuous waters around Kodiak), the road turned to gravel. With a certain fore-boding, I noticed that this gravel was mostly shale—the same rock the Indians used for arrowheads. And my low-slung rental car couldn't help but notice the road's washboarding. Also, the road had a coating of volcanic ash from the 1912 eruption of Katmai's Mt. Novarupta; it made the car, formerly green, look like a refugee from the Dust Bowl.

Since the land's skyward tilt put limits on that Alaskan phenom-enon known as homesteading, there weren't a lot of houses. The few that I saw looked like they'd been not so much built as slapped together from whatever scrap materials happened to be lying around. They were surrounded by terminally rusted pickup trucks, ancient plumbing fixtures, defunct appliances, and cordwood—Alaskan home landscaping.

Just beyond the turnoff for Pasagshak, I climbed out of the car to stretch my legs. Nootka lupines were blooming in violet-blue profu-sion, wild irises were everywhere, and the bright chartreuse of beach lovage seemed to ignite the whole shoreline. Snow-capped moun-tains cast perfect reflections of themselves in Chiniak Bay, and green islets and guano-streaked stacks rose from the bay's sparkling water like tutelary gods.

As if to put an exclamation point on this scene, half a dozen mag-pies were mobbing a goshawk overhead, and the harried bird flew down and—this is unheard of behavior in so dauntless a raptor—took refuge under my car.

After the lilliputian village of Chiniak (pop. 150), the road went from bad to worse. The potholes appeared deep enough to swallow my car forever, so I had no choice but to turn back before reaching Cape Chiniak. Part of me was disappointed, but another part was pleased to discover a place that so actively resisted automotive invasion.

And as if to confirm this resistance, I had a blowout. I replaced the stricken tire with the so-called donut, then on the liver-shaking drive back to Kodiak City the donut itself suffered a blowout. A man with the obligatory black lab seated in the rear of his pickup took me the rest of the way, saying: "Only two flats on that stretch of road? Hey, you haven't lived until you've had at least three . . ."

When I asked him why shale was being used as gravel, he shrugged and said, "Kodiak," as if that explained everything.

That evening I met my old friend Sven, who was now director of the Alutiiq Museum and working overtime to prepare for a forthcoming Smithsonian exhibit. He was tired and stressed-out, and he suggested that we retire to his brother-in-law's *banya* for a much-needed sweat.

The word banya is Russian, a testimony to the continuing influence of Kodiak's first European colonizers. But the Alutiiq had their own sweat baths long before the Russians fetched up on their shores. And however much they've lost of their culture, they haven't lost the tradition of incinerating themselves. Nor have they lost that tradition's healing component. An hour in a banya will cure any indisposition, even a hangover, one Alutiiq man told me. I didn't have a hangover, so I couldn't put this statement to the test. But I did want to rid myself of the frustration I felt from having been a slave to my car.

Sven fired up the stove, then we took off our clothes and sat down on the wooden bench to await the arrival of the heat. It arrived and then it kept on arriving, until the temperature in the banya was, I'm convinced, 200 degrees Fahrenheit.

"It's too hot," I told Sven.

"It's not hot enough," he said, dousing the stove with water and throwing in another log.

Now I seemed to enter a wholly different dimension, one where I found myself possessed by a sense of well-being so complete that it made the heat inconsequential. I felt like a new person, or maybe just a notably clean person. In this state, I made a firm resolve (a good sweat is supposed to help clarify your thoughts): to light out for a Kodiak where no car could ever go.

Afognak, the second largest island in the Kodiak Archipelago, is no stranger to human depredation. It has one of the world's ugliest clearcuts and a shoreline that suffered a significant hit of crude when the *Exxon Valdez* went aground in Prince William Sound in 1989. Yet the place where I was now hiking showed no obvious sign of human trashing except for the occasional wad of bathroom stationery, an item without which no wilderness experience in Alaska would be complete.

My guide, Luke Randall, pointed to a heap of fresh bear scat nearly as large as my recently jettisoned car. I exaggerate, of course; but by the standards with which I'm familiar (dog, cat, gerbil, etc), the mound was indeed huge. A bit of surgery indicated that the bear had been eating wild rhubarb, a plant that I noticed was growing all around us.

Luke carried a rifle, and being a sometime bear guide, he knew how to use it. Still, Kodiak bears are a lot less dangerous than their grizzly brethren elsewhere or, for that matter, a bad egg salad sandwich; their environment bursts with food resources, so they tend to be more or less tolerant of people wandering about in what they regard as their dining areas.

Soon we came to a river with a spawning run of salmon, although it was bald eagles, not bears, who were feeding there. In fact, I had never seen so many eagles in one place, and also never seen America's national emblem exhibiting such gluttonous behavior. One bird was trying to get its talons into a particularly large salmon, an act that made me want to shout out Miss Piggy's wise words: "Never eat anything you can't lift."

Raised on Afognak, Luke knew the island with an intimacy that belied his twenty-one years. His eye for seeing eagles camouflaged in trees was eaglelike itself. He showed me a delicate latticework of bones, all that remained of a long-tailed vole. Here was a depression among some ferns where a bear had been lying. And here was a not inconsiderable Sitka spruce broken almost in half—a macho statement from a male bear to its rivals.

At one point we stopped abruptly. Right in the middle of the trail was the front paw-print of a bear. It was twice the size of my boot, which meant that the bear in question would wear a Size 21 shoe, and that wouldn't even include the customized orthopedic extension for its claws.

By the end of the hike, we still hadn't seen a bear. Plenty of sign, yes; but not an actual bear. Luke proposed that we shift our search to Shuyak, the northernmost island in the Archipelago. Shuyak occupies a pivot point between the currents of the Gulf of Alaska and those of Shelikof Strait. This mingling of currents makes it such a nutrient-rich environment that, according to a naturalist I'd met in Kodiak City, much of the local wildlife suffers from obesity.

On the way to Shuyak, we saw humpback whales, fur-fluffing sea otters, and Dall porpoises. We saw horned puffins, tufted puffins, eider ducks, goldeneyes, rhinoceros auklets, and fork-tailed storm petrels. But the only really overweight creature we saw was a bull Steller's sea lion attending its harem at a rookery. Probably tipping the scales at a ton or so, it was shaped like a couch and seemed to have the same locomotion skills as a couch. Which just goes to show that size matters, at least to female sea lions.

As the boat approached the island, I noticed a large brown object near the shore.

"Bear!" I exclaimed.

"Boulder," Luke said.

While he was tying up the zodiac, I took a brief stroll. Giant cedar and hemlock drift logs littered the shingle beach like the lashed bones of dinosaurs. Half of Japan's material culture also seemed to be lying on the beach. There were Santory beer cans, glass fishing floats, sandals, a mouthwash bottle, hairspray, a sake bottle, mounds of netting, and a parachute rocket flare. I picked up one bottle and studied the lettering. It said, I'm convinced, "Please throw in water."

Now we set off. We crossed a broad green meadow that made most other meadows I've seen look like industrial waste sites. Then we hiked through a wind-stunted spruce forest whose every tree seemed to be draped with a wispy green lichen called old man's beard—a fitting complement to an old growth forest. Later we walked along the shore of a moraine-dammed lake.

But we still didn't see any bears. And, truth to tell, I didn't care. For I had taken in some of the purest oyxgen I'd ever tasted (it had an almost meaty flavor), and also gone into country where no car could ever go. Likewise, I was in privileged company: Luke told me that his father had taken Roy Rogers bear hunting forty years ago, and the King of the Cowboys had been skunked, too.

I liked the Alutiiq village of Old Harbor from the moment I arrived there, when I was picked up at the airstrip by the local mayor. "I don't need red carpet treatment," I told him.

"You're not getting red carpet treatment," he said. "I happen to be the only taxi driver in town."

But if there weren't any other taxi drivers, there were ATV (All Terrain Vehicle) drivers by the score. So abundant were ATVs, in fact, that they gave Old Harbor a cheerfully diminutive, somewhat cartoon-like aspect. And they weren't only in town. I constantly saw ATVs ascending and descending the vertiginous slopes outside of town. When I asked the driver of one of these gravity-defying vehicles what he was doing, he replied, "Just going for a spin."

Old Harbor had a whimsy, a funkiness, indeed a charm that made it feel quite different from most other Native villages I've visited in the North. In Kodiak itself, I'd found Akhiok, for example, a depressing place. Half the windows in its houses were broken, half the shingles on its roofs had fallen off, and the strips of salmon drying outside its houses looked utterly forlorn, as if they'd been abandoned. Perhaps they had been abandoned: Akhiok seemed like a ghost town waiting to happen.

You can evaluate an Alaskan community by the taste of its salmon, and in Old Harbor Sven's father gave me *sitkyuk* (half-smoked salmon) which was so good that I couldn't imagine it having been prepared without divine intervention.

Sven Sr. himself was something of a wag—a necessity, perhaps, in a place whose commercial fishery seemed moribund. He told people I was a journalist, and that I was going to put Old Harbor on the cover of *Rolling Stone*. Not surprisingly, several guitar-toting teenagers approached me for an audition.

Meanwhile, I was picking up tidbits of Alutiiq lore from local elders. I learned that the Alutiiq respected bears so much that they never called them by name, but always referred to them as "The Big Ones"; that a Sasquatch-like creature called an *ahulak* was seven feet tall and very fond of snuff; and that the sea had been created when a woman with a very full bladder relieved herself.

I also learned about Refuge Rock, where, in 1784, a Russian merchant-adventurer named Gregory Shelikof massacred some three hundred Alutiiq. This was the Wounded Knee of Kodiak, and a bleak day for the Alutiiq. Their spirit broken, they would soon become the slaves of Russian *promyshlenniks* (fur hunters).

The Alutiiq call Refuge Rock *Awa'aq*—"the place not to speak of." They say it's haunted, and that they can hear the weeping of their ancestors there. To get someone to go there with me was not easy. "It has the smell of death," I was told. Finally, an Alutiiq man named Jeff Peterson offered the services of his stepson Nolan. As it happened, Nolan was a non-Native.

Jeff dropped us off at Fox Lagoon on nearby Sitkalidak Island, and we began walking along the shore. That it was a grey, dismal, intermittently rainy day seemed somehow appropriate. For there are certain places where the weather ought to be lousy, and the place where we were headed was one of them.

After a mile, we came to a rock with what seemed to be a Russian Orthodox cross carved onto it. Nolan thought this cross might have been a gesture of atonement by early Russian missionaries. To me, it looked as if it'd been carved not by missionaries but by a glacier. No matter. After they arrived in Kodiak in the 1790's, Russian Orthodox missionaries did a reasonably good job of curbing the genocidal tendencies of their countrymen.

At last we reached Refuge Rock. Shaped like a recumbent whale, it was joined to Sitkalidaq Island by a narrow spit of land buried at high tide.

For an hour, we explored this historic chunk of geology, walking around the base and even clambering up to its sedge-tousled crown. I confess I did not find it ominous or uncanny, nor did I hear any sound other than the hum of a single-engine Beaver flying overhead—a ubiquitous sound in Kodiak. On the other hand, there was no reason why the departed spirits of the Alutiiq should reveal themselves to me, a White Person. For I was, after a fashion, the bringer of tears.

But one thing did reveal itself: the sun. It came out right after we left Refuge Rock, as if it had been withholding its blessing from such an unblessed place all this time.

When we'd been sitting in his brother-in-law's banya, Sven Jr. told me that Old Harbor people used to hike across the rough-and-tumble interior of Kodiak to attend dances in Larsen Bay, a distance of twenty-five miles. He'd made this hike himself a few years earlier, and it had taken him the better part of a week.

There's a stage in every journey I've ever made when I've felt the need to go off by myself and commune with Nature, or at least commune with the absence of people. I now decided I'd try to walk part of the way to Larsen Bay myself, with only a compass for company, So, having been dropped off at Barling Bay, I began trekking into the Kodiak National Wildlife Refuge, 1,957,000 of the most pristine acres in America.

There was a trail, although I couldn't tell whether it'd been made by bears or erstwhile dance-goers. It would vanish, reappear, then vanish again, barely surviving amid such a choking metropolis of vegetation. This metropolis included ten-foot-high cow parsnips, salmonberry bushes that were as profuse as weeds, and extremely dense alder thickets.

I disliked the alders at least as much they seemed to dislike me. Anyone who has ever done hand-to-hand battle with this apostate of the birch family knows why Jupiter transformed Phaeton's daughters into alders: no tree has a more unpleasant disposition, its branches snapping back with a lash usually in the face, and no tree is more resentful of human intrusion. If, instead of retreating to Refuge Rock, the Alutiiq had headed into an alder habitat, they would have had a natural barricade against Shelikof and his men.

Steadily climbing, I came out on a bare ridge—a relief after all that clutching, grasping botany. The view was spectacular, with knife-edged peaks, shimmering glaciers, and electric blue cirques in every direction. I thought: This is easily the most beautiful place in the world. As I began hiking down to one of the cirques, a pair of eagles turned in tight spirals above me and then flew away, apparently satisfied that I wasn't some sort of oddly constituted prey.

Suddenly I saw a cinnamon-colored object a hundred yards ahead of me. At first I thought it was another boulder, but no boulder has fur that ripples when it moves, and no boulder I've ever seen has the ability to stand up on its hind legs.

Encountering a bear in the wild, especially a Kodiak bear, is at once exhilarating and scary. You want to run, but you know that running instantly identifies you as prey; you want to stand and stare, but this only makes you feel like a 98-pound weakling tossed into the ring with a sumo wrestler. Two other thoughts might pass through your mind: (1) that the bear, if it's standing upright, looks not unlike a lusciously furred version of yourself, and (2) you're about to become sushi.

Slowly, I raised my binoculars. The bear was studying me with a high degree of interest, as if it was trying to figure out exactly what I was doing on its turf.

Then I heard a staccato huff, and the bear began running away from me. For some reason, it chose to head downhill rather than uphill, although a bear's forepaws are much better suited for climbing than descending. Maybe something about me was so unsettling that it threw caution to the winds. In any event, one moment its legs were moving like pistons, and the next moment it tumbled head over heels, landing unceremoniously at the bottom of the slope. It remained slumped there for maybe half a minute, then it got up and walked shakily away. Poor bear! I imagined a look of utter embarrassment on its face.

Right then and there I decided to turn back. I was less worried about a confrontation with another bear than I was about my own presence in a part of Kodiak set aside for wildlife rather than for me. That hapless bundle of fur at the bottom of the slope told me in no uncertain terms that I was as much an intruder here as a fly on a Vermeer painting. By all rights the bear should have held its ground because this was, after all, its ground. The only way I could apologize for disturbing the local status quo was to withdraw before I disturbed it again.

When I got back to Kodiak City, I mentioned my hike to Sven. "You took the wrong trail," he said.

This explained why I'd gotten hung up in that boreal jungle. Still, how could any trail that had led me into such remarkably unspoiled country (unspoiled, that is, except for me) be the wrong trail?

A day or two later I paid a visit to one of Kodiak City's more popular watering holes. Its walls were decorated not with *Playboy* centerfolds but with pictures of what were probably even more provocative to the bar's clientele—fishing boats. On a stool in the corner sat the same toothless old man with whom I'd talked at the beginning of my trip. I joined him, and soon I was describing my recent encounter with the bear.

"So your bruin didn't even make a false charge?" he said.

"Nope," I told him.

"Didn't do anything to show you that he's lord of creation in these parts?"

I shook my head.

"Well," the old man grinned, "you gotta be pulling my leg."

I shook my head again.

In Kodiak, tall tales have a peculiar habit of being true.

Looking for Henry Hudson

It could be a scene from a movie—a sort of boreal *Mutiny on the Bounty*. Nine figures huddle together in an open boat. One of them, the captain, has a look of numb surprise on his face. His teenage son reaches for his hand, perhaps to comfort him, perhaps just seeking a degree of warmth. One man is shaking his fist at unseen enemies; another is sobbing. The rest of the castaways, scurvy-sick, seem indifferent to their fate.

The camera backs off to reveal an old-fashioned bark with sails unfurled. The gap between the two vessels slowly widens until the smaller one is no more than a pinprick in the immensity of ice-flecked seas. Fadeout to, appropriately, white.

Our marooned captain now vanishes from history, at least official history. What became of him remains a mystery to this day, almost four hundred years later. Yet Henry Hudson's life before he went missing is something of a mystery, too. We mention his name every time we refer to a great bay, a town, a county, a strait, and one of the

29

world's most productive estuaries, but we know less about him than we do about his contemporary, William Shakespeare. There's not even a surviving portrait of the man who was probably England's most important maritime explorer before Captain Cook.

And yet Hudson bequeathed us a portrait of himself in the events of his four voyages. They suggest a man who was obsessed, self-absorbed, secretive, democratic, distrustful, intellectually curious, and paranoid. Likewise a captain who was a brilliant navigator, but whose very presence seemed to inspire mutiny in his crews. In spite of his flaws or maybe because of them, Hudson emerges from these voyages as a remarkably human figure.

We first encounter him in 1607 as the captain of a rotten bark, the *Hopewell*, en route to the legendary riches of the Orient by way of the North Pole. (The Pole's five months of sunlight blessed it with a warm climate, according to contemporary wisdom.) Scouring the Arctic from Greenland to Spitzbergen, he reached 81°N, the farthest north anyone would sail for more than two hundred years. His progress was finally frustrated by sea-ice—not exactly a warm climate phenomenon.

The following year Hudson sailed under the same sponsors, the English Muscovy Company, and this time tried to reach the Orient via the Arctic coast of Russia; ice again stopped him, so he turned his ship around and started looking for a western passage. Whereupon his crew staged what might be called a "soft" mutiny: perhaps homesick, perhaps simply sick of the intemperate North, they refused to sail a league farther. Their compliant captain turned his ship around again and headed back to England.

In 1609, we find him attempting the same northeastern route in the employ of the Dutch. Heavy ice near Novaya Zembla again brought out his crew's mutinous instincts. Another captain might have stuck to his guns, but Hudson gave in again. He preferred compromise to battle, a fact that seemed to make him an easy touch for the hard-bitten sea-dogs of his day.

So now he set his course on a more southerly route, much to the delight of his fair weather crew. He sailed his ship the *Half Moon* across the Atlantic, along the eastern seaboard of America, and into New York harbor. After anchoring somewhere off West 42nd Street, he began navigating the river that would later bear his name. Along the way he met a number of Delaware and Mohican Indians, and at one point threw a party for several of their chiefs; his guests got so drunk that their descendants were still talking about it 200 years later.

He would travel as far as the present site of Albany before concluding that upstate New York was not the gateway to China. But his voyage was not a failure, at least not for his employers, who now claimed the Hudson River Valley as Dutch property.

Back home Hudson was criticized for selling his services to a rival power, although not for long. He was England's most experienced Arctic hand at a time when England was looking for the shortest route to the putative riches of the East; and the shortest route, for such a relatively high latitude country, was across the Arctic . . . *west* across the Arctic, Hudson himself believed. So a syndicate of wealthy English merchants headed by Sir Dudley Digges and Lord Wolstenholme now gave him command of the most lavishly funded single-ship expedition of its day, telling him, in effect, "Go find the Northwest Passage."

On April 17, 1610, Hudson sailed the 55-ton bluff-bowed bark *Discovery* out of St. Katharine's Pool on his fourth voyage of exploration. This one would make the previous voyages seem like Sunday school picnics.

Twenty miles down the Thames, he touched at Gravesend and picked up a young protégé of his named Henry Greene. Greene was a wastrel, a libertine, and all-around rogue—a peculiar addition to the crew. Robert Juet, the mate, believed Greene had been shipped aboard to spy on the others. This may have been true: a good spy can nip mutiny in the bud.

The *Discovery*'s 23-man crew was certainly no worse than the usual ragtag-and-bobtail crews of the day. It included the sharp-tongued but seemingly reliable Juet; carpenter Philip Staffe, steadfast as his name; Abacuk Prickett, a London haberdasher and Sir Dudley Digges' valet; a rough but honest salt named John King; an able seaman named Robert Bylot; a young scholar, Thomas Wydowse, who'd signed on as a passenger; and Hudson's son John, one of the ship's boys.

A motley group, yes; but hardly a devil's brew.

Hudson sailed up the east coast of Britain to Iceland, then steered a course past Greenland to the tidal overfall at the entry to Hudson Strait. The strength of this tide-rip, first noted a generation earlier by Captain John Davis, suggested a possible passage between the Atlantic and the Pacific Oceans.

Pacific, indeed! Armadas of racing ice now buffeted the *Discovery* like a cockleshell, forcing Hudson to alter his course repeatedly. At last he took his ship south to Ungava Bay, where it got stuck in a crazy quilt of ice. The crew began to grumble. Anyone who has ever been stuck in sea-ice can sympathize with them; you feel like you might be stuck there for all eternity.

Hudson's crew couldn't go anywhere, so they really couldn't act on their grumbling. And little by little they worked the *Discovery* into open water. Hudson now set his course to the northwest. On August 3, he groped his way between two scoured, massive headlands (he named them, not surprisingly, Cape Digges and Cape Wolstenholme), and entered the vast saltwater reservoir of Hudson Bay.

Abacuk Prickett, who wrote the only surviving account of the trip, was not impressed with the local scenery. "A most barren place, having nothing on it but plashes of water and riven rocks, as if it were subject to earthquakes," he remarked.

But Hudson himself was pleased, at least initially. Having just passed through a strait longer than the Strait of Magellan, he felt that he had won the Passage. But as his ship moved southward along the derelict shoreline of Hudson Bay, he may have felt that he'd won only a booby prize.

By September, he'd entered the bay's bottom pocket, the mariner's bugaboo now known as James Bay (the Hudson Bay Company would later average a shipwreck a year there). James Bay is swampy, shoaly, mucky, and wind-whipped. It's so shallow that you can be out of sight of land and still touch bottom with a paddle. Wading ashore can be like wading through quicksand.

Hudson's already frayed nerves seemed to snap, and he took out his frustration on his crew. So when Juet mocked his belief that they would be in Java by Candlemas (February 2), he flew into a rage and condemned Juet's "abuses and slanders" as mutinous behavior. The mate was stripped of his rank and replaced by Robert Bylot, the former pilot. Boatswain Francis Clements was deposed on similar charges and replaced with a ruffian named William Wilson.

Obviously, Hudson was a man with mutiny on his mind. But whatever else he had on his mind he kept to himself. Back and forth, back and forth, he zigzagged between the low gaunt shores of James Bay. Each zigzag took him deeper into the season and farther from the south winds that might have liberated him from what Prickett refers to as "a labyrinth without end."

The first winter storms came and went, and still he continued his seemingly futile wanderings. At one point, he put his ship on the rocks—not a blunder you'd expect from such an expert navigator. At another point, he managed to lose one of the ship's anchors.

One day some of his crew went ashore and discovered footprints etched in the snow. You can imagine their astonishment at this sight: what manner of human being (if human being at all) could live in such a cold, dreadful, godforsaken place? They may have found in these solitary prints a kind of mirror image for their own increasingly unhappy state; they were mired in the cold themselves, and with a captain who seemed not only to have lost his way, but his marbles as well.

On November 1, both captain and crew gave in to the inevitable and hauled their ship aground in southeastern James Bay. By November 10 the *Discovery* was frozen in for the winter.

This was not the South Seas, the Spice Islands, or Cathay. Nor was it even England's green and pleasant if somewhat dank land. It was the cruel subarctic of North America, and no European had ever overwintered here before. Thus Hudson's crew hardly knew what to expect from the coming winter. Maybe they'd heard stories about Sir Hugh Willoughby's men wintering in Arctic Russia sixty years earlier and being frozen like statues. With their inadequate clothing, they may have wondered if they would end up in the same condition themselves.

Almost immediately, there was trouble. Hudson ordered the carpenter to build a house on shore. Staffe told him that it was too late in the year to begin a construction project: there was snow on the ground, the ground itself was frozen, and the cold would make his labor punishing. Hudson lost his temper and threatened to have Staffe, one of his most loyal crewmen, hung. Grumbling, Staffe built the house.

And then there was the case of the dead man's wardrobe. John Williams, the gunner, had died. The custom of the sea called for a dead sailor's garments to be auctioned off; Hudson violated this custom by giving Williams' coat to Henry Greene. When Greene went hunting with the recently maligned Staffe, Hudson took back the coat and offered it to Robert Bylot. And when Greene protested, Hudson gave him a violent tongue lashing.

"To speak of all the troubles of this cold winter," writes Prickett, "would be tedious." He adds that the cold "lamed" most of the crew, including himself. Actually, what lamed them was not the cold but "Herod's daughter"—the old seafarer's term for scurvy. With limbs swollen and barely functional, pulpy gums, and unhealing wounds, they must have looked a sorry sight; and when hunger forced them to emulate caribou and paw the snow for lichen, they must have looked an even sorrier sight.

Toward spring they had a visitor—an Indian curious about these pitiful strangers who were squatting in his land. Hudson gave the man, among other trinkets, a looking-glass. For the first time, the Indian could contemplate his own face. He must have liked what he saw, for the next day he returned pulling a sledge laden with furs. He wanted to barter a deer skin for a hatchet, but Hudson indicated that a hatchet was worth two skins. The Indian could tell a squeeze when he saw one and although he agreed to the trade, he never came back.

This meeting, presumably the first contact between Europeans and subarctic Amerindians, inaugurated the fur trade in Hudson Bay; a trade that would begin in earnest some sixty years later with the arrival of the Hudson Bay Company. Typically, the pale-skinned outsider tried to take advantage of the native.

The Indian must have passed along an account of the meeting to his people. Or perhaps the snowed-up land had eyes. For the pale-skinned outsiders entered the oral lore of the James Bay Cree. Many years later, Andrew Graham (c.1733–1815), the Hudson Bay Company's chief factor, wrote that a group of Cree called the Oupeeshepow were still telling stories about "the arrival and wintering of the unfortunate Captain Henry Hudson, as handed down to them by the tradition of their ancestors."

Prickett's journal is vague about where this singularly unpleasant wintering took place. But in 1668 a Boston captain named Zachariah Gillam sailed his ketch *Nonsuch* into Rupert Bay and found "the ruins of a house which had been built there above sixty years before by the English." If this house was in fact Staffe's (the time frame is right), then Hudson and his men spent the winter near the mouth of the Rupert River almost exactly where the present-day Cree community of Waskaganish is located.

With the ice retreating from shore, Hudson weighed anchor on June 12 and stood out to the north. A short while later, he deposed Robert Bylot as mate and replaced him with Philip Staffe, who was back in his favor. The rest of the crew were appalled: Staffe could neither read or write and had no knowledge of navigation. Since Hudson had already forbidden any of them to keep an account of the *Discovery*'s position, they now felt that, in Prickett's words, "the master and his ignorant mate would take the ship whither the master pleased."

And "whither the master pleased" happened to be a continuation of his search for the Northwest Passage. Hudson knew his crew had had enough of northern travel, but he seems to have thought they would behave themselves if he was the only man on board capable of bringing the ship home to England. He was mistaken.

Tongues wag on a ship, especially on a ship whose larder is almost empty. Somehow word got out that Hudson had a private reserve of food for himself and his so-called favorites. William Wilson asked Staffe about this, and the carpenter replied that certain members of the crew needed to be "kept up." Wilson must have wondered what would happen to those who weren't being kept up, those subsisting on meager rations, like himself.

You can envision the scene in the *Discovery*'s smoky, ill-lit foc'sle: a group of hungry, disgruntled men are lying in their bunks; they believe that their captain would like nothing better than to starve them out; they curse this captain with a saltiness of expression unique to their era; and while they're at it, they curse the ice, the cold, the winds, indeed the whole bloody North. If they ever want to see their homes in England again, there's only one thing to do . . .

With the ship trapped in pack-ice off Charlton Island, Wilson and Henry Greene crept into Prickett's cabin, told him of their plan to take over the ship, and enlisted his support. Prickett tried to dissuade them from doing "such an evil thing in the sight of God and man," or so he says (his journal can be read as a brief on behalf of his own innocence). Green cut him short: he knew mutiny was a hangable offence, but said he would rather be hanged at home than starved abroad.

The turncoat Greene was the plot's instigator, but he had the support of at least half the crew, including Juet, Clements, and even the cook. As eager as Prickett may have been to save Hudson's skin, he was considerably more eager to save his own, and he joined them.

Shortly after daybreak on Sunday morning, June 23, 1611, Henry Hudson stepped onto the deck. He was grabbed instantly and his arms bound. While he was struggling with his captors, the mutineers rounded up his favorites—his son John, the passenger Wydowse (what a lousy vacation this was turning out to be!), and quartermaster John King. Then "the poor, the sick, and the lame" were herded out of their cabins and bundled into the ship's shallop with

Hudson and the others. This last action seems to have been a form of triage: there was no point in wasting precious food reserves on men already at death's door.

There remained Staffe. The mutineers needed his carpentry skills for the long journey home, but he wanted no part of them or their mutiny, so he elected to join Hudson in the shallop. This display of conscience must have touched the mutineers, because they gave Staffe his chest, along with a musket, powder and shot, some meal, and a pot. Then they cut loose the shallop.

To have attacked the Arctic four times with such high-minded goals, and now *this*—we can only guess how Hudson must have felt as he watched the *Discovery*'s masts sink below the horizon.

For the moment, however, let us leave him in the shallop and return to the mutineers. Their journey home was a journey of attrition. At Cape Digges, a trading session (bells and jews' harps for venison) with the local Inuit suddenly turned nasty; Greene, Wilson, and three others were killed in the subsequent melee. Then Juet starved to death during a haphazard Atlantic crossing; the others survived by eating marrow from the bones of birds fried in candle wax. Only seven made it back to England, and those more dead than alive.

The survivors blamed the mutiny on their conveniently dead shipmates. But what probably saved them from the gallows was their claim that they'd located the elusive Northwest Passage. This may have been a ruse, or they may have actually believed that the capacious bay from which they'd so recently escaped had an outlet to the Pacific. In any event, you don't hang a potential economic windfall.

And there was an economic windfall, too. For the next 150 years, English ships poked around Hudson Bay in search of a thoroughfare to the Pacific. As a result, the Bay became the hub of the fur trade and thus a gateway to riches no less fabulous than the ones the exotic Orient was expected to deliver.

But what of the castaways themselves? Caught up in the Passage craze, Hudson's sponsors made virtually no effort to find him. Later travelers to Hudson Bay would bring back stories about blue-eyed men dressed in deerskins, wooden stakes carved by whiteman's tools, and English scalps decorating native wigwams. But such stories were inconclusive and often seemed like attempts to get the same kind of publicity that a person might get today if he suddenly announced, "Hey! I've found Amelia Earhart!"

Thus the nearly universal verdict: Hudson and his men died of cold and exposure shortly after being set adrift.

Yet I find it hard to believe that men who'd survived an entire sub-arctic winter couldn't have survived a while longer during the sub-arctic spring. Hudson himself possessed a tenacity that, in another era, might have put him on a lofty Himalayan summit or at one of the Poles; a tenacity that would not be diminished by the desire to get his son to safety. Also, he wasn't bundled into a mere dinghy. A typical shallop of his day ("chaloupe en fagot," as the French called it) might have been as long as thirty feet, and would have had at least one half-deck, high sides, and one or more masts.

Such a boat could have managed the open sea without too much difficulty. In fact, it's been claimed that Hudson sailed the shallop out of the Bay and all the way across the North Atlantic to, of all places, Spitzbergen. This claim is based on a freeze-dried corpse reputedly exhumed during a 1823 Spitzbergen expedition and somehow identified as Hudson's mortal remains. But the corpse probably belonged to one of the many whalers buried in Spitzbergen, since it's rather unlikely that a navigator of Hudson's ability would have missed England by more than 2,000 miles.

The mutiny seems to have occurred somewhere north of Charlton Island. Apart from Charlton Island itself, which still might have been surrounded by pack-ice, the nearest landfall for Hudson would have been the eastern shore of James Bay, perhaps twenty to thirty miles away, or one of the countless rock-ribbed islands between Charlton and the mainland.

But the nearest landfall might not have been the easiest or even the most likely one for a boat whose high freeboard would make its course subject to winds and drifts.

The current in James Bay is counter-clockwise and northward-tending. Even today, despite the alteration of flow rates into the Bay by Hydro Quebec's massive river replumbing scheme, the body of a person drowned in the southern part of James Bay always seems to wash up near the northern part of it. In some places, you can even see the currents' froth line zigzagging inexorably northward like a strand of runaway stitching.

Using the Canadian Hydrographic Survey's tidal prediction software, I checked out the tide for Charlton Island on the morning of June 23, 1611. So far as I can determine, the mutiny took place just as the tide was starting to ebb. An ebb tide with a pronounced northerly flow on it—Hudson would have read the writing on the water (so to speak) and ferried the shallop accordingly.

I dare say the trip would have been, if not a piece of cake, at least not overwhelmingly arduous. The mutineers had towed the shallop to open water before setting it adrift, but there still might have been enough ice around to act as a shock absorber on waves. Likewise the southerly winds that usually blow in James Bay at this time of year would have assisted the shallop in its northerly course.

Of course, all of this is conjecture. There might have been a hurricane blowing from the north on the morning of the mutiny; Prickett's journal could be unreliable; and the shallop itself could have even been downright unseaworthy. But that's what makes the Hudson story so interesting: there are so many question marks, so many "perhapses," "probablys," and "could have beens," that everyone becomes their own sleuth.

Now let's go back to our movie: Huddling together in the boat, the castaways notice the current turning like a rapids toward shore. Soon they find themselves entering a large bay littered with islands—islands whose rocky eminences seem to be painted a soft, beguiling red. Fadeout again.

This is the Paint Hills area of James Bay, and the Cree who live here today tell stories about a boatload of white men who fetched up on their shores a long time ago. That these stories are more or less fragmentary and that some of them are even a bit improbable (Henry Hudson marrying a beautiful Indian princess?) is not surprising: four hundred years can have a corrosive effect even on something so apparently immutable as an oral tradition.

The men in the boat (say the stories) were not in very good shape. Some of them looked as if they'd been beaten up. Their leader may have been thrown in the water. Several had bloated faces and feet—a sign of scurvy. One or two died just before or not long after the boat reached land. None of them were in any condition to travel, so they remained in the Paint Hills area and recuperated.

The leader had gold rings on his fingers, a curiously upturned nose, and—most curious of all—red hair. None of the local Cree had ever seen a man or even a *pwaat* (a white-skinned, hairy-faced being with cannibalistic tendencies) with red hair before, so they gave him the name Firebeard.

This may be the only known portrait of Hudson, although many of the Cree I queried did not know him by that name. One man told me: "Henry Hudson? Isn't he the guy they named the Oh! Henry bar for?" Another man said he'd always liked the way Hudson would stroll over to a woman he wanted to date and casually say, "Shall we?" I thought I might be onto something—Hudson's method of courting, perhaps—until I realized that he was talking about Rock Hudson, not Henry.

Now back to the stories. A few describe Hudson (or Firebeard) marrying the local chief's daughter. One story even has him heading north to Ungava and marrying an Inuit woman. In most of the others, however, he sails back to the place where he'd spent the winter on the assumption that that's where a rescue ship from England would go to look for him. He may have been so confident that such a ship would come that he didn't try to make the undeniably risky trip home himself.

No rescue ship came, of course, and Hudson and his fellow maroons were obliged to spend a second winter in James Bay. The following spring they set off inland for French Canada in the company of Cree guides. And here, abruptly, the stories end. Neither the guides or Hudson were ever heard from again.

In the 1950's, a rock with the inscription "H H 1612 CAPTIVE" was discovered near the Ottawa River in Ontario. Since one of the canoe routes to French Canada from James Bay would have been south via the Moose, Abitibi, and Ottawa Rivers, there's at least the possibility that Hudson might have been captured by Ottawa Valley Indians and held hostage; he could have even died in captivity. But whether he memorialized this captivity on a rock is another matter. In fact, the inscription's authenticity is somewhat dubious.

While I was in eastern James Bay, I heard about a place in the Paint Hills area called *Waamistikushiish*. This centipede of a word means "Young Englishman's Grave" in Cree. Elders in the community of Wemindji told me that the young Englishman buried there was Hudson's son, that he'd died in a drowning accident, and that his body had washed ashore not far from his final resting place. Or so the previous generation of elders had told them. There was even a rumor that Hudson himself might be buried in the grave, too.

The prospect of a Hudson grave—*any* Hudson grave—filled me with excitement despite the fact that none of my informants seemed to know how or when John Hudson had drowned, or how his father, who supposedly had left the area, could have ended up in the same grave. No matter: a bonafide grave might shed some light on the mystery of what happened to at least one of the Hudsons after the mutiny.

So, with a pair of guides from Wemindji, I traveled to the peninsula near the northwestern edge of Paint Hills Bay where the Waamistikushiish site was located. At the place where we hauled ashore our canoe, a seemingly endless rubble of rocks led up to an elevated terrace. Four hundred years ago this terrace would have been at sea-level, so we began our search for the grave in the open lichen-woodland forest immediately behind it.

The site's groundcover was the fructose lichen *Cladina rangiferina*, otherwise known as caribou moss. At times this spongy silver-grey lichen would assume the shape of an impassive head, or an entire gallery of impassive heads, and at other times a burial mound. More than once, in fact, I found myself approaching what I thought might be John Hudson's grave, only to realize that it was simply a mound of lichen.

Scattered around the area were the fire rings and collapsed *miichiwahp* (tipi) poles of old Cree campsites. Near one of them, a bear skull had been tied to the branches of a tree—a time-honored gesture of respect to the slain bear's spirit.

All at once I noticed a large pile of stones on a ridge. With thoughts of a certain fateful voyage, a mutiny, a drowning, and a possible double grave jostling together in my mind, I dashed over and began pulling the lichen away from the stones. The more I pulled away, the more stones I seemed to uncover. It turned out that I was excavating not an early seventeenth century burial cairn, but a deposit of glacial till.

If this had been a movie, we might have found two well-preserved bodies, one with reddish hair, under the next pile of stones we investigated. But it wasn't a movie, and all we found during the next few days was a relatively recent tobacco tin, some spent shotgun shells, and another bear skull. Finally, we gave up. The site was too overgrown, the pickings too slim, and the mosquitoes too voracious.

Yet as we left the site, I couldn't help wondering about all the stones we'd left unturned at Waamistikushiish. Perhaps there *was* a seventeenth century grave back there somewhere. But then again, maybe the stories weren't altogether accurate. Maybe John Hudson hadn't drowned at all. Maybe he'd stayed in the area and eventually gone native. And maybe his father had lived to a ripe old age, a doting paterfamilias surrounded by his red-haired Cree progeny. Or perhaps he'd starved to death while waiting for the ship that never came.

The answer lies buried somewhere in the Great Silent North that obsessed Henry Hudson . . . and that at some point claimed his life as part of its own.

The Dream People

N ight falls on Utshimassits, Labrador. Outside the tent, it's cold. Inside the tent, it's cold, too. Somewhere a dog or a wolf is howling, hard to say which. Or perhaps it's the wind howling down from the height of land. Two grizzled crones take turns spitting into an empty lard bucket. Then my host, a tubercular wraith of a man named Thomas Pastitshi, spits into this selfsame bucket and begins telling a story about the time Wolverine, trickster hero of the Labrador Indians, got stuck inside a bear's skull. His laughter, albeit accompanied by a bad cough, transforms the family tent into a voluptuous palace . . .

Very few people seem to know where Labrador is, apart from the fact that it presumably lies up there in the vast and inhospitable North. Even the Canadian postal service doesn't know where it is: Labrador's mail routinely ends up in El Salvador. Subarctic barrens, glacial erratics, and mosquito-infested muskeg would appear to have precious little human accessibility—certainly less accessibility than El Salvador.

As for the Labrador Indians, they're off the map, too. Who or what they are, or where they came from, is anybody's guess. Maybe they're a splinter band of Eastern Cree separated from the main group way back in Native American dream time. Or maybe they were dwellers of the deciduous woodlands driven north by the fierce Iroquois. Or maybe, just maybe, they're the last tatterdemalion remnant of a band of Ice Age hunters now wholly lost to history. Yet whatever their origin, they are among the least known, least assimilated, and least anthropologized Natives in North America.

Sometimes called Naskapi or Montagnais-Naskapi, though not by each other (Naskapi means "crude ones" in their language), nowadays Labrador's Indians call themselves Innu, a name which means "The People." It's a happily egocentric name which seems to consign everyone else to another species. It's also a name that invariably gets the Innu confused with their time-honored enemies, the Inuit. But whereas most of the Labrador Inuit inhabit one large town, Nain, the Innu live in two scruffy little villages, Utshimassits and Sheshashui, more than two hundred miles apart. And whereas the Inuit are now mostly employed as commercial fishermen, the Innu—at least the older, more entrenched Innu—still cling to a traditional hunter-gatherer lifestyle. Many of them camp out in the bush trapping and hunting caribou, from October until late March. That's a time of year when Labrador's temperatures commonly drop to fifty or sixty degrees below zero and the snow tends to pile up in Biblical proportions. The People seem to like such weather.

I first visited Utshimassits, otherwise known as Davis Inlet, in early September 1986. Before I went, a friend warned me to watch out for rocks. The previous year he'd tried to land there in his sea kayak and was repelled by rock-throwing teenagers. Rather than risk injury to his craft or his person, he'd made his landfall farther up the coast, in Shango Bay.

This story piqued my curiosity, maybe even my masochism (all writers seem to be masochists by nature), so the very next day I hopped the mail flight from Goose Bay to Utshimassits. The trip was an adventure, beginning with the NATO-F4 Phantom that nearly clipped us upon takeoff. Our plane got as far as Makkovik, kicked and buffeted by the boreal elements, and then seemed to break down. Actually, it ran out of fuel. The only fuel in Makkovik was helicopter fuel, for which a filter was needed. And as there was no filter in Makkovik, a special plane had to fly one in from Goose Bay. Bad weather in Goose Bay, filter delayed. Then when the plane did arrive, suddenly Makkovik's generator conked out. No power, no fuel. The pilot wandered off into the tundra to pick berries.

Ah, Labrador, I thought: where nothing is easy. Just as I'd resigned myself to spending the next day or two in Makkovik, the generator sputtered back to life. In another half hour, we were again airborne . . . and flying into a major storm. Sleet, snow, and ice pellets quickly rendered the windshield wipers useless and the front window opaque. The pilot, undaunted, kept rolling down the side window and sticking out his head to see where we were going. Each time he did this, the Innu man sleeping next to me would jerk awake and snarl what I assumed was the Inueimun version of *Shut the window, motherfucker* . . . Later, when I got to know a little of the language, I realized he couldn't have said that, for Inueimun has no approximation of "motherfucker." Probably the fellow had just been saying: *It's freezing in here!* A not unusual Labrador sentiment.

At last the plane touched down in Utshimassits. It was almost with relief that I braced myself for a pelting of rocks. The rocks never came. Too bad. I'd been hoping for perhaps a chunk or two of four-billion-year-old komatiite, the world's oldest rock and a rarity found only in northern Labrador.

Instead of stoning me, The People kept walking over and shaking my hand gratuitously. They seemed to regard me, a White Person, as a unique specimen of humanity. Doubtless that's because not too many of my race make it to this farflung Native fastness. Those who do are either social workers or government representatives. I suspect my kayaking friend might have been mistaken for one of the latter, which would explain the geologic missiles.

Within minutes of my arrival, a man with a cuprous, epicanthic face invited me into his tent; a tent which he rightly preferred to his uninsulated tract house next door. After he'd given me a cup of tea, he took out a bear patella and put it on top of the stove: if the patella moved, he said, today's hunt would be a success; if it didn't, well, it was back to bed. Meanwhile the man's wife was cleaning out their kids' noses the traditional way: by sucking out the mucal matter and spitting it on the floor.

I thought this a rather good introduction to the Innu. Yet by far the best introduction to a new culture comes from camping on the land where that culture itself is encamped. So it was that I left this man (he was going to bed anyway) and trekked off into the bush. Or, as it's referred to in these parts, "the country." Four or five miles north of Utshimassits, I stopped and pitched my own tent. The next few days I cultivated my solitude. Made bannock. Fought off insects. Studied my English-Innu dictionary. Made more bannock. Fought off more insects. And gazed up at a sky so clear, so unpolluted, so starkly blue that I felt I could reach up and touch it had I a mind to do so.

One thing I noticed during those few days: there was almost no wildlife. Apart from the black flies and mosquitoes, I saw only a couple of partridges and one lemming. Fortunately I didn't have to live off the land or I would have been very hungry, a plight which (alas!) would have enhanced my understanding of The People. For the desperate hustle for game is, or was, the driving force behind their existence. So sparse was this game that they'd often try to "dream" it; for instance, a dream of claw marks on a tree would indicate a hibernating bear inside a nearby tree. Or they'd try to divine it—the char on a burnt scapula bone would tell them the whereabouts of a particularly recalcitrant herd of caribou. If all else failed, there was always a certain unmentionable cuisine. Around 1900 the Hudson Bay trader Sebastien Mackenzie found an Innu woman who was pounding up the bones of her family for soup (she'd already consumed their flesh and entrails). That this woman had violated the deepest of human taboos is a tribute to her utter dereliction, along with the dereliction of the land.

Another thing I couldn't help but notice: this derelict land itself. It seemed to grow primarily moss and boulders. If you rotated the crops, you'd get boulders and moss. In more or less verdant areas, there'd be the occasional black spruce, a tree seemingly twisted by some complex inner torture. Such flora helps explain why The People never labored under the delusion, so dear to their Native brethren, that the Earth was their mother. For them, our planet was a lowdown, niggling place conspicuously lacking in maternal teats. Just to survive on it stretched all their resources. Small wonder that they turned the wolverine—that largest, most canny, most predacious member of the weasel family—into a sort of culture hero. The wolverine is the North's ultimate survivor.

I was not a survivor myself. After four days in the country, I retreated to Utshimassits, where I met a bilingual man named Uinipapeu Rich. That evening Uinipapeu and I visited an elder who spoke no English. Back in 1933, this elder, Tshinish Pasteen, found a set of bones that may or may not have belonged to Jim Martin, guide of the ill-fated Koehler Expedition. I was curious about this expedition, so I inquired about the bones. Uinipapeu translated. Tshinish shrugged. Whose bones they were he had no idea. A small White Man's. A large White Man's. He couldn't be sure. More or less as a consolation prize, he told me a story about how loons originated.

"You are interested in old stories?" Uinipapeu asked later. And he told me a story about a woolly mammoth which not only fetched me back to the early Pleistocene, but also suggested that this animal, extinct elsewhere in the world, was an active if not a downright malevolent force in Utshimassits.

LM: "That's kind of scary. A mammoth stomping people and then eating them."

UR: "Not as scary as the time I got trapped in a revolving door in St. John's, Newfoundland. *That* was scary, man. I'd rather take my chances with the mammoth . . ."

I decided to take my chances with the mammoth, too. So I started going to Uinipapeu's house for stories. Here, I thought, is the long-lost history of the Innu; a history made up of giants, monsters, and talking animals rather than mundanities like kings and world wars.

One day Uinipapeu told me one of his father's favorite stories, "The Shit Man," as a Hulk Hogan video was playing in the background. While Hulk was making mincemeat of a fellow wrestler more paunch than man, Uinipapeu's brood of kids looked on in silent wonder. No doubt they were admiring all that resplendent flesh: a thin physique, in their culture, is associated with starvation.

Ideally, Hulk Hogan is not the best context for Innu storytelling. The best context is the so-called country. On a winter's night. Around a campfire. With no evil spirits lurking nearby. But just then it didn't matter whether Hulk Hogan was headbutting someone into submission or Doris Day was singing "Que será, será." I was hooked.

So began a series of trips to Utshimassits and Sheshashui in search of stories. Almost every elder I visited seemed to have his own special repertoire. I heard origin stories. *Mistapeo* (shaman) stories. Cannibal stories. Scatological stories. Stories about humans and animals getting married. *Lots* of those. For in a hunting culture, marrying an animal is the natural extension of a hunter's hope and desire that game will give itself to him.

I became a kind of hunter-gatherer myself. Once in a while I'd strike out, as when an elder with a scantiness of tooth informed me that a White Man couldn't possibly understand an Innu *atnukan* (story) and in any event he was too senile, he said, to remember one. More often, I would get the equivalent of a home run, as when one man reeled off the entire Tchakapesh cycle in a single sitting.

In Sheshashui, I dropped in on a storyteller, Apinam Ashini, who was deep in his spruce beer cups. He was standing rather haphazardly among the animal bones, flip-tops, rancid caribou skins, and old snow-machine parts of his front yard. A purist might take exception to all this trash, but it's probably unfair to demand a suburban lawn ethic from a man whose people had no fixed abodes until a generation ago.

AA: "*Ehe!* They say God made the world. I think Kwakwadjec,

Wolverine, made it. I *know* he did. My grandfather told me so. He put his lips to a muskrat's ass and . . . blew. Out came the world."

LM: "Your grandfather put his lips to a muskrat's ass??"

AA: "No, Kwakwadjec. That's why the world is so much shit."

LM: "Well, maybe your people ought to be worshipping him Sunday mornings. Maybe the priest ought to be saying something like, Our Kwakwadjec Who art in Heaven . . ."

AA: "But Kwakwadjec is *not* in heaven. He's here, around here. Some twenty years ago, I saw him myself in a shaking tent on the Goose River. He danced around and he farted. Farted for, oh, two hours. Kwakwadjec was a great farter, friend. And a great one for poking his penis into *matweuns* . . ."

Part of this was Apinam's spruce beer talking. But another part is the unabashed ribaldry of The People. In their language, references to bodily functions and the genitalia carry no moral or immoral connotation whatsoever. Smut is White Man's invention, not theirs. As far back as 1634, Father Paul le Jeune, in his *Jesuit Relation*, complained: "In place of saying, through wonder, 'Jesus! what is that?' or 'My God! who has done that?,' these vile and infamous people [the Innu] pronounce the names of the private parts of man and woman. Their lips are constantly foul with these obscenities, and it is the same with the little children . . ."

Innu stories tend to be just as ribald as the Innu themselves. Here let me interject a brief polemic:

One of the myriad injustices perpetrated by White Man on the Indian is the theft of his lore and the subsequent whitewashing of it for puritans of all shapes and denominations. Especially puritan parents eager for prematurely puritan offspring. Cleaned up versions of Indian stories with much too cute drawings line the mythology/folklore shelves of libraries and bookstores. On those shelves, the well-endowed Ojibwa trickster Nanabozho seems to have lost his organ of generation. Coyote, the Hopi-Navaho culture hero, ends up losing his divinely-ordained ability to shit whenever and wherever he pleases. Even Wolverine has found himself airbrushed a couple of times. All because earthiness and scatology run counter to White Man's romantic image—romantic *and* patronizing—of the Indian as a brave, clean, sexless Child of Nature. Thus censored, the Indian becomes a sort of Bambi in Native drag, very, very unthreatening.

A good many of the stories I heard would have brought a blush to Father le Jeune's virginal cheeks. Others that are dirt-free might have disturbed the good Father owing to their triumphantly heathen point of view. Yet whether they're scatological or hygienic, Innu stories were not invented to entertain the Jesuits. The Innu themselves believe their stories originated in dreams, particularly dreams brought on by fasting or mega-doses of grease before bedtime. To dream is an essential aspect of Innu life. Even today a person will go to sleep and, upon waking, narrate his dreams to whoever happens to be around; if there's no one around, he'll tell them to the family dog. Anything to avoid the bad luck likely to bedevil a hoarder of dreams. From telling a dream to telling an *atnukan*—that's perhaps a difference time and a bit of license will take care of quite nicely.

Bad as it is not to tell your dreams, it's even worse not to act on them. You risk becoming a target for the most abysmal luck of all: death. I heard about an Utshimassits man who ignored his dreams, always refused to heed their advice, and who happened to step into a fox trap. When his body was found, it'd been nibbled to shreds by, it was assumed, foxes.

One day I was hanging around Sheshashui—trying to buy some snowshoes, I think—when an elder approached me and said. "I dreamed about you last night. I dreamed you were coming to my house tonight."

I gathered the man had spent much of the morning tracking me down. Which wasn't easy, given his lame, arthritic hobble. But Innu custom obliged him, nay, *forced* him to invite me to his house even if he hated my guts. I wonder what would have happened if I had refused to go there. Would the unfulfilled dream have revenged itself on him? Or would it have revenged itself on *me*? Anyway, I accepted the invitation and the man in question, John Michel, turned out to be just the sort of person I was looking for, a veritable fountain of stories and old lore. He knew cures, too. I'll always cherish his backwoods cure for a cavity: put a little gunpowder in the offending tooth and then a match to it, and BANG! the cavity's gone.

I joined John in his jerry-built, government issue house; a house that would have made a seamless fit in a Third World slum. Soon we were chatting about, not surprisingly, dreams.

JM: "All right, I'll tell you something. A person is born empty. Dreams fill him. It's just like you've got a skidoo. A skidoo can't go anywhere unless it's filled with petrol, eh?"

LM: "What about someone who hardly dreams at all? Like me?"

JM: "Why he'd be no better than a *bokageesh*. A black fly."

And so The People dream on. They dream stories, they dream the whereabouts of game, and they've even been known to dream a *bokageesh* like me. Yet what they seem incapable of dreaming is a future worthy of their own admittedly severe past. That past tilted them from one hardship to the next, one lean year to the next, and occasionally tilted them right into the lap of starvation. But at least it gave them a specific *raison d'etre*: Find some bloody food! Nowadays they're beset by a variety of bugaboos which, taken together, are worse, much worse than the specter of starvation—rampant alcoholism, low-flying NATO jets, hydro projects despoiling their land, test holes for nickel mining on their land, recreational hunters killing their caribou, huge clear-cuts in their forests, gas addiction, and suicidal despair among their teenagers. Recently, in Utsimassits, six young children whose parents were out boozing tried to heat their uninsulated house with a hot plate; the wiring was defective, the house exploded into flame, and the children burned to death. This is the stuff that nightmares rather than dreams are made of.

. . . and with a quick flutter of his hands, Thomas Pastitshi ends the telling of his story. The tent, briefly a palace, is once again only a wind-whipped heap of canvas in the immense subarctic night.

THE WOLF GIRL AND THE OTTER

Once upon a time a Wolf Girl asked an otter to marry her. The otter replied: "I can't marry someone who always has shit on her ass."

"If you refuse to marry me," the Wolf Girl told him, "I'll kill you."

When he heard this, the otter leaped into the nearest lake. The Wolf Girl waited by this lake until it froze over. There was just one breathing hole. The otter came up only to hear the Wolf Girl's voice: "Will you marry me now?"

"I suppose I'll have to marry you," the otter said, "since I have no wish to be killed."

So the two of them went to live with the Wolf Girl's brothers. Husband, wife, brothers—they all slept in the same tent. The otter thought he and his wife should have a tent of their own. "Not until you prove yourself a hunter," the brothers told him.

"I'll show you I'm a hunter," the otter said, "though my method is a little different from yours . . ."

Next day the brothers took the otter to the caribou grounds. He picked out a big bull and rushed toward it. The bull tried to run away, but the otter slipped into its ass and trampled its heart, thereby killing it. He came out the mouth.

The brothers were rolling on the ground with laughter.

"The caribou's dead," the otter said. "It doesn't matter how I killed it."

Every time they went hunting together, the otter would kill his caribou by slipping into its ass and trampling its heart. And every time that happened, the wolves would roll on the ground with laughter.

"I wish you'd tell your brothers to stop laughing at me," the otter said to his wife. She told them, but they refused to stop. They'd say: "Our brother-in-law swims in caribou shit." Or they'd say: "Our brother-in-law's nose is his *shimagin*." And then they'd be rolling on the ground again.

Finally the otter couldn't tolerate their ridicule any longer. He packed his gear and left. The Wolf Girl was very upset by this, so she set out looking for him. At last she found him in a little camp by a river. "Please come home with me, dear," she said.

"No," the otter replied. "Your brothers made fun of me once too often. Besides, I'm very happy with my new wife."

He pointed to a female otter.

Whereupon the Wolf Girl burst into tears and, it's said, cried herself to death.

WHY CERTAIN ANIMALS LIVE IN THE GROUND

Once there was a rabbit married to a lemming. The rabbit was a hunter. Every day he would go out to search for game while the little lemming minded the tent. Then came a time when the rabbit could find only enough game for himself. He would catch whatever he could and eat it before he returned home. When he got back, the lemming would ask him: "Any food?" And he would shake his head sadly, saying: "No, dear. Too bad. No food today."

With nothing to eat, the lemming began to get smaller and smaller. One day the rabbit came back and found the tent empty. For the lemming had gotten so small, she just slipped through a crack in the ground. The rabbit felt very bad about this. He thought: I must find my poor little wife and prove to her that I still love her. So he dug a hole in the ground himself, and went to look for the lemming. But he could not seem to find her. Even today he is still looking, deep down in the ground.

THE PENIS

A girl took a penis for a lover. Soon this penis was forcing her to haul him around in a *tabaskan*. As she hauled, he'd shout: "Faster! Faster! And if you don't shorten your lead, I'll find myself another girl."

Once the girl had to haul him around in a blizzard just because he was in the mood for a ride. Another time, when she didn't haul fast enough, he beat her until she felt her body would break.

One day the penis asked the girl to haul him up the hill north of camp. When she'd done that, he said: "That wasn't nearly as hard as I thought it would be. Let's try the hill south of camp. By the way, your lead is too long."

The girl bent down to shorten her lead. Suddenly she lifted up the *tabaskan* and the penis rolled off. He kept on rolling until he'd rolled down the hillside and into a frozen lake far, far below. He hit the ice with such force that he went right through it.

The girl skipped happily back to camp. I should have dumped that awful penis long ago, she told herself.

Next morning a penis came into her tent. The very same penis she'd dumped down the hillside the day before. He was all covered with frost and looked very angry.

"Try that little trick again, girl," he said, "and I'll kill you."

The girl cried. And then they went for a *tabaskan* ride.

Later the girl paid a visit to her old grandmother. "Granny," she said, "I've got a very cruel lover and I can't seem to get rid of him. What should I do?"

The grandmother brought out a bone-awl. "Try sticking him with this," she said. "That's what I used to do with all the men I didn't like."

That night the penis woke up the girl and asked her for a ride.

"And what if I don't give you one?" she said.

"I'll cut off your fingers one by one . . ."

Now the girl brought out the bone-awl and stabbed the penis with it. She stabbed him again. Again. Each time she stabbed him, a bit of grease would dribble out. She licked up some of this grease, saying, "Um-m-m, you taste good. For once."

The penis was writhing in pain on the ground. All at once he looked up and said: "I'm your father, girl. Your dear old father. How could you do such a thing to your own father?"

And then he died.

At last the girl was free.

THE DREAM PEOPLE

THE CANNIBAL LYNX

A lynx had a great fondness for human women. He'd marry them and, if there was no other food, eat them for his supper. He ate one wife after he was married to her for just two days. Another wife he ate even as they were making love.

After a while women seemed to catch on to the lynx. Maybe it was the way he tested their thighs for meat before he asked them to marry him. Or maybe it was the drool on his lips when they agreed to do so. Whatever the reason, he began to have some difficulty in finding a wife.

At last the lynx found a woman willing to marry him. She had a face like a porcupine's and so many lice on her head that they kept dropping into the stewpot. Yet she left him when he tried to put her at the end of his roasting stick.

Now the lynx was all alone. All alone and very, very hungry. He searched around for game, but he couldn't find any. No woman, either. So he said to himself: Maybe *I'm* good to eat . . .

He gnawed off one of his legs and put it on his roasting stick. Once he'd cooked the leg, he took a few cautious bites. Rolled the meat around in his mouth. Swallowed it. Well, he exclaimed, I don't taste bad at all. He ate the rest of the leg, including the bone.

Next day the lynx cut off the other leg and ate that, too. The day after that, he ate his arm. Then his other arm. Next went his loins, his shoulders, and his intestines.

Finally only one thing was left—his heart.

And he was still hungry.

So he tore out his heart, cooked and ate it.

That was the end of the cannibal lynx.

THE FIRST LOON

Long ago there were two lovers, a brother and sister. All night long they would fondle and embrace on their sleeping skins. This did not please their parents, who said: You can love each other and be first cousins, but not, certainly *not*, brother and sister.

"But why can't I love my brother?" the sister asked.

"And why can't I love my sister?" asked the brother.

"Because it's unhealthy, that's why," their parents said.

Hearing this, they loved each other even more.

At last the *mistapeo* spoke out against them: "A brother and sister who are lovers, that will bring a bad winter and plenty of starving."

The boy was forced to go into hiding. But wherever he hid, near or far, he'd only need to sing and his sister would hear him. And then she would come running.

Several months passed and the girl gave birth to a baby boy. She was carrying it in her moss-bag when one of her older brothers said: "I hope a lynx bites out its heart!"

"How can you say such a nasty thing?" the girl asked.

"Because your baby is unhealthy, that's why."

The girl did not understand this at all. To her, the baby looked as healthy as any she'd ever seen.

Now the girl's brothers decided to do something about the father of this baby. Although he was their younger brother, he was bringing shame on the family. The best way to get rid of this shame, they figured, was to get rid of the boy himself.

A while later the boy was singing for his sister. The girl put on her snowshoes and followed his song. The brothers tracked their sister all the way to the shore of Michikimau. And there, in the middle of the frozen lake, the boy was waiting.

"Look at the lovely baby I've brought you!" the girl exclaimed.

Just then one of the brothers shot an arrow directly into the baby's heart. "It's not lovely anymore," he said.

The boy knew they would try to shoot his heart, too. So he quickly sang a hole in the ice. He took off all his clothes and jumped into this hole. The next instant he was a loon, flying up out of the cold water. And as he flew, he cried mournfully, for his sweetheart would never come to him again.

THE DREAM PEOPLE

THE WOLF

Once upon a time a boy fell sick. When he tried to move, he felt pain. In his stomach was a howling which frightened people.

So an old *mistapeo* came to the boy's tent. Our son is dying, the mother told the man. The *mistapeo* listened to the boy's body, then he looked up and said: "This boy has swallowed a wolf."

"Swallowed a wolf?" exclaimed the father.

"Yes, and it's the wolf that's sick. The boy is fine."

"We must get the wolf out of him . . ."

"No," said the *mistapeo*, "you must not. The boy will die then. Instead the wolf must be cured."

Now the old man bent down and listened again. He said: "The wolf seems to need another wolf—a female."

"Isn't one wolf in my son enough?" inquired the father.

"He needs two wolves. Otherwise, the one will always be sick."

The *mistapeo* left the tent. He was gone for quite a while. When he came back, he had a young girl with him. "She has three wolves in her," he explained. "That's one wolf too many."

Now the girl put her lips to the boy's lips. All of a sudden there was a noise like a big animal moving from one den to another.

"Her wolf has gone to the boy," the *mistapeo* said, "which means his wolf will be all right now."

So it happened that the boy got back his health.

THE SHIT MAN

Once a big wind struck a camp and swept all the shit together into a man. This man stood up. Stretched his limbs. And began walking around. Wherever he went, people would say: "Take your awful smell somewhere else, Shit Man."

"I'll be glad to do that," the Shit Man told them, "if you'll give me some clothes to cover my nakedness."

Right away they gave him a nice caribou-skin shirt and some

leggings, moccasins with otter-fur fringes, and a beaded neck amulet.

"I'd like a canoe, too."

They gave him a freshly-sewn birchbark canoe, saying: "Here, take it, and get out of our camp."

The Shit Man took the canoe and paddled downriver until he came to another camp. A boy came out to see if he was friend or enemy. "I'll only talk to the headman," the Shit Man announced, puffing up his chest.

So the headman paddled out to his canoe. Ah, he thought to himself, this fellow must be very important, he's dressed so well. I'll bring him back and feast him, and maybe I'll get something out of it.

All at once the wind changed. The headman thought: My new friend smells bad, it's true, but if I mention this to him, he might be insulted.

Thus the Shit Man was brought ashore and a feast prepared in his honor. All the young girls gathered around him, for they thought he might make a good partner for the night. But when they smelled him, they quickly changed their minds.

In the midst of the feast, it started to rain. The Shit Man knew he would drip away in this rain, so he leaped to his feet and ran into the woods.

"It seems we've insulted our guest," the headman declared. "That's not good, not good at all, because he's so important."

And he went off in search of this guest. In a little clearing, he saw the clothes, moccasins, and neck amulet the man had been wearing, yet he couldn't seem to find the man himself. All he found was a fresh pile of shit.

THE ORIGIN OF SPRUCE SAP

Once two sisters had a camp to themselves. The younger girl was named Pitsu. Each could hunt, fish, and trap on her own, without help from a man.

One evening a man happened to visit their camp. He had nowhere to sleep, he said, and asked if he could sleep in their tent. It was quite cold outside, so neither Pitsu nor her sister had any objection to this.

The man slept right beside Pitsu. In the middle of the night, he placed his hand between her legs. She did not push it away.

"Do you like that?" he asked.

"Yes," she said, "but I don't know what it means."

"It means you're supposed to get excited."

Said Pitsu: "I only get excited when I see the northern lights children dancing across the sky."

This girl is really innocent, the man thought, but I know how to change that . . . He cut off one of his testicles and stuck it in Pitsu's vagina. Since he was a *mistapeo*, he could conjure up another one, no problem, whenever he wished.

"Why did you do that?" asked Pitsu.

"I did it to make you interested in men. Keep it there and you'll soon notice the difference. Maybe one day I'll come back and claim you."

Next morning the man left. Pitsu was eager to see what would happen when another man showed up. A couple of days later a pair of hunters, father and son, arrived at the camp and asked if they could spend the night. Be our guests, the elder sister told him. The father slept next to her while the son slept next to Pitsu.

The man right next to her made Pitsu very excited. In the middle of the night, she reached over and grabbed his hand and put it between her legs.

"Hey, woman!" the man exclaimed, feeling the testicle. "What's that you've got down there?"

"I borrowed it from a friend," Pitsu said.

The man was so upset by this that he woke his father and both decided to spend the night elsewhere.

Several days later another hunter, young and good-looking, came to the camp. It wasn't cold, but Pitsu asked him to stay the night anyway. As was her custom, she took his hand and put it between her legs.

"You seem to have grown a testicle, woman," the hunter said.

"What's a testicle?" asked Pitsu.

"Something only a man should have," he told her. And then he ran off into the night, too.

Poor Pitsu! Every time a man came to camp, she somehow managed to frighten him away. She thought to herself: If I can't have a man, maybe I can have a woman. So she asked her sister to sleep with her.

The sister had no objection to this. Indeed, she said she'd always wanted to lie down and fondle Pitsu's loins.

Soon the girls had pulled off each other's leggings.

The sister saw Pitsu's testicle.

"You shouldn't have *that* between your legs, dear Pitsu," she said. And she yanked out the testicle and flung it WHACK! against a spruce tree. It split right open and all the juices flowed down along the bark of the tree.

And that's how spruce sap came into the world.

Dog Day Revolutionary

(from *Last Places*)

While I was waiting at the Akureyri pier for the ferry to Grimsey, I began reading a book about the Danish soldier of fortune Jorgen Jorgensen. Icelanders refer to Jorgensen as their Dog Day King because he came to power during the dog days of one very remarkable summer in the year 1809. Actually, the island can't claim real dog days—days when the Dog Star, Sirius, shines just before sunrise and just after sunset—since the Midnight Sun runs interference with lighting conditions. But then Jorgen Jorgensen wasn't a real king, either.

A dockhand saw me sitting there and peered down to find out what I was reading. "Ah, Jörundur," he said, using the Icelandic sobriquet for Jorgensen. "*Hamingjan góða!* He was a man with a very strange story . . ."

Here is that strange story:

It is the year 1780, only two years since Captain Cook has discovered Hawaii and still three years before the end of the American War for Independence. In Copenhagen, Denmark, the wife of the royal watchmaker gives birth to a son named Jorgen. From earliest youth, perhaps because his father is so obsessed with time (Mr. Jorgensen has written books in Danish, French, and German about watches and chronometers), Jorgen seems to delight in disorder. He likes to see things broken, violated, ravaged—especially governments. Especially the government to whose court his father pays obeisance. Thus the single most satisfying event of his youth is standing with a crowd of onlookers and watching the king's palace in Copenhagen burn down. At the time of this happy event, he is fully nine years old.

But a person can hardly expect to make a career out of hating monarchy. Jorgen decides to be a sailor. At age twenty he journeys to England, land of sailors, and is wandering the docks at Southampton when he is impressed on board a Royal Navy vessel. Soon he is cannonading French frigates under the adopted name of John Johnson. For his cannonading abilities, Ordinary Seaman Johnson becomes Second Mate Johnson and joins the *Lady Nelson*, under assignment to explore the distant coasts of Van Diemen's Land, now Tasmania. In 1804 he arrives in Van Diemen's Land and helps lay the foundation stones for the capital, Hobart Town—a place, he remarks to a friend, he'd like to see again some day. Fateful words!

Next Jorgen is Chief Mate Johnson on a whaler, the *Alexander*, sailing from New Zealand to London with a rich cargo of sperm oil. Rounding Cape Horn, the *Alexander* meets up with one of those once-in-a-lifetime storms that blows it three thousand miles off course, to Tahiti. Tahiti, Jorgen finds, is even more congenial than Van Diemen's Land. Here he dallies with native girls whose mothers had given such a full-bodied welcome to the original *Bounty* mutineers. He meets a missionary (missionaries, he notes, "are selected from the dregs") who says that in all his years in Tahiti he has made only one convert, a retarded fourteen-year-old half-caste. He also meets King Pomare the Second, six foot five and bulky in proportion, who welcomes white visitors with "Master Christ very good, very fine fellow. Me love Christ like my own brother. Please give me one glass brandy . . ."

Dog Day Revolutionary

The *Alexander* at last returns to England with two Tahitians, who become instant ethnological specimens named Jack and Dick. Jorgen sails on to Denmark, only to find his country preparing for war with England (Denmark was an ally of France under Napoleon). As a sailor and navigator, he is given command of a Danish privateer, the *Admiral Juul*, with orders to blow up British brigs. Before he can blow up a single brig, however, he is taken prisoner and landed at Yarmouth, where he is set free on parole. Right away Jorgen hops his parole by heading up to London and purchasing himself a new wardrobe.

In London, Jorgen decides to look up his former charges Jack and Dick, who are currently being studied by the great naturalist Sir Joseph Banks. Jorgen and Sir Joseph take to each other almost immediately. Somehow the conversation shifts from Tahiti to Iceland, a country Sir Joseph visited thirty years earlier. Since that time the Danish administrators of the island ("You will pardon me, Mr. Johnson, if I speak harshly of your countrymen") have dissolved the Althing, symbol of a thousand years of democracy, and relegated its function to a local lawyer. And now, adds Sir Joseph, there is even more cause for concern, for Iceland is wholly dependent on Denmark for her imports and Denmark is presently engaged with the European war. Wretched people! Lately the Icelanders have been obliged to distill seawater for their salt. Sir Joseph has even heard stories about how some of them must perforce eat their own lice, like the indigenes of Kamchatka.

Jorgen has always felt a sympathy for the wretched of the earth. It isn't long before he has convinced a wealthy merchant, Mr. Samuel Phelps, to provision a boat, the *Clarence*, with salt, barley meal, and potatoes. Then in January 1809, he sails with Mr. Phelps to Iceland in the hope he can relieve some of the island's wretchedness. In Reykjavik he finds a motley of his countrymen in the town's lone tavern, smoking their clay pipes and drinking ale, a corrupt modern race indifferent to the ancient race over which they've gained ascendancy. Jorgen locates the factor and asks him for permission to trade, but is denied that permission because Iceland is a Danish monopoly and has been ever since the year 1381. Well do I know that, replies Jorgen, but I am a Dane, so trading with me would not be illegal. Permission again denied. The factor, slightly in his cups, laughs: "Here is a Dane arriving on an armed English vessel provided with letters of marque!" Jorgen sails back to England all the more determined to break the Danes, whom he's always hated with the passion of a native son and now hates even more.

In June 1809 another armed vessel arrives in Reykjavik. She is the barque *Margaret and Ann*, under the command of Captain John Liston, with Mr. Phelps, the young botanist William Jackson Hooker, and Jorgen himself on board. While Hooker sets off in search of flora, the others seize Count Trampe, the Danish governor, and march him back to the boat under armed escort. Captain Liston confiscates the island's entire arsenal—twenty-five antique fowling pieces. As for Jorgen, he walks up to Government House and blithely proclaims himself head of state: "We, Jorgen Jorgensen, His Excellency the Protector of Iceland, Commander-in-Chief by Sea and Land." He opens up Reykjavik jail and drafts the prisoners, primarily drunks, as his personal bodyguard. The next day, June 26, he issues a proclamation stating that the days of Danish rule in Iceland are over. Terminated. Gone forever. Henceforth his subjects will be free to trade with whomever they please. His Excellency himself designs a new Icelandic flag showing three dried codfish against a field of blue.

In his first and last public speech, Jorgen makes it clear that his coup d'état is a revolution and not a British occupation of Iceland. This seems to surprise a number of his subjects, who had always thought revolutions required lopped heads, like the French one, or a healthy body count, like the American variety. In this revolution, though, only twelve men have been employed, not a drop of blood shed, and not a single shot fired (except by one of the prisoners, who got drunk and accidentally shot himself in the leg).

Now His Excellency mounts his horse and travels across the island to observe the daily life of his subjects. His journey takes him past salmon rivers and bilberry-covered heaths, over lava fields, and into the snowy realm of mountains from which glaciers tumble like frozen cascades. Along the way he stays in native farmhouses and samples native cuisine (pickled ram's testicles and horse steaks). In these farmhouses the farmer, his wife, their children, and the hired help all sleep in the same bed, the better to keep themselves warm at night. Not infrequently Jorgen joins them in these same beds. From now on there are rumors of little Excellencies playing in the ashes of native hearths.

Seldom has a less likely sovereign graced the corridors of power. Jorgen thinks taxes are boring, believes in paying teachers well and judges badly, and thinks redistribution of wealth a capital idea. Of course, the gentry whose wealth His Excellency is busily redistributing think much less of the idea; one man, Judge Isleif Einarsson, ends up in jail when his plan for a counterrevolution is divulged. A magistrate from the Skaftáfell district named Jón Gudmundsson declares that if Jorgen and his entourage ever appear east of the Jökulsá á Fjollum they will be treated as common outlaws. The grand old man of Icelandic politics, Magnús Stephensen, despises Jorgen, the revolution, and the codfish flag alike. He even invites His Excellency to dinner with the express intention of making his displeasure known, though his advocacy of Danish rule loses its edge somewhat when he sits down at table and his chair collapses under him.

On the evening of August 14, events take a decided turn for the worse. This, indeed, is a crucial date in Jorgen's career. Henceforth he will be bucking an uphill course against the dictates of power and his own self-destructive impulses, and as he bucks that course, his idealism by slow degrees will fade away. On this evening the British man-of-war *Talbot* sails into Reykjavik harbor under the command of the Honorable Captain Alexander (Paddy) Jones. Captain Jones is an Irish snob with the prejudices of an English snob, and Jorgen's butterfly escapade of a revolution is plainly not to his taste. This taste he can back up, if necessary, with a crew of five hundred men and numerous cannon. His Excellency, he concludes, has played the traitor to both England and Denmark; he has acted in open rebellion against both countries, but especially against Denmark, which Captain Jones apparently feels Britain cannot afford to irritate even though the two countries are fighting each other tooth and nail. Soon Captain Jones is lowering the codfish flag, obviously a joke. Not a joke? Well, so much the worse for Mr. Johnson.

On August 22 His Excellency Jorgen Jorgensen, a.k.a. John Johnson, is forced to abdicate. His army of eight is disbanded, and all Danish property and valuables are redistributed to their former owners. The dog days—and their king—have fled with the summer itself. Iceland digs in for the long winter, restored to its former capacity as a Danish colony, which it will remain until 1944.

Back in England the former Protector of Iceland is sent to Toothill Fields Prison, where he falls in with a checkered crew of cardsharks and gamblers who educate him in the intricacies of their trade (or has he been a gambler, of a different sort, all along?). After four weeks he is removed to a pestilential prison ship, the *Bahama*, where he takes up his pen and writes a defense of the Icelandic Revolution in the form of an autobiographical novel, *The Adventures of Thomas Walters*. Then he writes another novel, *Shandaria*, which combines Iceland and Tahiti into a single Utopia vaguely described as situated in Asia just beyond the dominion of the Great Mogul—a Utopia with no poverty, no prisons, no drunkenness, no lawyers, no doctors, no policemen, and no communication with foreigners. In short, no evils whatsoever. *Shandaria* he dedicates to his old friend, the botanist Hooker.

Hooker himself at last secures the Protector's release from the *Bahama*. Jorgen heads directly for the gaming tables where he promptly loses everything and is thrown into Fleet Prison, the debtor's prison. Prisons seem to bring out his literary side. In Fleet Prison he meets a fellow inmate recently returned from Afghanistan and cribs a memoir of that country based loosely on his friend's exploits. The memoir somehow falls into the hands of the foreign secretary, Lord

Castlereagh, who reads it with interest, for its author seems to be describing precisely the route the Russian czar would take if he elected to invade British India. This fellow Johnson, Castlereagh realizes, is exceptionally clever. He engages the former Protector of Iceland as an agent in the British Secret Service and sends him to the Continent to spy on France.

The best vantage point for spying on France, Jorgen decides, is the gaming tables of Paris, to which he repairs upon his arrival. He promptly loses his shirt, as well as his jacket, gaiters, and shoes. A bleak December morning in 1814 finds him quitting the French capital on foot, penniless and nearly naked. Yet before the end of the day he's posing as an Irish pilgrim en route to the Holy Land and receiving much-needed alms ("I thank ye, and Our Lord Jesus Christ thanks ye, your honor") from devout country folk. He heads east into Germany and gets an audience with Goethe, introducing himself as the exiled king of Iceland, now sadly reduced in circumstances. Likewise he meets Prince Püchler von Muskau, who takes him up in a hydrogen-filled balloon. Someday, he tells the prince excitedly, everybody will travel by air. That is not likely, my friend, replies the prince, who cannot imagine anyone but aristocrats like himself taking to the air. Meanwhile Jorgen is scribbling away at a top-secret report for Lord Castlereagh which blames Napoleon for every penniless beggar and every ruined gambler in Europe.

Back in England the former Excellency is arrested for trying to pawn his landlady's furniture. He lands in Newgate Prison, whereupon he begins work on a history of Madagascar, plundering information from another prisoner, a former captain of a French slaver. This time no one in the foreign service seems interested in the manuscript, so he begins a history of the Christian faith, which seems a more marketable subject than Madagascar. One day while he's working away at this latter tome, he learns that the Court of Appeals has granted him a pardon on condition that he leave Britain and never return. *Never return!* What, he wonders, has he ever done to justify being banished like this? But he's delighted with the pardon, which he celebrates by hitting the gaming tables again and once again losing everything. Back in Newgate Prison, this time he's sentenced to be hung. "In a rather dreadful scrape," he writes his friend Hooker, who by now must have wished he'd never met His Excellency. But once again Hooker comes to his aid: instead of being hung, Jorgen is to be transported to the Antipodes for life.

On April 26, 1826, Jorgen arrives with the convict ship *Woodman* in Van Diemen's Land. The irony of his situation does not escape him. He has returned in a state of degradation to the very colony he helped establish twenty-four years earlier and is to be billeted in a town, Hobart, whose very foundation he helped to lay. Even worse: Hobart has not yet developed to the point where it has any gambling salons . . .

Jorgen's spirit is crushed, his wanderings pinioned to one spare cushion on the global map. Home is the sailor, home from the sea, wrote Robert Louis Stevenson, and these words describe the later career of the former sailor and revolutionary, who, unfortunately, has found a home. He's found a job, too—Governor Arthur makes him a policeman. A policeman! The man who excluded the police from his Utopia! In his new role he hunts down bushrangers. He commands a unit of Governor Arthur's infamous Black Line and hunts down the last of the Tasmanian aborigines. He drinks.

Eventually Jorgen marries an Irishwoman named Norah Corbett and settles into a *ménage à trois* with her and John Barleycorn. All too frequently Hobart Town is treated to the spectacle of the ex-Protector of Iceland being chased through its streets by his drunken spouse. Or that spouse being chased by the drunken ex-Protector. To his credit, Jorgen doesn't auction off Norah to the highest bidder, which would have been considered quite proper in the colony. Instead he haunts the taprooms where his associates bow and call him "Your Icelandish Majesty."

Toward the end of his life he is greeted by a ghost, or the son of a ghost, from the past. Joseph Dalton Hooker, son of the botanist, shows up in Hobart Town with the HMS *Erebus*. In a few years the

Erebus will be sailing into oblivion in the Canadian Arctic with her captain, Sir John Franklin, but now she's rigged out for a voyage of discovery in Antarctic seas. The young Hooker seeks out Jorgen and finds him at the taps, ill, destitute, and disheveled. When the young man identifies himself, the ragged figure seated at the table bursts into tears, after which he starts to ramble, on and on, barely coherent. Senile dementia, thinks Hooker, and writes his father that Jorgen is "quite incorrigible . . . irreclaimable . . . hopeless." Later the hopeless old man joins the cheering crowd at the docks as the *Erebus* sails off toward the last unexplored continent. How he must have envied young Hooker his adventures! Two months later, on January 29, 1841, he raises his own anchor and falls dead in a roadside ditch. Perhaps his last thoughts have returned him to Iceland, the dog days of summer, and the good times.

Like Mozart, Jorgen Jorgensen lies buried in an unmarked pauper's grave.

Getting My Goat

andelaria, Ecuador, is thirty-five miles southeast of the popular watering hole of Baños, at the end of a tortuous, looping track. There are only two reasons to include it on your itinerary: (1) If you happen to be a Peace Corps volunteer looking for work. (2) If you're climbing L'Altara, the 18,000-footer that lies directly behind the village. I'd come for the latter reason—to test my limbs against the steepdown pinnacle of L'Altara.

Yet before testing those limbs, I needed to fuel them. I stopped an Indian bent under a bundle of faggots and asked him where I could grab a bite to eat. For every Andean hamlet, no matter how dingy, has some sort of restaurant. The Indian pointed a finger toward a low-slung, mud-and-wattle dwelling with a dead dog a few feet from its front door.

The place did not inspire confidence. But since I wasn't exactly looking for haute cuisine, I figured I could take whatever local specialty the restaurant dished up. So I walked over, stooped, and entered what turned out to be a musty room lit by a single flickering candle. There was only one item of furniture—a semi-collapsed bench on which sat an old *campusino* drinking from a bottle of hooch. At the other end of the bench an enormous cockroach was drinking from a syrupy puddle. I sat down between them.

A slight, dark-hued man was staring at me. "I'd like something to eat, Señor," I told him.

The man smiled. "Antonio," he said, shaking my hand.

"Larry."

"You are perhaps climbing L'Altara, Señor Larry?"

"I am. Tomorrow."

Antonio told me about Hermann, a Swiss climber who fell off L'Altara last month and got battered on the rocks below. "Dead?" I asked. "Dead as mutton," he smiled.

Funny he should have used that phrase. A bit ominous, too. It was mutton that I planned to ask him for, thinking it the most readily available meat in these parts. Immediately, I switched to goat.

"You shall have it." He shouted *Manuel!*, and a boy emerged from one of the back rooms. He gave the boy a few sucres. "My son will get *chivo* from the village. Meanwhile, you would perhaps care for a drink?"

"Yes," I said. "*Malta.*" Malta was a dark beer with the proverbial egg mixed into it.

"I have no malta."

"*Naranjilla*, then." This is an Ecuadorian fruit juice that has the not unpleasant flavor of bitter orange.

"I have only *agua.*"

"Well, agua it is. Bottled."

"You shall have it." He brought out a large transparent flask that bore only the slightest resemblance to a bottle. Its so-called water was slate-grey in color and doubtless harbored an army of amoebas poised for attack.

"On second thought," I said, "I'll pass on the agua."

Now I settled back on the bench. Soon I noticed an incredibly wizened crone hunched up on the dirt floor and staring at me.

"That is my mother, Señor Larry," Antonio said. "And the person sitting next to you, he is my father." (This guy runs a family restaurant, I thought, or maybe he's just running a family.)

Half an hour passed. I tried to study my topo map of L'Altara, but there wasn't enough light to make out a single contour, much less the lay of the mountain itself. On the other hand, there was quite enough light for my host's clutch of offspring, stationed at every doorway, to study me. Four boys, three girls, and several unclassified infants, all staring with the abnormally large eyes of Mexican children painted on velvet.

"You don't see many gringos around here, do you?" I said to Antonio.

"Very few. The last was Señor Hermann. He was battered on the rocks."

"Dead as mutton."

"You have it."

An hour passed. No Manuel, no chivo. I was beginning to think this a not very satisfactory dining experience. It was fine, of course, if you liked being stared at. Otherwise, it suggested famine and drought, with a dash of pestilence thrown in as well.

"Señor Antonio," I said, "your son has been gone for well over an hour. Why is he taking so long?"

"He must take long. For you, Señor Larry, are an honored guest and he must find you the very best chivo in the village. That's what the boy is doing now. Bargaining for your chivo."

"How much longer will he be bargaining for my chivo?"

"Not more than two hours . . ."

Two more hours of this and I'd be a slavering idiot. Not only a slavering, but a pretty damned peeved idiot, too. So I implored Antonio to feed me some food, *any* food, while we were waiting for Manuel. He seemed to ponder this request, mentioned a *sopa de maíz*, but then went on to say that it really wasn't good enough for an honored guest like me.

"It'll be good enough, I assure you."

Within fifteen minutes Antonio had brought out a bowl, which I quickly lifted to my lips, only to discover that he'd been right: the soup wasn't good enough for me. It tasted like postage stamp glue. This, in itself, was not surprising, since postage stamps are gummed with corn and cassava, two items always present in sopa de maíz. The soup tasted worse than postage stamp glue. What's more, it had enough salt in it to clog the arteries of a blue whale. I exploded:

"What kind of restaurant is this? First you can't locate a goat in a land overrun with goats. Then you serve me this soup. No wonder you don't have any customers here . . ."

"Restaurant?" said Antonio. "But this isn't a restaurant, Señor Larry. It is my own home."

"Your . . . home?"

"Of course. If you want a restaurant, there is a small one next door."

I felt lower than the lowest mite on a llama's backside. To think: I'd mistaken this poor man's abode for an eatery, making uncivil demands on him even as he was doing his best to treat me like a visiting dignitary. I muttered a few hopelessly inadequate words of apology. Then (God help me!) I lifted the bowl once again to my lips. And God must have indeed helped me, for the sopa de maíz began to taste, if not actually good, at least more palatable. I nodded my approval.

"Taste good?" Antonio said.

"Like heaven," I replied.

A short while later Manuel returned from his quest for the ultimate goat. Apparently his father had given him only enough sucres for a very ordinary goat, so he'd come back, sad to say, emptyhanded. I tried to give him a few more sucres for his trouble, but Antonio brushed away my hand, saying:

"Oh no. It's been our pleasure, amigo."

"On the contrary," I told him, "it's been my pleasure."

So ends a cautionary tale of dining out in the High Andes. Well, not quite. I still had to mount an exit that would not hurt anybody's feelings. Smiling and shaking hands all around, I performed this task with some success, but then as I stepped from the house, I tripped over the dog. The poor animal let out an alarmed yelp and went running down the road. It wasn't dead, after all.

In the Land of the White Rajahs

One morning in Sarawak I found myself wandering through the jungly extravagance of Gunung Gading National Park. The heat was formidable, and the humidity even more so. Working together, they comprised a pas de deux that made me feel like I was at once drying up and drowning.

In my discomfort, I almost wished I was back in Kuching, where I'd spent the last few days. Kuching, Sarawak's capital, is a charming town of wood-slatted Anglo Malay buildings, ornate Chinese temples, and narrow labyrinthine lanes. It has a museum with a world-class exhibit of Iban *palangs* (penis pins) and another museum devoted exclusively to cats. For me, however, the town's main attraction was its McDonald's. There I would take refuge not because I was subject to Big Mac attacks, perish the thought, but because it had air conditioning.

As the morning progressed, the heat grew steadily worse. I began thinking of it as vengeful; I felt it wanted to teach me, a sometime

75

Arctic hand, an unpleasant lesson in climatology, or perhaps punish me for the expletives I'd been using at its expense. Meanwhile, the humidity had become nearly as thick as bechamel sauce.

At one point I noticed a dazzling indigo-colored bird hopping from tree to tree, but I couldn't identify it because the sweat was pouring off my brow in veritable cascades and blurring my vision. Then I saw something long and thin slithering across the path.

"Giant centipede," announced Akhri, my Malay guide. "One bite from him, and you die. But not right away. Maybe in about five minutes."

A heartening thought: for if the sweltering conditions finally proved too much for me, I could always caress one of these venomous arthropods, and then I'd at least go quickly to my so-called reward rather than in tortuous increments.

But the local flora seemed to appreciate the hothouse conditions. Growth was almost visible, and its lushness made the sky almost invisible. From this sky, wherever it was, dangled lianas that a Tarzan would kill for.

Onward we trudged, stepping over masses of exposed roots that were like an ebony giant's fingers. Somewhere in the forest canopy a monkey cackled, presumably at the sight of two fellow hominids demented enough to wander about in the mid-day heat. Suddenly I blinked. Blinked again. Wiped the sweat out of my eyes and blinked yet again. Directly in front of us was a vinaceous red flower three feet wide and boasting a deep spike-studded nectarium seemingly inspired by a medieval dungeon.

I tried to place the flower's distinctive odor. Ah, yes: dead caribou.

We'd happened upon a rafflesia, described by one of its discoverers, nineteenth-century English botanist Thomas Arnold, as "the greatest prodigy of the vegetable world."

He was not mincing words. No flower in the world is bigger or heavier—rafflesias have been known to tip the scales at twenty pounds avoirdupois. Doubtless no flower is more bizarre in its habits or physiognomy: it feeds only on the roots of the *Tetrastigma* vine, has neither stalk or leaves, and reputedly bursts from its cabbagelike bud with a triumphant popping sound. Certainly, no other flower has such a rank odor. And no flower is as languid in its promotion of itself—one rafflesia bud brought to Kew Gardens took thirty-five years to blossom.

Something curious happened as I was staring at this prodigy: I forgot all about my discomfort. For I'd been transported to a realm wholly different from the one I'd inhabited just a few minutes earlier; a realm so exotic that even its swelter was exotic. It was as if I'd somehow fallen into the flower's capacious opening and ended up, like Alice after her tumble down the rabbit hole, in Wonderland.

In my childhood imagination, the island of Borneo occupied a privileged place. Especially in math and citizenship classes, I would journey to its distant jungles in search of hair-raising, pith-helmeted adventure. I would become chums with impenitent headhunters, idly shoo away poisonous snakes, and cross slippery log bridges with the aplomb of a ballet dancer. Stricken with malaria and shaking like an aspen leaf, I would compose my face into a stoic smile; after all, malaria came with the territory.

If, in the midst of my daydreaming, I'd been asked to invent a history for Sarawak itself, I doubt that I could have come up with anything quite as romantic or improbable as the saga of the so-called White Rajahs.

James Brooke was an English gentleman-swashbuckler, maybe even a pirate, who arrived in Borneo in 1839 and promptly helped the Sultan of Brunei crush a local rebellion. In return, the grateful Sultan gave him the northwest province of Sarawak. Brooke, now Rajah Brooke, proceeded to govern his newly acquired domain with no greater outside force than a shipwrecked Irishman, an English doctor, a translator, and his manservant.

In 1868, the aging Rajah bequeathed his kingdom to his eccentric nephew Charles, who ruled it for nearly fifty years. Charles had a glass eye originally made for a stuffed albatross (or so the rumor went) and a habit of watering the plants at the Istana, his Kuching residence, by urinating on them. No less eccentric, in an age dedicated to White Man's Burden, were his efforts to protect Sarawak's native people from harmful European influences.

The Brookes realized a colonialist's dream. Imagine: to be at once potentate and proprietor of a large equatorial kingdom . . . and to have your subjects actually like you. Thus when Vyner Brooke, the last of the White Rajahs, ceded Sarawak to the British Crown in 1946, not a few of those subjects felt as if they'd been flung to the dogs. Even now, with Sarawak a state in Eastern Malaysia, you can still find people who would gladly hand it back to a Brooke whether he wanted it or not.

I can't help thinking that a century of relatively benevolent rule made Sarawak a kinder, gentler place. Its Bornean neighbor, the Indonesian territory of Kalimantan, is a periodic hotbed of religious and ethnic strife. In equally multi-ethnic (Malay, Chinese, and numerous native tribes) Sarawak, the only strife I encountered came on Bako Island, when a long-tailed macaque rushed me after I refused him a fried noodle handout.

I confess I felt a bit guilty about chasing off the macaque. For no one in Sarawak had refused me anything, not even when I made an obviously outrageous request. For example: when I mentioned to one of my guides that I wanted to see an *oran utang*, he obligingly located a sad-eyed, somewhat disreputable-looking man for me to gaze upon—orang utang means "debtor" in Malay, while the arboreal ape is an *orang utan*.

And in this supposedly dangerous part of the globe, the most dangerous behavior I encountered was, well, my own. Toward the beginning of the trip, I was chatting with some Bidayuh men about the catholicity of their diet (python, fermented wild boar, various insects, and so on) when one of them asked me if I'd like to try some smoked cat. I shook my head vigorously and took an involuntary step backwards, whereupon my leg slipped into a crack between the bamboo-slatted floorboards of the longhouse; it took the men several minutes to extricate me.

After this last contretemps, I could easily imagine the Bidayuh wondering if there was any log bridge in their country off of which I was not capable of falling or any poisonous snake safe from my heedless tread.

"This is a remote control area," one of the Bidayuh men informed me, his slightly uncertain English being a testimony to the presence of television in his longhouse. But it wasn't really that remote; his longhouse, Anna Rais, was less than two hours by road from the bustle of Kuching.

I wanted a genuine remote control area, somewhere that would cater to my childhood jungle fantasies and perhaps even include a few impenitent headhunters as well. So that's why a day or so later Akhri and I found ourselves in a motorized dugout canoe on the Lemanak River, heading into Iban country.

"You are from the land of our old Rajahs?" the boatman, an Iban, asked me, concluding that since I spoke English, I must therefore be English myself.

"No, from America."

He uttered a few words in Malay to Akhri, who turned to me and said, "He's too polite to ask, but he wonders if you could introduce him to Rambo."

I wasn't surprised by this request, for the Iban have a reputation for being somewhat pugacious themselves. Their most important god, Sengalang Burong, is a god of war, and from him all Iban trace their descent. For such people, Rambo would be a more likely celebrity than, say, Pee Wee Herman.

The river was an incessant series of rapids, snags, and oxbows, with the result that the boatman was constantly opening and closing the throttle of his antiquated, minimally horsepowered motor. But at last we pulled up alongside several other canoes. High above us loomed our destination, Nanga Kesit longhouse.

Now I heard howls of laughter and the stomping of feet. A *gawai* (festival) seemed to be in progress. I figured I might get to see a dusty skull brought out and a cigarette stuck in its mouth, or hear an Iban bard chant *mengap* (sacred poems), or at least observe the ritual sacrifice of a rooster.

No such luck. On the longhouse verandah, a group of lively, bibulous European visitors were performing what looked like an Iban war dance, while their hosts looked on with, I thought, commendable patience. One of the visitors seemed to be making a feature-length video of an Iban woman's bare breasts. Another was trying to show off his prowess with a ten-foot blowpipe, but his aim was so bad that he had everyone scurrying for cover.

The Iban knew a good thing when they saw it. Some of the women had spread out a mat and were doing a brisk trade in handicrafts. Not all of the handicrafts were local, however. I picked up an exquisite carving of a rhinoceros hornbill and read "Made in Taiwan" written on the bottom.

As I was debating whether to buy this unusual cross-cultural artifact, an Iban man drunk on *tuak* (rice wine) approached me. Would I like to see his palang? he said. (A palang is a traditional Bornean sex device inserted in the penis and designed to stimulate one's female partner.) He offered to drop his loincloth and show it to me for twenty Malaysian *ringgit*. Then another man offered to show me his palang for only ten ringgit, adding that it was made with a shear pin from an outboard motor.

"Evinrude or Mercury?" I asked.

"Yamaha," he said.

"This place seems to be full of exhibitionists," I told Akhri, who was doing the translating.

"Tourist longhouse," he observed tartly.

Before we left, I noticed a bundle of old skulls hanging in a rattan bag from the longhouse ceiling. The Iban believe that when a skull is displeased or offended, it will grind its teeth together. Was it my imagination, or did I hear the unmistakable sound of grinding teeth from inside the rattan bag?

If at first you don't succeed, try, try again.

A few days later Akhri and I were climbing up the notched log ladder to Nanga Okun longhouse in the Batang Ai area. At the top, we took off our shoes and padded along the roofed verandah. Some Iban men mending a nylon fishing net smiled at us, but did not offer to sell the net. I thought this a good sign.

Each of the thirty or so *bileks* (apartments) in the longhouse had a honeycomb tacked on its door as a safeguard against *antus* (evil spirits). Antus are mathematically challenged; they'll stand at a door and try repeatedly to count the holes in the honeycomb before giving up in frustration.

"No honeycomb on your door, and you are—how you say it in English?—'dead meat,' " Akhri told me.

The chief now appeared in front of his bilek. He was a lean, sinewy man in his mid-fifties whose extensive circuitry of blue-black tattoos made him look like a giant thumbprint. "Welcome," he announced. "We were expecting you."

Apparently, someone had seen a magpie robin an hour or two earlier, which meant visitors, probably visitors from a distant place, would be coming.

"Bird omen," said Akhri. "Very important for the Iban. It's good they did not hear the little bird that sings, 'I will scratch your eyes out, I will scratch your eyes out . . . ' Then maybe they would not be very nice to us."

Soon we were seated on a woven rattan mat beside the chief, drinking tea so laden with sugar that it was almost viscous. Half the longhouse seemed to be gathered around us. There was an old woman with generously distended earlobes, a man with the Royal Malaysian Airlines logo tattooed on his upper chest, wide-eyed children, the local *manang* (shaman), and girls so eloquently beautiful that any one of them would make a *Vogue* model seem like a toothless hag.

Akhri and the chief were talking rapidly in Malay. "I told him you would like to stay here," Akhri said to me, "and he asks for how long, and I say only for a few days, and he says fine, but forever would be okay, too."

Although forever seemed a bit too long, I was, I confess, touched by the invitation. Here I was, a scruffy stranger wearing a "Shiitake Happens" T-shirt and scribbling God knows what absurdities in his notebook. If it had been me, I would have turned myself back at the door. But the magpie robin seemed to like me, and that was good enough for the chief.

Indeed, the bird must have been prodigal in its praise, for the Iban treated me like a White Rajah on an official visit. At dinner, a cicada with misguided ailerons crashlanded into my plate of glutinous rice, and half a dozen hands immediately reached down to remove it. The chief offered me a post-prandial smoke—a large funnel-shaped cheroot made from local tobacco. Then someone offered me a glass of tuak. Someone else noticed I was having problems with the heat and began fanning me with a nipah palm leaf.

If my skull ends up in a rattan bag here, I told myself, it will never have cause to grind its teeth.

Actually, I was curious about the custom of taking heads, especially as I'd met a number of people in my travels—Parisian waiters, for instance—far more inclined to whip off the occasional head than my hosts. So I asked the chief if anyone in his longhouse still did a bit of headhunting.

"The Iban have not hunted heads in many years."

"Not even to stay in practice?" I inquired.

"We have different trophies now."

In his grandfather's day, he said, an Iban man couldn't get a wife unless he brought home an enemy's head as a trophy. But today there were other, less sanguinary ways to get ahead (so to speak) with a woman. One way was for a young man to take a job in Brunei,

Kuching, or Peninsular Malaysia. He would bring back an outboard motor or a sewing machine, and that would impress a woman just as much as a head might have impressed her in the old days.

I turned to the young woman seated next to me and asked her which she would prefer, a sewing machine or a freshly plucked human head. She chose the sewing machine.

Evidently, the chief thought I had more than a researcher's interest in the subject, because he asked whether I was married.

"No," I told him.

"Then perhaps you would like a wife?"

And before I could answer, a girl who couldn't have been more than sixteen years old was brought forth for my inspection. I won't say she looked at me imploringly, but neither will I say that she wrinkled her nose in disgust.

Now the girl's father spoke. He would be willing to let me have his daughter for either ten chickens or a new chainsaw, whichever would be easier on my budget. In addition to the daughter, he would give me a share of his rice padi and a bilek at the far end of the longhouse.

It was tempting offer, I admit: I could easily lose myself here, forget about deadlines, forget about the IRS, and forget about unpaid bills. Likewise, I could realize a refined version of my youthful Bornean fantasy, with genial ex-headhunters as my companions and an enviable domestic situation as well.

"Give me a day or two to think it over," I said.

That night I lay down on the verandah. The humidity was at least one hundred percent. Dogs were barking, cocks crowing, and pigs rooting around noisily under the longhouse. Nightbirds screeched, and cicadas were exercising their typically strident vibratos. Doubtless there were a couple of antus prowling about, too.

Even so, I slept the sleep of the blessed.

Certain images crowd my mind when I think of my visit to Nanga Okun: the morning mist lifting to reveal the blue mountains of Kalimantan almost close enough to touch; a python falling through the longhouse roof, only to be dispatched by two small boys with sticks; children staring at me as I went about my evening ablutions ("Astonishing! He washes himself much the same way we do . . . "); and an elderly woman shaking my hand for a full minute, less a tribute to me, Akhri observed, than to my white-skinned predecessors, the Brookes.

One day I noticed a very nasty rash around my ankles (from a run in with an antu, I was told), but the manang applied a poultice from a larkspur-like plant to it, and lo! the rash went away in a few hours. I was so effusive in my gratitude that he gave me a tour of his pharmacy—i.e., the jungle.

He showed me a lanceolate leaf that he used for bladder problems and a shiny one that helped ease the pain of a toothache. This root would cure a hangover, this one was an antidote for snake bites, and a decoction from this plant was a tonic for diarrhea. With a rakish grin, he pointed to a plant called *tongkat ali*, "the viagra of Borneo," in Akhri's words.

"Ask him what he recommends for writer's block," I said to Akhri.

It was obvious that the manang had never been asked about this occupational disease before. But he looked around and at last pointed to a small yellow-brown mushroom which I recognized as hallucinogenic.

"He say this *kulat* maybe very helpful for such a block," said Akrhi.

Now I asked the manang about edible fungi. Right away he pointed to a Split Gill (*Schizophyllum commune*) and licked his lips, saying that it was highly prized by the Iban.

This was the first time I'd ever heard of anyone eating Split Gills, which have the consistency of leather and, I would have assumed, the flavor to match. But the Iban also considered monkey eyes a delicacy, and I found them somewhat unappetizing as well.

I ate several of the Split Gills that evening. They did have the flavor of leather. *Bad* leather. In a flash, I knew I could never be a longhouse dweller. My own tastes, culinary and otherwise, were just too different from those of the Iban. Yet how to convey this without offending my would-be bride or her father, not to mention the matchmaking chief?

Akhri came to my rescue. "Mr. Larry lives in the Arctic," he declared, "and the heat here would kill him."

The chief gazed at me sympathetically, as did the girl and her father. That I was unwilling to spend the rest of my days in their long-house did not seem to offend them. In fact, the girl's father looked relieved—for what self-respecting descendant of a war god would want an easily overheated wimp like me for a son-in-law?

As I was leaving, the chief shook my hand for at least a minute, then uttered this benediction: May all your omen birds be nice ones . . .

My fantasy jungle would be, if not wholly intact, at least logged so gently that no bird, beast, or human being would have cause for complaint. Here, particularly, Sarawak refused to conform to my idealization of it. For large swathes of its rainforest have fallen to the chainsaws and bulldozers of timber companies. In my flight from the oil boom town of Miri to Gunung Mulu National Park, I saw country that seemed to have undergone an anti-botanical blitzkrieg, and rivers so filled with runoff from the denuded land that they looked like soapy brown sludge.

Then the plane touched down in an opulence of green.

Remarkably lush in its vegetation and even more remarkably profuse in the variety of its wildlife (more than 20,000 different bird, animal, and insect species), Mulu seemed a fitting place for me to conclude my journey into Borneo's Wonderland.

The Park did not disappoint me. On my inaugural hike, I saw a snake no bigger than an earthworm and a frog with webbed phalanges gliding elegantly from tree to tree. My Kelabit guide Elis pointed to a lantern fly, an insect with a long snoutlike projection seemingly borrowed from Pinocchio. Here were orchids as delicate as origami and a tree, the *ipoh*, so indelicate as to exude a potentially lethal sap. And what made that odd noise? It was a black hornbill, perhaps the only bird in the world that sounds like a pig throwing up.

"Any poisonous snakes around here?" I asked Elis.

"Yes, but they are hiding from us," he replied. "You see, they believe people are poisonous."

One creature eagerly sought us out. Leeches seemed to be everywhere, on twigs, leaves, and on the ground, not to mention affixed to our bodies. Some would actually jump onto us, those on the ground would loop toward us in graceful sinuosities, and others would rear up like miniature cobras at our approach. One species, the tiger leech, had stripes of the brightest yellow, thus proving that in Borneo even the leeches are exotic.

"You know any good leech repellent?" I asked.

Elis shook his head, and while doing so plucked a leech off it.

And then we were standing in front of an enormous hole in a limestone cliff. This was the opening to Deer Cave, which, according to one of my guidebooks, widened into a passage large enough to accommodate London's St. Paul's Cathedral five times over. Soon a few black specks emerged from the opening, then a few more, and then a virtual tornado of specks. The specks were wrinkle-lipped bats, millions of them, and they were going out to dinner.

"On a good night, they will eat nine tons of insects," said Elis.

Twisting and turning, swivelling and undulating, the stream of bats appeared to be without end. Day turned to night, and still it continued, accompanied by an audible thrumming of wings.

On our walk back, I listened to the nocturnal music of the jungle: the loud vibrato of cicadas, a frog whose croak sounded like the horn of an old Model T, and the soft reiterated "mm-papas" of the white-crowned hornbill. A host of fireflies provided their version of a magic lightshow, almost but not quite illuminating the trail. Elis, too, produced a magic light show. At one point he focused the beam of his flashlight on an armor-plated gecko, and at another point on a pair of gently swaying branches—two giant stick insects mating.

So entranced was I by all these sights and sounds that when we came to a log bridge, I stepped right onto it. Not having the aplomb of a ballet dancer, I tottered briefly and then slipped off, landing in the mud a few feet below.

Another fantasy shattered.

But I didn't mind. I didn't mind at all.

Elis was busy with a group of German filmmakers, so on my last day in Mulu I went for a hike by myself. My destination was Clearwater Stream, which, according to a local legend, makes a person a year younger every time he takes a dip in it. I planned to hop in and out of the stream's salubrious waters fifteen or twenty times.

All of a sudden a Penan man with rattan ringlets around his arms and legs appeared on the trail. He was short, maybe an inch or two above five feet, and he carried a blowpipe that towered above him. His feet were calloused and spatulate from what was doubtless a lifetime of walking barefoot in the jungle.

"How are you?" the man said, waving his blowpipe as if in greeting.

This turned out to be the extent of his English. And since my knowledge of Penan was even less extensive, I couldn't ask him whether he was one of the few remaining Penan who were still nomadic, or whether he'd been settled in a government-built long-house like most of his fellow tribesmen.

"How are you?" the man repeated with a smile, and then he disappeared into the jungle. Can I be forgiven for wanting to follow him? For I wanted to tell him that despite the heat, which was insufferable, and the leeches, who were unbearable, and the mountainous heap of hornbill shit recently planted on my trousers, I was just fine.

The Last of the Wandering Bards

(from *Our Like Will Not Be There Again*)

Anthony Fergus alowly descends the stairs of the doss house, his left foot the victim of an automobile accident. From beneath a black Stetson hat, which time has flattened into a near-beret, his gray-blond hair droops like unwashed fleece. His teeth are yellow and broken, like those of an old horse. And red spiderwebs cling to his cheeks; their intricate patterns illustrate his fondness for drink.

Anthony is eager to put the story right as to the precise nature of his accident. His hands flutter in front of his face like a pair of birds as he talks. It seems that he was taking the bus from Ballycastle (near where he makes his home) to Sligo for the funeral of his sister, a nun, and because he had taken drink, he had gotten off at Ballysodare, thinking it was Sligo, though he had been in Sligo dozens of times, and once he realized his mistake, he proceeded to travel the remaining five miles to Sligo on foot, in a state of mild mourning. Almost there, he was walking on the margin of the road, and a lorry driver stopped to ask him the whereabouts of the turnoff to Ballymote ("Do you know that song, 'Old

Ballymote'?" he interjects. "It goes this way—'In County Roscommon through hailstones and rain,/I was crossing the fields on my way to the train . . .'"), and after walking up to tell him, he must have continued on in the middle of the road, for the next thing was, a motorcar with an Ulster plate had come and gone, mashing his foot in the process.

"That is the manner of story," he concludes, "that Homer would probably be opening up his ears to."

Where has he heard of Homer?

"Just before it, I was sitting on the bus, and I was sitting next to a young novitiate priest, and he was reading one of Homer's books. He tells me what, that this Homer is the greatest poet afield and afoot. Do you know now, is this Homer living at present? Because if he is, I'd like to swap poems, some of my own poems, with him."

Anthony has decided not to attend his sister's funeral; he'd feel too gauche now, with a makeshift poultice of the *Irish Independent* wrapped around his foot by a hay rope. Also, being a proud man in the matter of religion, so he explains, he wouldn't want the nuns to see him "big with drink." Would he like to see a doctor about his foot, then? No, he just wants to go back to Ballycastle now. I accept his invitation to drive him back.

After he has clambered into the car with a tipsy indeterminacy of movement, he begins to shrug off his accident: "I am more fortunate than the Kennedys, because I'm alive and those poor people are dead, because they had too much money. If they were just living something like myself, they would have been alive today. If they had done that, nobody would watch them to kill them. They were all killed as young men, and I don't think that they had committed a crime. They should have gone back to where they started before it was too late."

He is truly Ptolemaic in these pronouncements; all global events are shrunk to his own size, where they can be dispatched with the same ease as a pint of stout. Hermetically sealed off from the rest of the world, he can define his limits where he pleases, which he does, and no one will know the difference—least of all himself. Hence, he adopts this tone of familiarity with the rich and the famous; they are just extensions of himself, and he has never asked of himself, Am I enough?

But, as with the features of certain animals on the brink of extinction, some of Anthony's personal traits have developed to a fantastic degree. The great Irish elk grew antlers so large they were unsupportable; Anthony's own extravagance, as befits a man who often calls himself "The Last of the Bards," consists in his not being able to control his poetry—if poetry it is. In that sense, he is all antlers. A good many things draw him back to some shadowy bardic notion of himself. Even as the car passes a boggy skein of lakes black as death-tarns, he abruptly bursts into song:

> *I wish I was by that dim Lake,*
> *Where sinful souls their farewell take*
> *Of this vain world, and half-way lie*
> *In death's cold shadow, ere they die.*
> *There, there, far from thee,*
> *Deceitful world, my home should be:*
> *Where, come what might of blood and pain,*
> *False hope should ne'er deceive again.*

That is Thomas Moore, and Anthony goes a trifle soft when his name is mentioned.

Actually, Anthony juggles his self-appointed titles somewhat promiscuously. One day, he's "The Last of the Bards," the next day he'll be "The Last of the Minstrel Boys," and then on another day, he might be "The Last of the Wandering Minstrels." One thing is constant: he is preoccupied with his own lastness. Will there ever be another like him, "at least in this part of Mayo"? He is fairly convinced that there won't be, and this elicits from his lips a bold lament: "After me, it'll be dead. Poetry, I mean. They'll never know it again in this country. It's all money now, money, money, money. Money and tablets and land speculation."

He uses this same high heroic tone to suggest "a few jars" when we come to a pub on the side of the road. He hasn't any of "this money" on him at the moment—would I mind buying him a drink? Anthony won't beg for what instinct tells him is his right. He won't become whiny and accommodating; instead, he puts both his hands on the steering wheel when the car shows no sign of stopping.

Nowadays, Anthony's bardic activities are limited to the songs and recitations he performs in local pubs for drink. Many of these are of his own devising. "I've made up hundreds on top of hundreds of songs and verses and all that stuff, and sometimes I fit them to old airs, and sometimes I don't. Take a verse like

> Your journey here is short, my man,
> It climbs up to the stars,
> And the road where Saint Peter stands,
> It has no motorcars.

"You could hardly improve that by putting music on it, or at least, that's my opinion."

In these pubs, he is just barely tolerated, and his prospective audiences often buy him his "jars" if he'll promise to be quiet, an offer he is quick to take. Thirty years ago he could lay more claim to his honorific titles; in those days, he traveled from town to town in Mayo, Sligo, and Leitrim, singing in the streets for a few shillings and playing his concertina. Fair days, he says, were the only days he had enough money for "great boozing." Yet he drank much less in those days, too. And he seems to have been more widely tolerated as well.

"I had 'stage-houses,' friends who'd put me up and feed me. Grand friends who'd appreciate what I was doing, the life that I was leading. A hard life. The traveling musician and the poet man couldn't make a living at it, he just kept going, kept going. I had an old concertina I used to play, but in the end, there was no keys in it, and I'd be pulling it in and out, and there was no notes, only nonsense. So I had to stop."

To be the "last" of the bards implies an unbroken line of them, and at least in his own family, Anthony cannot even trace it back as far as his own father, "a small farmer and nothing else, never making anything of himself. Only he drank a lot, and I suppose you could say I got that from him. His drinking made for some good cracks, man. Once he was stumbling down the road to Ballygrady in a terrible way, and this priest, a Father Quinn, walks up to him and says, 'You're drunk again,' and my father says, 'So am I, Father.' He was in such a bad way, he thought the priest was after saying that *he* was drunk! In the end, 'twas drink what killed him. He was eighty or thereabouts.

"My own idea is, the whole business just rose up in me like the furze that does be in the fields. Now!"

This "idea" he tosses off with a cavalier nod of his head. But maybe, he does suggest, it goes all the way back to the *very* old times, to the old kings and clan leaders, to the time when minstrels and bards and gleemen wandered "our four green fields" and when some nobleman would have been proud to be patron to men like himself. It is too much! Anthony can only celebrate this possibility by breaking into song, Thomas Moore again:

> *Let Erin remember the days of old*
> *Ere her faithless sons betray'd her;*
> *When Malachi wore the collar of gold,*
> *Which he won from her proud invader,*
> *When her kings, with standard of green unfurl'd*
> *Led the Red-Branch Knights to danger—*
> *Ere the emerald gem of the western world*
> *Was set in the crown of a stranger.*

Listening to him sing these lines, I think: Perhaps he *is* the last of the wandering bards, the last voice out of a tradition that has turned lush with eccentricity in its final stages and now has gone on one last spree before joining the great cattle drive to uniformity. Perhaps tradition, as it lies dying, becomes a voluble crank. In nearly everyone's view, Anthony has gone to bits and pieces with his craving for drink and his various obsessions. Yet wandering back and forth inside his own enchanted vacuum, he may be all that's left now. The other Minstrel Boys to the wars have gone.

Anthony's own attitude toward tradition is at the very least paradoxical. On the one hand, he likes to think that he is very much a part of it; on the other, he invokes Moore's *Irish Melodies*—slight Anglo-Irish stuff, really—as though they were Columbkille's Prophecies. And when I ask him if he can sing any song in Irish, he fulminates against the very idea of it: "Damn the Irish language! I don't want to hear the Irish language, let alone sing it. Leave everybody to theirselves, that's the way God left them. A language is no good to the majority of people that doesn't know it." Irish had nearly vanished from his part of Mayo by the time he was born; most people had come to regard it as the speech of the backward and the uneducated, and that's the view Anthony, who considers himself an educated man, takes of it today.

He reserves for the tramp and the "travelin' beggar-man" the sort of high esteem that in other quarters is often lavished upon native Irish speakers. These men—Anthony calls them "the Lord's bards"—he met on the roads during his own traveling. He'd often (he says) recite one of his poems in exchange for a song he hadn't heard before, defying them to come up with a song he *hadn't* heard.

"Many of those men were high-strung persons, real aristocrats, and some were even educated, often in schools. You could tell from talking to them that they weren't the ordinary type of man at all. No, not at all ordinary."

Perhaps to some extent, these "bards" are Anthony's conscious models—the "furze" rising sharp within him. "If you want to talk of freedom," he observes, "those men had it. They didn't have to answer to anyone. Whether to go to Donegal town or to Enniskillen, the choice was in their own minds. That's why I call them 'the Lord's bards.' They had no master but the Lord."

The tramp, for him, is the apotheosis of all the old Irish traditions, a past master of the bright saying, a man with "every good crack and story that ever came about."

"One of those fellows I had met during my own travels came in on me back in Ballycastle about half a year ago, to stay the night, and he coughin'. 'A terrible cough, man,' I says to him. 'Yeah, 'twas cold in that barn last night.' 'You slept in a barn last night and it snowin' and hailin', Christmas time?' 'Yeah, yeah,' this was his speech, you know [Anthony speaks through his nose to imitate it], 'I'm Michael Walsh, Belmullet, County Mayo, yeah, I slept in a barn last night, 'twas cold.' 'My god, you'll get pneumonia, man, and die.' 'No, no, I couldn't die—I have never lived.'

"There was another fellow, a little raggedy man named O'Brien I met outside Claremorris sitting at the foot of a hill. He was closing his boot, and he had but one eye. 'Everybody must bear his cross,' he said, 'but 'tis strange, I can see more with my one eye than you can see with your two.' I heard one-eyed people say that before, and I never believed them before, so I says, 'Ah no, that's impossible for you to say.' 'All right,' he said, but will you bet it?' 'I will,' I says. He put two shillings down, and I put two shillings against it, and he beat me. He explained the case to me. 'I see your two eyes,' he said, 'but if you were looking at me, you can't see but one!'

"If you were talking with them till tomorrow, they could beat you. That was their lives, you see, between that and studying nature. And those men, I'm not coddin' you a bit, they were the purest gentlemen in the whole entire country! You wouldn't get a man with twenty servants and a landlord's big estate to touch them, for manners. They wouldn't harm a fly nor a flower. 'Twasn't a gentlemanly thing to lift my two shillings off me like that? Well, I ask you truthfully now, which is more gentlemanly, to lose two shillings to a beggar man, or to have the government take the lot of your money off you with taxes and high costs?"

Anthony jumps from here to a harsh indictment of the present government. Why, he asks, don't they raise subsidies for struggling bards like himself? Instead, all they seem able to raise is the price of a pint until no one can afford it. He spits out the car window to show his contempt, and the wind blows it back on him. He is not accustomed to riding in motorcars.

When we reach his bungalow in Ballycastle, Anthony invites me in to share the simple comforts of his hearth, but advises me in advance that they really are simple, "because I have no chairs inside." In fact, I soon discover that there are no furnishings of any kind inside, only a lone mattress soiled to a rich golden-brown, the product of years of not washing. An odor of almost medieval rankness clogs the air, and the only light ("Long ago," says Anthony, "my electricity was taken away from me for nonpayment of it") is that which the sun manages to scud in. It is the sort of home that only a person dedicated to his own homelessness could love; the four walls are just an illusion, concealing just more Mayo bogland, which also surrounds them.

If Anthony is not proud of this domestic setting, neither is he ashamed of it. "A man could live in a dung pit and love it, I believe. In fact, I even knowed a man that lived in a public lavatory in Castlebar once. Would lock himself in a stall at night, pull his feet up when the guard came in to close it up.

"And a man could live in a barrel and love it, there's no doubt about that." He finds a half-empty bottle of Guinness on the floor, and hoists it to his mouth, and then in an effusion of scrappy phrases and asides, he goes on to describe his own past tenure in a barrel, "a grand ol' barrel I put up right near here." He had just returned to Ballycastle from his five years of musical wandering, and what should he discover but that the roof of his ancestral cabin, the home of his father and his grandfather, had caved in from neglect? That was all right; he just began to live in this fishmonger's barrel he "put up" on his property, behind the original house. At least it provided him with a roof over his head. As for the other attractions of home, they could be obtained at the local pub.

(In the long run, he indicates, what difference will it make where he slept during that time? "There's no sleep in any of us that won't be sleep when we come to God." His religiosity increases the more drink he's taken.)

He continued his residence in this barrel for the better part of a year. The end came suddenly. He never was able to brave the regimentation of turf cutting, and after sacrificing all the timber from his fallen house, he needed something else to burn, particularly with the advent of winter. So, he began raiding his neighbors' store of firewood, and also was not beneath taking the odd handle from a spade, for it made excellent seasoned kindling. Anthony speculates that one of his victims didn't take kindly to this last practice of his; late one night, he returned from the pub to discover a pile of charred wood where his barrel had been. Somebody had burned the barrel down. "I spent the next two days with a bottle of methylated spirits," he says, "I was that far gone with the sadness."

Anyway, the County Council took pity on him, and built him the bungalow where he now lives, and they supplied him with such furnishings as a respectable burgher might require. But within a week (and he refers to this with just a twinge of regret), he had sold everything but his mattress for "case after case of good Irish whiskey," which it took even him several months to drink. In that way, he transcended the sudden burden of middle-classness.

I gaze around the interior of the bungalow now, nearly twenty years after these events just described, and what the place seems to resemble most is—a cavernous barrel. Anthony has slowly staged a return to the days of his former glory, crawling back into his barrel as nearly as circumstance will allow. He has purified his living conditions of all nonessentials. Of the essentials, however, I am told to be very careful: Anthony says he never removes his boots anymore, for fear of stepping with his bare feet on the broken shards of bottles islanding the floor.

Custom usually dictates that a country person keep a tidy house, unless he's a bachelor and then be might be considered somewhat disreputable (too "delicate") if his house is tidy. Anthony's neighbors consider him disreputable anyway. They give his bungalow a wide berth; their general attitude is a little like that of the old mariners who refused to navigate the unknown regions that their maps labeled with "Here Be Monsters."

"He's like a hippie or some suchlike person, he's so filthy."

"He's the worst man for booze I've ever met with."

"He let the house of his family fall in ruins without a bother about it. Was that nice?"

"He's made a madhouse of his head."

Neighborly complaints like these have brought a regional social worker to Anthony's door on more than one occasion, and he has not exactly warmed to this show of humane interest toward his predicament.

"This chap from Ballina, he had been here before and each time, 'twas a bit messy in the house. 'Well,' he was a man with a starch collar and a clean new suit. He came here about a month ago and told me I should submit to 'psychoanalysis,' and I asked him, 'What for?' and he said, 'Because we need to get you back to normal,' and I says, 'I am normal, I've always been like this,' and he says, 'But you need to talk to a doctor about your problems.' 'Well,' I says, 'I got no problems, only I'm a fond man of the pint, and sure, there's nothing wrong with that.' He says, 'We'll pay for your sessions and you'll see, they'll make a happy man of you,' and I says, 'I'm not an unhappy man and this psychoanalysis business, I don't know now but it mightn't make an unhappy man of me.' 'All this dirt and filth you're living in,' he says, ' 'tisn't fit for man nor beast,' and I tells him, 'I'm taking it the way God gave it to me, dirt and all.' So he kept goin' on with the analysis stuff, like, and then he tells me, 'That's what's getting our race into trouble, your kind of thinking,' and now he's made me angry, you see, fuckin' angry, a stupid thing that was to say to anyone, so I told him, 'I'm not the fuckin' race, I'm meself, and I don't want any of your fuckin' analysis even if the whole race is doing it.' He says, 'You can't go on like this,' and I says, 'I'll go on all right, the same as you, except you're going first,' and I threw him out, told him to go away and not come back if he's going to talk such rubbish, about getting analyzed, imagine it."

At moments like the one he's just described, when the madness of the outside world seems to creep to his very doorstep, Anthony wishes he still had his concertina, for playing it "would clear the air of that nonsense." But having left this keyless instrument "somewhere on the road to Killala," he usually honors the departure of Benevolent Officialdom with a new verse. Or if it's the summer, he might find a degree of solace in one of the "hippie wanderers from all parts" who pass through and detect in him possibly some archaic counterpart to themselves. They've even given him marijuana seeds, and though he's sowed them, the plants were eaten by some sheep; this has happened twice, and Anthony therefore concludes that "sheep must be very fond of the marijuana." Yet he fears that even these people, sympathetic as they've been to him, might be rather put off by his habits: "There was a young Danish hippie-man staying with me for about a week, and he wanted me to go to his country and go on the tele for to be some sort of performer, because whatever I said, I made him laugh. He was trying to teach me the Danish language, you see, for that purpose. A flaming smart lad, yes—but I think he must have been used to another way of living than what I'm doing here, and when he left, he told me I should see a 'vocational guidance counselor.'

"What is a 'vocational guidance counselor'?" Anthony asks me.

Others have suggested that he try his hand at a profession, even engage himself with a bit of farming, like his father did, but Anthony feels that this might very well conspire against the dignity of the heroic past that he imagines for himself, deflating it with mundane sweat-work. And being the guardian of the bardic tradition, he is accountable to his fellow countrymen as well. He mustn't sully his role in society.

In fits of sobriety, however, and only then when he's presented with the gift of a young puck-goat, he might make a *bodhrán* (a skin drum played by traditional musicians), which might bring him fifteen pounds. But he can't bring himself to make an industry out of it with the purchase of a herd of goats. Such long-term investments are obviously not his style. Even, the purchase of an individual animal poses a nearly metaphysical problem for him: it is commerce in its rudimentary stages, and he cowers at the thought of it seizing him.

The skin of a greyhound, Anthony claims, will make the best *bodhrán*, because it is so thin, and a few months ago, he made one from an old greyhound belonging to a neighbor who was going to send the dog out to stud. The ensuing row landed him in court, where he was let off with a small fine by promising not to steal another greyhound. His day in court was a traumatic experience for him; since then, he hasn't made a *bodhrán* from any species of animal.

Anthony has been on the dole so long, remark his neighbors, he can't even remember another method of acquiring money. He himself likes to perpetuate the story that he hasn't worked, except in the bardic sense, since the last war. "I am the idle rich," be observes facetiously, then begins to sing a song whose words I find completely unintelligible.

The raven bleeds around the eyes during coition. Anthony Fergus is a bird of a somewhat similar feather, for his own eyes are bloodshot from the intensity of his own indulgences. Except that for him, there has been no coition, not once by his own count; he remains untainted by that form of commerce as well.

"The closest that ever I came to courtin' came when I was a lad of twenty-five years and living at home. I had a pony, and this pony got sick with me, frosty, after Christmas it was, and there was nothing in it, only the bones. He couldn't eat nothing, and I used to be trying to give him old bran and turnips, one thing and another, and a sack over him for covering at night.

"Well, this one night, I was lying in my bed under the window, and I heard a horse galloping outside, and I looked out, and here was a big mare, the grandest mare, I never looked at a nicer one and she all snow-white and blue spots, and up upon the saddle was a young girl with long yellow hair. I never seen the like of her, lovely. She beckoned to me to come on, get up behind her, and what did I do but get up the way I was and it winter. Away we went, terrible cold weather.

"The next thing was, I came awake from my sleep and there I was, in my skin, no shirt or nothing, and I was on the back of my old pony between two big old rocks, no sign of the girl or mare or nothing. And we went down the rocks and between the old furze and I seen we were on a hill I knew very well, Knockannamaurnach they calls it.

"We went down the road about a mile where an old man lived. 'Twas about seven in the morning, and the old man said, 'What's wrong with ye at all?' 'I'm after comin' down from the mountain,' says I. He gave me a bad raggedy coat and terrible raggedy trousers, only one leg in them, and away I go in my bare feet leading the pony down the road to my own house here.

" 'Oh where have you been off to?' says my father. I was ashamed to tell him about the girl, do you see. 'I must have walked in my sleep or something,' I says.

"You see, that pony was sick and couldn't go nowhere, and there were bushes and rocks in it you wouldn't do in a week, the three miles in a week up to the top of that hill."

Anthony recites this tale with pride. He is glad to be detached from the rank and file of common courters. It is as if other peoples' accounts of the courting experience were only so much fabrication.

In his younger days, he was handsome enough, in a craggy way, to attract women from beyond this evanescent horsey set. Once or twice, he was even mistaken for Spencer Tracy on holidays. After the film *Boys' Town* first came out, one American lady, visiting relatives near Ballycastle, addressed him as "Father" and inquired how the work was going back in Nebraska. Anthony replied that indeed it must be going well, for the fine weather would mean the lads were all out cutting turf. The joke was lost on him until the local priest, informed of Father Flanagan's recent arrival in his parish, descended on him and warned him against impersonating men of the cloth.

He was handsome enough, except for one deformity: North Mayo. "By the time I was a grown lad, all the girls had gone away." That succinct sentence tells nearly the whole story; the remainder of it comes from the fierce love of celibacy men often pursue in the West as an alternative to loving not even *that*. Where there's scarcely a marriageable women around for miles, of what use is it to belabor the issue with hope? Instead, a man can become a monument of eccentric freedom, unfettered by a woman's influence. After a time, his desires will have dissolved as perfectly as a wafer in the mouth.

Of the fifty houses within a two-mile radius of him, Anthony notes that half of them lodge aging bachelors, stuck to their paltry holdings. In the same vicinity, there isn't a single aging spinster.

"My brother Pat is living in Pittsburgh in America and he has eight children and I have none. I've often wondered why the Creator wanted such a complete imbalance as that."

Despite his wondering, his face grows tenebrous at the prospect of some woman luring him to the altar. After all, he's the last of the bards. What business does he have marrying? "Poetry and females, you wouldn't want to mix them together." He could not have accomplished all that he has, he states, if he had allowed himself to take the matrimonial plunge. The very thought of it causes him to wince, and brings a curse to his lips: "Women, they're bad news." Then, from the place in his mind where he stores such things, he breaks into a description of the bizarre practice of "spanceling," which an elderly man told him was common in Mayo "right up to a hundred fifty years ago."

"Ugly women that wanted a husband would work the spancel as a charm. They used to take the skin off a carcass of a person that was just after being buried. A band of skin from the waist right around the back, that was the 'spancel.' Dig up a dead man or woman from the burying ground for that purpose, to get the spancel. Then this woman would creep in and wrap the spancel around the waist of her intended man whilst he was asleep in his bed. The poor fellow, he wouldn't have a chance. If he didn't wake up while she's doing the wrappin', he'd have to marry her before the end of the year. And if he did wake up, then it's all over and he'll die before the end of that year. So you see, 'twas a very poor bargain altogether for the man."

I ask him if he thinks the odd ugly woman might be at it still.

"Well, it died out altogether. About the time of the Famine, that's when it would have died out. I expect 'twould be the contagion on the corpses put a stop to it."

But he is not amused, or not much. Spanceling has such far-reaching implications, the concept of it alone comes close to sobering him. It would seem to be the human condition, in a nut-shell. Anthony has offered this little anecdote like a cautionary tale. His serious countenance seems to suggest that he thinks the *spirit* of the spancel lingers on in women—but he has had too little contact with them to know for sure.

"I wouldn't let no woman do me with marriage," he states, and as though to make certain that no woman is now approaching his bun-galow with that thought in mind, he glances out the window over the giant navel-holes of his bog. No one is coming. The barren vista affirms yet another claim he can make to being the last; a line stretching back to the beginning of time will end with him.

The sudden downpour of rain does not deter Anthony from his ever-lasting pursuit of the pint. He whips into a long black frieze coat (which makes him look a little like Dracula), and we begin to negotiate the windy, well-nigh longitudinal rain for the mile-long trek to the nearest pub. Despite the wet, Anthony says that he prefers to walk this distance because walking may bring back life to his injured foot.

At the bar are two youth hostelers instantly identifiable as Cana-dians by the abundance of maple leafs emblazoned on their ruck-sacks, jackets, and jeans. In the past, Anthony has found that Canadians are a good "touch" for marijuana. He walks up to one of them, shakes the fellow's hand vigorously, and inquires, "Have you brought any of the green grass of home with you?" The fellow shakes his head; he doesn't quite understand. Anthony has to explicate the metaphor for him, which he does in a booming voice. No, neither of them carries that sort of thing. Then the boy's companion whispers something to him, and the two of them, indicating that they'd like to sit down, move to the opposite side of the room.

It is the odor of urine from Anthony that has done it; the original tanning properties from his coat (the wool for frieze is cured in urine for a year) have been released by the rain, and the smell has formed a nimbus around him for several feet. The other patrons of the bar are beginning to move away too, but that doesn't appear to bother Anthony, who is well used to their distance. He takes a long draft from his stout and looks at the bottle with the sort of intimate stare other men sometimes reserve for their women. Then suddenly he closes his eyes and recites what turns out to be his most recent composition, "The Football Match of the Fairies," machine-gunning the words in a manner that parodies radio sports announcers. It dramatizes a game of Gaelic football between a north Mayo team and a team made up exclusively of pookas, goblins, leprechauns, and assorted sprites. The mythical creatures win by one point; a Pyrrhic victory for the oral tradition.

Death on Ice

n 1911, a young man named George Street made a decision that must have inspired a good deal of tongue wagging among his mates with the New Northwest Exploration Party. "Street's crazy," you can hear them saying. "To spend three years with that Radford fellow—why, I'd rather spend three years with a bilious grizzly. Or three years in a lunatic asylum . . . "

Strong, persistent, perhaps a bit stubborn, Street had proven himself an invaluable member of J.J. Crean's surveying party. He was a fine hand with an axe, a first-rate driver of dogs, and a superb canoeist. On portages, he could carry two hundred pounds, the normal tump-line load for a seasoned packer. But the twenty-two-year-old Ottawan was burning to make a great trip. A great trip far to the north of Smith's Landing, Alberta, where the Crean expedition was based.

And now here was Radford offering him just the opportunity he was looking for. He would join the American in one of the most ambitious Arctic expeditions ever planned; they would paddle all the way from Fort Smith to Chesterfield Inlet on Hudson Bay, sledge north to Bathurst Inlet, cross the Arctic Ocean to Fort MacPherson on the Mackenzie Delta, and end up in the Yukon. Part of this route would take them through unexplored country; some of it, especially the area around Bathurst Inlet, might even have uncontacted Eskimos.

It was an offer Street could hardly refuse, even though Radford had asked him to sign a rather unusual contract: he was supposed to protect Radford's life, if necessary, at the risk of his own; he would receive less than his share of food if food became scarce; and he would keep no diaries of the trip (Radford wanted exclusive rights to it himself).

Street probably identified the somewhat older man with his demanding, quick-to-anger father, and this may have given Radford's contract the veneer of, if not respectability, at least familiarity. Yet Street would have signed any contract, however oppressive its terms, for the opportunity to spend three years in the Arctic. At his age, I might have done the same thing—the prospect of adventure, particularly adventure in far off lands, makes youth even more blind than it already is.

A wealthy New York sportsman and erstwhile editor for *Field & Stream*, Harry Radford ("Adirondack Harry") had come north in 1909 to collect zoological specimens for the U.S. Biological Survey and the Smithsonian Institution. From the outset, his swagger rubbed Northerners the wrong way. In fact, it inspired a celebrated joke at his expense. In the summer of 1909, he was a passenger on an Athabaska River steamboat. The steamer's captain had grown a bit weary of Radford's portrayal of himself as a Great White Hunter. All of a sudden Captain Barber pointed to a large bear roaming around on the shore. Radford stalked the bear and, upon getting close, emptied the magazine of his .30-.30 rifle into it, only to discover that it was a log dressed in an old fur coat and rigged on a rope and pulley. "And with that," read a contemporary newspaper account of the incident, "the North country started to laugh, and has been laughing ever since."

Despite his success with this "bear," Radford was no more than an indifferent marksman, which is probably why so many of his specimens in the Smithsonian's collection are "pickups" (animals already dead). That he did manage to shoot a 2,402 ton wood bison, the largest ever killed, is no doubt a tribute to his inability to miss it. This trophy animal was Radford's ticket to self-proclaimed fame and may have led him to think he could make Arctic history. Actually, he did make Arctic history, although not as an explorer of the first order, which is how, strange to say, he saw himself.

"This gentleman is utterly helpless and can do nothing for himself"—such was the verdict of Mounted Police Corporal Mellor in Fort Smith. How Mellor reacted when he heard about Radford's proposed expedition is not known. Perhaps he just laughed. After all, this was the same man who turned up his nose at the three time-honored B's (beans, bacon, and bannock) and claimed he could live exclusively on a diet of milk chocolate while traveling in the Arctic. Or perhaps Mellor repeated what he'd said about an earlier journey of Radford's: "A trip of this arduous nature is simply madness for him to tackle."

On June 27, 1911, Radford and Street lowered Radford's nineteen foot Peterborough canoe *Hope* into the Slave River at Fort Smith. Paddling with the current, they reached Fort Resolution on Great Slave Lake in three and a half days. Here a nun gave Street a bottle of Holy Water to protect the expedition from storms. A charm to protect it from Radford's rages might have been a better idea. But there were no rages yet, except possibly toward local wildlife: by July 9, he had already collected sixty-seven mammals and twenty-two birds for the U.S. Biological Survey.

Three weeks and 325 miles later, they reached Artillery Lake. Here they hired two Yellowknife Indians to, Radford wrote, "lighten the load of my fine cedar canoe [with their birchbark canoe] which otherwise would be in danger of swamping should high winds be met on the large lakes." Then they set out for these lakes via the Hanbury and Thelon Rivers, a route pioneered by Mounted Police Inspector Ephrem Pelletier in 1908.

So far, so good. But in mid-August, the Indians deserted. Hard work seems not to have agreed with them—or maybe Radford didn't agree with them. A few months later they showed up at Fort Resolution, complaining of ill treatment. "We are not dogs to work like that," they said. Radford was a hard man, they added. A hard man who used hard words.

Street regretted the loss of the Indians more than his partner. Due to their departure and the fact that Radford had an infected arm, he now had to navigate their canoe single-handed, running rapids and packing their entire half ton outfit over rough portages. They reached Chesterfield Inlet too late in the season to continue on to Bathurst Inlet, so they decided to winter over with a group of Eskimos at Schultz Lake. Here they arranged for lodgings in a sort of annex to the igloo of the local headman, Akulak.

Street was now in his element. He was not bothered by the cold, the caribou stomach dinners, or his hosts' kitchen hygiene (their method of washing dishes was simply to let their dogs lick them). Quite the contrary. His letters home, which he cautioned his family not to publish (the contract . . .), show his delight in the frozen world around him. They also show his keen interest in the particulars of Eskimo life. "Eskimo children are espoused when only five or six years old, and often a boy of six or seven has two wives already," he writes. And: "The reason the chief [Akulak] gave for not wanting to die was that he would not be able to eat any more."

Radford, meanwhile, was trying to locate a guide for the spring sledge trip to Bathurst Inlet. This wasn't easy, since the Eskimos in Akulak's camp considered the land north of them starvation country. At last two men named Cockney and Bosun reluctantly agreed to make the trip. Yet when Radford refused to provide for his family in his absence, Bosun refused to go. Whereupon Radford grabbed a rifle and threatened to shoot him if he didn't obey orders. "Go ahead and shoot," Bosun declared, and Radford backed down. An ominous moment.

At last, with Akulak himself as guide, the Radford-Street Expedition, Part II, set out for Bathurst Inlet. They made the six week journey without incident, certainly without starvation, arriving at their destination in early May.

Radford now began mapping what he called "the last strip remaining unexplored of the continental coast of North America." Soon the two explorers were encountering Copper Eskimos who had never seen a white man before. In a letter to the American Geographical Society, Radford wrote of these people: "They possess no rifles, and hunt, as of old, with the bow, spear, and harpoon . . . They speak a dialect very different from the inland Eskimos and those that dwell near Hudson Bay; and Mr. Street and I find it difficult to communicate with them."

And then the two men seemed to vanish. For a year, there was no news concerning their whereabouts; no sightings and no letters back to civilization. It was as if the Arctic, an eager grave for the gallant and not-so-gallant alike, had swallowed them up. Then, on June 11, 1913, Akulak appeared at the Hudson Bay Company trading post in Chesterfield Inlet. The story he told H. H. Hall, the post's manager, slowly made its way southward, until most of Canada knew that Harry Radford and George Street had been murdered by the Bathurst Inlet Eskimos.

Within several months, Canada's privy council authorized an expenditure not to exceed $70,656 for a special police patrol to investigate Akulak's story. This was a huge sum of money, especially for murders which, according to Akulak, had been provoked. But the issue at stake was not just murder. If the police could track down the Eskimos responsible for killing Radford and Street, then the country's control over its own central Arctic coast—an area virtually off the map—would be more or less established.

On July 31, 1914, Inspector W. J. Beyts of the Royal Northwest Mounted Police, along with Sergeant-Major Thomas Caulkin and two constables, sailed from Halifax in the steamer *Village Belle*. It was a miserable trip, beset by storms and icebergs. The *Village Belle* barely escaped shipwreck half a dozen times. Beyts reached Chesterfield Inlet too late in the season to do anything more than erect a portable shelter for the winter.

For two years, the Mounties battled the unfriendly Arctic in an effort to reach Bathurst Inlet. Their oil stove wouldn't work; their kerosene lanterns broke; their tent caught fire; incessant storms battered them; and their hungry dogs devoured fourteen sets of harness. It was no consolation that the local Eskimos were in even worse shape, having lost almost all of their dogs to starvation. "In one instance," reported Beyts, "I saw a party moving camp with one dog, two women, and a native hitched to the sledge."

Beyts's difficulties left him exhausted, and in the summer of 1916 his superiors in Ottawa relieved him of his command. Mounties, at least in literature, always "got their man." All Beyts had gotten for his efforts were pleurisy and bronchitis, from which he never really recovered.

Beyts's replacement, Inspector Francis H. French, looked the perfect model of a Mountie—he was thirty-two years old, handsome, generously mustached, and athletic. He was also a nephew of the Force's first commissioner, George French, and the son of Captain John French, who'd helped put down the 1885 Northwest Rebellion—a good pedigree for leading what was now being called the Bathurst Inlet Patrol.

On March 21, 1917, Inspector French, Caulkin, three Eskimo doghandlers, and an Eskimo woman named Solomon mushed westward from the police detachment at Baker Lake. This was the start of a trip that would have confounded even their wildest dreams.

The misfortune that had dogged Beyts soon began to dog the new patrol. First, a pack of wolves attacked their camp. Then they were stormbound for a week. Later the dazzle of the sun made the entire party snowblind. But French and Caulkin were blind in another sense, too—their maps were inaccurate, and on April 10 the only one of their Eskimos familiar with the route decided to go home. They were now traveling without a guide through virtually unknown country. Their compass was no help; mineral deposits caused its needle to gyrate uselessly.

And there was more. For six days, they sledged around in dense fog trying to locate the outlet of the Back River to Beechey Lake. Because of melting snow, they were now forced to follow tortuous courses along the still snowed-in bottoms of ravines. Luckily, they met an Eskimo named Angingat who, for a rifle and ammunition, agreed to take them to the coast on a considerably less arduous route, via the Ellice River. Unluckily, the ice on this route made their dogs lame; Solomon now had to sew *kamiks* (boots) not only for the patrol's human members, but for its canine members, too.

On May 7, with a northwest blizzard blowing and the temperature thirty-five below zero, Inspector French made a significant entry in his diary: "Came within sight of Arctic Ocean at east side of Kent Peninsula at 6:30 P.M. and camped." Then he added, almost as an aside, "Living on deer [caribou] meat straight. All civilized grub gone. Oil out." Raw meat, which was fine for the Eskimos, made both French and Caulkin sick.

On May 10, another storm struck and kept the patrol igloo-bound. Two days later, the same storm came back and halted their progress again. By now French may have wished he was pursuing his duty in a more temperate part of Canada. Or maybe not. A Mountie is not a Mountie if he doesn't accept tough physical conditions as an unavoidable part of his job.

A day or so later, they noticed a good sign—fresh sled tracks. They followed these tracks in a southwesterly direction and at last came to a Copper Eskimo camp at the mouth of Bathurst Inlet. It was now three years since Beyts had sailed from Halifax and nearly five years since the murders were committed.

There were only women in the camp when the patrol arrived. They fled immediately to their igloos, which isn't surprising. French and Caulkin may have been the first *qallunaat* (white men) they'd ever seen. At most, they would have seen only three others—the English adventurer David Hanbury, Radford, and Street. And their experience of the latter two would not have been a pleasant one.

The women reappeared when members of the patrol raised their hands high above their heads, the traditional friendly greeting among Eskimos. Their men were seal hunting a short distance away. Upon seeing the strangers, they dashed toward them with their spears and snow knives in menacing attitudes. French and Caulkin must have wondered if they were going to end up like Radford and Street.

They needn't have worried. The men put down their weapons the moment they saw the hands-over-head gesture. Soon another group arrived from the west side of Bathurst Inlet. Up went their hands over their heads again. French found the Eskimos in this new group quite amiable. They even supplied him with *kudliqs* (soapstone lamps) and bladders of seal oil, for which he must have been grateful, since he now could cook his meat. Unfortunately, this method of cooking was so slow that he had to abandon it after what he describes as an "all-night vigil."

But French had more important things to do than eat a hot meal. He now began traveling up and down Bathurst Inlet, asking about the deaths of the two white men. The Eskimos he met responded freely and openly to his questions. In the end, he took down sworn depositions from eleven men and women, most of whom had been eyewitnesses to the murders. All of them told his interpreter, Police Native Joe, exactly the same story:

About five winters ago, the two qallunaat came to North Quadyuk Island in Bathurst Inlet. The older man's name was Ishumatak (lit., "the man who does the thinking") because he seemed to be the leader. The other one was known as Kiuk ("Wood") because of his great strength. Ishumatak had such an unusually bad temper that some people thought he might be possessed by a *tornrak* (evil spirit).

It was not possible to communicate with either of them except through signs.

The qallunaat wanted two guides to travel west with them. Harla and Kaneak agreed to do this. Harla had already started off in his sledge when Kaneak decided not to go. His wife had fallen down on the ice and hurt herself, and he wanted to stay with her. Ishumatak got very angry at him and began talking loudly, but no one could understand him. All at once he began beating Kaneak with the butt of a dog whip. He beat him on the head and face many times. He was *ningasaituq*—completely out of control. Kiuk tried to restrain him, but could not. Ishumutuk dragged Kaneak over to a hole in the ice, as if he was going to push him in.

Now a man named Okitok grabbed Ishumatak and another man, Hulalark, stabbed him three times in the back with a snow knife. Kiuk began running toward his sled. There was no time to decide whether he was going for a rifle or just trying to get away. Okitok ran after him and held him, and a one-eyed man named Amegealnik stabbed him between the shoulder blades and in the back with a snow knife. Kiuk died right away. Ishumutak was still alive. Hulalark slit his throat so that he would not suffer. The two bodies were covered with caribou skins and left on the ice. Their rifles were broken up and used as hand tools.

French questioned every Eskimo he met, but neither he or Caulkin, who spoke their language, could find any flaws in this story. Asked about Radford, his informants were unanimous in saying that he'd treated them badly. There was even an earlier incident where he'd picked up a knife and chased a man with it, threatening to kill him. But Street, they kept saying, was an *inoqiktok*—a good man. No one had wanted any harm to come to him. (Amelgealnik later offered missionary W. H. B. Hoare the pick of his white fox pelts and asked Hoare to deliver them to Street's family—the only way he could think of to atone for what he'd done.)

Neither Amelgealnik or the other murderer, Hulalark, was in Bathurst Inlet at the time of French's visit. Apparently, both were still at their winter hunting ground. Where this was, no one seemed to know—maybe "the big island across the salt" (Victoria Island), maybe somewhere else. But it wouldn't have mattered even if they were sitting in the igloo next door, since it was obvious that they had acted in their own defense. That being the case, and since he'd been instructed to make no arrests in the event of provocation by either Radford or Street, French exonerated the two men *in absentia*.

Nowadays Amelgealnik and Hulalark probably would be slapped with a manslaughter charge. But in French's day Eskimos were not so much above the law as beyond it: they were considered uncivilized, often admirably so, and thus not subject to the same legal standards as other Canadians. This attitude, at once liberal and condescending, would change in a few years, with increased contact between whites and Natives. And with that change, the Arctic would pass from Eskimo hands into the hands of the proverbial Great White Father.

Before he left Bathurst Inlet, French warned the Eskimos that his verdict in the Radford-Street case would be the last verdict of its kind they would ever encounter. If they killed or molested white men again, he said, "the culprits would be taken away and would never return." These words had a quite powerful effect on his listeners. For the very worst thing they could imagine, worse even than starvation, was to be somehow taken away from this austere, unforgiving land, their home.

During French's inquiry, old Elatchak, Bathurst Inlet's resident *angakok* (shaman), revealed that he'd seen a bad spirit following the patrol's sleds into his camp. Either this spirit went from bad to worse, or French's luck deserted him. For his trip back to civilization makes his not necessarily easy trip to Bathurst Inlet seem like a mere country outing.

It was now late May. With the warmer weather, French's igloo collapsed on top of him. An amusing incident, perhaps; but it indicated melting snow, which in turn indicated an early end to sled travel. Even more worrisome, the patrol was now subsisting on half-raw caribou meat. This diet could only get worse, since they had only a few rounds of ammunition left for their .303 rifles. Also, their tattered clothing did little to keep out the various Arctic elements.

French badly needed to reprovision his patrol. From the Eskimos, he learned of a trading ship frozen in on the coast somewhere west of Bathurst Inlet. He decided to strike out for this ship rather than return to Baker Lake. His superiors had already waited five years for a verdict in the Radford-Street case; he figured they could wait a while longer.

Coastal travel turned out to be a nightmare. The patrol found itself alternately sloshing knee-high through meltwater or plunging through cracks in the sea-ice. By June 8, when they reached the schooner *Teddy Bear*, they were all suffering from cold and exposure. To this can be added disappointment, for the schooner's captain was underprovisioned himself. They continued on to the Hudson Bay Company post at Bernard Harbor, only to learn that the post's manager, Mr. Phillips, was almost out of supplies, too. No matter: the Company's supply ship was expected any day now. They waited all summer in Bernard Harbor for this ship. Due to ice conditions, it never came.

"The hardest trip I ever made," French wrote in his diary. And this was just the beginning. He still had another Arctic winter to look forward to.

French finally bought two small rifles and a handful of cartridges from Mr. Phillips, and then moved his patrol to the mouth of the Coppermine River. Here they overhauled their outfit, dried a batch of fish for their dogs, and waited for a snowfall deep enough for their sleds. On October 2, French scribbled a note to "any member" of the Force or "any white man" and gave it to some Indians heading south to Great Bear Lake. This note described his proposed itinerary to Baker Lake and included these words: "If we able to kill deer, we will be able to make out all right." That "if" must have loomed large in his mind.

On October 16, the patrol returned to the coast, where the usual travails greeted them—thin ice, howling blizzards, and wet snow that soaked them through to the skin. Almost a month later, they reached Bathurst Inlet. The Eskimos were astonished to see them again, and perhaps a little worried too: Had they unwittingly made trouble for more qallunaat?

Having very little food for their overworked dogs, they set out for Baker Lake with the equivalent of a fuel tank close to empty. Wolves ("The biggest specimens I have ever seen," noted French) began to follow them again, seemingly aware that the patrol was on, if not its last legs, at least quite weak ones. At one point they found a batch of semi-putrid caribou carcasses being feasted upon by wolves and ravens.

Here follows a scene you'll never see in films featuring King of the Royal Mounted, Renfrew of the same, and Sergeant Preston of the Yukon: two Mounties, French and Caulkin, fighting off scavengers, indeed becoming scavengers themselves, in order to get some highly odiferous meat for their patrol. Nothing could have been less romantic . . . or more useful. For the weather was now so calm that any sound they made carried for miles, warning any potentially edible animal of their presence.

Meanwhile, the days were getting shorter, with fewer hours for travel and hunting. Also colder: the temperature on even the warmest days never rose higher than ten degrees above zero. Their clothing was now more or less continually frozen. Likewise their boots. Likewise their bedding.

Not even the world's greatest masochist would have wanted to exchange positions with these skin-clad specks of humanity slowly creeping over the vast spaces of the Arctic. By early December, they had almost no oil to cook with, their faces were frostbitten, their feet were numb, and their ragged clothes were stiff as cardboard. Patches of their skin were dropping off. No doubt their fingernails were dropping off, too. And, of course, they had very little food. Anything more? Yes: they were less than halfway to Baker Lake.

On December 13, their dogs ate the last of the caribou and then went hungry. To have the "legs" of your expedition without food is almost as bad as going without food yourself. For if dogs don't eat, they don't move; and if they don't move, you're stuck wherever they've stopped, often a not very pleasant place. On December 17, French shot five of his weakest dogs to feed the rest, and a day or so later he killed five more. This measure, he reported, "struck deep into all of us," adding: "In this country, a man grows to love his dogs." He doesn't say it, but the loss of these dogs doubtless left the patrol with a sense of loneliness they had not anticipated.

Now comes the sort of thing you might expect from an old-fashioned serial, where the hero is hanging on in desperation in one episode and rescued, albeit temporarily, in the next. The patrol's Eskimos had gone off hunting. And on Christmas Day, they returned to camp with two sleds piled high with musk-ox meat. Never mind Christmas dinner—now everyone, dogs included, would have something to put in their empty bellies. This, at least, was a cause for celebration.

Whatever merriment they may have had on Christmas quickly dissipated with the series of blinding blizzards that inaugurated the New Year. Day after day, windblown snow clawed at French and his party from out of the winter's darkness, never slackening, never letting up. Running low on food again, they couldn't afford to wait out the weather, so they traveled nearly eighty miles off their course. French was obliged to abandon a sled. He killed three more dogs to feed the others. A bitch had seven pups: the other dogs immediately devoured them. Temperatures went from being merely punishing to downright lethal, averaging sixty degrees below zero during the day and somewhat lower at night.

By mid-January, their Eskimos still had seen no familiar landmarks and were convinced the patrol was lost. Not only lost, but actually heading in the wrong direction. If that was the case, nothing could save them. Maybe nothing could save them anyway. Most of the fur had fallen out of their caribou skin clothes, with the result that the wind swept right through the holes. They were cold beyond any possible imagining. And their only food was a thin soup made from old caribou bones: starvation grub.

On January 24, the temperature dropped to seventy-two degrees below zero, and French was so weak he could barely talk. "It looks like our last patrol," he wrote in his notebook. Dutiful Mountie that he was, he must have been especially upset about the possibility that his verdict in the Radford-Street case might not survive him.

Then a miracle happened—they sighted a herd of caribou. "We shot ten after some smart maneuvering," French wrote. They ate the meat themselves, and fed the heads and guts to their few remaining dogs. Now the Arctic gods seemed to be smiling on them. Several days later they found themselves at the southwestern extremity of Baker Lake. And on January 29, 1918, they arrived at the Baker Lake police post, where they were greeted like men just returned from the dead. In a sense, they were.

And so it was over—the longest, most arduous manhunt in the history of the Mounted Police, maybe in the history of any police force. The two patrols, Beyts's and French's, had taken place not only during World War I, but had taken almost as long as World War I, too. French himself had traveled an extraordinary 5,153 miles, most of them walking or running with his dogs through country that resisted his every step. This remarkable feat of endurance earned him the coveted Imperial Service Award from the Canadian Government. It also undermined his health; in 1924, the seemingly indomitable Inspector French had to be invalided out of the Force.

Like Beyts, French did not "get his man." If he had, the story of the Bathurst Inlet Patrol might be as well known today as the Arctic adventures of Peary or Stefansson. But French got something perhaps better than fame—justice for a couple of Eskimos living at the end of the world.

In 1996, I visited Bathurst Inlet myself. Whereas it had taken Inspector French almost two months to get there, I managed the trip from Yellowknife in less than three hours. But a twin-engine Cessna would not have been an option for French.

The local Inuit, who call themselves Kingaunmiut (People of the Nose: the name derives from a distinctive noselike hump in the landscape behind the settlement), seemed to me still rather traditional, although perhaps not quite as traditional as in French's day. For instance, they no longer expect a hands-over-the-head greeting from visitors: a simple "hello" will suffice. Also, it's unlikely that they would kill a latter-day Radford if he happened to be abusive toward them; they would just pack him onto the next plane bound for Yellowknife. For they've grown accustomed to erratic behavior from qallunaat. Prospectors, the Hudson Bay Company, the inevitable missionaries, even tourists—all have passed through this remote Arctic fastness in the wake of French.

Perhaps because murder, even justifiable murder, is not something to be particularly proud of, the Kingaunmiut don't like to talk about the Radford-Street incident. But in asking around, I did meet one man who volunteered to show me where the murders had been committed. So it was that on a bright, typically mosquito-plagued day, we traveled to the gaunt pyramidal strip of North Quadyuk Island in his motorboat. After we landed on the island, we wandered along the shore for a few minutes, and then the man suddenly pointed to the ground.

"*Tavva!*" he exclaimed. "Right here!"

But how did he know this was the precise place?

"Because this plant grows wherever blood has been spilled," he told me.

On the rock where he'd been pointing, there was a scurf of red-spotted lichen (*Haematoma lapponicum*)—the plant in question. The spots did in fact look like blood. But the same lichen seemed to be growing everywhere, which made me wonder whether the island had hosted some event that was considerably more violent than the murder of two wayfaring white men.

There was nothing else on North Quadyuk Island to indicate that it was the site of a disastrous clash of cultures eighty-four years earlier; no monument, no memorial cairn, and certainly no graves. Indeed, the only place in Bathurst Inlet with any record of the killings is South Quadyuk Island. There, securely pegged into a diabase cliff overlooking the sea, is a simple bronze plaque that contains these words:

IN MEMORY OF

THOMAS GEORGE STREET

OF OTTAWA

AGE 23 YEARS

WHO DIED GOING TO THE

AID OF HIS FRIEND

JULY 12, 1912

Very nice. Too nice, in fact. Street did not die going to Radford's aid, although his contract would have required him to do so. He died running in the opposite direction from the man who, in all but physical deed, plunged the fatal knife into his back.

The Great Winter

On Hrolf, son of Baldur, nearly every sort of darkness fell. Both his parents he lost within the same year. His mother ate unripened shark's meat and died raving about the fires of hell that dwelt inside her. His father he lost to the fretted heights of Glissa. Though no more supple than a stern-post, he went up there in search of missing sheep. He stumbled into a lava-pit and, helpless, died of hunger. His body was not found until after the ravens had picked at it and nothing was left but bare bones. The boy Hrolf collected these bones in his father's canvas satchel and carried them to Arnes for burial. They were placed with his mother's remains in the same pauper's grave.

The boy was brought up by his elder brother Petur. Petur was a somewhat better herd than his father. It was told that he could bring down sheep from their upland pastures in less time than it would take any five men on horseback, and Petur himself only on foot. There were even a few *rimur* composed about this. But the madness of winter never seemed very far from him. Long hours he would sit staring at the hearth; or he would thrust his flensing knife again and again into the wooden rafters. Then one night, with the aurora winding across the frozen sky, Petur went berserk. He howled and screamed, and he said: "We have not enough blood in this house." And he killed his two younger sisters, Anna and Thorey, and gutted them as though they were sheep. For this Petur Baldursson was sentenced and beheaded in Kuvikur in the year 1704. The family holding, Botn, fell to Hrolf. He was fourteen years old at the time.

Now Botn was in the shadow of Kaldbakshorn, which kept the sun away except during summer solstice. This gave Hrolf a rather grey complexion—but not so grey as the holding itself. For Botn was hardly more than a jumble of scree borne down the slope of Kaldbakshorn by avalanches. It was a farm without furrow. Nothing could be tilled that wasn't already seeded by rock. The land was so wretched that the stock had often to chew the lichen off the very stones or nibble at scurvy-grass along the salt-bitten cliffs. Travellers who lodged there would say: Nothing grows in Botn but the length of winter.

In his twentieth year, Hrolf pledged to marry Sigurlaug, daughter of Jon Tyrdilmyri, who lived on Isafjord Deep. Jon offered a fourth part of his farm to Hrolf, but this fourth part was rock-ridden and boggy and if possible more barren still than Botn. At last he offered (and Hrolf accepted) a wintering of hay and ten fjordungs of whale-belly. Jon was willing to pay this much dowry because Sigurlaug had no other prospects. Nor would she—no one else would want a woman so disfigured by smallpox that her face (folk said) was like a bad mountain path. She was also considered ill-mannered and disagreeable. However, it was said that there was no finer hand at the loom in all of Strandasysla than Sigurlaug Jonsdottir.

Hrolf and Sigurlaug were wed in the church at Arnes. The priest blessed them in return for a suckling lamb. He told the couple never to forsake Him who breathed life into their poor husks. He said Providence would be closest to them just when they thought it was the most remote. Then he made this sermon:

"A dairymaid takes the milk and pours it into a churn. She thumps it and shakes it, and batters it with a plunger. Then she separates the higher from the lower; that is, the butter from the whey. The whey she pours into a bowl, while the butter she puts up on the larder shelf . . ."

"God does the like with us. He thumps and shakes us, and batters us with the plunger that is His cross. Then He separates the higher from the lower, the soul from the body. The body He lays in the grave, while the soul He raises up to His heavenly larder . . ."

Afterwards the couple rode to their home in a cold rain.

God did much thumping and shaking Sigurlaug's first year at Botn. The snows fell until the month of June. A strong northern wind came and keened and seldom abated. It whipped the snow already on the ground into strange whorls and shapes, and blew it in all directions at once. A cruel, hard frost clamped the ground, splitting rocks. Grazing was all but ruined. No berries grew in the highlands. And not a single eider egg could be found along the cliffs—perhaps God had collected them all and put them in His heavenly larder.

Hrolf would say: "Bad winters seem all the fashion in this part of the country. We must just tighten our belts and hope for the best."

And Sigurlaug would reply: "Well, tighten them any further and we will be tightening only air."

The next year the fjords were choked with ice for the first time in memory. And this ice made much mischief. It consisted partly of ice-mountains which floated in from the open sea and announced themselves with loud crashes, and partly of floe ice of the depth of one or even two fathoms. No boat could venture out in such a cluttered sea, with the result that fish could neither be sold, salted, or brought to table.

Folk cursed this ice more mightily than ever they cursed each other. It caused such cold that Hrolf's horse dropped down dead on account of it. The cold made the grass so scant that many sheep were seen to eat at each other's wool.

Said Sigurlaug: "Perhaps we should slaughter a few ewes . . ."

"Only farmers in the South eat their own sheep," Hrolf growled.

Now poor though it was, Botn was the only farm between Naustvik and Nes, and thus the only lodging travellers going north to the Hornstrands could obtain of an evening. At one time these travellers would sit by the hearth, and one of them might announce, "I will relate to you some of the great deeds of Olaf Trygvasson, King of Norway by grace of God," and the night would be nearly exhausted before the deeds were done. But now, in darker times, it seemed as though all talk concerned lack of food:

"We have only raven-gruel in Kjorvogur."

"Ourselves? We are only just like the sheep—we crawl about on the cliffs searching for scurvy-grass."

"In Drangsnes, there is naught but the rock itself. And a little seaweed."

"Please, God, deliver food for my poor children . . ."

One evening a young Danish gentleman arrived who was on his way north. He had shallow fish-eyes and wore a fine lambskin pelt over his shoulders. He said he never knew such beggarly people could exist as he had seen in his travels. What could good King Haakon have been thinking of when he took over this godforsaken country? And when Sigurlaug ladled the man a gruel of horse-meat, he pushed it away. He said he would not be surprised if the farmer and his wife, like Greenlanders, scraped the dirt from between their toes and offered it to their guests as a garnish. He said this lightly, but Hrolf took offence. He ordered the man out into the night.

"But I'll die of cold," the man protested.

"Better to die of cold than eat our homely fare," Hrolf said.

Thereupon the man exclaimed: "Well, I'll see justice done, so I will. My uncle is merchant in Blonduos. I'll see that he confiscates this holding and puts you in irons!"

"The Devil take you and your uncle both! This holding belongs to me, and will always belong to me or my kinfolk . . ."

After the man had left, Sigurlaug told him that he should not have behaved in such a way.

"And why not? The fellow insulted me in my own house."

"You know that it is bad luck to order away a guest. And besides, there is some truth in his words. We seem to be little better than beasts . . ."

"The only truth is, you wish you were gentry yourself. Yes, even with that face of yours, you wish you were born a Dane . . ."

"I did not come here to starve, Hrolf Grey. I could have done that well enough at home."

"Hunger is a burden only to those who've never known it."

"Trolls take your words! I call it a burden to eat—and to require others to eat—the wormy flesh of your father's old horse. Tell me if that is not a burden!"

"You would be a Dane, wouldn't you?" Saying this, Hrolf tore yarn and distaff from her hands and flung them to the floor.

And as it happened, such was the luck of the young Dane that he met with only a high wind and no snow, and he made it easily to Nes by the next day.

The following year, the storm-hounds bayed ever louder. Snow fell and kept on falling. In the month of July, a whole mountainside of snow broke away and thundered down on the farms of Sunnudalur and Gufadalur. The battering wind smoothed and rounded the track of the snow so that it lay at the foot of the mountain like a newly born spur of land. Buildings, men, beasts—all vanished. Not a few folk said it might be better to be buried like this than to await the slower workings of Providence.

In Nordurfjordur, a horse was found frozen to death in a standing position—a very bad omen. And now polar bears were walking the ice-floes from Greenland in order to ravage the sheep flocks.

Hrolf slaughtered the last of his sheep so the bears would not get them, and so he and his wife would have something to eat. His heart at this task was so heavy that he could barely bring himself to thrust the knife. For he was of the opinion—as was his father, and his father's father—that killing a sheep was nearly a greater evil than killing a man.

Old people began to speak of doom. They said the *Fimbulvetur*, the Great Winter, the winter to end the world, was at hand. It was foretold in the Vala's prophecy. Three terrible winters would pass, when blizzards drove from every quarter, frosts would be iron-hard and winds sharp, and mountains would tumble headlong from their foundations. Nor would there be any light but snow-light, as the Fenris-Wolf would devour the sun and the Moongarm take the moon. Brother would slay brother in an axe-time, a sword-time. Then would come vast sea-floods and they would billow toward shore a vessel made from the uncut nails of the dead. It would not be a happy thing, the old people said, to lay sight on this vessel.

One evening Sigurlaug caught Hrolf with his gaze fixed on the sea. "I am looking for the black sail of the nail-ship," he told her.

"It would have some difficulty managing these ice-floes," she replied.

He turned to face her. And now for the first time his empty eyes showed that he had joined with the doom-sayers. He said: "I have checked the byre—a fjordung of liver *pylsa* and four sheep's heads. We might be able to find a little scurvy-grass. Or sorrel leaves. After that, nothing . . ."

Sigurlaug put down the birdskins—there was no longer wool— which she was sewing together. Her voice became like a fist. "This is a bad time to give up, Hrolf Grey. We must find food somewhere. We must look under the very rocks, if necessary. Because I do not want to lose the child I am carrying . . ."

She had not mentioned the child before. And though she mentioned it now, her husband's eyes did not change.

That night Hrolf dreamt he saw his two dead sisters lying on the floor, their throats gashed open. And he saw his brother Petur bending over their bodies and drinking of their blood with as great a gust as though the blood was wine. Petur gestured him over to join him and Hrolf rose from his bed, a monstrous thirst upon him, to do so.

Hrolf woke Sigurlaug and related this dream to her. "There is no hope," he said. And later she knelt down and prayed to the Almighty for sustenance—if not for herself, at least for her infant. She could not help but remember that the woman at Melar had starved to death with her baby at suck—by the time they were found, the child was eating the mother's breast. "Please let my child live," Sigurlaug prayed, and she remained kneeling the whole night.

The next day there appeared at the door a certain Augusta. She was a beggar-woman who shuffled from farmhouse to farmhouse, demanding food and shelter. None dared deny her hospitality, for it was told that she possessed a powerful evil eye and that a farmer in Drangsnes who turned her away died mysteriously in the midst of apparent health. It was also told that she had sold favorable winds to mariners—or, on a whim, sent them violent ones.

This Augusta said she was quite hungry. And could the farmer and his wife give her a shakedown for the evening? She had travelled the distance of three parishes with the wind in her teeth.

Hrolf and Sigurlaug stood in the door, gaunt and hollow-cheeked. The woman knitted her brows at them. She was a stout, big-boned creature who did not seem too badly off—at least not as badly off as the two of them. Hrolf told her that they had not provision enough to welcome her.

But Sigurlaug declared: "No, my husband. We must share what little we have with her. It is only good manners to offer hospitality to a guest, especially a guest who has travelled the distance of three parishes since break of day. And besides, this woman I've heard brings good fortune to whoever shares his table with her."

And so they took in the beggar-woman.

Augusta, daughter of Axlar, was never seen or heard of again. Folk wondered why she no longer darkened their evenings with her evil looks and wild mutterings. At last word got around that she had frozen to death in a cave in the fjalls.

Another traveller who came for lodging was a man named Gunnar. He informed the couple that he was born and raised at Seljanes, but he had married into a well-to-do farm in the South. And now he was headed home to attend the funeral of his old father, who died (Gunnar said) never knowing the touch of a silver crown in his hand. As it happened, Gunnar never attended his old father's funeral. No one knew what became of him. It was thought that perhaps he lost his footing on the mountain path to Seljanes and fell to his death in the sea.

Likewise disappeared the tax-collector Simon Briem. There were many who would have been glad to do away with him, as tax collectors were not very popular in the district. In the time of Bishop Jon, some farmers from Inn-Strandir had tied up the tax collector and traded him to pressers from an English ship for a barrel of grog. And closer to the present, a Dane named Gustafson was force-fed a mare's afterbirth until he agreed to say that the outlaw Bjarni had robbed him of all his tax-money.

The High Sheriff of Kuvikur decided to make an inquiry into Simon Briem's whereabouts. Despite the snows, the Sheriff's man went to nearly all the farms in Strandasysla. He even came to Botn, and there Hrolf received him cordially. The farmer remarked that he'd laid aside his wool, but he had not yet met a tax collector this year. The winter had been terrible and the fjalls so treacherous, there was no telling what became of the fellow. Did the Sheriff's man hear about a certain Gunnar, who lost his way in a squall of snow and wandered right into the sea? Listen to the wind howl even now. Like a ravening wolf, it is . . .

And Sigurlaug said to the visitor: "The afternoon is nearly dark, and you must be weary from your travels. We would be honored were you to bide the night with us."

The man tipped his hat and replied: "It would be my honor to bide here, Sigurlaug Jonsdottir. For I have not been well received in this district. The folk do not seem to care for this inquiry. I would not be surprised to learn that they had banded together and thrown the tax collector in the sea."

Said Hrolf: "Nor would I be surprised to learn that, either."

Later Sigurlaug fed the Sheriff's man a meal which he ate with great gusto. He was famished, he said, and none of the paupers whose houses he had visited that day had offered him so much as a single bit of dried fish. Yes, indeed, famished. But what was this meat he was so busily stuffing into his mouth?

"It is sausage, of course," Sigurlaug said.

"Of course," the man replied, and went on to admit—perhaps out of gratitude—that it was the best sausage he had ever put in his mouth.

"Well," she said, "We are but poor people and we do the best we can with what God has given us."

At break of day, the Sheriff's man thanked Hrolf for his many kindnesses. To Sigurlaug he added: "And may the child you are carrying be sturdy and strong of heart, and may he fear only God."

"Such is my own wish," she replied.

The man rode north to continue his inquiry. And word quickly spread that Hrolf Baldursson and his wife did not need to scrape for weeds along the cliffs, and that they ate well and often. When Pall Jonsson from Naustvik asked Hrolf about this, Hrolf answered him: "If you had slaughtered your sheep, Neighbor Pall, instead of letting them die or be eaten by bears, you too might have meat in your belly." And he gave the man some liver sausage to bring home for his children.

Time passed. And come spring, Sigurlaug gave birth to a son. She named the boy Gudmundur, God's Gift. The boy was born the night of the new moon, which hung like a sickle in the cold night sky. The next day the sun shone brightly, as though Providence was acknowledging the name she had bestowed on her son—acknowledging him with shafts of Heavenly Light.

And the boy was taken to Arnes to be baptised. The priest wrapped him in his cloak and sprinkled him with water. "I anoint thee Gudmundur, son of Hrolf, son of Baldur, son of Einar . . ." he said as he kissed the infant on the forehead. Then he remarked on how robust the boy looked, as most babies born nowadays were little more than bony skeletons, if they survived birth at all. Or perhaps they would be splotched in some untoward way. These are not healthy times, the priest said. Those who are not struck down by disease succumb of famine, and those who miss out on either of these seem to vanish without trace in the night.

Said Sigurlaug: "He is healthy because God's grace is upon him."

Hrolf paid for the baptism with some smoked meat, at the sight of which the priest drew in his breath. "You are a very fortunate fellow, as just today I talked to a man who had to cook his skin clothes and eat them without sauce."

"Prudent is the man who slaughters his sheep in season," Hrolf replied.

"And to look at you," the priest said, "one would think you were a different man. We shall no longer be obliged to speak of you as Hrolf Grey . . ."

With light steps did the farmer and his wife journey home from Arnes. They laughed and joked together. Hrolf admitted that he hadn't expected to witness the day he would have a son baptised.

"Yes," said his wife, "You were even ready to throw in your lot with the nail-ship . . ."

Some months later the mysterious disappearances started up again. This time they were not travellers from outside (who had become few, owing to bad weather and worse reputation)—not travellers at all, but folk within the district itself.

There was a widow-woman named Gudny who lived alone in Stor-Avik. Whatever befell her, befell her cleanly. The house was in perfect order, as though she had only just gone out to the well for some water. But the same could not be said of Naustvik, which was a scene of great carnage. If the hearth could talk, it would have a most awful tale to tell. All was blood-soaked—the beds, the ground, even Pall Jonsson's silver snuff-horn. And of the family, Pall, his wife, their four children, not a trace. Certain it was that they had not been drawn from their house without a struggle. But a struggle with what?

Could a polar bear have found its way to their height of land? folk wondered. No, for if it was a polar bear ravaged Naustvik, at least someone would have been able to escape and tell of it.

Many people cited Naustvik as further evidence of the Great Winter. Such was the blood-age prophesied by the Vala, when men would redden their axes on each other's throats as once they had used those same axes to hack timber for their dwellings. The hellhound Garm seemed at last to have broken loose—him that had been chained in the bottomless cave of Gnipa. Would not the stars now turn in their steadings in the sky? Would not all bridges crumble? Rains come down the color of blood? When would grinning corpses tramp the fjalls? And having fought in life, conquer each other in death. Soon the whole world would be torn asunder, and the high sky as well, and then darkness, forever darkness.

The Governor in Bessastadir, however, no more believed in prophecies than he believed in trolls. It was his view that some madman was loose in the Westfjords and was responsible for the gore at Naustvik and perhaps a few of the disappearances. He told the Sheriff of Kuvikur to find this madman and find him soon, else the Danish king would have to be informed that everyone in Iceland had vanished.

And so the Sheriff himself rode out from farm to farm, from parsonage to parsonage, as his man before him. And he met with the same luck as his man before him. No one could offer him any clue as to the cause of the strange happenings in Strandasysla. The priests complained that each missing parishioner was likewise a missing tithe. And the farmers—they were so affrighted that they could hardly be persuaded to open their doors and speak. Some were of the opinion that a shape-shifter was causing all the trouble, and that the Sheriff himself might even be that shape-shifter disguised as the Sheriff.

At last he reached Botn. Hrolf greeted him and invited him to come in out of the cold. Sigurlaug was sewing skins together with sinew-thread. She put down these skins and said: "Welcome to Botn. We are at your service."

131

By the hearth, the boy Gudmundur was playing with rib bones. His child's face was knitted with great concentration and he was talking to himself. Though little more than two years old, he was as big as a boy of four or five. He was red-haired and very well-made. And when he saw the Sheriff, he halted his play and stood up and mouthed this one word: "Meat."

"He has not eaten since morning," Sigurlaug explained.

And the Sheriff replied: "Pall Jonsson's boy Stephan does not seem to have that worry . . ."

"Now, I think," began Hrolf, "the very Turks who pillaged the Westmann Islands are the cause of these troubles. They are once again hauling off Icelanders . . ."

"Well," sighed the Sheriff, "that is one possible explanation."

"Yes, and those same Turks have gone back to the Barbary while you are still looking for them here."

By and by the Sheriff was thanking the farmer and his wife for their help. And now, he said, he was riding to Nes where he would spend the night. They wished him Godspeed. And as he made ready to go, he noticed a white bandage sticking through Hrolf's thread-bare jerkin. "What have you done to your arm?" he asked.

"Oh, it is nothing. I was hewing some wood and the axe slipped. It will heal soon, no doubt."

"That seems an odd place for a right-handed man to wound himself—on the left shoulder." The Sheriff made a motion as though to strike his own shoulder. "You must have wanted to do harm to yourself . . ." he said.

"It was wood I was cutting," Hrolf repeated strongly.

Then Sigurlaug broke in: "Listen to our Gudmundur! He is a bard born. Listen to him! He will be another Egil Skallagrimsson . . ."

The boy was hitting the rib-bones together and chanting these words:

"Birds of prey   fly thick
to the body stack for eyes to pick

and flesh to hack   The raven's beak
is wondrous red   and wolves go seek
their daily bread . . ."

Said Sigurlaug: "I have been teaching him some of the old rhymes. He only sings them and does not follow the sense yet, for he has but two winters on him. But the sense will come, God willing."

"God willing," the Sheriff said.

As he rode away, he considered these people. He thought there was something very strange about them. Perhaps it was that they seemed so healthy, all three.

The Sheriff was still thinking about this when he arrived at Nes. And at this farm, he was greeted by a scene that took his stomach away, a scene very much like that at Naustvik. All was in turmoil—chairs overturned, household goods scattered everywhere, clothes ripped nearly to rags. There had been fearsome blows struck. Blood lay on the earthen floor like pools of water after a heavy rainfall. And of the family, no sign or trace. The Sheriff wandered back and forth, rubbing at his lower lip with the back of his hand. Then slowly he sank to his knees and gave forth a long, baleful groan. The farmer had been a kinsman of his, Bjorn Haraldsson, his brother's stepson, and the farmer's wife was Ingibjorg, than whom there was no more gentle a soul in the western fjords. "I will see justice done," the Sheriff whispered.

The butchery at Nes was followed by a similar happening at the remote farm of Skord. And now the mood in Strandasysla grew so sombre, neighbor would not regard neighbor, fathers and sons cast suspicious eyes on each other, and folk sat in their houses like the living dead, awaiting the World's End. Those who dwelt near the sea kept a ready gaze on it, expecting at any moment the black sail of the nail-ship. To very few could the priests offer any solace. Most turned from the Church as from an adder-snake, and bowed toward the dark gods of the past, for (they said) the Wolf had long since devoured Christ on His cross.

But summer came, and no nail-ship came.

The Sheriff met Hrolf Baldursson in Kuvikur. Hrolf told him that he had come to do barter. He had plentiful meats, he said, and wished to sell them to the Danish merchant Sophus Hansen. For folk in Kuvikur had money and they would pay dear for a good flank of mutton. He also had a few hearts and would not the Sheriff himself care to buy one?

"Those are rather large for sheep hearts, aren't they?"

"Oh, I didn't say they were sheep hearts. They are pig hearts, and very tasty. But be sure you cook them for a long while."

Later in the day he saw Hrolf again, this time in the company of a large black dog. The farmer smiled and said: "I have done well today, my friend. I have touched coin for the first time in ten years. And see, I even bought this dog. His name is Hrafn, Raven. He will be a fit companion for our Gudmundur."

Afterwards the Sheriff thought: I have seen his silver-buttoned tunic before, and it was on someone else. By end of day, he was still wondering, Now where, where have I seen it? He cooked the heart and ate it, although it was tough and very bitter. And then he went to sleep and dreamt of the gore that had been at Nes. He saw blood rise up like a tidal wave and he saw himself struggling to stay afloat in it. And he saw Bjorn Haraldsson of Nes lying dead in his silver-buttoned tunic . . . The Sheriff woke up with his mind keen as a knife edge. Hrolf had also been wearing Bjorn's doublet! Could there be any doubt now who was behind the evil doings in Strandasysla? The Sheriff declared: "You will not live to touch coin again, Hrolf Baldursson! I will see your own pig's heart torn from out of your body. And I will see your soul rolling down to Hell like sheep-droppings on a slope of hard snow . . ."

And he collected his man and five others, and that same night they headed north to the fjalls. They rode in silence, with a mizzling rain in their faces, and they reached Botn by late morning. From the scent, they could tell that there was meat smoking in the byre. Soon they heard a voice of cheer. It was Gudmundur and he was frolicking with the dog Hrafn. The dog was dragging along a woman's head by its flax-colored hair. Upon seeing the men, the boy grasped the head and offered it to them.

"It is Ingibjorg of Nes," one of the men softly said.

"Eat . . ." said the boy. And the look on his face was the hopefulness of childhood.

On the morning of June 17, 1718, in bright sunshine and a high wind, Hrolf Baldursson and Sigurlaug Jonsdottir were beheaded in Kuvikur by edict of the Great Assembly. Then their bodies were sundered and their bodily parts buried under six separate cairns, so their spirits would not walk after death.

Before he was executed, Hrolf said: "I am a man who was brought up in the dark of Kaldbakshorn. I know no other place. My father and mother died before I could learn from them. My brother Petur, he was brought here himself not many years ago. He was my teacher. May the Lord Redeemer have mercy on my soul!"

And Sigurlaug said: "May God judge us not for what we've done, but for what we were. We have been good Christians. Our only sin was want. We were hungry people. After death our innocence will be shown . . ."

There was shouting and hooting from the crowd.

Sigurlaug continued: "I have but one request: That some Christian soul among you will take and raise my son so that he will never know this hunger."

Just as she had finished these words, an old man named Svein— a man of nearly a hundred winters—uttered a loud oath and pointed out to sea. A murmur ran through the crowd. For there seemed to be a black sail idling in the fjord. "It is the nailship!" this Svein exclaimed.

"Oh no," someone answered, "It is only the shadow from a cloud. It happens often on days like this."

"Clouds don't have triangular sails . . ."

Then the sky went dark and the earth grey as the rock that had riven it. A sharp wind whipped through the air. The horses frisked. A lone boulder clattered down the mountain Vigaberg, down, down, down to the sea. Some rain began to fall. Was not this rain the color of human blood? old Svein asked.

"The Wolf has taken the sun," a woman named Birna shrieked, beating at her chest.

"We are doomed!"

"See how the Earth cries out in pain!"

"The Great Winter! the Great Winter!!"

"Christ is not risen!"

Then spoke the Danish gentleman whom Hrolf had thrown out into the night. He had come to Kuvikur to witness the execution. Having bought a new lambskin pelt for the occasion, he would not be cheated: "Look up there, you people. Don't you see that it is only a dark cloud passing over? The sun will be back again soon enough . . ."

And then the sun did come back and it shone down on them like so many warm feathers stripped from their shafts. The light lay bright on the water, turning and gleaming and whetting itself. The black sail was nowhere to be seen.

"So much for doom," the Sheriff said. "Now we can enjoy a bit of justice." Whereupon the headsman raised his weapon on Sigurlaug's neck.

Off by himself, mindful of only his own small games, sat the boy Gudmundur. He was chanting the rhymes his mother had taught him:

> "Let peace be torn   by rushing spears
> let bows be drawn   men raise their ears
> The yew-bow shrills   the edges bite
> The hero kills   to defend his right . . ."

Thus ends the story of Hrolf, son of Baldur, upon whom much darkness fell, and his wife Sigurlaug, the daughter of a poor farmer.

Murder Will Out

There are islands that are nice, and then there are islands that are too nice.

At first Prince Edward Island struck me as being in the latter category—the locals were courteous to a fault, the landscape was picture-book pastoral, and the villages looked like they'd been modeled on Brigadoon. I concluded that the only mischief ever perpetrated on the island had been caused by a fictional character, Anne of Green Gables.

But then I began to notice cracks in the island's placid exterior. One of these cracks turned out to be, in a manner of speaking, me. Near Mininimegash, I found myself talking with an elderly man about the harvesting of Irish moss in his area. "Your name's Millman, eh?" the man said. I nodded. He looked at me, I thought, rather oddly.

More or less the same scenario occured several times during the next few days. In Kensington, I introduced myself to a man with whom I wanted to discuss traditional farming techniques. He immediately stepped back from me as if I were carrying the plague. Another man performed a similar maneuver when I offered him my card.

And then there was the old woman in North Rustico who, upon hearing my name, exclaimed: "My God! The Millmans are back!"

I mentioned these reactions to a folklorist named Wendell Boyle. "What's going on?" I asked him. "Your fellow islanders are treating me like my name was mud."

"You don't know, then?" Wendell said.

"I don't know what?"

"Your name *is* mud. It's the same name as one of the most famous murderers in Prince Edward Island's history, Willie Millman. He lived over a hundred years ago, but in a place like this, that's just like yesterday."

Whereupon he began singing one of the ballads composed about my murderous namesake:

"*Come pull down your curtains, look silently on,*
While I sing you the Millman and Tuplin song . . ."

Later, at the Institute for Island Studies, I researched my namesake's not very nice story. Apparently, Willie Millman was concerned that his seventeen-year-old girlfriend Mary Tuplin might tell people that he'd made her pregnant, so he shot her twice in the head with a handgun, put an eight pound anchor stone around her waist, and dumped her body in the Southwest River. Now her lips were sealed. So, too, was his own fate. On February 6, 1888, the twenty-year-old farmer's son was convicted of murder and sentenced to be hung.

I confess I felt a mounting sense of unease when I read about Willie's blindfolded march to the scaffold, and my hands went reflexively to my own neck when I read about the actual hanging. For there was a part of me that identified with the man. After all, the two of us shared the same name. We may have even shared the same blood—my family's history was so obscure that I couldn't discount the possibility that Willie and I might be distant cousins.

My exchanges with islanders now became somewhat self-conscious.

I would omit my surname when introducing myself or utter it so softly that it would be inaudible. To one man, I apologized for Willie's vile deed. It turned out that he knew nothing of the deed in question, and he now gazed at me as if I might be protesting a bit too much: could I perhaps have done away with the landlady at my last Bed and Breakfast?

At one point I went to the murder site, a lovely spot at the junction of two mill streams and surrounded by woods and gently rolling pastures. There I tried to recreate in my mind a certain fateful summer evening in the year 1887 . . .

A pair of lovers are walking together, hand in hand. All of a sudden the woman raises her voice, and the man raises a revolver—the temperamental Millman gene declaring itself. Scarcely aware of his actions, he puts two quick bullets in her head. "Good God, Mary!" he cries. "What have I done?" Overcome with grief, he puts the gun to his own head but does not have the courage to pull the trigger.

But however I replayed the scene, I couldn't get Willie off the hook. Nor could I get myself off it, either.

One day toward the end of my trip I found myself in Margate and remembering Mary was buried in the local cemetery, I paid a visit to her grave. There were no dates on the stone, no mention of a life suddenly cut short, no decoration of any kind. All it said was "Mary Pickering Tuplin." But those three words seemed to me far more poignant than any homily or expression of bereavement.

I now placed a bunch of chanterelle mushrooms I'd gathered earlier in the day on the grave. An unconventional offering, perhaps. But I hadn't brought any flowers, and I wanted to leave Mary something that would show I was sorry for my namesake's bad behavior. I also wanted to assuage some of the guilt I felt at being his unwitting accomplice.

The next afternoon, as I left the island, I reflected on my trip and realized that I'd learned a valuable lesson: that no matter how prosaic (or worse, how nice) a place might seem at first glance, there's always a Millman lurking somewhere in its woodpile.

Wanderer

Hassoldt Davis, whose books I press on friends at the slightest provocation, chose the road least traveled from the beginning. The *very* beginning—at birth, he refused to breathe even when the doctor in attendance held him by the heels and spanked him repeatedly. At last a nurse anointed him with alcohol, and he bawled with life.

Davis grew up in the fashionable Boston suburb of Wellesley Hills. His father, a greeting card magnate, gave his family every amenity, thus making Bill (he used Hassoldt, his mother's maiden name, as a sort of nom de plume) hate amenities. The boy chose Tarzan of the Apes, who also seemed to hate amenities, as his role model. Indeed, he became so obsessed with Edgar Rice Burroughs' arboreal hero that he even tried to look like him; he took a Charles Atlas physical-culture course and did in fact win a magazine prize for being "The Best Developed Boy in America." But this wasn't enough. At thirteen, he packed a slingshot, a few maps, and a compass, then set off for Africa. He got no closer to the Dark Continent than Tremont Street in downtown Boston. Even so, he established a paradigm for his subsequent adventures: shoot for the proverbial moon, for the risky, the distant, and the exotic, rather than the cozy world next door.

Romantic interests inevitably replaced his desire to swing from tree to tree. In 1926, at the age of nineteen, he traveled to Paris and promptly took up with a model named Dodo. His father wouldn't have approved of Dodo. So much the better. Meanwhile, he was taking artistic photographs of tramps and prostitutes. The bohemian idyll ended when he joined a public protest against the execution of Sacco and Vanzetti and was expelled from France as an undesirable alien. Back home he entered Harvard, boxed, and wrote poetry. Then came the incident that changed his life: he took some nude photographs of his seventeen-year-old sister Aline.

Actually, the pictures in question are pretty tame even by the standards of their time. I can say this because Aline, who is now over ninety, showed them to me. Done with a lens screen and opal printing paper, the pictures show her wearing a scarf around her waist and balancing a hoop, her back demurely to the viewer. But her father, who was very possessive of her, found them totally indecent and kicked Bill out of the house. So began his career as a grand itinerant.

He went to San Francisco, where he worked alternately as a journalist and a maker of death masks. He also boxed professionally under the name Victor Vitallis. But the urge to travel was much stronger than the urge to earn a living, so he shipped aboard a Pacific-bound steamer. In Tahiti, he met Nordhoff and Hall (authors of *Mutiny on the Bounty*), the great documentary film-maker Robert Flaherty, Paul Gauguin's son, and any number of obliging native women. Inspired by Flaherty's tales of even more exotic islands, he went on to Fiji, the Celebes, and Bali; he traveled deck class in order to experience the rough edges of shipboard life. Footloose and seemingly fancy-free, he wrote to Aline: "The future will take care of its bastard self."

From these early travels came the first Hassoldt Davis book, *Islands Under the Wind*. Brimming with purple, no, ultra-violet prose, *Islands Under the Wind* is not a particularly good book. Apart from a splendid description of a shark fight in the Celebes, it is chiefly remarkable for its sexual frankness; its author both kisses and tells, a combination somewhat unusual in a travel book and even more unusual for a travel book published as long ago as 1932.

There's often a fine line between travel and exploration, and Davis crossed that line in the late 1930s when he signed on as writer, still photographer, and self-styled whipping boy with the Denis-Roosevelt Asiatic Expedition. Led by filmmaker Armand Denis, the expedition spent eight arduous months in the most isolated parts of Burma, northern India, and Nepal. Davis wrote up this experience in *The Land of the Eye*, a book vastly superior to his first one. Here, for the first time, he exercises his passion for the bizarre and the grotesque; a passion that became one of his trademarks. He describes what it's like to have hundreds of leeches clinging to your body; reports on an aphrodisiac composed of owl dung, powdered snakeskin, and bone dust; and gives a detailed account of the ritual decapitation of a water buffalo in Nepal, after which "My moccasins squished with blood."

Writing does not seem to have been his favorite pursuit. "You sit by yourself all day long," he says in his 1957 autobiography *World Without a Roof*, "and, if you get tight enough, half through the night, living with the ghosts of memory or the imagined ones of fiction, hoping the telephone will ring, that your most calamitous friend will drop in on you, forgetting your work to call up women you really don't give a damn about . . . " Like Ernest Hemingway, who became his friend (they would ring each other up and complain about women), he considered himself a man of action at least as much as a writer. And to a large extent he was a man of action, perhaps more so than Hemingway.

Hemingway went to great lengths to prove he was a war hero, but Davis actually was a war hero, albeit in a French rather than

American uniform. In 1941, he joined the Free French forces of General Leclerc in French Equatorial Africa and was soon serving as a combat captain with a crack Spahi (Moroccan cavalry) regiment. He saw action all over Africa and, eventually, in Europe. His war-time memoir, *Half Past When*, describes his many brushes with "Papa Death," a phenomenon he seems to have been more than half in love with. Still, *Half Past When* is an uncommonly modest book. If you blink while reading it, you might miss the fact that its author won both the Legion of Honor and the Croix de guerre (twice) for conduct under fire. Maybe its author won something else, too—the knowledge that he was no longer a villain in the eyes of the country which had once expelled him.

After the War, in New York, the much-decorated soldier met a professional photographer named Ruth Staudinger. Ruth was a blonde, and Davis had once stated in print that he didn't care for blonde women because they smelled like boiled milk. Ruth was different, however. She smelled like caramel and hot rum, or so he remarks in *World Without a Roof*. Likewise she was adventurous, a first-rate cameraperson, and very attractive. She became the second Mrs. Davis (the first was a temperamental Russian woman named Hinny, about whom he wrote: "We didn't want each other, but loneliness was the colder choice.").

"Where were you to turn, Explorer, in a world so shrunken by war—mapped, exposed, foul . . . ?" Davis now inquired of both himself and Ruth, newly adopted as an explorer. To the Francophile and aficionado of the world's most unpleasant places, the answer came immediately: French Guiana. Ruth, to her credit, was not put off by the idea of a honeymoon in what her husband cheerfully referred to as "rotten country."

France has always been a bit peculiar about what she chooses to colonize: what other nation would have tried to colonize the Sahara? Pestilential, bug-ridden, and covered with dense jungle, French Guiana is—or was—hardly less daunting in its own way than the Sahara. Its infamous penal settlements were at least situated on a group of offshore islands. Known as the Iles du Salut (Islands of Health), these islands got their name not because they were healthy, but because the colony's interior was so unhealthy.

This interior was what Davis wanted to explore. He proposed to paddle up the five-hundred mile Maroni River and then trek into the remote Tumuc-Humac Mountains, the presumed location of Sir Walter Raleigh's lost city of gold, El Dorado. This plan had certain risks. For one thing, the Maroni boasts eighty or so rapids, most of them white-water with a vengeance. For another, the local Indians had a reputation for being not very good hosts—the Oyaricoulets, for example, had killed all but one member of a recent expedition to the Maroni's headwaters (the lone survivor had been asleep in a tree). But travel, for Davis, wasn't satisfying unless it contained an element of risk.

The couple arrived in French Guiana without their provisions, which had been held up by a dock strike in Martinique. Having little else to do, they began talking to the colony's convicts, many of whom were on restricted parole. One convict cut Davis' hair without, he was happy to note, cutting his throat. Another would sing hymns of praise to his blanket, the only thing in the world that was truly his. Yet another was a disgruntled author who'd killed his publisher.

In *The Jungle and the Damned*, the book he wrote about the trip, Davis seems to devote an inordinate amount of space to these convicts—the "damned" of his title. A reader impatient for vicarious thrills and death-defying adventures might be inclined to say, "Get on with it, give me some action, enough about these bloody prisoners . . . " But Davis was a writer always willing to bend a narrative out of shape to accommodate a good story, and the convicts' stories are often very good indeed (I especially like the one where the disgruntled author describes how he did away with his publisher). Yet I suspect there might be another, more personal reason why he gives so much ink to the convicts: he identified with them. Kicked out of his home, he was a societal reject, a sort of convict, too. And in telling one story after another about unrepentant felons, he may have been telling his own story in disguise.

At last their provisions came, and off the Davises went into the colony's interior. Their paddlers were Boni, descendants of African slaves who'd escaped to the bush years earlier. Later they hired a group of brightly painted Roucouyenne Indians to serve as guides. For Ruth, who was filming the expedition, the daily presence of these two relatively traditional ethnic groups was a photographic boon. But there were not many other boons on a trip that seemed to go from bad to worse with each successive paddle stroke. The Boni constantly threatened mutiny, the expedition's cook was demented, and the guides were untrustworthy . . . and this was just the small stuff. "I sat snarling at the fire," writes Davis of one particularly bad day, "wishing I had brought along just one person whom I could sock in the teeth from time to time . . . "

But a book is not the same as the experience it recounts, and *The Jungle and the Damned* offers triumphant proof that the world, far from being shrunken, is a quite bountiful place. It takes a trip from hell, so-called, and turns it into something rich, strange, and often very funny. In reading about such trips, you invariably find yourself saying, "I'm glad I stayed at home, but I'm even more glad the author didn't."

After the French Guiana trip, they returned to New York. Ruth edited her film, which Warner Brothers later picked up and released, much to her disgust, as *Jungle Terror*. As for Davis himself, he wrote, lectured, helped with the film, and grew increasingly bored. He could tolerate neither domesticity or staying put, so one day he spun the globe and a spark from his cigarette dropped on West Africa, specifically on the Ivory Coast—another splendidly unhealthy place.

Less than a year after they got back from French Guiana, he and Ruth landed at Abidjan, capital of the Ivory Coast, and then headed into the bush in search of a reputed school for witch doctors. Along the way, they spent time with the Guerre tribe, whom Davis refers to as "competent cannibals." But, he adds, "we were safe because they didn't like white flesh." Whenever they did happen to be in danger, Davis would set off firecrackers; for firecrackers, he believed, were a lot more effective than firearms in frightening away hostile natives. (The nineteenth-century American paleontologist Edward Cope had an even more effective method—as a Quaker, he refused to carry a gun, so he scared off hostile natives simply by removing his false teeth.)

The witch doctors themselves were not fey little Harry Potters transported to the African bush. They seemed to have real magical powers, and Davis experienced these powers personally after he fired one of his guides. The very next day he found himself paralyzed along his right side from the top of his head to the sole of his foot. Aureomycin didn't help him, nor did vodka. The paralysis lasted for a whole week, until his ex-employee, who'd paid a witch doctor to hex him, ran out of money. Or so he says in his rip-roaring book about the trip, *Sorcerer's Village*. But Davis, like almost every writer I know, was not beneath gilding a good story to make it a better one.

And then they were home again. But since home, for Davis, was anywhere but home, his Fifth Avenue apartment was not so much a residence as it was a repository for his travels. He filled it with African tribal masks, Tibetan trumpets, prayer wheels, poison arrows, tom-toms, leopard skins, and hundreds of other artifacts. Pets included a large rattlesnake and a tortoise named Consuela whose shell he regularly shined with shoe polish. As a gesture toward permanence, he kept a French perpetual soup on the stove; every week or so, he would clarify the soup with egg, throw in vegetable waters and marrow bones, sometimes even lobster shells, and then set the pot to simmer again. The soup sat on his stove for years, scrupulously tended by friends when he was away.

As Davis grew older, his whims grew more peculiar. For instance, he developed an urge to taste human flesh. So when a doctor friend brought him a hand snatched from an unclaimed corpse, he eagerly cooked and ate it, pronouncing it excellent: could the doctor bring him its mate?

I can't help but think that there's a quality of *épater* about such behavior. But since the person he wanted to outrage, doubtless his father, was dead, Ruth got the brunt of it. In the early years of their marriage, she put up with her husband's oddities, but now she found herself resenting them, particularly when he mixed them with alcohol, of which he was a passionate devotee. Every morning he would drink orange juice crowded with vodka (he claimed he couldn't have food on an empty stomach). At last she divorced him. She returned to Africa and made a name for herself by running a gallery in Nairobi that showed only the work of untrained artists.

Davis once described Ruth as "an excellent jungle wife." I'm not certain he wanted a wife whose talents extended beyond the jungle. Still, he felt her loss keenly. Jokingly, he talked about the need for an organization called S.A. (Satyrs Anonymous) that would "cure us chronic addicts of love." His other addiction, liquor, was no joke; he was now drinking more or less all the time. His work floundered. He took a trip around the world on a tramp steamer, but wrote almost nothing about it. Perhaps the trip was unadventurous by his standards; or perhaps he was no longer at home even when he was away from home, and no longer at home with himself.

There's a certain symmetry about Hassoldt Davis' life. Alcohol helped him enter the world, and alcohol dispatched him to his grave. On September 15, 1959, he died of its effects, leaving his last work, a biography of Pan, unfinished. One might regret the fact that he was only fifty-two at the time, but I have a feeling Davis himself would have preferred it that way. For it's unlikely he would have tolerated the infirmities of age or indeed anything else that would have kept him from lighting out for the farflung Territory.

Mountains of Sulphur

I t was a typical May morning in Iceland's Eastfjords, with snow pellet showers, sleet, glowering skies, and gusty winds. The snow pellets sounded like buckshot hitting my anorak; the wind-whipped blobs of sleet attacked me horizontally; and the wind itself was rapidly turning my flesh to pumice, a substance not uncommon in these igneous parts.

It could be worse, I thought. There could be a volcanic eruption or an earthquake, both of which are common in these parts, too. And so, having more or less consoled myself, I continued to trek along a rugged mountain road north of Bakkagerdi. After a few hours, I began to climb a slippery, nearly vertical footpath. Finally I came to a small white bungalow located at the bottom of a scree slope. Here lived the man I was looking for—an eighty-nine-year-old retired surveyor named Sigurdur Bjornsson.

Sigurdur greeted me at the door. He was a great hogshead of a man with a bellying laugh that seemed to shake his entire body.

149

He looked perhaps thirty years younger than he actually was. He also looked like he'd be strong enough to wrestle me into submission if he had a mind to do so.

Icelanders consider it extremely rude for a visitor to state the purpose of his visit until at least an hour after his arrival, so I asked Sigurdur about avalanches. There was rock-strewn evidence of them all around his house.

"Jájá," he said, "we get plenty of avalanches here. You see that avalanche fence up there? It does no good at all."

Then I asked him about *huldufolk* (hidden people). These are pesky, gnomelike beings, the Icelandic version of leprechauns, who reputedly inhabit lava fields.

"We have plenty of *huldufolk* around here, too," Sigurdur informed me. "My own grandson saw a pair of them, a male and a female, only a few days ago."

At last I got to the point of my visit: my host's father, Bjorn Thorgeirsson, had been one of Sir Richard Burton's guides on the occasion of the Arabian Nights adventurer's 1872 visit to Iceland.

Sigurdur smiled when I mentioned Burton's name. "Jájá," he said, "I know a few things about Mr. Burton. He spoke Latin with an English accent. My father spoke it with an Icelandic accent. They did not communicate very well . . . "

As he was talking, I noticed a faded photograph of Burton on the wall. The face, or what I could make of it, had a faroff, visionary glow, as if fondly recalling some beloved heap of Arabian sand. I'd been intrigued by Burton for years, ever since I visited London's Mortlake Cemetery and happened upon his tomb, a gimcrack Bedouin tent made from marble and boasting a crucified Christ on its lintel. And now here was a man who possessed something akin to a filial bond with him.

"My father was a young theology student at the time," said Sigurdur, "but since he had already guided other Englishmen, he was asked to be one of the guides for Mr. Burton. My father figured this Mr. Burton would be just another Englishman. You see, we got rather a lot of them in those days."

"Why did you get so many Englishmen?" I inquired, my eyes still on the photograph.

"They came because of the British Museum. It was offering a big reward to anybody who could bring back a *geirfugla* (great auk). Of course, no one knew that the last pair of geirfuglar had been killed on Eldey Island in 1844."

Burton himself wasn't looking for anything so romantic as an extinct bird. Rather, he was looking for sulphur, an almost universal mineral on this volcanic island. At the time sulphur was industrial gold, the primary ingredient in pesticides, soap, bleach, and gunpowder. Burton's mission was to report on the prospects for its commercial exploitation by the English.

"Mr. Burton liked to eat cow meat," Sigurdur continued, "so he made his guides bring cows along on the trip. Cows were not intended for our hard lava paths, and they slowed him down. Mr. Burton beat them, my father said, and then they slowed him down even more."

"What else might he have eaten?" I said.

"Sheeps' heads. Rams' testicles. Whale steaks. All good Icelandic foods. But he preferred to eat cows."

Burton made a complete, albeit arduous circuit of the island in three months. It was not a very congenial trip. His horses kept breaking down, the weather was consistently bad, and Iceland's "humbug" geyser would not erupt for him. To make matters worse, the sulphur turned out to be altogether inferior in quality to European sulphur. Burton was not amused.

But then if you were the august personage who'd entered Mecca in *jubbah* disguise, penetrated to the source of the Nile and looked on while Mormon leader Brigham Young gorged himself on raw eggs in an effort to cure his impotence, you probably wouldn't be amused, either.

"He wrote a book about the trip which was so nasty that my father would not allow it in the house," Sigurdur said.

I nodded. The book in question, *Ultima Thule*, is in fact quite nasty. In its pages, Burton exacts a blistering revenge on Iceland for forcing him to suffer so many indignities. He calls the celebrated volcano Hekla "a commonplace heap" and Thingvellir, site of the world's first democratic parliament, "a mere ditch." He condemns the midnight sun because it would play havoc with a devout Moslem's hours of prayer. As for his guides, he refers to them as "couthless Calibans who are worse even than the Irish help in the United States . . ."

I mentioned the remark about "couthless Calibans" to my host, who did not seem pleased by it.

"Mr. Burton is describing himself with those words," he said. "He treated his guides like he treated his cows. Maybe he thought they were from the lower classes. But Iceland is not like England. We do not have a class system. Here, if you beat a guide or even a gelder of pigs, it's no different from beating a bank president."

"Well, he was known as Ruffian Dick," I remarked.

"My father thought he was one of the crudest people he'd ever met."

"Did your father tell you anything else about Burton?" I was hoping for some kind of revelation: an amorous liason, for instance, or perhaps a secret admiration for Hekla.

"Yes. He told me that Mr. Burton spoke very bad Latin. A five-year-old Icelandic child speaks better Latin, he said."

Now my eyes returned to the picture on the wall. Somewhere I'd read that Burton subscribed to the Moslem belief that a camera deprives a person of his soul. For every soul swept into the lens, the photographer must beget a child or he'll get into big trouble with Allah later on.

I mentioned this to Sigurdur.

"Oh, that's not Mr. Burton," he told me, fetching snuff first into one nostril, then the other. "That's Tyrone Power. I took that photograph myself. You know Tyrone Power, the film actor? He flew a two-engine Dakota plane to Reykjavik in 1947. Everybody went wild over him. You see, he was the first film actor ever to visit Iceland . . ."

Mingulay

I n distant time The MacNeill of Barra dispatched a certain steward named MacPhee to the isle of Mingulay, for rents were due and long since due in that lorn scrap of rock. He told the steward: "From the larger crofts, bring me two barrels of shearwater fatlings. From the smaller crofts, bring me one barrel. There is no use asking for anything but seafowl from Mingulay."

MacPhee and six galley-men took ship at Baile Mhicneill and headed southward, past the big white sweep of Vatersay Bay and Ben Guier. Scarpnamutt was a ghost in cerements of fog. They passed the red fort at Rosinish, on Pabbay, and the old chapel at Beagh Ban. After that they were in open sea and the foam curled before them and hissed along their sides. Their mast creaked and the stays stretched taut.

"Pah!" said a galley-man named Alisdair Mór, spitting salt from his mouth. "The MacDonalds of Uist would not send men on such a stupid mission. A boatload of seabirds! Pah!"

A man from Kentangaval, one Rory Dubh, said: "The MacDonalds of Uist would not own a place that was bare of even an ale-house."

"I have heard the women of Mingulay have dugs that are long and twisted, like jerked beef," remarked a third man.

They went past the Heiskers, low, mean rocks that were like hounds forever straining at harness. Now the rocks of Mingulay Sound greeted them. Sgeir nan Uibhein, Rubha Domhain, Rubh' an Droma—not names that invited fond feelings. Finally they came to sheltered water. A group of black houses stood along the strand. The men did not see smoke from any of them.

"There is some trouble here," MacPhee said. Because it was not easy to effect a landing, only he left the boat. He leapt overboard and swam ashore and then walked to the nearest house.

"I smell death," Alisdair Mór said, grabbing a lump of peat and lighting his pipe with it.

As quickly as MacPhee would enter one house, twice that quickly he emerged again. He ran like one distracted. Soon he was heading back to the water.

"It seems The MacNeill will have no *fachaich* this Eastertide," said Rory Dubh.

MacPhee swam to the boat like a water-horse was after him. "Perished in their houses, they are, all of them," he gasped, and clutched at the gunwales. "Reddish skin-spots . . . the plague . . . "

At that the galley-men lashed out with their oars and struck his fingers smartly and he tumbled back into the water. They told him they would not have him on board. What if he were carrying the contagion himself now? They did not care to die like the folk of Mingulay and they still in the first strength of their manhood, with bairns yet at suck and enemies still to hack and hew. MacPhee could only gaze up at them, a hare at the mercy of a pack of hounds. They said they had no choice but to leave him behind. A smoldering peat was flung to the shore so that he might kindle a fire.

"Hen-hearts! *Maidhm sléibhe anuas ort!* A mountain landslide down upon all of ye!" MacPhee cursed them. But it did no good.

They raised sail and made for Baile Mhicneill with the gruesome tidings that on Mingulay the steward had not found a living soul.

MacPhee knew they did right. Better to be marooned in this broken ground than smite the whole of Barra with contagion.

Back the man went and gathered tinder, then took the lump of peat and built a fire on the strand. He pulled up some marram grass and ignited the dry roots and into the thatch of the nearest house he hurled it. Firebrand after firebrand he threw onto the roofs of Mingulay. By this he hoped to scourge out the plague. And soon the village was a pyre of smoke and flaming thatch. The hum that began to foul the air did not smell earthly. MacPhee's stomach was in his mouth and pressing to be out. Gagging, he climbed upwards along the village burn to fresher air. He reached the green height of Carnan and lay down among the nesting fulmars and there he fell into exhausted sleep.

The shrill cries of sea-fowl circling overhead drew the steward to keen wakefulness the next morning. *Ma-krill! Ma-krill!* Burly bees buzzed near his face. He was lying in a patch of sheep-sorrel, upon which he began to breakfast hungrily, and as he did so his eyes rested on the village, which looked as though sea raiders from Orkney had gone through it and ravaged it. Here and there was still a twist of black smoke. But then he saw, to the south, the isle of Berneray lifting its mountainy head from the blue silken sea, and to the north, the isles of Fladay, Pabbay, Sandray, Lingay, and then the whole humpbacked torso of Uist, all radiant and glittering, laid out in the sun like a string of colored jewels. The dead village grew small in his mind.

The man thought: Bitter ranns have been recited against Mingulay, but there are many places held by the Lords of the Isles that are worse by half. Sula Sgeir has no well. Rona has neither wood to hang a man or soil to bury him. Rhum is thick with clegs and Hellisay thick with rats. They are heathen on St. Kilda and Englishmen on Skye. And on Scarba, one false step could land a man in the whirlpool of Corrievreckan.

That noontide MacPhee knocked limpets from the rocks at Hecla promontory and feasted on them and also on the wild celery that he found along the burn. He dared not touch the potato crop for fear of taint. But chickweed and rosewort grew in profusion around the grave-yard. At Leac na' Langich he gathered pearlwort, which wise women call "the cure for all aching."

Some weeks passed. Daily the man climbed Ben Gunnary and set his eyes to the north, but naught could he see of galley or longboat battening the waves for Mingulay. He would shake a fist and wish a high windy gallows to the clan of MacNeill and then he would walk to the ledges at Lianamul, where the sea-fowl were like files of sol-diers standing at ease. There could be few sights more wondrous in all the Isles. In a twinkling, he had a wealth of razorbills and puffins broken-necked and ready for his stewpot.

It was at these cliffs of an evening that he first saw her, a woman among the wraithlike shadows of Ben Gunnary. She was moving toward him. In her hand she held a spray of celandine and moon-wort. Strange in the telling! A woman! Who could have guessed that he wasn't alone? He figured she was newly exiled here by the MacLeods, who often sent women displeasing to them to lonely and desolate places. The bard Mary MacLeod they banished to Scarba, the better to cool her verse. And the wife of Hector, chief of the MacLeods, was put on Soay that she might grow more affectionate to him.

"May God welcome you to this island," he called to the woman.

But as he approached her, she drew back behind an old cairn. She was nowhere to be seen when he got there.

Now he began to see her often. She would always have some plant or herb, storksbill and sorrel, dwarfwillow or vernal squill, coaxed to her breast. Whatever she held he would seem to find there on the ground. Often she came close enough for him to see her big grey-pupiled eyes, like foxglove her cheeks. Yet whenever he paid her heed, she would steal off to Skipisdale or to the kame of Geod-hachan or to some steepdown ridge where he could not follow her.

In time the steward learned that words and only words would not drive her away. It would be no lie to say that speaking to her gave him pleasure. " 'S olc an aimsir so," he would say to her. "Bad weather from the West." And she would nod as though she understood him. "It blows hard and there are big white horses riding the Minch. We are in for a season of it . . . "

To keep the edge of winter off his bones, the man set about to construct a sheiling. "Will ye come down to the strand with me?" he inquired of the woman. Stone after heavy stone he carried from the village and always she seemed to be there with him. He decided to give her a name. He called her Mary, *Mhairi mo Chridhe*, Mary of my Heart. That she might be a specter or perhaps a creature made up from his own solitude did not trouble him.

After a year and a day The MacNeill softened his heart toward MacPhee. To Mingulay he sent his new steward, Alisdair Mór, with tidings as generous as they were laggardly. Alisdair and his men sailed around Rubh' an Droma and dropped anchor near the strand. Once ashore, they met a raggedy sort of person who was chipping away at a block of stone and paid them no attention.

Alisdair Mór addressed the man: "The MacNeill has it in his mind that you should come back to Barra. He is prepared to offer any unwed woman there to be your wife, and also to offer you a holding in Eoligarry."

"My wife is here," MacPhee said.

Alisdair Mór laughed at such a jest. Then he said: "But do you not care to own a croft that contains the land of twelve cows and that is so rich you could eat it with a spoon?"

"Mingulay is my croft," the man answered. And he walked toward the house he was making with the stone in the cradle of his arms.

Tundra

Near Ferguson Lake, N.W.T.

Here in this unadorned geology there's no getting away from last things. Several miles from my tent I find a caribou skeleton with its girders caved in, innards gone, and only a few forlorn tags of fur and skin to indicate that it wasn't born this way.

But then I see a few black flies hovering around the carcass like artists admiring their handiwork. In the dying wind I watch these few begin to multiply. All at once the air possesses an unnatural stillness. The sky seems to turn yellow, then a pocked, insectual black. And then these ravening lords of the tundra strike, mobbing my every available pore and drinking from my fountain. Each bite—not painful, but worse—sends a sharp pinprick of torment straight to the kernel of my bodily being.

I sprint off over broken ground, over esker and glacial rubble, lateral moraine and terminal moraine, heading in the direction of my tent. Rock after hard rock my feet waken from an early Pleistocene sleep. I plead with my Maker: I'll give up anything, Maker, Old Chap, sloth and gluttony, maybe even lust, only please, *please* deliver me from this plague of insects. There's no response except a thrumming acceleration of interest from the plague itself. Either God's bailiwick does not extend to these lovely abysmal parts, empty, powerfully empty of human habitation, or He shies away from encounters with rival lords.

Now I leap rivulets and splash through shoaly ponds, slop across bogs and tromp *tripe de roche*, until I reach, at last, long last, my glorious tent. Which, ingloriously, is nowhere to be seen. So again I splatter, plunge, hop, tramp, and slosh until I locate the tent in its rightful place a few feet from a riverine embankment. Cheek by jowl with a dwarf pillow patch. Not far from an ancient kayak stand. Surrounded by a bumper crop of Labrador tea. Except it isn't there again.

Where's the north wind when you really need its vindictive keen? My weary feet crunch a sedge meadow inlaid with a handsomely stitched tapestry of jewel lichen, but I'm far too fly-besotted to appreciate it. By now my morale is wholly unstrung, and I'm feeling the onset of histamine shock. Just give up, I tell myself, and let them drink their fill . . .

All at once I see the aquamarine dome of my tent in the distance. I run to it, trip, fall, rise again, and crawl inside, my own girders still aloft (barely). Then I quickly anoint my body with the magic of citronella oil and carbolated Vaseline, a dope guaranteed to distinguish my fate from the fate of my late caribou brother.

By such thin coatings we live and die.

A Walk on the Wild Side

(from *Last Places*)

I n Eric the Red's time, you could hop an open-decked merchant ship or possibly hitch a lift with a Norwegian bishop for the five-day run to Greenland's Eastern Settlement. Nowadays the connection isn't quite so easy, as I learned when I wandered the Reykjavik docks in search of a Greenland-bound boat. Neither cargo ships nor passenger ships like the *Norröna* made the run between the two islands, and trawlers weren't supposed to take on travelers like myself. A skipper who was a friend of a friend offered to bring me along as a paying stowaway, but he warned me they might not actually land; last time out, they caught their cod and steamed directly back to Iceland, much to the disappointment of the crew, for whom fishing off Greenland often meant a visit ashore to sport with native girls.

Finally I realized I'd have to fly if I wanted to reach Greenland before the onslaught of winter. By flying, I would be violating my original plan. The Vikings probably wouldn't have flown even if they'd had the chance. They were a seagoing, sea-hearty people who always traveled with their worldly goods; doubtless they'd have balked at the prospect of herding their cattle into an aircraft. On the other hand, native Greenlanders have always used the jet stream. Stories about their inspired aviations abound. An old *angakok* (shaman) named Angerlerduaq once took to the air by rapidly beating a pair of guillemot wings over his head, and two other *angakut* named Ayiyaq and Uitsaleqangiteq used to stage aerial competitions for the benefit of spectators. And the mountain hermits known as *qivigtut* were able to fly simply by placing their thumbs in their nostrils and wiggling their index fingers; once aloft, they would float one leg behind them like a rudder and use the other to steer. Robert Petersen, of the Inuit Institute in Nuuq, once told me he'd heard about a man who could fly just by bending one leg slightly and flexing his little fingers back and forth—a major breakthrough, Petersen thought, in the science of aerodynamics.

And so it was that I went to Greenland more or less in native style.

On previous visits I had fallen crazily in love with this capacious island, shaped like a colossal stockinged foot, with a land area four times the size of France and a population slightly smaller than Wauwatosa, Wisconsin. I had fallen in love with its high-flying natives, a race of people who call themselves Inuit (Real People) or Kalladlit (Real, Real People), but never Eskimos, which is a Cree Indian term of disdain meaning "eaters of raw fish" (Frenchmen don't like being called "eaters of garlicky snails," either). I had even fallen in love—for a night—with a young woman who possessed by far the finest pair of eyes I'd ever seen, thus confirming an old northern seafarer's adage that the only two beings in all the world with human eyes are seals and Greenland girls.

I'm not usually inclined to betray an intimacy, but I feel obliged to say a few words about this last-named love because it was as much a cultural liaison as an amatory one:

I had gone to the tiny East Greenland village of Igateq to meet an old man named Salluq, reputedly the last impenitent heathen (others had converted to Christianity by the late 1920s) in the country. Unfortunately, Salluq was sailing from Igateq to Angmagssalik with a cargo of sealskins just as I was sailing from Angmagssalik to Igateq. We never met. And now I found myself stuck in Igateq. The village was draped along a rocky eminence whose hard-used beauty lay wild around it like contours on a map (the perfect place, I thought, for a last heathen). I pitched my tent in the lee of this eminence and settled in for the evening. I was just making a good gut-cauterizing pot of coffee when a young woman suddenly appeared beside me. According to the explorer Knud Rasmussen, Inuit women move with the silence of the ages, and that's exactly how this woman had moved—I hadn't even heard a crunch of silt and gravel to indicate her approach. She was just there, as if by magic. Now she smiled. I smiled. She smiled again, saying: "*Kusunsuaa unsukkapiq?*" (Do you have a nice penis?) I was a little taken aback, as this wasn't the sort of question I was accustomed to in my country. Here, the woman explained, "a nice penis" meant I didn't have gonorrhea. I said my penis was fine, yet I must admit I had no idea what her mission was. Perhaps she was the village nurse carrying out some sort of medical survey.

The woman departed and an hour or so later came back with her husband, a man whose neat tapered body seemed ideally designed to fit into a kayak. He grinned and whacked me on the back, spilling half my cup of coffee. *Ela!* he exclaimed, My little wife fancies you. Glad to know it, I mumbled, still a bit confused, wondering why she fancied a fleabag camper like myself. And, he added, I would be honored if she and you had sexual intercourse tonight. At which point I nearly spilled all the rest of my coffee, too. *Tonight?* I said, buying time to think it over. He nodded pleasantly and whacked me on the back again. I peered up at his little wife, then back at him, and—being young, adventurous, and perhaps even a little naive—agreed to take him up on his very generous offer.

And so I was introduced to the Inuit custom of wife swapping in its modern incarnation. In the old days the custom satisfied bodily desires even as it kept the wolf from the door. If a man loaned out his wife, he could expect to get meat from her lover once his own cache of meat was gone; the resulting tie was as deep as a kinship tie, and lovers who didn't share their meat often died under very mysterious circumstances. Today, however, there's no need to share one's comestibles—a person can always drop by the Royal Greenlandic Trading Post and purchase a few tins of South African pilchards or a plasticized smear of Danish ham. Yet Greenlanders remain free and easy with each other's charms, as if their mind-set had not quite caught up with the times: I was being *given* a wife with no strings attached. Whether it was because I appeared to be lonely or the woman simply liked my looks, I never found out.

We went back to their two-room shack and I spent the night with the woman Katrina's brown, wondrous eyes gazing up at me and her smooth flesh blended into mine. It was the sort of night when every part of your body has a sense of belonging to every other part as well as to the naked globes and grasses of the carnal Universe itself. But what I most remember about that night was the husband seated at a table in the next room, cheerfully cutting cards, CLACK! CLACK! CLACK! over and over again. Next morning he thanked me for my visit and gave me a send-off in the form of a succulent haunch of seal.

I returned to my tent and didn't see either of them again. Several days later I was in an outboard heading back to Angmagssalik when the man at the throttle turned to me and inquired whether Katrina made love softly, in the Greenlandic manner, or noisily, in the manner of Europeans. I hesitated and then said: In the Greenlandic manner.

But Greenland itself. I would be a rather shameful lover if I blinded myself to its enormous swarm of problems, not least of which is the apparent irreconcilability, inside and outside bedroom walls, of Greenlandic and European manners. For three hundred and fifty years the island was a perennially underachieving colony of the Danish crown. While African and South American colonies were working overtime on behalf of their European proprietors, Greenland managed only to be a drain on the Royal Danish Treasury. Yet the Danes persevered, if only because they thought there had to be something akin to a resource under all that ice; even then they were less greedy than most colonial proprietors. They dragged their huge woebegone charge from one age to the next, providing social and medical services, religious instruction, and the best European education a non-European could possibly desire. With the best of intentions, they made European victuals available to all, from canned foods to sugary glop, not realizing that imposing a shift in food habits would leave a subsistence-fueled people with not much to do anymore. And with slightly less than the best of intentions (they still hoped there'd be *something* under the island's interminable ice or in its unfathomed seas), they gave Greenland a sort of phantom Home Rule in 1979, retaining for themselves control of all preeminent policy decisions. Greenland is free; the Danish raj lives on.

Our plane made a very spirited landing at Narsarssuaq, the only airstrip in southern Greenland long enough to receive a fixed-wing aircraft. Many of my fellow passengers were Icelandair employees who showed neither the patience nor the steadfastness of their ancestors. Whereas the Viking colony had lasted five hundred years, they planned to stay in Greenland only half an hour. They had no interest in the island itself; their plan was to fly directly back to the Keflavik airport and clear out a few shelves of duty-free booze, available only to international passengers, which, in their transit from Iceland to Greenland and back again, they would become.

I could hardly blame the Icelanders for choosing to leave Narsarssuaq the instant they arrived. It was a disagreeable place—just a runway and a hotel at the head of a long claustrophobic valley. Once a U.S. air base, it became a demobilization hospital during the Korean conflict and quartered the saddest and most pathetic of the war wounded, men whose viscera had been blown away or whose faces had been left behind on the battlefield. Most of them died, and their bodies were cremated and ashes scattered in the glacial silt of the so-called Hospital Valley. A friend of mine once visited here and came across the brainpan of a man who doubtless did not expect to end up in Greenland when he signed on for Korea.

As I stepped into the warm sunny afternoon, I was greeted by the local welcoming committee, taking time off from their busy schedules to salute my arrival. Perhaps they had just been mobbing a musk ox to distraction, or forcing a reindeer to make a suicidal leap from a cliff top, or taking their time with the murder of a brooding bird or two. Whichever, they were now giving me the full-bodied benefit of their attention. I refer to that tiny celebrant of all warm-blooded life, the mosquito (*Aedes rearcticus*), whose remorseless presence makes much of the west coast of Greenland buggier than Amazonia.

On warm days like today, *Aedes* rise up from bogs and willow thickets in enormous, noisy clouds. The males are gentlemen, hovering lazily and buzzing each other with stray tidbits of insectual wisdom, like perpetual bachelors at the firehouse. But the women are whining peevish viragoes capable of penetrating jeans, underwear, and skin with a proboscis as sharp as a needle and as subtle as a drill bit. Bloody persistence! Once I even saw a female *Aedes* probing for a capillary through an eyelet on my hiking boot. Yet the victim deludes himself if he thinks his hemoglobin is the staff of their life. Not true at all. The arctic mosquito can get all the sustenance she requires from the juices of willow herbs, but she needs blood to condition her reproductive equipment and so allow her to become a mother to hundreds more like her.

In a 1966 article in *Meddelelser om Grønland*, Danish scientist Erik Nielsen described how he once counted a landing rate of eighty-three "individuals" per minute on a person—himself—sitting in the shade at Narsarssuaq. Just now, as I stood in the sunlight, this did not seem like very many. I was encompassed from head to foot and naturally tried to reduce their numbers by slapping a few of them to perdition. The more I killed, the more rose up in apparently endless maternal relays. As genocide didn't seem to be the answer, I decided to show a little respect by rubbing on some Tiger Balm. A good many

Greenlanders swear that this Singapore-made panacea for rheumatism, headaches, and gout is the best mosquito repellent on the market—much better than seal oil or overdose quantities of Vitamin B. Others think repellents only make a bad situation worse. Tiger Balm does stop mosquitoes from eating you alive, but it doesn't stop them from getting stuck in your ears and nostrils, stepping into your eyes, getting tangled in your hair, and jumping to their dooms down your throat. Hold the Tiger Balm and they'll just suck and depart. Apply the Tiger Balm and you'll get a swarming, gossipy mass of mosquitoes as everlasting consorts, along with the odor of camphor.

My present destination was Igaliko, former clerical headquarters of the Vikings (Igaliko means "Abandoned Cooking Place"—the Greenlanders who named it thought empty pots more eloquent than an empty cathedral) and point of embarkation for eleventh-century trips to Labrador and Newfoundland. The boat for Igaliko did not leave until the next morning. As I had no desire to linger around the airport or take a room in the overpriced barracks calling itself the Arctic Hotel, I walked toward Hospital Valley. What I saw along the way was not a pretty sight.

Narsarssuaq lost its usefulness in the mid-1950s, after the Army Corps of Engineers built the Thule Air Base to provide American paranoia about the Soviets with an outpost in the Far North. The GIs left in 1959, and the Danes sold much of the scrap from the base to a Norwegian scrap merchant—much, but not all. There is still enough heavy metal lying around to make Narsarssuaq a first-rate tourist hangout for William S. Burroughs: a terminally rusted B-52 resting on its back like a fallen pterodactyl; military vehicles stripped to their essential nakedness; the corpse of an old asphalt factory; vestiges of antiaircraft batteries; snakelike fixtures with coiled necks rising a foot or two off the ground; and convoluted bits of machinery whose only purpose would seem to be their own purposelessness.

I had no interest in camping among all this dead technology, so I continued walking for several miles along a pebbled glacial plain carpeted with gray-green moss. I walked until I came to a river so silted up it looked like chocolate milk. On the bank of this river I pitched my tent, with only a few "rogue" mosquitoes (it was now too cool for most of the little fiends) to gnaw at my skin and nerves. Directly ahead of me stood Qorqup Sermia, a tongue of the ice cap that resembled a long roughfronted wall. Directly behind me was the jungle, thick copses of dwarf rowans and dwarf willows with seed-pods like delicate gray earrings. A few bluebells lay scattered about, though they seemed positively harassed, cringing close to the ground as if they remembered the head-pincering gales of winter and expected them to strike again at any moment. It was an odd sensation, first looking at the great white ice cap and then turning around to see so much vegetation.

That evening I pondered Eric the Red's color-coding scheme for the North Atlantic. Eric is supposed to have adopted a sales pitch that presented Iceland as icy, white, and awful, and Greenland as green and inviting. Being a murderer, perhaps he found that the Madison Avenue style came easily. Yet Iceland in the tenth century did have fourteen more glaciers than it has today, and the southwest coast of Greenland—where, after a trip as far north as Disko Bay, Eric elected to settle—did have fjords ostensibly more suitable for raising stock than the coastal fringes of Eric's volcanic homeland. Also, southwest Greenland gets a nudge from the Greenland Current, an offshoot of the Gulf Stream, and some of its valleys can be strikingly green in summer. If Eric had visited here during what meteorologists call a static depression (a prolonged period of low barometric pressure), he might have thought himself transported to the greenest, loveliest land on earth, a land where photosynthesis goes on twenty-four hours a day and where every petal on every plant seems to grow almost visibly. A land, in short, that speaks eloquently, if seasonally, of Thor's plenty.

Early next morning I took the *Aleqa Ittuk*, a little ten-knot passenger ferry, from Narsarssuaq to Igaliko. We chugged along steep-flanked Tunugdliarfik Fjord toward the blue height of Nunarsarnaq, a mountain shaped like a miniature Matterhorn. The skipper, a Greenlander with a cleft palate and cracked sunglasses, neatly circumnavigated solitary chunks of drift ice that had been carried southward from East Greenland glaciers by the cold East Greenland Current, around the horn of Cape Farewell, and into Davis Strait—a long haul, and they'd been properly whittled down by it.

It was this drift ice that bottled up fjord entrances during the so-called Little Ice Age of the fourteenth century and severed the European connection for latter-day Viking colonists. Right now, though, the ice wasn't bad and we made a fairly smooth passage. The only incident of any note during the trip occurred when a Greenlander's drunken girlfriend flung his sneaker overboard. (The victim merely shrugged and flung the other one overboard, too.) After two hours the boat bumped against a little landing place. Two Swiss hikers joined me on shore, reconnoitered their gear (they had enough to outfit a small sporting goods store, in Zurich), and trotted off briskly into the mountains.

At two miles the rock-strewn, up-and-down track to Igaliko is one of the longest roads in a country where any road at all is a curiosity. I followed this track to the village through a series of abrupt swivels and switchbacks that made me feel as if I were wandering around inside a vast intestine. Toward the end I began to see the linty forms of grazing sheep, all apparently unaware that this was Greenland, not the plains of Wyoming, and they weren't supposed to be here.

I've often thought the Home Rule government encourages sheep farming in order to keep its constituents from being sucked dry, since the Arctic mosquito refuses to live near sheep. Whatever the reason for this aversion (bad odor? wool too thick to penetrate? a preference for more intelligent forms of life?), I've never once felt the tell-tale incision of a mother-to-be while visiting a farm in Greenland. Yet this dearth of mosquitoes may be the lone agricultural virtue of trying to raise sheep on an island whose spectacular winters always seem to kill off about half the stock.

Being the Viking Vatican City, Igaliko had the Viking equivalent of

Saint Peter's, a cathedral dedicated to Saint Nicolai, the patron saint of sailors. I walked through a field thick with chamomile and came to all that remained of this cathedral—a few scattered blocks of red sandstone. It had been relatively large, ninety-five feet by fifty-three feet, and also rather ornate, with windows of green glaze instead of the usual stretched calves' stomachs. Dust to dust: Now it looked so ruinous you'd be paying it a compliment by calling it a ruin. Over the years the natives had dismantled it block by block for their own significantly more modest red sandstone dwellings. This meant that each of the fifty or so Greenlanders in Igaliko was living in, however shabby, a consecrated dwelling.

I pitched my tent half a mile or so from the village, down by Igaliko Fjord, where I could be watched and evaluated. This was an old Indian practice whose wisdom I value: Never move in on your hosts unless distinctly invited to do so. Strangers are, by definition, untrustworthy—they want your land, your artifacts, or your women. I know I wouldn't take kindly to anyone putting up a tent like mine, part Christo and part Buckminster Fuller, in *my* backyard.

That evening I did receive an invitation, of sorts. I was admiring somebody's lawn, all ragged oil drums and old fish bones, when a ten-year-old kicked a soccer ball in my direction. Soon we'd adjourned to a nearby soccer field, which was just as thick with chamomile as the old Viking churchyard. Possibly I should have made myself some tea on the spot, for chamomile tea is very soothing and might have helped me deal with the bloodthirstiness of Greenlandic soccer.

Before long we were joined by two other kids. In time a match was suggested. Since none of them showed any enthusiasm for being on my side, I ended up playing against all three, a White Man outnumbered by the natives. Right away I realized they were just as inclined to kick me as kick the ball. One of them would block me out, another would bash away at my shins, and the third would drive the ball triumphantly to a goal. Or all three would dedicate themselves to bashing away at my shins, forgetting about the ball. The underlying message seemed to be "Off the White Guy." The great wide world of getting and spending—*things, things, and more things*—may be his, but now we've got him on the holy ground of our soccer field and let's see who's boss. I figured I was getting what they got every day in their Danish-oriented schools, taught by Danes who (for the most part) hate Greenland; I figured this especially when the mockery of a match was over and one of them—he couldn't have been more than eight years old—called me a lousy Dane. I told him I was a lousy American, not a Dane. This seemed to jam his circuits, for in all probability he'd never seen an American except on his TV.

Back at my tent I nursed my wounds and briefly considered a return match; *mano a mano*, wherein I transformed these kids, each in turn, into Inuit gelatin. But as the bright, lustrous evening wore on, I began to shake off my irritation. A trail of opaline clouds crowded the horizon like vistas in a Piranesi drawing. A couple of wayward icebergs rested contemplatively in the fjord, and the fjord itself had turned a rich Mediterranean blue. Once when I looked up, I happened to see a sea eagle poised on magisterial wings above the knurled summit of the mountain behind my tent. It was a scene of peerless tranquility, tossed out in Nature's devil-may-care way, which says: just open your eyes, my friend, and I'll astonish you every minute of your life.

Next day I awoke to rain as intense as an Asiatic monsoon, except it was much colder and, wind-driven, flung itself around Igaliko in big horizontal sweeps. I've always thought Greenlanders were born water-proof (often you see them sitting outside in snow or rain as if they are sunbathing), but this was too much even for them, and everyone— including the cheerfully demented old man who had stood beside his house and played his concertina all during the previous day—seemed to have retreated indoors. I decided I would use this opportunity to try and locate a guide for my overland trek to Qaqortoq.

Qaqortoq (Greenlandic for Julianehåb) was a six- or seven-day walk from Igaliko and the trip took in several Viking farm sites as well as the old Hvalsøy Church, possibly the last Viking stronghold in Greenland. The route was not without its perils, ranging from lack of paths to suddenly plunging couloirs, but it was probably no more perilous, merely longer, than my previous trek to Hornbjarg. Yet here—especially here, in this polyglot, puzzle-headed, much-imperialized country—I felt I needed someone to serve as ombudsman between myself and his land, else I'd be violating one of the oldest of all travel rules: The native knows best, and even if he doesn't know best, at least he'll manage to get you into the same trouble he's always gotten into himself.

I visited a man named Gustav Olsen, who possessed a smile as calm as a sheltered inlet. But when I told him where I wanted to go, he quickly swallowed his smile and shook his head, saying he was afraid ("*Niangiannatuk!*") of the *qivigtoq*. This *qivigtoq* inhabited a little gulch called Itigvitaq only a mile or so from my chosen route. He told me this story:

Fifteen years ago three friends went out to hunt seals in Igaliko Fjord. Each of them had been drinking heavily for several days, case after case of beer, and they had a rather exalted notion of how many seals they'd get. Several hours out of Igaliko they rammed their speedboat full throttle into a submerged ice floe, and the boat capsized. Two of the men drowned, but the third, Anda, reached the shore suffering badly from exposure but even worse from shame. His two companions had died, but he had not died with them. He realized it would be impossible for him to hold up his head in human society anymore, so he elected to live out his days, alone and shame-ridden, in Itigvitaq.

"The fellow doesn't sound so frightening to me," I remarked. "A little sad, but not frightening."

"Would you be frightened if you knew he could change himself into a polar bear? *Ela*, would you?"

"I suppose so . . ."

"*Assâssakâq!* He can. It is well known. Would you like Anda to eat you up, White Man?"

By the end of the afternoon I still hadn't managed to locate a guide from among Igaliko's housebound citizenry. Some were afraid of the *qivigtoq*; others, of unpleasant weather. Some said they'd be too busy tending their sheep; others, their idleness. Hardly anyone wanted to miss Friday's *kaffemik* (coffee orgy), a sort of party where everybody sits around drinking cup after cup of strong coffee until eventually their hearts blast out of their chests like rockets from a launching pad.

At last I met Paulassie Egede, a raw-boned, dimple-cheeked, gap-toothed man in his early thirties. Paulassie lived with his girlfriend Meqqoq in a house whose walls were papered with hundreds of yellow labels from Dole pineapple cans. When I commented on this, he told me he'd been drunk one night and had seen a large shipment of canned pineapple sitting on the dock; he was so impressed by the decorative potential of the brightly colored labels that he tore them all off and covered his walls with them. The canned contents he threw into the fjord, at whose bottom they presumably still lie.

Paulassie was something of a wag, both worldly and a little old-fashioned. He grew cannabis—thin, scraggly, awful-looking plants obviously ill at ease in a Greenlandic window—and claimed he'd be perfectly content to spend his whole life hunting ravens and ptarmigan, soaking up welfare *kroner* from the Danish taxpayer. He asked me where I came from and seemed genuinely disappointed that it wasn't Alabama, because his most cherished possession—apart from a 70 Winchester .270 rifle with a twenty-two-inch barrel—was a University of Alabama sweatshirt he'd bought in a Copenhagen shop specializing in American sweat items. Someday, he said, he hoped to visit Alabama, if only to see what kind of place he was promoting with this shirt.

Paulassie's relaxation in his body bordered on laziness, not a quality you ordinarily look for in a guide. But he did know the mountains, and he had helped some Danes excavate the old Viking farmstead at Sigssardlugtoq last summer. Also, he was not afraid of the *qivigtoq*, nor dedicated to sheep, nor interested in the coffee orgy (he preferred beer orgies).

"Ela," he said with a grin, shaking my hand. "You are Mr. Peary and I will take you to the Pole . . ."

That evening I was brushing my teeth in the rain when a snow bunting dropped down and perched on my tent and gave me the strangest look, as if to say: What in the name of reason *are* you doing, White Man?

July 26. A bright, almost tropical day. As we walk, the Greenland Shield seems to shed more of its thin vegetative garb in favor of naked granite. We skirt the mountain Nujuk, which Paulassie says is unclimbable, owing to scree that always brings your best intentions down with a rubbly flourish, and carry on along a brusque, serpentine ridge. At every col and gully there's a thicket of dwarf Arctic birches, dwarf rowans, or dwarf willows, none higher than eighteen inches, through which we have to stomp, a process quite a bit more arduous than boulder hopping.

Every fifteen minutes Paulassie stops and drinks a lingering, salutary draft of stream water. Every half hour he disappears to rustle up a ptarmigan for supper, returning ptarmiganless but—I suspect from the sound of the ricochet—having shot a rock or two. His sneakers have holes in them, as do his sweat socks. Every hour or so he pauses to give both these sets of holes a rest. Sometimes he just pauses and doesn't drink water and doesn't rearrange his footwear. What's up? I inquire. I'm thinking about my girlfriend, he says. She has a very fine *utsuuq.* But he also says his grandmother always told him to proceed slowly in the mountains, since they're full of evil dog-headed creatures called *erqigdlit.* (While *he* wasn't really too worried about these *erqigdlit,* he says his feet sometimes seemed to be quite worried.) Continuing on, we hike past clumps of rosewort and gay rosettes of purple saxifrage with petals flared eagerly toward the sun.

I hardly mind our leisurely progress, since I'm not in a hurry to catch the 5:17 to Poona Junction, the 6:09 from Grand Central, or the evening Aeroflot to Tashkent. One of the purposes of travel is to avoid your destination at all costs (once you're there, you're there, and you'll never be permitted that long bated breath of anticipation again), and once in a while Paulassie does point out to me the most extraordinary things. For example: We shinny our way up the polished chute of a defunct waterfall, ascend and descend a mountain called Akudlipqaq, and then enter a remote, handsome, seemingly unfathomed valley, when Paulassie stops dead in his tracks and draws my attention to—four Carlsberg lager cans! My own, he says proudly. I came to this place two years ago to hunt ravens. *Sóruna*, I tell him, and you've made it ugly. Beer is not ugly, he protests.

Midafternoon: We take our lunch on a ledge overlooking Igaliko Fjord. I'm gazing down on the fjord, a blue fallen peacock feather, when Paulassie interrupts my reverie to tell me that I'm sitting on some of his ancestors. I peek through the interstices of an apparent pile of rocks to observe three dearticulated human skeletons stacked up inside like logs, with a snow bunting's nest built in one of the rib cages. One of these skeletons is a child's; a few thin wisps of black hair cling to its tiny lemon-colored skull. The other two have patches of green moss growing on them like a close-cropped fuzz of hair (nothing inspires a bryophyte more than the proximity of a good human skull). A family of famine victims, Paulassie says. Probably starved to death a hundred or so years ago. Are they buried above ground because of upward pressure in the permafrost? I inquire. No, he replies, they're buried above ground so they'll have a beautiful view for all eternity.

Later we pitch our tents beside a cirque of unprecedented turquoise called Tattersuit, which has gullies of snow dotting its shoreline like exclamation points. Tattersuit is an almost impossible lake to read since it has no obvious plant or insect life, just a few wasted silver-gray cattails sticking up like beacons. But in half an hour I've caught eight full-grown arctic char, each seven inches long, with a Dardevle lure. These char have precious little to feed on in Tattersuit, mostly just plankton, but that turns out to be enough for them to continue living even though they hardly grow at all. Paulassie is less pleased with these *erqalut* than with the can of beans he's extracted from my pack. He's never tasted beans before, so he flings the can into our dry willow root fire and PLONK! it soon explodes. The beans are cooked to perfection. Unfortunately he insists on boiling the char for almost an hour, which gives their delicate pink flesh the consistency of an old Goodyear tire.

A cold, lovely evening. Ripples like frost heaves on the lake. Tent rustling softly in the wind. The distant bark of an arctic fox. A few random mosquitoes browsing around our campsite . . . even *they* seem to contribute to the evening's general beneficence, for *Aedes rearcticus* cannot perform its surgery—wing muscles won't function properly—unless the temperature is a minimum of fifty degrees, which it isn't right now.

"Happy is the camp that doesn't possess mosquitoes," I observe, citing an old Micmac Indian proverb of incontestable wisdom.

"I will tell you a mosquito story, Allaut," says Paulassie. He has taken to calling me Allaut (Pencil) because every time he looks up, I seem to be scribbling something with my no. 2 Ruttledge word processor. Here is his story:

Once upon a time all the mosquitoes in the world lived on a little island in Igaliko Fjord called Qerqertarssuaq. They kept entirely to themselves, never leaving the island, just paddling their kayaks around it occasionally. On the mainland there lived a man named Niliq who made a habit of robbing, stealing, and cheating his friends. The last straw came when Niliq stole a boat full of whale meat. He rowed the boat over to the mosquito island, where he assumed no one would be able to find him. But his friends followed him by the scent of the whale meat. They decided to put an end to Niliq's thievery once and for all, so they beat him to a pulp and left him lying dead on the rocks. The mosquitoes, who had been going through a period of very poor hunting, approached the man and started to drink his blood, whose flavor they liked very much. After that the mosquitoes left the island and forever after hunted people, for once they had tasted human blood, they preferred it above all else.

July 27. Late in the morning we climb down a lateral moraine undulating to the fjord and come upon a lush meadow of dandelions. You can always tell the old Viking farms in Greenland by the presence of this common suburban lawn pest. The land may have been undisturbed for hundreds of years, but dandelions are perennials that respond enthusiastically to the labor of earlier times; the original laborers and their livestock may be dust, but the dandelion still extends its powerful taproot to near-permafrost levels and still raises its bright yellow head in June and July.

At this site, Sigssardlugtoq, Paulassie worked for part of last summer with two Danish archaeologists and one other native hand, disturbing the poorly aerated soil yet more by putting it in a bucket and then shaking it over a sieve. He points to a Viking longhouse, revealed only by its rectangular embankments, and a few scattered stones, either a church or a cow byre, hard to tell now. He says the Danes found evidence of a spring flowing through a stone channel to a basin on the longhouse floor, and then another channel where the overflow could be diverted under a wall. Running water! That was a luxury nobody in Igaliko possessed seven hundred years later . . .

I search around for artifacts and manage to locate an empty potato chip bag, a rusted tin of pilchards, some toilet paper, a scattering of shotgun shells, and another mound of beer cans. Greenlandic kitchen midden, circa 1986. "This time not me," Paulassie declares, pointing to himself and then to the cans (he knows his own litter like he knows the back of his hand). I guess that a couple of seal hunters stopped off here and enjoyed a picnic of potato chips and beer among the warty-fruited dandelions, and I leave their artifacts exactly where I found them. Maybe some future archaeologist intent upon reconstructing the late twentieth century will be grateful for my foresight.

An aside on litter: In the Ecuadorian Amazon, I once followed a trail blaze through the jungle of Shuar Indian homework. Mismanaged sums, botched multiplication tables, and mangled long division, all stuck in liana vines marking the path. The source of this detritus? The kids trek in each morning to get their schooling and each afternoon they happily throw this schooling away. But a few days later, when I passed through again, every last wretched piece of homework had been snatched up by the glutinous Jungle Madre, digested and gone forever. In Greenland, however, it's been estimated that a piece of paper might survive intact, with all the print still legible, for a minimum of five hundred years, whether or not anyone is present to read it. For Dame Permafrost refuses to dine on the nondegradable software, hardware, or any other ware belonging to the modern age. Impossible to digest the stuff. In this she shares the good taste of a Greenlander who doesn't want Carlsberg empties and used toilet tissue—not to mention soggy insulation, unsinkable polystyrene fish boxes, and eviscerated mattresses—lying around his house. Trouble is, she doesn't want that litter in *her* house, either. So it just sits outside in limbo, abandoned and unloved, brooding everlastingly on itself, with a half-life scarcely shorter than uranium.

Back up the same moraine, higher and higher, using rock climber's logic: Take it easy if you have any interest in knowing what ledges, precipices, jams, or cracks the future holds for you. We camp near an unnamed lake whose rocks press together on its clear bottom in a deep hug of silence. Rowans and birches grovel among the lichen, and one immaculate pale yellow arctic poppy peers forth demurely from a sprinkle of glacial till.

Another lucent evening. Ptarmigan, crowberries, and bannock for supper. The bannock (my recipe, tried and true, with wheat germ and a dash of cinnamon) Paulassie proceeds to fling into the air and shoot down like a clay pigeon, declaring it the very worst thing he's ever eaten. Far worse, he says, than the green juices the old people would scoop from a dead walrus's stomach and use as a garnish. I'm honored by the compliment. Slept so soundly, mummified in my sleeping bag, that I might have been winging my passage along one of the back roads of Eternity.

July 28. On an escarpment whose scoured surfaces give it the candor and toughness of the very old. We leap across a torrential, exhilarating river of melt-off no more than a foot and a half wide, then slide along slabs of granite laid out like enormous planchets of sheet metal. Paulassie pauses to contemplate his girlfriend or shoot something, hard to say which, and I scramble on alone up a deep fretted ledge to get a closer look at a waterfall frayed into dreadlocks by the wind. From the top I can see the snow-streaked mountains north of Nanortalik, seismic skips seventy-five miles away; directly below me, icebergs ride silently in the fjord, like motes of dandruff on a blue serge suit.

Now I catch sight of an arctic fox loping off on its uneven course, a figure in a frieze jauntily come alive. I'm startled. We haven't met with too much sentient life on this trip other than our occasionally sentient selves. Just snow buntings, a few ptarmigan, some errant sheep, the char, and the mosquitoes. It's safe to say that Boston Common on a good afternoon boasts more wildlife. So too do the books of certain writers, wherein the North seems to be a logjam of wildlife—as it can appear if you're traveling from herd to herd in a flying machine. But if you're merely walking or getting a lift with a hunter, you'll see northern landscapes from the very different perspective of your stomach, and then you'll be glad you brought along those desiccated strips of whale jerky or that freeze-dried ersatz.

Once upon a time Greenlanders made their big empty land less lonely by providing every last pawky scrap of its furnishings with a soul. Every animal had a soul, and a hunter needed to pray to that soul directly after killing its bodily component or it would take offense. Plants had souls. Drops of water had souls. Even human beings had souls—two souls, in fact, each no bigger than a medium-sized snow bunting, the first located in the throat, the other set in a bubble of air in the groin. Even laughter and sleep had souls. Thus a person could never travel anywhere without some sort of companionship, nor could he travel anywhere and presume that his medium-sized snow buntings were better than Mr. Nepheline Syenite or Mrs. Gabbro, upon whose bodies he was being permitted to tread. Better than a rock? Better than a warty-fruited dandelion? *Tássaqa!* (Not too likely!)

Up until the year 1721 a Greenlander could converse amiably with his own sleep and maybe even his insomnia, but in that year a Danish pastor named Hans Egede arrived on the island looking for the ice-trapped Viking colony, to whose long-pent-up spiritual needs (he assumed the Vikings had retreated into heathenism) he hoped to minister. Egede didn't find any Vikings, but he did find a group of heathens, so he aimed all his High Church artillery in their direction, daily preaching against the sins of gambling and profiteering, which did not exist in Greenland. He did not win many converts until he started to whip the *angakut*. Then people seemed to appreciate his point of view, though they still wondered what this "daily bread" was they were supposed to be asking for. Egede changed that to "daily seal," yet he made it clear to them that seals didn't have souls. Nothing had a soul unless it first submitted to baptism, and he wasn't about to dunk a ringed seal in holy water. Only human beings were allowed that treatment. One by one Hans Egede baptized these human beings—whereupon Greenlanders got the chance to be just as lonely as everybody else.

July 29. Tonight I'm a little shaky. Can't get to sleep for a change. The events of the day keep coming back to me like a melody I can't thrust from my head. I'm writing these notes by flashlight inside our tent, with a rising wind and Paulassie's deep hoarse snores to punctuate them.

Toward midday we were approaching Itigvitaq. At the last moment, Paulassie wanted to steer clear of Anda the *qivigtog*'s gulch, all crow's feet and prattling rivulets, but I offered to raise his guide's fee by adding on the return ticket from Qaqortoq to Igaliko if he'd make the detour. He relented, yet he was obviously uncomfortable about it, the first time I'd noticed him ill at ease on the entire trip.

We first spied Anda from a considerable distance, a tiny gnome-like figure squatting in front of a heap of stones. Every few paces Paulassie called out, in traditional fashion, We are friendly, we are friendly, we are friendly. No reply. At last we stood opposite him. He peered up at us with little discernible interest.

Anda's wrinkled parchment skin carried a few stray whiskers—he looked a bit like a Chinese mandarin. He was dressed entirely in sealskins that even the mosquitoes seemed to find a little rancid. *"Qaqqislunga qatangajualaq,"* whispered Paulassie. (He has not wiped off his snot in many years.) From inside the hovel of stones wafted the odor of burnt oil and ancient, petrified sweat.

Slowly his mouth opened to reveal a long tooth extending fanglike from his upper jaw. Then he asked me for tobacco in a voice that sounded cracked at the joints from disuse and bad weather. I offered him some of my Balkan Sobranie, which he grabbed immediately and stuffed into his short-stemmed pipe—the pipe of choice in the North because it allows less time for smoke to condense and it burns like a furnace.

"Qujanaq. Perhaps you will give some food to an old man?"

I rummaged in my pack for something he might consider edible, putting aside a few packets of freeze-dried camper's cuisine. Apparently he thought I was giving him these packets, for he grabbed one of them—beef stroganoff—ripped it open, and poured the powdery contents into his mouth, smiling gratefully.

"Qujanaq. I have always liked White Man."

Now it was his turn to play host. He crawled into his heap of stones, returning with a thermos of ice-cold tea. Drink, he instructed us. We drank straight from the thermos (he seemed to have no cups) even as I wondered what diseases unknown to modern medical science I might pick up from a man capable of turning himself into a bear. The tea tasted like a decoction of swamp water and acid indigestion, yet custom decreed that we not offend him by spitting it out or getting sick.

We were his first real guests, Anda told us, since two Danish hikers dropped by nearly a year ago. I asked him where he got the tea and he said it came from his son Søren, who visited in the spring and the fall, hauling up supplies of tea, sugar, and flour along with batteries for his tape recorder. Now he inserted a cassette of music by the early 1970s pop group Seqijaq (Good-for-Nothings) into this recorder, and we were treated to a sound not unlike a herd of wildebeest in heat. Evidently he hadn't cleaned the tape heads in a long, long time.

"*Ela.* How many winters do you think I have?"

"Seventy," I replied, trying to be diplomatic.

"I am forty-seven."

All at once he burst into tears and retreated into his hovel, where I could hear him crying with the softness of a child. My diplomacy had failed miserably, and now I felt rather miserable myself. I had not wanted to hurt this man: to be alone for fifteen years in these unnurturing mountains ranked him, in my mind, with the Desert Saints. It didn't matter that he set new records in the categories of filth and bedragglement or even that he was maybe a little crazy. To me he was genuinely heroic in his pursuit of a fate hardly more sup-portable than the antlers on the great Irish elk (they weighed the animal down and eventually killed it).

Anda appeared at the doorway with a battered old Lee-Enfield rifle aimed directly at my head.

"Go! Leave me with my shame . . ."

We went. Fifteen minutes later I looked back, and my last glimpse of Anda the *qivigtoq* was of a man older than the hills squatting beside his stones and smoking his pipe in apparent contentment.

July 30. Snow: like tiny parachutes of eiderdown floating from the sky. I'm still feeling somewhat uneasy about yesterday's incident. Also a little scared. The twin adrenal meatballs keep you aloft for a while, but when they have finished with their edifying work you splatter down messily to terra firma. Twenty-four hours later, Anda's stubby brown finger on that trigger seems to have been etched in my mind just a few minutes ago. Only now do I recall that he had some sort of ring—a wedding ring?—a joint or two down from the bluish dirt under his nail.

"You see, Pencil?" says Paulassie. "It is not a good thing to steal another man's solitude."

July 31. Slow descent down a slope seamed with gullies. Then through a thicket of dwarf rowans a foot high and possibly two hundred years old, full of ptarmigan burbling sweet nothings to each other. Finally we come out on a tidal estuary and head west along Hvalsøy Fjord. The island Arpatsivigaq rises up on one side of us like a vast brooding joss-house idol and the mountain Qaqortoq rises up on the other, higher still, the deity to whom the idol is offering homage.

Then we see the old Hvalsøy Church resting in a field of bright buttercups. It's a church after my own heart, being humble (about the size of a medium-sized chicken coop), disused (since the fifteenth century), and ruined (very). Roofless, too. It reminds me of certain ramshackle Irish abbeys whose stonework the local farmers are not beneath shifting to their garden walls. Nowadays God enters such abodes directly through the clear open air rather than through the more difficult and oft-haphazard mediation of an earthly appointee. And when there's not a soul around, as here, He simply readjusts His sights and infiltrates the souls of rocks and the ever-present souls of mosquitoes.

On September 14, 1408, the last Viking marriage of which any record exists took place at this church. After that ceremony, silence. A haze of last things. The newly married couple, Thorsteinn Olafsson and Sigrid Björnsdottir, stand for a single halcyon moment among the buttercups and then disappear forever. Their descendants disappear forever, too. Atoms have been smashed, artificial life installed, human life spawned in petri dishes, and the Moon walked upon, yet the fate of these last ice-bound Vikings in Greenland remains a mystery. Did the absence of new blood doom them to a slavering idiocy? Were they perhaps kidnapped by Barbary pirates and peddled in the white slave trade? Might they have been wiped out by the Black Death? Did they travel across to North America and, as the explorer Vilhjalmur

Stefansson once suggested, mingle their debased genes with the rather better genes of the so-called Copper Eskimos? Or were they simply eaten alive by the mosquitoes? History fails to provide an answer. European history, that is. A little over a century ago, an old Greenlander named Abraham told the Danish folklorist-mineralogist Heinrich Rink the following story, which he'd heard from his father:

In distant time Greenlanders and Vikings lived together on the shores of Hvalsøy Fjord. One day a Greenlander was paddling off to hunt birds when he met a Viking standing near the water. The Viking said: "Silly man! Do you actually think you can hit a bird with one of those little darts? Why, I bet you can't even hit *me* with one of them . . ." The Greenlander obliged him with a dart between the eyes. This killing infuriated the other Vikings, so they raided a Greenlandic camp and killed everybody, including women and children. Now the Greenlanders were infuriated. They paddled their kayaks to Hvalsøy Church, which they set afire. Inside the church the Vikings were tossing the head of a Greenlandic woman back and forth as if it were a ball. So intent were they with this game that they didn't realize the church was on fire. They continued to toss the head back and forth until they burned to death. All except Ungartoq (Ingvar), their leader. He leaped from a window with his young son under his arm, warding off arrows with his bare hands. A Greenlander named Kaissapê pursued him into the mountains, where Ungartoq paused for a moment to fling his son into an icy tarn (better the boy should die by his father's hand than the hand of an enemy). Finally Kaissapê caught up with Ungartoq in the shadow of Igaliko Cathedral. He shot arrow after arrow into the man, but to no apparent effect. Yet he had one last arrow, which came from the lamp rack of his barren wife and was endowed with magical powers. Kaissapê shot this arrow into Ungartoq's heart and thus the last Viking in Greenland fell down dead . . .

Later, while inspecting the church, I notice quite a lot of old char on its worn granitic blocks, as if someone had indeed attempted to torch it long ago. I tell Paulassie old Abraham's story, which he has never heard before. He merely shrugs and says:

"My people and your people, Pencil, they never did get along together."

August 1. Final day. It's warm and windless, which means a diaphanous bonnet of mosquitoes around our heads. They scent out every little morsel of flesh where the Tiger Balm hasn't been applied and then they dig in with an enthusiasm that suggests we might be their last chance for motherhood. Paulassie says the best antidote is beer, lots and lots of beer. I'd heard of smearing seal oil or reindeer fat on your skin, but this was a new one to me.

"You rub *beer* over your body?"

"No, you stupid White Man. You drink it and then you will forget all about the mosquitoes."

At the lake Olserssuaq we observe our first human beings in almost a week not begrimed with filth or supernaturally endowed. And what human beings! They're a bunch of young girls cavorting naked in the lake, giggling, laughing, splashing, and sometimes even swimming in the upper six inches of water (below that is hypothermia country). Paulassie and I glance at each other and nod appreciatively. After so many rough albeit rewarding rocks, so many undulating moraines, so many yellowing bones, these girls are like a vision of earthly delights visited upon the last place on earth you'd expect to find it—a secluded glacial valley with an icy glacial lake and a few ground-hugging white rhododendrons which seldom bloom for more than two weeks a year and are blooming right now . . .

Whereas most towns in Greenland seem to represent urbanization on the South Bronx model, Qaqortoq (pop. 1,700) represents the Danish provincial model. Perhaps that's because it has a fairly large population of provincial Danes to keep it free, more or less, from Greenlandic urban blight. ("Qaqortoq has no recreational homicide," a local friend of mine once quipped.) The town is quaint, safe, and pleasantly dull. It even has Greenland's only village green. All in all, it seemed like a perfect place to rest my weary limbs after our long trek. But shortly after we arrived, I dropped by the shipping office and learned that the MS *Disko* would be docking here tomorrow en route to Nuuq and wouldn't be coming back for another two weeks. If I didn't take it, I'd be stuck in Qaqortoq for those two weeks, which seemed like rather a long time to spend staring at Greenland's only public fountain.

I bought Paulassie, a bit belatedly, a good pair of hiking boots and treated him to a whale steak at the Nanoq Restaurant.

"Where are you going now?" he asked me. Tomorrow he'd be heading back on the *Alega Ittuk* to his Dole pineapple-labeled house in Igaliko.

"To Nuuq. Your capital. The Western Settlement of the Vikings."

"It is very bad in Nuuq. They say it has the most suicides of any city in the world."

"I've heard the same thing said about Aasiaat."

"Aasiaat is not a city . . ."

After dinner I walked him to a dance that was being held in the local recreation hall. We promised to stay in touch, but I knew we wouldn't. The wilds exalt camaraderie only when you're passing through them, and it's a far more intimate camaraderie—no bodily odors barred, nothing sacred, and virtually nothing private—than the fellowship of the city. But we weren't in the wilds anymore and even now I could feel my friendship with Paulassie ebbing gracefully. His mind was already on the girls he'd be meeting at the dance; my mind was on the boat trip up the coast. He picked up a package of condoms at the door (condom machines were no good; they froze), turned to me and said, *"Ingerlalluariarnat, Allaut!"* (Safe journey, Pencil), then walked in. He did not look back.

Before I turned in, I watched a hunter flensing a ringed seal down by the dock. The animal's dead eyes stared up at me, and its flippers lay at its side like futile baby hands. The hunter was just beginning. First he took out the gall bladder so it wouldn't explode and taint the meat; then he removed the liver, a culinary delight of the first order, especially when it's raw and still steaming; then he reached in for the intestines. While his countrymen were being trained by the Danes for the high-tech future (or the sheep-farming nonfuture), here was this man seated happily in a puddle of gore, with the startlingly thin intestines of a seal like a cat's cradle in his hands. He wiped his greasy fingers on his anorak as if he were trying to waterproof it.

We chatted. The man spoke without looking up, in rhythm with his work, as if each word were a sinew. He told me this story:

Once a raven and a seagull got into a fight over a piece of meat. The raven was on the Inuit's side, the seagull on the side of White Man. They fought for days, for weeks, even for months. Whoever won, his side would be the stronger. They tore and bit furiously at each other. At last the seagull won: White Man would be stronger and more plentiful than the Inuit. But by the time he flew away with his piece of meat, it had become quite rancid.

The man told me this with such quiet conviction that I knew it was the truth.

Our Man In Everest

If Maurice Wilson had not existed, it's highly unlikely that a member of the scribbling trade would have thought to invent him. Instead, we'd beseech our Muses to come up with someone a bit less outrageous, like, for example, Sir Edmund Hillary. But Maurice Wilson did exist, strange to say. And even stranger to say, he continues to exist, a testimony, of sorts, to the human spirit.

Born in Bradford, Yorkshire, in 1898, the son of a well-to-do woolens manufacturer, Maurice seemed headed for the same kind of stolid career as Wilson père when the Great War intervened. The young man fought at Ypres, after which he suffered fatigue, depression, inexplicable aches and pains. No doctor could help him, so he turned to a homeopath, a man with decidedly Eastern whims.

Food's the problem, always is, this doctor informed Maurice. Food's bad for a person's body. Just fast for a couple of weeks, old chap, and you'll be as good as new.

Maurice had nothing to lose, so he subsisted for thirty-five days on a diet of rice-water, with a few slugs of meditation thrown in. By the thirty-fifth day he indeed seemed to be, if not as good as new, at least better than he'd felt in a long, long time. Shortly thereafter he had a vision in which an unusually thin but otherwise robust God appeared to him. The Supreme Being seemed to be taking the cure, too.

From then on Maurice set himself the task of bringing this cure before the eyes of the world. One day he happened on a newspaper cutting about the ill-fated 1924 Everest expedition. He read it through with interest, deciding that if mountaineers Mallory and Irvine had only fasted, they would have reached the hitherto unreachable summit of Everest, lived to tell the tale, and likewise been able to forgo the hateful task of high-altitude cookery. To prove his point, he concocted a plan for his own personal Everest expedition. He would fly solo to the mountain, crash his plane on East Rongbuk Glacier, and—dosing himself with rice-water—trot up to the summit, Union Jack patriotically in hand.

There were just two practical objections to Maurice's plan. He knew nothing about mountain climbing and he couldn't fly a plane. Mere details. He bought a secondhand Gipsy Moth, rechristened it *Ever Wrest*, and proceeded to take flying lessons at the London Aero Club. That he earned his pilot's license is indicative of the loose if not downright unfettered standards of the time. As for climbing, he made a few modest scrambles in Snowdonia and pronounced himself fit. The prospect of altitude sickness didn't trouble him. For he reasoned that the less food his body took in, the more room it'd have for oxygen, a commodity he knew to be rather more scarce on Everest than in North Wales.

By April 1933 he was ready to gatecrash the mountain Tibetans call Chomolungma, the Mother Goddess of the Earth. But first he decided to say goodbye to his parents. En route to Bradford his engine cut out and he crashed into a farmer's hedgerow. He was unhurt. Undaunted, too. A month later, he was ready to try again. But now the Air Ministry caught wind of his eccentric plan and sent him a restraining order in the form of a telegram. He tore up this telegram and off he flew. Somehow *Ever Wrest* managed to sputter and wheeze a passage as far as Darjeeling, India, but there it was impounded. Well, I'll just have to walk the rest of the distance, Maurice announced. The British refused him permission to enter Tibet on foot, too. So he simply disguised himself as a Sherpa and, as promised, walked the rest of the distance.

On April 12, 1934, Maurice reached Rongbuk Monastery. Two days later he set off by himself to ascend the Mother Goddess of the Earth. His most important item of gear was a shaving mirror. This he intended to use as a heliograph from the summit, so the world would know of his success. With an ice-axe borrowed from the head lama, he began hacking steps, none of which led in the direction of the summit. At one point he found some discarded crampons, but such was his ignorance—nay, innocence—that he just threw them away, having no idea what they were for. His haphazard ascent was finally brought to a halt by whiteout conditions. In his diary he wrote: "No use going any further . . . It's the weather that has beaten me—what damned bad luck!"

Back at the monastery he engaged the services of two local Sherpas, Rinzing and Tewang, for another assault on the mountain. They'd show him the proper route to the summit, he reasoned, and then he'd be able to carry on by himself.

So it was that the slightly revised Maurice Wilson Everest Expedition made the ascent to Camp III. Here they discovered a food cache left behind by Hugh Ruttledge's expedition the previous year, and Maurice—late of the rice-water persuasion—happily gorged himself on anchovy paste, Ovaltine, sardines, King George chocolates, and other goodies from Fortnum & Mason's. One can imagine the erstwhile faster turning to his Sherpas and guiltily pressing a chocolate-smudged finger to his lips.

For the next three days a ferocious blizzard pinned them to their tents even as it threatened to blow those tents away. Then, on May 21, the blowing abruptly ceased. Rinzing and Maurice started up to Camp IV, not trotting, hardly even climbing, but mostly just clawing at the iced-up mountain. Maurice queried his companion as to the whereabouts of Ruttledge's ice steps, made the previous year. They'd found Ruttledge's chocolates, hadn't they? He seems not to have realized that a good wind can whittle ice steps into oblivion in scarcely more time than it takes to read this sentence.

Around noon they parted: Rinzing went back to Camp III while Maurice climbed on by himself. In the next few days, he distinguished himself by starting an avalanche, sliding backwards over two hundred feet of icy verglas, breaking some ribs, and accidentally destroying all his matches. When at last he staggered back to camp, he was considerably more dead than alive. But defeated? Not bloody likely! He'd just come back to pick up his Sherpas, who, he figured, might be of some use in his assault on Camp IV. But the Sherpas refused to climb even another fifty feet with him. For they'd come to the conclusion that their sahib was, at the very least, a loony.

So it ended for Maurice Wilson exactly where it began: a man alone against a mountain. No fellow climbers, no superfluous technology, not even a piton. No rice-water, either. *Alone.* The most stubborn Yorkshireman in the world against the most stubborn mountain in the world. Now we watch that man trudging wearily through the snow. Now he stands at the foot of the North Col and gazes up . . .

The following year Eric Shipton, Charles Warren, and H.W. Tilman were themselves trying to reconnoiter a North Col route to the summit. It was the morning of July 9 and Warren was walking a little ahead of the others. A few hundred yards above Camp III he spotted a perfectly good pair of boots lying in the snow. Soon he saw a crumpled green tent torn from its guy ropes, along with an equally crumpled Union Jack. He thought this might be an earlier expedition's dump site until he saw the body itself, huddled in the snow. "I say," he called out to Shipton, "it's that fellow Wilson . . ."

Maurice was wearing—well, that's where accounts seem to differ. According to Warren, he was wearing a mauve pullover, lightweight flannel trousers, and thin socks, attire somewhat more suitable for high tea in Mayfair than the high elevations of the Himalayas. But in the next few years, another story spread: Maurice had been dressed in silken panties and a brassiere, possibly heels, too. Though the story has never been officially verified, a woman's high-heeled shoe was in fact found close to Camp III by a later expedition. Whatever Maurice's sartorial preferences, it was clear that death had come about as a result of exposure, not starvation. Which, one feels, is how this devotee of starvation would himself have preferred it.

Near the body Shipton located the weather-beaten diary in whose pages Maurice had recorded his perpetual struggle with the mountain. The entries were nearly all of a piece. "No food, no water . . . terribly cold . . . dead tired . . . must somehow go on . . ." But of how he occupied himself toward the end, or roughly when that end might have come, the diary provides not a clue. Nor does it bother to mention the deceased's taste, maybe bizarre, maybe not, in wearing apparel.

Shipton and Warren wrapped the body in its tent and slid it into a nearby crevasse, where, by all rights, it should have remained. But you can't keep a good man down. Over the years Maurice has surfaced with macabre regularity, thrust forth by the movements of Rongbuk Glacier. In 1960 Chinese climbers found him and dutifully reburied him. More recently, he's been sighted by Japanese, German, and yet more Chinese climbers. It's as if the Mother Goddess were offering her myriad visitors a bit of advice by repeatedly putting Maurice on display, as if she were telling them: Dance to the beat of your own drummer, my friends. Follow your star wherever it may lead you. And above all, keep the faith, as this gentleman himself seems to have kept it, even unto his own very cold end.

The last entry in Maurice's diary, penciled thinly but clearly, in a shaky hand, reads: "Off again, gorgeous day . . ."

Feeding My Demon

Suddenly my hand felt it. A bump that squatted hard and dime-sized near the middle of my balding pate. I gently nudged it, but it did not go away. Then I picked at it, rubbed it, kneaded it, even gave it a tentative knock or two. Though it still refused to go away, I did manage to learn the lay of its geography with a certain intimacy. For instance, the bump's north slope was steep, almost vertical, while its other slopes consisted of soft billows and more moderate inclines. There was some sort of nodule, cairn-like, on the summit.

I couldn't recall being bitten by a black fly, mosquito, or other insectual bump-producer. Nor could I recall walking into an open door which should have been closed or a closed door which should have been open. Nor had anyone struck me with a rock, at least not lately. The bump seemed to have erupted all by itself, the result of some perhaps significant flaw beneath the surface of my skin.

The more I thought about this possible flaw, the more worried I became. My writing began to suffer, then my appetite, then my personal hygiene. Even my table manners suffered. For it's not easy to wield a knife and fork while simultaneously feeling a bump on your head. So frequently did I feel the bump, in fact, that it acquired a rich lacquerlike finish.

My worry still needed to be grounded in the ink-dark reality of print. So I picked up the medical encyclopedia that occupies pride of place next to the O.E.D. on my desk. Since there were no entries in the index under "bump," I went straight to the hard stuff. Soon I had reduced my options to either an ivory oseoma or a Ewing's sarcoma. Reading through the descriptions of these cranial protuberances, I did not encounter the word fatal. But it was my job, not the book's, to maneuver that word into its appropriate position. And once maneuvered, my job to put the proverbial coppers over my eyes.

I performed this job flawlessly, if I do say so myself. First I cancelled all my social engagements. Best not to keep friends and relations waiting for the eternity that always accompanies one's demise. Then I took to my bed. For I figured it would be a good idea to prepare myself for my Last End by simulating its recumbent posture. I was just beginning to negotiate a peace settlement with my Maker when the telephone rang. Not wanting someone's jolly voice to violate my perishing condition, I didn't answer it. Even the thought of jollity made me feel a little less ill, thus a little more ill.

As it happened, I didn't perish. My deathbed turned out to be only my unassuming futon, with no metaphor, mortal or otherwise, attached. But that's another story, one which I'll save for later. Right now I want to say a few words about the condition commonly referred to as hypochondria. It is a condition described by James Boswell, himself a notable hypochondriac, as "incidental to all sorts of men, from the wisest to the most foolish." Charles Darwin was a sufferer. So was Percy Bysshe Shelley. So too was a certain unnamed gentleman from the Italian town of Senes, who, according to Robert Burton (in *The Anatomy of Melancholy*), was "afraid to piss lest all the town should be drowned; the physician caused the bells to ring backwards and told him the town was on fire, whereupon he made water and was immediately cured."

But I never use the word hypochondriac to describe myself, not even on those rare occasions when, relatively affliction-free, I can be objective. If Hell is Other People, then hypochondriacs are Other People, too. Highstrung, self-absorbed, highly neurotic people. People like that curious gentleman from Senes. People like my own grandfather, who once checked himself into a hospital because he thought he was pregnant.

What makes me different, more or less a special case, is my demon. *It* bears the responsibility for my damnable condition. I know: putting the blame on a demon ("My demon made me do it") is a defense serial killers and mass murderers often use to justify their line of work. All I can say in my own defense is that the only person I kill serially is myself.

This demon has staked out my entire body, from bregma to toe, as its lair. When it gets tired of the solar plexus, it burrows into my heart cavity or liver. It even rummages around my groin area. At least once it gnawed a huge hole in my left metatarsis. But it is by nature secretive, so secretive that I've never laid actual eyes on it, although I suspect it is covered with a thick bristly pelage, has a rather bulbous belly, and possesses fangs, claws, or at least something extremely sharp. Also, its gender would seem to be masculine.

One thing is certain, however—my demon's disposition is quite disagreeable. Seldom does a day go by when it doesn't send up an ache, a migraine, a strained muscle, heartburn, or an enigmatic jolt of pain. By doing this, it appears to be saying: *That's to punish you for keeping me a prisoner of your physiognomy.* Or maybe it's punishing me simply for owning a physiognomy.

If I don't feed my demon, its disposition becomes even worse, so I feed it morning, noon, and night. Best of all, I feed it when I'm sitting at my typewriter (no computer for me—all those noxious rays!), pecking away. Such an innocuous action, and yet my demon thrives on it because it's like a metronomic reminder of mortality. Back and forth, back and forth the keyboard shifts, from upper case to lower case, from imminent decease to eminent disease. *There!* Now I've got a brain tumor. And though this brain tumor pays less well than an article, the act of creating it doesn't require nearly so much sweat.

I suffer no shortage of friends who believe I can rid myself of my demon. Recently one such friend, a woman versed in Jungian lore, mentioned active imagination. You should practice it, she said. But I've already been practicing active imagination, I protested. Not the positive kind, she replied. I felt slightly nauseous upon hearing the word positive. Just a little reflex of mine. Even so, I listened while she told me how to call on a guardian spirit capable of battling the demon.

All right, I thought, I'll give it a try. I settled back on a comfortable chair, let my mind go mystically blank, and lo! who should appear but Wolverine, trickster-transformer figure of the Naskapi Indians (one of my books is about the Naskapi). Wolverine created our world by putting his lips to Muskrat's ass and blowing heaps of inchoate mud out of Muskrat's mouth. Surely he could wrestle one man's obstreperous demon into submission. So off I sent him on a journey into my own unexplored interior. It wasn't long before he came back, tail between his legs, whining pathetically.

Reason the demon out of existence, others suggest. Tell myself that one little bump is not a microcosm of the body's intricate and glorious mechanism. Nor does that bump a grave make. Remember what Yogi Berra, that equable man, once observed: It ain't over until it's over. Not only that, but even when it appears to be over the body can always snatch victory from the jaws of defeat with a late inning rally.

But my demon inhabits a time that precedes Reason, precedes the ancestral loincloth and the rough adze, precedes even the invention of language itself. Which is probably why my words never have any effect. They seem to hit a solid wall out there in millenial space and then bounce right back to me, albeit with not a shred of their original meaning still intact: Death has to start somewhere, they now inform me, and an unnatural growth on the skull is as good a place to start as any.

Maybe I'm not trying hard enough to get rid of the demon. Or maybe I don't really want to get rid of it. We've been together for so long, my demon and I, that we've developed a close if somewhat morbid relationship. O the times we've shared, the situations, the near calamities! Through thick and thin it has been my staunch familiar, unswerving in its loyalty, like a faithful dog, and never less than consistent, like a faithful scorpion. To whom would I turn if it took up residence in someone else?

There have been times too when I feel genuinely sorry for it. I mean, solitary confinement in a human body can't be much fun, but solitary confinement in *my* body must be downright miserable. Doubtless that's why a low, mournful keen occasionally seems to escape its lips. This cry from the depths never fails to wrench my heart. Whenever I hear it, I feel obliged to feed the demon even more lavishly than before. And then it has been known to respond with a generosity that I'd hardly expect from so loathsome a creature. In fact, it is most generous not when it giveth but when it taketh away.

Consider my bump. It went away after only a week. Vanished into the same subcutaneous mystery out of which it originally came.

Needless to say, I felt jubilant about this. Now I could start up the business of living again. I also knew a reprieve when I saw one, so I vowed to change the error of my ways. Henceforth I would support more noble causes, recycle all my garbage, be more charitable to the homeless, stop being rude to Republicans, even be nicer to my demon.

But scarcely had the bump gone away when I detected a lump under my right armpit. Lumps are worse, obviously, than bumps. At the very least they indicate lymphatic cancer, particularly if they happen to be of the armpit variety. It was all I could do to drag my three-quarters defunct body to the doctor's office.

"It looks like a mosquito bite," my doctor said.

"You mean it's not cancer of the lymph nodes?"

"It's a mosquito bite. Or maybe a bedbug bite. Nothing to worry about."

"Assuming you're right, what happens if it gets infected?" I had an image of my armpit somehow being amputated.

"We'll zap it with a course of antibiotics," the doctor told me. Then he said, more or less as an afterthought, "Believe it or not, you're one of the healthiest people I've ever met."

Ah yes, I sighed sadly: that's exactly the trouble.

An Arctic Cave Man

've never been particularly attracted to the luminaries of Polar exploration—Commander Robert Peary, Frederick Cook, Captain Robert Falcon Scott, Rear-Admiral Richard Byrd, even Sir Ernest Shackleton. They seem to me an unpleasantly obsessive bunch, and with the exception of Cook, who was a convicted felon, a rather colorless bunch as well. At least one of them, Peary, had the disposition of a predacious corporate tycoon. "Mine at last!" he exclaimed upon attaining (or not attaining) the North Pole, as if he'd just engineered a hostile takeover.

John Hornby was not really an explorer, although he covered more ground in the Arctic, much of it unexplored, than Peary ever did. In fact, it's hard to say exactly what Hornby was. One thing is certain, though: he was a dangerous man to travel with. And yet I would have rather traveled with him than with one of the goal-driven stars of the Arctic pantheon . . . as long as I could clear out at the first sign of catastrophe.

Born on September 21, 1880, at Church Minshull, Cheshire, Hornby came from an affluent cotton-spinning family and was by education a Harrovian. His mother was the daughter of Sir Herbert Ingram, publisher of *The Illustrated London News*; his father, Albert "Monkey" Hornby, was one of the country's most celebrated cricketers and a friend of Edward VII. The family moved easily in the world of social privilege. John Hornby himself grew up amid an endless succession of lawn parties, cricket matches, and fox hunts. He also grew up in a large house, Parkfields, whose chief characteristic seems to have been the oppressively dark trees which surrounded it.

Hornby later claimed to loathe civilization. In making this claim, he was probably confusing civilization with his own background, which he loathed, too. He made his break with this cushy, somewhat rarified background when he left England for Canada in 1904, thereafter returning home only for brief, obligatory visits.

But there was another reason he didn't return to England. He'd fallen in love, although not with a woman. Women, for Hornby, were more or less dispensable. What he fell in love with was an entire geography, the Canadian North, and especially that rugged, desolate, heroically beautiful part of the North known as the Barren Lands (a.k.a., Barren Grounds or just plain Barrens). With its tumbled heaps of tumulus, sweeps of tussocked sedge, and ridges of frost-shattered rock, this is a landscape perilously close to the bone. And whoever goes into it usually comes out closer to the bone himself, wiser and with less cheap shine, if he manages to come out at all.

Hornby made his first trips in the Barren Lands with such capable northern hands as Cosmo Melvill, Guy Blanchet, George Douglas, and Vilhjalmur Stefansson (whom he insisted on calling Stevenson). Once he became more or less capable himself, he began heading into the bush alone or with a few hard-bitten Barren Land trappers. From the beginning, he seems to have been a sort of proto-Outward Bounder, a man who could tough out any situation, however adverse. A veteran trapper who knew him told me: "Jack Hornby could go further on a diet of snow, air, and scenery than a car can go on twenty gallons of gas."

Hornby was fond of saying that he wished he'd been born an Indian, which is probably another way of saying that he wished he hadn't been born with a silver spoon in his mouth. Yet the way he lived was similar to an Indian's in at least one respect: it was guided more by whim and improvisation than by foresight or the demands of comfort.

Indeed, he couldn't have cared less about comfort. If a trek wasn't difficult or a portage backbreaking, he would make it so either by choosing the trail of most resistance or by shouldering packs that were twice his weight. He would live in caves or the rudest of rude cabins. And not for him the overcooked fare of his countrymen: he preferred his meat raw or, even better, putrid. He once ate some bread on which a skunk had squirted, gleefully pronouncing it "the meanest eating I ever encountered." Such habits invariably contributed to his reputation as "The Hermit of the Arctic."

Unlike most of his contemporaries, however, Hornby wasn't searching for any particular Arctic Grail. He had no interest in the North Pole, the Northwest Passage, or in converting the Natives to an alien faith. Nor did he tend to pursue will-o-the-wisp dreams based on the discovery of precious minerals. What Hornby wanted was simply to meet the rough integrity of the North with an equally rough integrity of his own . . . and with no safety nets whatsoever. He regarded hardship and the ever-present specter of starvation as, if not exactly virtues, at least conditions to be accepted and then over-come—English pluck with a vengeance. So it was that he would pro-vision his bush trips with little more than a rifle, a gill net, a bag of flour, and tea.

Hornby had some close calls, of course. Darcy Arden, Jr., a long-time resident of the Arctic bush himself, told me this story: "My father found Jack at one time digging in the snow near the east arm of Great Slave Lake. He seemed pretty well gone. He told Dad, 'I'm looking for a wolf skull that I threw out a while back.' He was going to cook down that skull for his supper since he had nothing else. Dad gave him some food and probably saved his life."

Old-timers like Darcy often use the word "bushed" to describe Hornby's behavior. When they say someone is bushed, they mean he's gone off the deep end as a result of spending too much time in the backcountry. And yet I wonder if at least some of Hornby's behavior can be attributed simply to eccentricity, a trait the English seem to have perfected. For Hornby was an undeniable eccentric. Wherever he went in the Barrens, he would carry a crumpled evening suit in a satchel. He would turn up at the National Museum in Ottawa wearing this suit, then empty its pockets of mouldy and mummified mouse carcasses, which he somehow believed were valuable scientific specimens. For reasons he never really explained, he refused to travel with anyone who didn't have blue eyes.

But whatever sort of person John Hornby might have been before World War I, he was a very different person afterward. In 1914, he joined the 19th Alberta Dragoons and departed for the War in Europe. In 1915, his unit survived the German assault at the Second Battle of Ypres. Later he received a commission as Lieutenant with the Second Lancashire Regiment. On July 4, 1916 he was wounded—and probably shell-shocked—at the Battle of the Somme. This wound was sufficiently severe that he had to be evacuated to London.

The War convinced him that the world had gone completely mad. In 1917, he returned to the relative sanity of northern Canada. Those who knew him, like explorer George Douglas, said that whereas he had been steady, albeit a bit erratic before the War, he was now unpredictable and unreliable, a man whose screws seemed to be working their way slowly loose.

Enter Captain James C. Critchell-Bullock. An Englishman, a descendant of wealthy Wiltshire farmers, and a graduate of Sherborne, his background was not unlike Hornby's. But there the resemblance ends. In contrast to Hornby, who happily gutted animals over his sleeping bag, Bullock was a military man with a military man's sense of discipline and decorum. During the War, he'd been the official cameraman for General Allenby's triumphant entry into Aleppo. It was while serving in Allenby's Palestine campaign that he contracted the malaria that eventually forced him to resign his Army commission. And in 1923 he went to Canada for a rest cure. What followed was neither a rest or a cure, but a typically harrowing trip with Hornby.

In 1924, the two men set off on an expedition to the Barren Lands. Darcy Arden recalls seeing them in a scow on Great Slave Lake toward the start of the trip, and what struck him most was the apparent tension between the two men: Hornby was "talking up a storm," while Bullock was silent and seemed a little sullen. Bullock, in fact, was quite upset with his partner. Since he'd financed the expedition, he regarded himself as its leader. Hornby, however, had already decided he was the leader. This, after all, was *his* country; and a certain part of him wanted to protect it from bounders like Bullock. He also took a dim view of all the photographic equipment that Bullock had stashed among their provisions. For him, the crucial thing was to travel light . . . and now they were traveling heavy rather than light.

In accordance with Hornby's cave-dwelling propensities, they found an esker near Artillery Lake and excavated it to make a ten by seven foot shelter. A more comfortless place to spend the winter would be difficult to imagine. There was almost no light, snow blew in on them, and glacial till from the ceiling drifted down more or less constantly. Being something of a troglodyte, Hornby seems to have been delighted with this accommodation. Bullock was not. Nor was he delighted with Hornby. In the film footage he shot of the trip, there's almost no evidence of his esker mate.

Their spring escape from what Bullock described as their "hole" was vintage Hornby—a journey that embraced mishap and hunger almost, it would seem, by choice. They took arguably the least convenient route available to them, eastward via the Hanbury and Thelon Rivers, rather than west down the Casba and over Pike's Portage, which was the way they came. By the end of the trip, they may or may not have been wiser men. Certainly, they were much thinner ones. Much more egalitarian diners, too—at one point, they were obliged to eat a wolf, innards and all.

On their canoe trip out of the Barrens, they passed a stand of spruce trees near a sharp double bend on the Thelon River, sixty miles southeast of the Thelon's junction with the Hanbury River. The spot seemed like an oasis to the two men; they hadn't seen any trees other than dwarf willows and birches in over a year. Hornby remarked to Bullock that he'd like to come back some day and winter over there. "Not with me," Bullock informed him tartly.

Enter two "greenhorns," Harold Adlard and Edgar Christian. Adlard had wanted to join the previous expedition, but Bullock turned him down on the grounds that he was physically unfit. Edgar Christian was Hornby's first cousin, an 18-year-old schoolboy with no previous wilderness experience. The boy idolized Hornby, so his father asked him to include "dear Edgar" on his next expedition, in order, he said, to make a man out of him. Frank Christian knew that his cousin had made numerous trips to the Great White North; he did not know that Hornby was a very risky man to travel with.

So it was that in 1926 John Hornby embarked on his final Barrens trip, accompanied by Adlard and Christian. Their destination, he decided, would be the oasis on the Thelon he'd seen with Bullock. Shortly after they started out, he broke open a couple of bottles that he'd planned to use for his so-called scientific specimens. Then he proposed a toast to the expedition with (in the absence of champagne) glycerine and neutral grain spirits. This toast set the tone for a trip that would become increasingly dominated by missing ingredients. The last person to see the Hornby party alive, a trapper named Fred Linde, later reported that the group had no provision of meat with them, in fact no food at all except for a few bags of flour. This was intentional; Hornby had wanted them to live entirely off the land.

In time-honored Hornby fashion, the party traveled in such a desultory manner that they missed the annual caribou migration southward. This error of judgement probably didn't matter too much to Hornby. For he seems not to have been content unless he was playing Russian roulette with his life. Now, of course, he was playing it with the lives of two other men, both of whom looked to him as a sort of northern guru.

Two winters of silence followed. On July 21, 1928, a group of geologists traveling down the Thelon noticed a rough-hewn log cabin a short distance from shore. They called out. There was no answer. Called out again. Again, no answer. The geologists approached the cabin and found a pair of bodies, Hornby's and Adlard's, wrapped in red Hudson Bay blankets just outside the door. Inside, they found another blanket in a bunk. One of the men, Kenneth Dewar, gave this blanket a slight pull and a skull rolled out. The skull was Edgar Christian's. "I'm sure the four of us getting out of that cabin would have been a sight to behold," Dewar later wrote.

The geologists reported their gruesome discovery to the Royal Canadian Mounted Police when they reached Chesterfield Inlet several weeks later. It was too late to do anything that year, but the next year three police officers arrived to bury the bodies and recover their effects. While inspecting the cabin, they found a piece of paper with this barely legible inscription written on it: WHO . . . LOOK IN STOVE. In the stove was Christian's diary, which described how each of the men, Hornby first, then Adlard, and Christian last, had starved by slow inches in this oasis on the Thelon. From its pages, Hornby emerges as an altogether heroic, selfless person; just the kind of person you would entrust with your life. And in his last hunger, maybe John Hornby was exactly that sort of person, too.

Almost seventy years later I traveled down the Thelon and visited the same rough-hewn cabin myself. Scarcely more than a heap of rubble, it was in the process of being reclaimed by what passes for ground cover at this latitude. A hundred feet away were the graves of the three men, each marked by a simple wooden cross—the cross with "J.H." written on it was tilted at a very precarious angle. I found it hard to imagine any sort of tragedy occuring here. The sky was giddy with blue; bright fritillary butterflies were fluttering about; a robin was caroling; and delicate Arctic wildflowers seemed to be everywhere. I remember thinking: what a lovely place to spend a bit of time . . .

Certainly, John Hornby's last expedition accomplished little beyond its match-up of three pitifully ill-equipped travelers against the pitiless Barrens. On the face of it, the earlier trip with Bullock was equally lacking in consequence. It didn't add anything new to science, resulted in no new maps being drawn up, and did not come back with any ethnographic data on the Natives. It was not even remarkable by the standards of previous Barrens trips: the English gentleman-adventurer David Hanbury, the brothers James and Joseph Tyrrell, and Police Inspector Ephrem Pelletier had already traveled a roughly similar route.

Yet the story of the Hornby-Bullock expedition does not end here. After he left the Barrens, Hornby stopped off in Ottawa and gave the National Museum the usual mouse carcasses. But he also gave Hoyes Lloyd at the Department of Interior a manuscript entitled *Report of Explorations in the District Between Artillery Lake and Chesterfield Inlet.* This sixteen-page, single-spaced report made a simple recommendation: that immediate measures be taken to protect the wildlife of the Barren Lands from human exploitation.

Lloyd took Hornby's report seriously and passed it on to the Advisory Board on Wildlife Protection. They, in turn, passed it on to the Dominion Government for approval. On June 15, 1927, the Governor General of Canada put his signature on an order creating a sanctuary of 35,000 square miles in the Upper Thelon region. The Thelon Game Sanctuary thus became Canada's first official wildlife preserve. Today it remains the country's largest tract of protected wilderness.

Had he lived, John Hornby—a man who valued wilderness above all else—would have been quite gratified by this.

A Visit to the Zoo

Setting out from the town of Terrace in British Columbia, you drive northwest over washboarding seemingly calculated to destroy your transmission. Likewise you try to avert potholes so deep that they should be signposted with "Abandon Hope All Ye Who Enter." Suddenly, in the middle of an apparent nowhere, you come upon a medley of tents and tarps, converted school buses, trailers, teepees, Winnebagos, and rough plank shanties. Welcome to Cranberry Junction, pop. 250. Or at least that's what the name on the road sign says. But nearly everyone in these parts calls this seasonal bush settlement The Zoo.

"This place has lots of animals, but they've all got two legs, and they're all here to pick mushrooms," says one of The Zoo's residents, an eroded-looking, fifty-something man who goes by the name of Alberta Al.

Mushrooms—specifically, the large creamy-white to bronze-colored mushrooms called matsutakes—are in fact The Zoo's raison d'etre. In Japan, matsutakes are symbols of fertility, wealth, and happiness. The Japanese also prize them for their subtle flavor and unique odor, described by one mycologist as "a provocative compromise between red hots and dirty socks." Since the Japanese demand for matsutakes far exceeds the local supply, wildcat buyers descend on the rain-soaked Pacific Northwest each fall and pay pickers top dollar—cash up-front, no records kept—for this fungal delicacy, often as much as $300 a pound in good years. In bad years, well, there's not much overhead on a teepee or plank shanty.

Not surprisingly, The Zoo is a bit like a Gold Rush town, with fortunes made, broken, or drunk away almost as fast as you can say matsutake. Its citizens are a bit like Gold Rush characters, too. They include hirsute sons and sturdy daughters of the forest, the unemployed and the unemployable, certified eccentrics, the disenfranchised, the opportunistic, and wanderers with no fixed abode. There's a man named Wormy Pete who boasts that he hasn't had a bath in at least a year, and a toothless but otherwise attractive woman who cheerfully lowers her jeans to reveal a matsutake tattooed on each buttock.

In front of a rundown trailer sits a huge barrel of a man who calls himself Tiny. Tiny has come all the way from Truro, Nova Scotia, more than three thousand miles across the continent. "This is about freedom, man," he says, making a 360 degree sweep of his hand. "Freedom to roam where you like, sleep where you like, and do what you like."

After a pause, he adds: "I haven't paid a penny in taxes in five years."

His pause is not without significance; mushroom harvesting is probably Canada's most noncompliant underground economy, so pickers tend to be somewhat reticent about speaking with outsiders, who may or may not be representatives of the law.

The Zoo has a cookhouse which offers, according to a piece of cardboard tacked to the door, "Three Coarse Meals." It has two churches, both nondenominational and neither much bigger than one of the community's port-a-loos. It also has several illegal saloons operated by bootleggers. Supposedly, there's even a brothel.

The town is more or less deserted during the day, when pickers are roaming the steep, forested slopes of the nearby Skeena Range in search of mushroom bounty. Then, in the late afternoon or early evening, the pickers return and make a beeline for the shanties that serve as both buying depots and local hangouts. In one of these shanties, you might hear snatches of conversation like the following:

"Some bastard raided my patch, and all he left me with was three empty beer cans and a Snickers wrapper."

"Every mushroom I found was slushed out or full of bugs, but then I tripped on a deadfall and landed with my nose right on top of a Grade 1 pine [matsutake] . . ."

"I got a real mother lode today. Probably forty pounds of hooters [buttons] and only two or three flags [mushrooms with open caps]."

"Just look at this beauty—a seventy-five-dollar matsie!"

". . . chased down a mountain by a bear, but luckily I didn't lose a single mushroom . . ."

Buyers sort the mushrooms into six grades, weigh them, and pass wads of bills into the hands of pickers. The thickness of the wad depends on the condition and grade of the mushrooms, the current Asian market, and whether there's a price war going on among the buyers. It might also depend on a buyer's mood that day: if a dog bit him, the price might be lower than usual, and if his girlfriend declared her undying love for him, it might be considerably higher.

Prices can shift dramatically during a twenty-four hour period. Today's price may be almost twice yesterday's, and vice versa. There's a story about a picker who got lost in the woods for two weeks, and when he was found, he was suffering from severe hypothermia. Even so, he was still gripping his bag of by now rotten mushrooms. According to the story, the man's first intelligible words were: "What's . . . today's . . . price?"

Each night the closing of the buy stands is announced by a volley of gunshots. This usually occurs around nine o'clock, so the night is still young. There isn't a lot in The Zoo you can spend your money on, no fancy restaurants, for instance, or movie theaters, so what's a picker to do? Being somewhat thirsty by nature, he might get boozed up. Then you might see a few punches exchanged, or someone who's imbibed not wisely but too well sleeping it off in a rain puddle. And since liquor lubricates the tongue, you might also hear the occasional tall tale, like the one about the matsutake so big that it could be removed from the ground only with a winch or chainsaw, but alas! the picker who found it had neither implement with him.

"Despite everybody having knives and some having guns, there's not a whole lot of violence around here," observes a man named George, who refers to himself as the Mayor of The Zoo. "Well, there was an incident last year when two guys got into a fight, and one ended up killing the other. But they were fighting over a woman, not mushrooms. Somehow I think they got their priorities mixed up."

Increasingly frigid temperatures and even snowfall would not deter stalwarts like George, Alberta Al, Tiny, or a woman who calls herself The Iron Maiden, but frost and snow do deter matsutakes. So it is that when the weather turns wintry, the pickers pull up stakes and either go home or head south along the mushroom trail, to places like Bella Coola and Boston Bar in British Columbia, and then later in the season, Washington and Oregon.

Whereupon The Zoo, bereft of its nomadic menagerie, once again becomes Cranberry Junction, a mere potholed crossroads in the back of the Great Northern Beyond.

A Gigantic Mythopoeic
Literary Volcano

Some years ago, in the slate-quarrying village of Blaenau Ffestiniog, Wales, I paid a visit to Phyllis Playter, the longtime companion of the writer John Cowper Powys. She was a tiny, ancient woman whose skin was stretched like parchment over her bones. At one point I asked her how she met Powys. She said: "It was in Joplin, Missouri, in 1921, and Mr. Powys was lecturing on Dostoevski. The lecture was so powerful that three people in the audience fainted. I knew he was the man for me."

I fell for Powys myself, although not quite in the same way. In college, I was fed a steady diet of professor-friendly, eminently deconstructable texts, many of them seemingly written for classroom exegesis. I yearned for, if not stronger stuff, at least less polite stuff, and acting on a tip in Henry Miller's *The Books in My Life*, I began reading Powys. I started with a 1929 novel called *Wolf Solent* because I thought it might be about wolves, possibly in the manner of Jack London. It couldn't have been less about wolves. It concerned an extremely introverted man, Wolf Solent, and his courtship of two very different women. The supporting cast included a lecherous sausage-maker, a peddler of antiquarian pornograpy, a homosexual clergyman, a voyeuristic country squire, a teenage boy who kisses trees, and a mad poet. Here, I thought, is God's weird plenty.

What struck me when I reread *Wolf Solent* recently was not its weirdness, but its compassion for the down-and-out, the aberrant, and the misbegotten. What also struck me was its casual attitude toward polymorphic sex. "Natural or unnatural," says one of the characters, "it's still nature. It's mortal man's one great solace before he's annihilated . . ." I can't imagine anyone else of Powys's generation writing those words. Certainly not D. H. Lawrence, who was a veritable reactionary about matters of the flesh compared to Powys.

You don't read Powys so much as enlist in him. *Wolf Solent* is over six hundred pages long. Two later novels, *A Glastonbury Romance* and *Porius*, are nearly twice that length (in hardcover, they make formidable weapons). Even the shorter novels invite the Jamesian description of "loose, baggy monsters." Powys himself detested James and often, when asked about a writer he liked, would mention Homer, although sometimes he mentioned Sir Walter Scott. His own writing is epic, grandiose, often wildly rhetorical, and probably undeconstructable. He was not, in other words, a *petit maître*. He could be guilty of absurdities, as when he describes Tom Barter's soul leaving his dead body in *A Glastonbury Romance*; and yet he was also capable of exquisite moments, as when, in the same novel, a drowning John Geard can think only of "snuffing the sweet sweat of those he loved."

"A great modern novel consists of and ought to include just about *everything*," Powys wrote. In including just about everything himself, he was a maximalist writer in an increasingly minimalist age. Among recent writers, I can think of no equivalent to him except, perhaps, Patrick White. Both seek the transcendent in the ordinary, and both occasionally spin their wheels in trying to evoke such an elusive quarry. But White received a Nobel Prize. Powys never received any prize at all except a bronze plaque from the Hamburg Free Academy of the Arts a few years before his death.

To certain readers, Powys is a long-winded, bombastic bore, an almost pathological celebrant of oddball sex and chthonic realms. To most, he is an unknown quantity. His name seldom comes up in discussions of that dreary academic figment known as The Novel, and I know a number of well-read people who've never even heard of him. Over the years, he's had some reputable allies—Henry Miller, Robertson Davies, Angus Wilson, George Steiner, Iris Murdoch, J.P. Priestley, Elias Canetti, and Philip Larkin, who referred to Powys as a "gigantic mythopoeic literary volcano." But he remains, in the phrase of Martin Amis, "a monument of neglect."

Perhaps if he'd been a member of a fashionable literary movement like the Bloomsbury group, he might have achieved more recognition. But I find it difficult to imagine a man who described himself as "a born Camp-fire or Cave-fire storyteller" having tea with Lytton Strachey and Virginia Woolf. In fact, Powys avoided literary company; he would no sooner have taken part in a writer's conference than in a gathering of morticians. A triumphant solitary, he avoided nonliterary company, too. He didn't serve in the Great War because he had a phobia about urinating in public . . . or so he says in his *Autobiography*. With Powys, you sometimes can't tell whether he's pulling your leg or pulling his own.

Yet he did belong to at least one literary group—his own family. Of his ten siblings, seven ended up writing books. Theodore, probably the best known of these siblings, wrote short stories and novels (*Mr. Weston's Good Wine*); Llewelyn wrote rather florid nature essays and memoirs; Philippa wrote a novel and poems; Littleton wrote autobiographies; and Bertie wrote about architecture. All together, the innumerable Powyses produced well over a hundred books.

Born in 1872 in Derbyshire, England, John Cowper himself had a typical upper-middle class upbringing that shuffled him methodically from his father's vicarage to Sherborne School, Cambridge, and a career as a country schoolmaster. Then, in 1904, he did something wholly atypical: he traveled to America and turned an innate talent for the histrionic to good use by becoming a freelance lecturer.

His lectures must have been remarkable, especially the ones on literary figures. "With almost an erotic emotion, as if I were indulging myself in a kind of perverted love affair," he wrote, "I entered the nerves of Dickens or Henry James or Dostoevski . . ." At the same time he never ceased to be John Cowper Powys, a high-strung, perpetually dishevelled Englishman. Once, when he was getting ready to lecture, his hostess whispered to him that his fly buttons were undone. "Madam," he replied, "I wear them that way." I suspect this was true.

One reason Powys went to America was to escape the English class system, whose snobberies, restraints, atrophied manners, and cults of discretion he hated. He hated them so much, in fact, that he devised a sort of reverse class system. "The deepest emotion I have is my malice against the well-constituted as compared to the ill-constituted," he declared in his 1934 *Autobiography*, adding: "Dwarfs, morons, idiots, imbeciles, hunchbacks, degenerates, perverts, paranoiacs, neurasthenics, every type of individual upon whom the world looked down, I loved, admired . . . and *imitated*."

A word about this unusual *Autobiography*: it is a record not of Powys's achievements, but of his various inadequacies. In it, he describes his manias and phobias, his "idiotic" mouth and "Neanderthal" brow, and particularly his sexual failures. He discusses "the sickening moments of dead sea desolation that come to me from my ulcerated stomach" and his chronic constipation. He calls himself "a scarecrow Don Quixote with the faint heart of a Sancho." And yet the *Autobiography*'s mood is not gloomy or self-pitying. After all, this is a book written by a man who finds it desirable to be "ill-constituted."

No doubt Powys's feelings of inadequacy contributed to his being a comparatively late bloomer as a writer. He was forty-three when he published his first book, a collaborative memoir with his brother Llewelyn entitled *Confessions of Two Brothers*. There followed two Hardyesque novels, *Ducdame* and *Rodmoor*, and then *Wolf Solent*, each written primarily on trains as he was traveling between lectures. At last, in 1930, he settled down with Phyllis Playter outside the town of Hillsdale in New York's hardscrabble Columbia County. At age fifty-eight, he began to earn his living, or what passed for a living, as a writer.

By now his ulcer had become, as he put it, "rampageous." A diet of raw eggs, milk, olive oil, and bread crusts did little to assuage it. Also, his bowels were so out of whack that he had to have an enema every third day. But he thrived, or at least his Muse thrived, and in his four years in upstate New York, Powys wrote *A Glastonbury Romance*, another novel of epic proportions entitled *Weymouth Sands*, and the *Autobiography*, along with a book of idiosyncratic popular philosophy called *A Philosophy of Solitude* (sample quote: "When you think in a seated posture, you think with your rump, not your soul").

In 1981, while staying in nearby Austerlitz, I visited Phudd Bottom, Powys's improbably named upstate retreat. It was not very different from dozens of other clapboard, slightly ramshackle houses in the area, but just down the road I noticed a house that *was* different. It was surrounded by a fence on each of whose pickets there appeared to be a decapitated human head. The owner turned out to be a retired dumpkeeper who'd cut off the heads of plaster saints, dolls, and sculptures discarded by locals and impaled them on his fence as decoration. He was an elderly man, and as it happened, he remembered Powys.

"Now there was one strange guy," he said. "Used to walk around in the snow in his bare feet. He'd say he just forgot to put his boots on. And then you'd sometimes see him banging his head on the mailbox. Strange guy."

Actually, Powys didn't bang his head so much as tap it against the mailbox, a ritual he believed would insure the safe delivery of a letter. He'd also utter lengthy incantations while bathing, walk exactly the same route every day, and bow to exactly the same trees and stones. One of these stones he named "the god of Phudd." Another he named Perdita. Perdita, he wrote, was "the only daughter

I shall ever have"; he once felt obliged to kiss his geological offspring nine times because his dog had peed on it (her?).

Nowadays such behavior probably would be called obsessive compulsive and classified as a disorder. Powys didn't think of it as a disorder, however. He indulged in it, exulted in it, flourished it like a standard, and ultimately used it to his advantage as a writer. For the flip side of kissing stones or tapping your head against the mailbox is a volcanic talent for putting words to paper.

In 1935, Powys moved to Wales. This was not only a physical move, but also a journey into his own past. Wales was the land of his distant ancestors as well as home to the sixth century magician-cum-bard Taliesen, who'd been a sort of role model for him since childhood. In fact, he sometimes called himself as a "tatterdemalion Taliesen."

Powys was at heart a primitivist for whom virtually every modern invention was anathema. As early as *Wolf Solent*, he referred to airplanes as "spying down on every retreat like ubiquitous vultures." He never drove a car and never used a typewriter. He thought television was pernicious. He refused to talk on the telephone because he didn't want his words violated by a tangle of wires. So it's not surprising that after his move to Wales, he looked to the inviolate past, especially the inviolate Welsh past, for inspiration.

He was now working on a novel about Owen Glendower's failed rebellion against Henry IV of England—the same event Shakespeare dramatized in *Henry IV, Part I*. An enormous novel (the first chapter, in manuscript, was three hundred pages long) set in fifteenth century Wales was not the most practical of projects for a financially strapped writer in his late sixties. And he was *quite* strapped: at the time his publisher Bodley Head accepted the novel in question, *Owen Glendower*, Powys had less than fifteen pounds in the bank.

To call *Owen Glendower* and his next book, *Porius*, historical novels would be a bit like calling *Moby Dick* a sea story. The former includes scenes of rather dubious historical accuracy, including one in which Owen shares his thoughts with a merganser (the merganser reciprocates by sharing its thoughts with him), while the latter starts out more or less realistically in the Edeyrnion Valley in the year 499 A.D., but then quickly shifts to a sort of Welsh Never Never Land.

Porius is, I think, Powys's masterpiece. It calls to mind novels as diverse as *One Hundred Years of Solitude, Finnegans Wake,* and *Alice in Wonderland.* At times it reads like an extended study of what Powys called "the three incomprehensibles" (sex, religion, and nature); at other times, like a magical mystery extravaganza. In one chapter, an owl metamorphoses into a bird-maiden; in another, the hero, Prince Porius, mates with an aboriginal giantess while her father is plucking corpses off a battlefield with cannibalistic intent; and in another, the bard Taliesen (Powys's mouthpiece) chants verses about "The ending forever of the Guilt-sense and God-sense/, The ending forever of the Sin-sense and Shame-sense . . ."

I can imagine the alarm at the offices of Simon & Schuster, Powys's American publisher, when the novel's 1,589 page manuscript arrived. The author, always somewhat intemperate about book length, now seemed to have gone totally round the bend. Not surprisingly, Simon & Schuster declined to make an offer on *Porius,* as did every other American publisher Powys's agents approached. A reader for Bodley Head insisted that the manuscript be trimmed by at least a thousand pages. At this Powys, a man normally compliant with publishers' requests, howled. He was an organ of communication for the departed spirits of the sixth century, he said, and didn't that count for something? Only Powys could have invented a ploy like this.

Except it might not have been altogether a ploy—he may have actually thought Taliesen had spoken to him, albeit from inside his own skull rather than a distance of fifteen centuries. For he believed that his "ichthyosaurus-ego," as he called it, could draw on a store of memories that date as far back as the dawn of human experience, maybe back even farther. Powys is not the only one who held this conviction. Dr. C. G. Jung of Zurich believed more or less the same thing, but without the dinosaur designation.

Porius was published by Macdonalds in an abridged edition in

1951 (the complete version didn't appear in print until 1994). Although Powys was now close to eighty, he did not go gentle into the so-called good night. He went eccentric into it. He would entertain visitors by acting out the stoning of St. Stephen for them. Immediately after getting up in the morning, he would pray to a host of heathen deities, including Demeter, the Greek goddess of agriculture, and Cybele, the Phrygian goddess of nature.

And he kept putting pen to paper. Indeed, Powys's literary output in old age was so voluminous that upon learning he died in his ninety-first year in 1963, you're almost inclined to say: "Yes, but did he stop writing?"

His last books are loopy, free-form fantasies in which anything can happen. The venerable Odysseus can travel to the lost continent of Atlantis, for instance, or Time can suddenly materialize as "an enormous black slug." In his final work, *All or Nothing*, a science fiction story apparently written for children, someone called the King of the Milky Way wanders about the solar system with his penis slung over his shoulder. Silly stuff, perhaps; but silliness, for Powys, was an antidote to the numbing effects of machined logic.

Powys spent his last years as a semi-recluse, seldom leaving the obscure Welsh mining town where he lived. But he was not a forlorn figure. Quite the contrary. There's a certain majesty in the image of this craggy, rumpled old man, foolscap tablet in his lap, writing, endlessly writing, as if the world depended on his words. He may have been a monument of neglect, but he seems not to have cared whether he was neglected or dutifully fêted. What mattered to Powys was pursuing his own bliss, and this he did right up to the end.

On my visit to 1, Waterloo Place in Blaeunau Ffestiniog, I couldn't help but notice the waterfall just behind the house. I found its noise disconcerting, even annoying, since I could barely hear my hostess's frail voice above the clamor and din of plunging water. When I mentioned the noise to her, she said, "Well, Mr. Powys found it essential . . ."

The Preserved Woman

The town of Loudon Falls was starved for a good woman. Oh, it had Molly Billingsly, who was far too old, and Pumpkin Anson, who was far too generous, and it had a few drunk and miserable squaws who turned up one day after the Southport Indian Reservation collapsed into the sea during a winter storm. But the good women, they pulled up their stakes at the very first opportunity and headed down the coast. Soon even the bad women got to be pretty scarce. Dull listless eyes—the same eyes, men's eyes, boys' eyes, darksome children's eyes—greeted the traveler from every window. Then Madeline Corrigal was discovered. She was six feet one inches tall in her bare feet and had a wasp waist and her hair set in a neat bun, and she must have been some beauty in her day. Barney Ames dug her up in his blueberry bog.

As Loudon Falls neither had nor desired nor could afford a law enforcement officer, Barney took the news of his find to Armand Anson, the selectman.

How long do you think she's been dead? Armand inquired.

Oh, I'd say a hunnerd years or more.

She isn't all decomposed?

Not in the places I've looked. There's worse looking women walking around in Ellsworth and married, too . . .

I guess it's that acidy bogwater. Keeps a body good as new. Better than embalming fluid, that stuff.

A check of the town records showed that the woman was Madeline Corrigal, who died for love in the year 1871. A traveling salesman arrived in the district and courted her. Seeded her and left her, poor girl. When she saw she was to become a mother, she was so overcome by shame that she killed herself. Took a dose of rat poison. For this she was buried in unconsecrated ground. And there she lay, preserved in the bog, her resting place unmarked and her sad tale forgotten. Until now.

Well, said Armand. We don't need the state coming up here and making all kinds of ruckus. Who knows what filth they'd unearth? My advice to you, Barney, is just keep quiet. Don't tell a soul about her.

Barney nodded. He was a naturally reticent man and it was no difficult matter for him to keep quiet about Madeline. Armand himself only told his daughter Pumpkin. Pumpkin was the town pump, acne-ridden and shapeless and under the age of consent though she was. Few parts of her were as loose as her lips.

After seeing Armand, Barney went home and covered up the woman with bog. To him it was like she didn't exist anymore. But for Madeline Corrigal, it would be her last night on a century of calm. Next morning Barney was driving fence posts on his back forty, and he happened to glance up and there was Edge Boatwright excavating away at his bog. He hastened over to where Edge—the town dowser—was shoveling soil right and left in a kind of frenzy.

Looking for a well, Edge?

Edge said he couldn't control his curiosity. He had to come and see the preserved woman. That's what he called her. That's what Pumpkin Anson had called her. The preserved woman. A woman taller than any man, better looking than any female you'd see on the streets in Ellsworth, silver ringlets in her ears, feet pointed and delicate like slippers.

Well, I suppose I oughter show you then. As you've made the trip all the way out here. An' so you won't be carryin' back tales about silver ringlets and beauty contests . . . Barney threw back the dirt till Madeline lay exposed in all her glory to Edge's goggly eyes.

Jesus Baldheaded Christ! the dowser gasped. I can't rightly fathom if she's the most beautiful thing I've ever seen or the ugliest.

The rat poison, Barney said. It messes up the innerds, but it keeps the outside pure.

Rat poison?

Yep. She killed herself for love.

Edge went on staring like it was the peepshow at the Fryeburg Fair. When Barney decided the man had had enough, he tossed the dirt back over Madeline. Much obliged, Edge said. On his face was a look of visible pleasure.

Quickly, with Pumpkin's help and Edge's, Madeline Corrigal became legend around Loudon Falls. Neighbor told neighbor about her, and with each telling she took on a new character. She was an old-timey free-love advocate who lived on rats and died of an overdose of them. Or she was not real at all but manufactured from a mass of molding clay by—who? Rewt Stringer? He liked to create strange sculptures in his yard from auto parts. Or she was a Negress—her skin *did* have a rather darkish hue—who died of loneliness in these light-skinned parts. Someone said she wasn't dead at all but in a deep coma and told Johnny Cope to put his lips against hers and see if she didn't turn into a princess. Now Johnny Cope was a little soft in the head. And he hadn't yet been so lucky as to kiss a woman—only goats and a few heifers and his brother lost-at-sea's gravestone. Right away he fell in love with Madeline though he didn't know her from Adam's off ox.

From their decayed colonials, their tarpaper shacks, from out of the very woodwork, folks emerged and they headed for Barney's to dig the woman up. First, like Edge Boatwright, they were only curious. Then they began to come for the sport of it, young and old alike.

Hey Hank. Me an' some of the fellows are goin' down to have a look at the preserved woman. Why don't you come an' join us?

Well, I promised the boy I'd take him fishing . . .

Bring him along instead. It'll be an education for him . . .

A few of these visitors would dig Madeline up, gaze on her for a bit, and bury her right back again, same place. Most of them, however, would leave her fully exposed to the noonday sun. By now Barney was getting a little ruffled. On a decent Saturday afternoon, his blueberry bog would resemble a football gridiron after a game. It did no good to bury her in another part of the bog. They always managed to find her again. Barney figured that they posted a sentry somewhere. One day he caught Johnny Cope with Madeline in his arms, kissing her wildly, his eyes all hope and enthusiasm. That was the last straw as far as he was concerned. He could tolerate the invasion from town no longer. He cuffed Johnny across the ear and told him to go home.

She's still the same, Johnny whimpered. She ain't no princess.

Get on home, boy. You're trespassing.

Maybe I ain't kissed her enough . . .

Here now. You're stepping all over my berries.

You only want her for yourself, the boy pouted.

You got the squirts, boy. Get out of my field or I'll see you buried here yourself. Go on, scat. At last the halfwit got the message and took off pell-mell and rackergaited for home.

Barney hoisted Madeline up over his shoulder, like she was either plunder or a wedding partner. She wasn't very heavy. Barney found he could hold her and cross the blueberry plain at a steady trot. He intended to bury her where she wouldn't be subject to Saturday afternoon sports. He settled on an area near his workshed, safeguarded from prying eyes by the shed itself as well as his house. The first time he dug, he struck rock. He moved over several feet and struck rock again. The ground would not accommodate a burial unless he blasted, and he couldn't blast without the whole town knowing about it. So he took her around back where the soil ran deeper, set her down gently, and commenced digging again. But he halted almost immediately. He was no more than ten feet from the privy. It wouldn't be fair to the woman, interring her next to a privy.

You might say he was beginning to take a proprietary interest in Madeline. Just like she was a crop of blueberries, he wanted to keep her out of harm's way. But he couldn't very well take her back to the bog and lay her with the blueberries. And it appeared that he couldn't bury her next to the house, either. Like many a man in his predicament, Barney merely reached into his pocket for a wad of snuff. He inserted the snuff between his gum and lip, then let his mind go completely blank, the better to ambush a passing thought.

Now Barney Ames was only a poor turdknocker. He wouldn't have recognized wealth if it bit him on the left testicle. He always kept his sights set low as the lowbush blueberry that he grew, cultivated, pruned, and picked. At that level he could spot a tussock moth at thirty paces. He could sniff out gray mold blight or powdery mildew a mile away. But Jesus Smuttynosed Christ, it was a pauper's life! Barney thought of all the people crowding his plain for a look-see at Madeline. If only he could put up a fence and turnstile and charge admission . . . Then he had a brainstorm. Turning to Madeline, he chuckled: You an' me's gonna make some money, sweetkins . . .

The woman, she showed no interest at all. And the way she smelled, even money would have given her a wide berth. Barney wanted to attract customers, not flies. So he got himself a bucket of bogwater and gave her leathery body a good washing. Something came off in his hand, a flap of skin or old clothing, hard to tell. But she did look better all scrubbed and clean. And she smelled less like a rotten mattress than like the earth from whence she came.

Next Barney headed into town and asked Rewt Stringer for a big glass case with a sliding door. He handed Rewt the specifications. And make it airtight, he said.

Credit?

I expect a bumper crop this year, said Barney with a smile.

Several hours later he was driving back with the case tied tight to his pickup. He paused by his mailbox and beside it he put a placard that read:

SEE THE FAMOUS PRESERVED WOMAN OF WASHINGTON COUNTY
ONLY 25 CENTS (CHEAP)

He stepped back and scratched the stubble on his chin. Squinted. He was not a whole lot satisfied. Madeline Corrigal had been a good woman, and a good woman should be worth more. Barney crossed out the 25 cents and wrote 50 cents on the placard. That was better. He didn't feel like he was shortchanging her now.

In the beginning, business wasn't bad. Hosy Cutwell came, and he hadn't been seen all year; many took him for dead, in fact, till the prospect of Madeline coaxed him out. Milt (The Real) McCoy, who raised turkeys, put in an appearance; likewise Turkey Bigelow, who torched his barn but ended up burning down his house and wife instead; Edge Boatwright twice; Josh Applegate, the manure-broker; Mem Bragdon, who distilled rotgut by the light of the moon; the Billingsly twins, Mort and Mack, hale and hearty in their ninetieth year; and the local Congregationalist minister, Mr. Ashley.

Ezra Adams, the undertaker, brought his whole family. He took a professional interest in Madeline. He gazed at her admiringly. Couldn't do a better job myself, he said.

It really wasn't me, Barney told him. It's just that she's a natural . . . And he looked with pride at the glassed-in woman. She was seated on a large blueberry crate with her hands folded demurely in her lap. In those hands he had placed a lily. He had combed her hair as best he could and wrapped a shawl that had been his mother's over her shoulders. All in all, she seemed quite comfortable. A person might even have construed on her ancient lips the makings of a smile.

And then, of course, Johnny Cope came. The town albatross. Only a matter of time before he showed up. Barney winced. Sorry, Johnny, he said. Only paying customers . . .

Johnny Cope grinned a great, beaming, full-mouthed grin. He

emptied his pockets into Barney's hands: a dead fieldmouse, a fish-hook, a moist hanky, a spent shotgun shell, and a return ticket stub from the State Farm. God's plenty. Johnny allowed as how he was the payingest customer of all.

The boy was so eager, Barney let him enter the house. And enter he did, embracing Madeline's glass case with a full-bodied hug. Barney had to restrain him. Now you just sit down here, he said, pulling up a chair. And Johnny sat in front of his lady love eyeing her the whole livelong day. Ever so often, he'd mumble cryptic things to her in his idiot tongue. Barney vowed not to let him come back. The genuine customers would object to him. *He* objected to him. The boy gave him the creepy-crawlies staring like that. And so when Johnny returned the next day and held out a dead sparrow and an old Canadian Pacific Railway menu, Barney barred the door.

Hey Barney Ames. I want to see my princess.

She ain't yours, Barney said. She's mine. An' you better not pester me anymore 'less you got four bits.

I want to see her.

Barney answered him by waving his .30-.30 Winchester out the window. Your carcass better be outa here by the count of three, he said. One, two . . . And he exploded with laughter watching Johnny light out across the field.

Toward the end of the week his business trailed off. Only a few lowdown and morose-looking gents from the barrel-hoop factory across the county stopped in to see the preserved woman. They peered at her and then departed without a word. Afterward Barney discovered that one of them had left a couple of iron washers in the till. Another put in a token that permitted the bearer two meals for the price of one at a defunct diner. Real lowdowns, Barney thought.

What had happened? He met Edge Boatwright practicing his dowsing beside the town water supply. He asked him what the explanation was for Madeline's sudden decline in popularity.

Edge said: My guess is, it has to do with that Pumpkin Anson girl. She's startin' to charge for her favors. It's all folks can do to come up with the money. She's got 'em on all fours, so she does. They don't have anything left over for your preserved woman.

Pumpkin Anson's flatter'n a pair of pieplates. Folks *pay* for her?

Sure do. Church collection yestidy was next to nothing. Saturday's her big night, I hear.

Christmas, what a world!

Yeah, an' I believe she got the idea for charging from your own little operation, fellow . . .

Barney spat out his snuff. He was ashamed to hang his hat in a town where a Pumpkin Anson could outdraw a good woman like Madeline Corrigal. His shame forced him to lower his asking price to twenty-five cents a visit. He even decided to launch a Pay Later Plan. His placard advertised family rates. But there were no takers. Madeline could have been lying neglected and forlorn in her bog for all the interest the fickle town now took in her.

And Barney's troubles still weren't over. One day Rewt Stringer drove up in his Studebaker-Packard-Dodge pickup mix. He said he needed the money right away. Else he'd have to repossess the glass case.

Don't got it, Rewt. Wait till berry season's underway.

Sorry, old pal. Jem Bragdon wants a phone booth for his store and this is as good a casing as any, I'm thinking. Now, would you mind removing *that*?

Barney knew better than to argue with a man who was the town tax collector. So he removed the offending body and helped Rewt load the case into the pickup. Before he drove off, Rewt mentioned an odor strong enough to flatten a bull elephant.

The preserved woman did seem to be less preserved than before. Barney decided to carry her back to her original resting place. This he did with a twinge of regret. All his moneymaking plans had come to naught.

A couple of days later, a foreigner from Massachusetts pulled up in front of the house, flashed his press card, said he was a newspaperman. He wanted to photograph the preserved woman for his paper. He was willing to offer ten dollars for the privilege. Needless to say,

Barney jumped at the offer. With this kind of publicity, he might be able to compete with Pumpkin Anson. He might even be able to corner the out-of-state market, which Pumpkin could never do. Pumpkin was at best a local attraction. Madeline was universal, a woman for the whole world to see and admire.

Briskly he set out with the newsman across his blueberry plain. They reached the spot where he had buried the woman. As the man stood poised with his camera, Barney heaved up shovelful after shovelful of bog. He dug to a depth of five feet, but Madeline Corrigal was nowhere to be seen. She'd gone and vanished on him! Flustered, he couldn't stop digging. Maybe he was mistaken about where he buried her. But he knew he couldn't be mistaken about a thing like that. He knew this bog like he knew his own face. At last the newspaperman coughed. Said he hadn't come all the way up here just to watch a man dig a new cellar hole.

She ain't where I put her, Barney shrugged.

The man called the whole story a hoax and drove away in a huff.

I'll get her back for you, Barney yelled after him. He dashed into the house and phoned up Armand Anson and told him that he'd been robbed. The selectman seemed to be in one of his dour, legalistic moods. He said: Strictly speaking, Barney, she isn't your property at all. Not at all. She belongs to the government.

The government?

Right. If you found, say, buried treasure on your property, the U. S. of A. has a claim on sixty percent of it. The rest is yours. But as this preserved woman can't be divided, being a person separate and entire, the U. S. of A. owns the whole lot of her outright. And it chooses—through me, its lawful representative—not to conduct an investigation as to the woman's whereabouts. Sorry, old poke. See you at bingo tomorrow evening.

Barney cursed the man under his breath. He figured that Armand was in cahoots with his daughter. Pleased as punch to have a monopoly on the local business now. Lord knows what rake-offs he was getting from Pumpkin. You're not going to see that woman's like again, leastways around here, he remarked to the selectman, and the blue dolefuls were in his voice.

Now a few folks said it was the exposure that finally got the best of Madeline Corrigal. She'd been dug up too much, she'd seen too much sun, and her antiquated system couldn't take it. Proverbial decay snatched her, they said, and ground her to dust in practically no time.

Others were less sure. Ezra Adams claimed she was put on display at some fair or freak show where she'd be more widely appreciated than she was in the town of Loudon Falls. Edge Boatwright heard that she had made it to the mummy division of the State Museum and he planned to visit her first chance he got. No, impossible, someone told him. All that manhandling had forced her out of her coma like a butterfly from its cocoon and she just rose up and walked off, just like that, left her bogland to seek her fortune elsewhere. Turkey Bigelow agreed. He had observed her or a woman very much like her, a tall woman and brownskinned, hitting up strangers for meal money in Ellsworth. Held for ransom! declared Roger Holly. Hell, no! Local hooligans got her, tore her to shreds, and fed the pieces to the gulls. Even a few people claimed it was Johnny Cope who did it, stole her and hid her so he could have her all to himself. Johnny was looking unusually blissful of late, like at last he'd managed to turn her into the princess of his dreams.

Whatever happened to Madeline, it was a given fact that Barney Ames never had a decent stand of blueberries again. If they came up at all, the berries would be bitter and withered and hardly fit for the hogs, every last one of them. The leaves would always be wilted and black like a hard frost had hit them. But no frost ever hit those parts in the middle of summer. It was all highly mysterious. Barney almost felt like something vital, some nutrient or other, had been sucked out of his soil.

Daughter of the Wind

A t times during my visit to the Mediterranean island of Pantelleria the wind sounded like a pneumatic drill gone awry, at other times like the high-pitched howling of Eskimo sled dogs, and still other times like a melancholy riff from a blues man's sax. Once it managed a pretty good imitation of Frank Sinatra crooning "I've Got You Under My Skin," albeit with an uncharacteristic vibrato. Another time it whisked off my cap and deposited it unceremoniously on a nearby Bronze Age tomb, laughing shrilly as I went to retrieve it.

Alternately bullying, keening, buffeting, and whistling, the wind on Pantelleria blows at twelve knots or more virtually every day of the year, including the day I arrived. On that day, a *sirocco* was scattering bits of the Sahara around the island. This legendary ill wind, sometimes referred to as "the African pest," reputedly causes indolence, insomnia, and even depression, so I asked the waiter at my hotel whether he was feeling any of its effects. Perhaps he regarded diners through a fog of ennui?

He shook his head rather more vigorously than one is supposed to shake a head when a sirocco is blowing. "Pantescans feel out of sorts only when there's no wind," he said.

A mistral blew in that evening. A cleansing wind, it swept away all evidence of the Sahara. I went out for a post-prandial stroll and instead of being blown north by the sirocco, I found myself blown in a southerly direction, which became southwesterly with the arrival of a levanter. I braced myself against being picked up and flung to Tunisia, whose flickering fairyland of lights forty miles away looked almost close enough to touch.

I know what you're thinking: that not even the wind-god Aeolus, try as he might, could have flung me all the way to Tunisian shores. But on an island where 2,500 year-old cisterns are still in use, donkeys move with nineteen different gaits, and the fabled voyager Ulysses is spoken of like a contemporary, anything is possible, even a levitation across forty miles of sea.

So it should not seem altogether surprising that when I woke up the next morning, I heard the wind imitating the Three Tenors in a knockdown, drag-out fight (Pavarotti, being the biggest, won).

At first I felt a bit disoriented, although not so much by the island's bravura winds as by its apparent borrowings from other places. The volcanic landscape reminded me of Iceland, the architecture suggested the Old Testament, the baking sun suggested Africa, and the stone wall traceries put me in mind of Ireland's Aran Islands. Jets of steam issuing from the ground made me think of Yellowstone, while the place names—Bukkhuram, for instance, or Farkhikhala—seemed to have been stolen from the Arabian Nights.

This curious hodgepodge is in fact part of Italy—the part that fell off or perhaps was blown away. Most of my traveled friends had never heard of it; one, a waggish Irishman, said, "Pantelleria? Sounds like a good place for stealing knickers off clotheslines." (The name is actually a corruption of the Arabic phrase *bint al Rion*, which means "daughter of the wind.") Another friend *had* heard of it: his first wife had run off with an Italian nobleman, and the place they chose to hide out from the world was Pantelleria.

Once upon a time, however, the island sat so squarely on the map that everyone had heard of it. Bronze Age people from North Africa, Phoenicians, Romans, Carthaginians, Vandals, Byzantines, Arabs, Normans, Turkish sea-raiders, Spanish, and Bourbons—all passed through its continually revolving door, marauding, setting up a government, working the island's obsidian deposits, or just pausing from their travels for a while. Such is the virtue, or the burden, of being located at the intersection of time-honored Mediterranean shipping lanes.

In 1860, Italy annexed the forty-five square mile island and began sending political undesirables there. In the 1930s, Mussolini referred to it as "The Black Pearl of the Mediterranean" and, in an unusual use for a pearl, made the island a military base, with the result that the Allies carpet-bombed it during World War II. The port town of Pantelleria was flattened; after the War, it was rebuilt in ugly low-rise ferro-concrete—to bomb it again, an unkind person might say, would be a mercy.

After so many assaults and flattenings, you might think this would be a paranoid island: What unwanted visitor will batter at our door next? But Pantelleria is more or less free from neurosis. "I embrace everything," it seems to say, and then proceeds to assimilate whatever fetches up on its shores, be it an architectural style, a foreign physiognomy, or a method of cooking fish. In doing so, it has managed not only to keep its sanity, but also, paradoxically, to remain *sui generis*.

Consider the island's traditional *dammuso* houses. With their barrel vaults, white stucco domes, three foot thick walls, and cube shapes, they speak of distant invaders—certainly the Arabs, possibly the Phoenicians, and maybe even Bronze Age Sesioti, who constructed mausoleums similarly domelike. At the same time dammusi seem so peculiar to Pantelleria, so spare and basaltic themselves, that they suggest not human influence so much as a geology that's taken a skilled architectural turn.

If the world's a beach, then the world has bypassed Pantelleria, since it has no beaches. Instead, its shoreline consists of basalt sufficiently fierce that a person who elects to lie on it runs the risk of impalement. So the wise visitor does as Pantescans themselves do: he looks inland, away from the invader-dark sea, for sustenance.

Thus it was that one day I went for a backcountry trek with a local naturalist named Giuseppe. Giuseppe's English was nearly as bad as my Italian, a fact that quickly became apparent when a trumpet-colored mutt tried to mate with my leg. "This god wants sex," Giuseppe observed. No matter: he possessed the innate Italian talent for making gestures speak as eloquently as words.

From the village of Siba, we walked north into the teeth of a wind that sounded like an amalgam of Philip Glass and flapping laundry. Within half an hour, it had shifted to the mellow throatiness of early Billie Holiday.

But it could not shift enough to benefit local agriculture. Olive trees looked like bonsai versions of this usually hardy Mediterranean evergreen; they'd been trained to grow outward rather than upward in order to avoid being snipped off by the wind. Nearby, grapevines were surrounded by windbreaks of cactus stem; where the cactus had blown over, the poor vines looked like victims of an anti-botanical blitzkrieg.

In the same vineyard, Giuseppe bent down and picked up a white terracotta shard. "Punic," he said. A moment later he picked up a reddish piece of ceramic. "Roman," he declared. Then he pointed to a few blue-and-white tiles and told me they were Arab, probably from around the year 1000 A.D. All of the island's variegated influences seemed to be at our feet.

"Is this an archaeological site?" I asked.

"No," he said, "just an ordinary Pantescan vineyard."

We passed several dammusi so Middle Eastern in appearance that I half expected to see the involuted forms of Arab script on their walls. Their domed roofs, designed to collect rainwater and channel it to underground cisterns, gleamed in the midday sun like giant white bubbles. In front of one, a large-paunched man with burst singlet buttons was splayed over a bench and drinking heartily from a flagon of wine—an image straight out of Brueghel.

Mediterranean *macchia* soon replaced the terraced vineyards. Its resinous scent, comprised of bush oak, maritime pine, rock roses, honeysuckle, myrtle, and various xerophytic shrubs, nearly lifted me off my feet. I also saw enough wild herbs (thyme, fennel, rosemary, sage, oregano, borage, etc.) to stock a kitchen cabinet. Giuseppe pointed to some pale pink mallow flowers: Did I know they made a superior herbal tea? Then he pointed to some rue (*Ruta chaliepensis*) and said Pantescans use it as an unguent for hemorrhoids.

Later I read that the island hosts more than 570 varieties of plants. All thanks to the incessant winds, usually less than beneficial, for blowing such an abundance of seeds here from Europe and North Africa, and for bringing relief to local hemorrhoid sufferers.

We now began climbing a partially collapsed volcanic cone called Gelfiser. There was black scoriaceous rock everywhere, including the inside of my hiking boot. Where there wasn't rock, there were fissures in the rock—Gelfiser means "Fissure Mountain" in Arabic. I stepped into one of these fissures and ended up with a colorful souvenir of the island on the lower part of my leg.

At one point I looked around, and there seemed to be nothing but unspoiled, untrammeled Nature in every direction. "Marlboro Country," Giuseppe announced with a sweeping gesture of his hand. Yet we were no more than a few miles "as the cow flies" (in Giuseppe's phrase) from the modest bustle of Pantelleria town, and even closer to an American hill-top radar facility.

At last we arrived at our destination, a large cave extending deep into Gelfiser. Recently, a friend of Giuseppe's had descended into the bowels of this cave and discovered a rusty Norman sword sticking upright in the rock—shades of Excalibur! Now Giuseppe wanted to search for other relics, possibly bits of ceramic, possibly bones, that might help explain what the mysterious sword was doing here.

We began rappelling into the cave's gloom. The passage was tight, and it soon got tighter. All at once I felt violently claustrophobic. It was too dark for me to read my Italian dictionary, so I just yelled out the word claustrophobia in English. As it happened, the word was almost exactly the same in Italian.

"No more *caverna* for you, my friend," Giuseppe said after we were outside again. Well, that wasn't entirely true. We investigated another, less deep cave and found a scattering of Arab tiles just inside the entrance. I got the impression that you can bend down almost anywhere on Pantelleria, even seemingly inaccessible places, and pick up some sort of artifact.

As we hiked down, the Mediterranean suddenly came into view. Peacock-blue around the island, it clung to the horizon like a filament of liquid silver. "*Bello*, eh?" I said.

"*Puah!*" Giuseppe exclaimed, half in jest but half seriously, too. He said he'd grown up with such a strong dislike of the sea that he never learned to swim and, to this day, refused to eat seafood, even the Pantescan specialty *couscous di pesce*. It was because a member of his family had been kidnapped by Turkish sea-raiders. He gestured northwest to indicate where they'd come from.

I asked him when this unfortunate incident had occurred.

"Not long ago," he said, adding: "In the seventeenth century."

Wherever I went on Pantelleria, I felt vigilant eyes gazing in my direction.

The chinks in the Bronze Age tombs at Mursia seemed to be squinting at me as if they were trying to figure out whether I was friend or foe, harmless visitor or rapacious sea-raider. Dammuso windows seemed to look at me hopefully, as if I might turn out to be another Giorgio Armani. In Gadir, the underwear-to-evening wear designer had bought and renovated a set of dammusi, thus providing them with a life considerably more elegant than the one to which history had accustomed them.

Pantescans themselves often gazed at me as if I were from another planet. Once, when I was clambering down from the hill of San Marco, site of first a Punic, then a Roman acropolis, an old woman interrupted her journey to the well, set down her buckets, and gave me a stare that must have lasted a full minute.

At the time I assumed the woman was only registering her curiosity about outsiders. And with my Ouje-Bougoumou Cree cap, my "Shiitake Happens" T-shirt, and my diligent scribbling, I was a slightly more flagrant outsider than most. But when I discovered a dead fritillary butterfly floating in my cappuccino the next morning, I became concerned. Then in short order I wrenched my knee doing the gentlest of sidestrokes in Specchio di Venere lake and nearly got blown off the vertiginous cliffs at Salto della Vecchia by a sudden gust of wind.

Aha, I told myself, you've been given *malocciu*, otherwise known as the evil eye.

People who believe in this affliction say it can reduce whole cities to ruin. I didn't feel like waiting around to see whether I would be reduced to ruin myself, so I paid a visit to a squat, ancient woman named Angela. Angela was one of the island's evil eye doctors.

The first thing Angela did was ask me more or less the same question I'd been asked on small islands in the Pacific, the Caribbean, and indeed all over the world: Did I know her cousin in Brooklyn? She seemed astonished when I told I hardly knew a soul in Brooklyn.

Then she got down to business. She brought out a pasta bowl and filled it with water, added a dash of salt, and then held it next to my chest, and began uttering a succession of barely audible *Pater nosters* and *Ave Marias*. After making the sign of the cross over the bowl, she put three drops of olive oil in the water. If the drops dispersed over the surface, I'd been *pigghiatu ad occiu* (lit., "struck by the eye"), she said; if not, I was just having a run of bad luck.

The drops formed solid globules on the water.

I was relieved. More than relieved, exultant. Seldom have I been so pleased with my own bad luck. I offered Angela several thousand *lira*, but she said she never accepted money for her services. So, in return for those services, I promised to phone her cousin in Brooklyn when I got home. (Note: I did make the call, only to learn that the cousin had died some years ago. News travels slowly to outposts like Pantelleria.)

As for the woman who'd given me such a lingering stare, I later found out that she was half blind and probably thought I was one of her pigs escaped from its pen.

"We are not Sicilian," Pantescans declare, adding that their immediate neighbors to the north are either arrogant or mafiosi, and sometimes both. Certain Pantescans will even deny being Italian; their ancestry is Arab, they'll tell you, or if not exclusively Arab, at least an Arab-Italian mix, with perhaps a dollop of Spaniard thrown in for good measure.

In regard to their hospitality, Pantescans did in fact strike me as being more Arab than European. I could imagine them wining and dining Mother Teresa and Attila the Hun with equal devotion to their respective needs. Certainly, they looked after my needs in much the same way a desert Bedouin might look after a famished guest.

For instance, I'd inquire about the taste of moray eels, a local delicacy, and the next day a toothsome fillet of moray would appear on my plate. Or I'd wander into a bar, only to have a glass of vintage *passito* wine pressed on me with the bartender's compliments. Or I'd have peanut butter graciously put before me at mealtimes on the assumption that it was my national food.

At one point I mentioned my interest in mushrooms to one of my guides, and an hour later he showed up with a bucketful of mud. Apparently, my pronunciation of *funghi*, the word for mushrooms, sounded not unlike *fanghi*, the word for mud, and rather than question my sanity (the guest is always right), he'd gone out and gathered the choicest mud he could find.

But it was the offerings of wine that I'll most remember. Along with capers, wine is Pantelleria's most important export, and I often felt I was being considered for the role of the island's North American jobber. I'd be marveling at some local sight, a two-thousand-year-old Punic cistern, say, or the artful stonework of a so-called Arab garden, and there'd be a polite tap on my shoulder. The next thing I knew, I'd be seated on the shaded veranda of a farmer's dammuso with a beaker-sized glass of wine in front of me.

Pantescan wines tend to be heady. *Very* heady. For the passito version of a muscatel, the aromatic zibibbo grapes unique to the island are spread out to dry for three weeks. As they lose their water (passito means "past it"), their flavor intensifies and their sugar content increases. The result is a high octane wine whose alcohol content is typically fifteen percent or more.

The island's passito reputedly put the notorious rake Casanova in a libidinous mood. It did not have that effect on me. After two or three glasses, I wouldn't have recognized my libido if it'd announced itself with a flourish of trumpets. Also, I couldn't always tell whether I was being buffeted by blasts of wind or swaying back and forth of my own accord. Doubtless some of what I took to be Pantelleria's bluster was really the consequence of my visits to dammuso verandas.

I felt obliged to drink less prudently than I would have drunk at home. For, as one of my guides informed me, "It's bad manners to stop with just one glass. The farmer will think you don't like his wine."

Eventually, I began taking to the high country so as not to seem unmannerly. Even there, I was not immune from local hospitality. Late one afternoon I encountered a farmer tending his vineyard on the upper slope of Montagna Gibele. Just coincidentally, he happened to have a bottle of homemade passito in his donkey's saddle-pack. I can't remember drinking the bottle with him, but I'm sure I did, because when I looked out to sea a short while later, I saw a Roman trireme approaching the island.

I blinked. The trireme turned into the passenger-and-car ferry that links Pantelleria with Trapani in Sicily. I blinked again to make sure. The ship remained indisputably modern.

Still, this is a place with at least one foot in the past, although perhaps not the past of Roman triremes. It seemed to me to occupy a space in time somewhere in the 1930s, or so I felt after seeing faded photographs of Mussolini in several of the island's bars. One of the Pantescans who regaled me with wine—a sweet-spirited, leprechaunish man in his early eighties—told me he ranked Mussolini with Garibaldi and Count Cavour as the three greatest Italian heroes.

I confess that I wasn't troubled by this enthusiasm for a man whose rating elsewhere isn't very high. The picture of Mussolini I got from older Pantescans is not of history's strutting despot, but of a public-minded padrone who improved local schools and helped fund the island's first real roads.

"Il Duce looked after us, *signore*," my leprechaunish friend told me. He said he presented Mussolini with a bottle of passito on the occasion of the dictator's visit to Pantelleria in 1936. On hearing this, I had a sudden vision of Il Duce staggering back and forth in a merry dance that belied the grimness of fascism.

Partially because of its leisurely, old-fashioned pace, but also because my wrenched knee continued to bother me, I became a lumbering creature on Pantelleria. One of my guides told me the best way to unwrench my knee was to go swimming in the same place where I wrenched it, the Specchio di Venere lake, so named because the goddess Venus used its mirrorlike surface to gaze on her own lovely visage.

I returned to Specchio di Venere one bright, levanter-blown day. The lake was so churned up that Venus, had she gazed in it, would have seen only a murky image of herself. Undaunted, I waded through mineral-packed ooze and began paddling around in the highly alkaline water.

The sulphurous smell reminded me of similar lakes, likewise old volcanic craters, in Iceland. The lake also had the roundish shape of a volcanic crater. With this in mind, I wondered where I would come down if an eruption occurred. Tunisia? Palermo? On top of Signor Armani's dammuso?

But an eruption did not occur, and after an hour or so of sulphur and alkalinity, my knee felt better. Much better.

I shouldn't have been surprised by the knee's improved condition. After all, Pantelleria's geology has long been known for its healing powers. Near the main town, there's a saunalike cave whose steam has eased bodily aches and pains since Roman times. In Benikhula, there's another cave whose hot vapors are a balm for rheumatism sufferers. All over the island, in fact, there are caves, hot springs, miniature geysers called *favare*, and thermo-mineral waters where you can sweat, burn, or rinse away your ills.

And on the island's west coast, there's the Grotta di Sataria (Cave of Good Health), popularly known as Calypso's Cave. Here, according to legend, the Homeric wanderer Ulysses spent seven years cavorting with the sea-nymph Calypso, a prisoner of her seductive powers. Nowadays the inhabitants of the nearby village of Scauri use the cave for their own romantic trysts.

Toward the end of my trip, I found myself reclining in a pool of hot water at Calypso's Cave. Time seemed to dissolve, past and present merge, and a few feet away I noticed Ulysses and Calypso—or was it a couple from Scauri?—locked in an amorous embrace. Roman centurions dropped by for a soak, and gossiped about their emperor's various excesses. Arabs knelt toward Mecca. A certain leprechaunish old man proffered a beaker-sized glass of wine.

Earlier in the day, the wind had been in a tumultuous mood, but now it was singing something blithe and airy by Mozart. Resting in the pool, I felt blithe and airy myself, and also more than a little envious: What a lucky fellow Ulysses was to be stuck for seven years on this most salubrious of islands.

In Banda

ike most scrutable Occidentals, I tend to be a bundle of fallacies and clichés about the so-called inscrutable East. Something to do with Charlie Chan movies and overly generous doses of Dr. Fu Manchu at an impressionable age, I suspect. About Indonesia, however, I seem to have fewer stereotypes than I have about other Eastern places. Probably that's because island-rich Indonesia is not so much a single place as it is 13,667 distinct places, some so obscure that even the government in Sakarta doesn't seem to know about them. Take the Banda Islands. When I informed a well-traveled friend that I was visiting Banda, he said:

"Hastings Banda? The doyen of discretionary nonalignment? The man's older than sin. Actually, I thought he was dead."

Whereupon I confessed that I wasn't visiting the President-for-Life of Malawi, but a group of small islands in the Moluccan archipelago in eastern Indonesia. Banda, I added, was a stomping ground for the *tjoelik*, a ghost whose specialty is nipping off peoples' heads, along with the *laweri*, a fish with a built-in flashlight.

"Ah, you old fantasist," my friend said. "Now I know you're making it all up. You *are* visiting Hastings Banda, aren't you?"

Shortly after this conversation, I hopped a series of increasingly smaller planes until I touched down on Neira, the capital island. Here in the flesh was a genuine Banda, quite obviously neither an aged African potentate or a figment of my imagination. Almost the first sight that greeted my eyes was a large crowd of locals gathered around an open-air TV; they were watching an old *I Love Lucy* rerun dubbed in Bahasa Indonesia, even as a muezzin's voice from a nearby mosque was inciting them to prayer.

Such an image suggests a cheerful little backwater wholly removed from the pulse of modern life. Maybe this image is true today, but the Bandas weren't always cheerful, nor were they always a backwater. No less a celebrity than Christopher Columbus may have even been searching for them when he discovered, much to his disappointment, America. And the usual roll call of European empire builders—the Spanish, the Portuguese, the English, and the Dutch—all tried to colonize them at one time or another. At last the Dutch prevailed, largely through the efforts of a soldier-adventurer named Jan Pieterszoon Coen, who put to death every male Bandanese over the age of fifteen.

Why such interest in a bunch of remote, pinprick islands? Because the Bandas grew nutmeg, the "gold" of the spice trade, in astonishingly profuse groves. That this spice inspired the homocidal instincts of the normally mild-mannered Dutch is, I suppose, a tribute to its former versatility—it was used as a seasoning, a meat preservative, a source of mace, and a cure for madness and sciatica. Also, nutmeg is a mild hallucinogen, a fact presumably not lost on the sailors who were transporting it all the way back to Europe.

My first day on Neira I took a little stroll and noticed some curious reminders of the long-departed Dutch. Inside the old jail, there was a badly warped but still serviceable ping-pong table. There were tumbledown *perkenier* (planter) homesteads whose tiled floors had been invaded by poinciana trees and whose shallow marble steps were covered with maidenhair ferns: former stately mansions transformed into botanical displays. Then there were all those cannons— cannons by the roadside, cannons in gardens, cannons in tidal flats, and even one forlorn cannon still guarding the battlements of Fort Belgica. If nothing else, these slightly absurd relics showed how much easier it is to get rid of a colonial master than colonial ironmongery.

I was photographing a cannon that seemed to be growing in somebody's banana grove when a policeman approached me. Uh-oh, I thought, not three hours here and you're already in trouble with the local gendarmes. I'd heard stories about the Indonesian police casually jailing trespassers, jaywalkers, and other small-time felons, so I wondered if I was going to inaugurate my visit to Banda with a shakedown in the old jail. If that were the case, I decided I'd at least request a cellmate who played ping-pong. But this particular policeman simply asked me whether I'd like a banana. And before I could respond, he'd plucked down a ripe *pisang susu*, renowned for its milky flavor.

Later I wrote these words in my notebook: "Indonesia is a land of contrasts. In Timor the police machine-gun you. Here they offer you bananas."

Taken together, the ten Banda Islands cover only twenty square miles of dry land, or roughly 1/25,000 the total area of Indonesia. The largest island, boomerang-shaped Lontar, is seven miles long and scarcely a mile wide; the smallest, Kapal, is a blunt outcropping of rock. Neira itself is small enough that even the most torpid walker can negotiate it in a few hours. Small wonder that cartographers occasionally turn their talents to more momentous places. On the other hand, if you remind yourself that the Bandas rise 22,000 feet sheer from the bottom of the Banda Sea, that they are in fact the merest tips of abyssal volcanoes, then they seem pretty momentous themselves.

Of all the Bandas, Gunung Api is the one most likely to resent being called a "tip," since its Fuji-like centerpiece, Fire Mountain, is a full-fledged, still active volcano, complete with a resident fire goddess, Pele, who reputedly has a more or less conjugal relationship with the mountain. It's also said that whenever any sort of invasion force arrives in Banda, she persuades the mountain to blow its top. In 1615, Fire Mountain erupted just as a Dutch fleet sailed into the strait between Gunung Api and Neira. It erupted again in the 1790s to mark the coming of an English expeditionary force. The most recent eruption, in May of 1988, forced a mass evacuation of Gunung Api and all the islands around it. There wasn't an invasion this time— not unless you consider a visit by Jacques Cousteau an invasion.

An ascent of Fire Mountain is almost an official act for the visitor, so I hired a guide named Ali to take me up and down this pyramid of living rock. Like many Bandanese, Ali was something of a demographic jumble; Dutch features fought Javanese and Arab trader features for supremacy on his face. For my purposes, he also happened to be the local equivalent of a Sherpa.

Ali and I started our ascent at 5:30 a.m. to keep from being fricasseed by the midday sun. We followed a path uphill that led through a dense nutmeg plantation. Immediately I began to hear the booming "Aw-w-w, aw-w-w, aw-w-w" of the nutmeg pigeon, a handsome, green-collared bird celebrated by Alfred Wallace in his classic travelogue *The Malay Archipelago*, but much disliked by the Bandanese themselves. Indeed, they dislike it so much that they represent it as the Bird of Death in their mythology. No doubt they'd make even the chickadee a Bird of Death if, like the pigeon, a single chickadee consumed a dozen or so nutmeg "nuts" a day.

The actual climb wasn't difficult. It was just that the human creature isn't accustomed to getting down on all fours and crawling up a slope of volcanic rubble like an early primate. But that's the only way to avoid sliding two steps backwards for every successful step forward. Likewise it's the only way to avoid ending up with an imprint of lava on your person. The lack of interest in this sort of painful imprint is probably why the first European ascent of Fire Mountain didn't occur until 1821, a relatively recent date.

At last we made it up to the summit, a place of smoking rock, barren and sulphurous, that reminded me a little of Iceland. But the view was distinctly not Icelandic—both the near Bandas and the far Bandas spread out on a sea so azure, so pellucid that it made every other sea seem dingy by comparison.

I asked Ali if he knew about Pele.

He nodded. "Sometimes we sacrifice a kitchen to her," he said.

"A kitchen? Hard to haul a whole kitchen up these slopes."

"Not hard, easy," he replied, adding: "We cut its throat, too."

"You cut the kitchen's throat?"

He nodded again. Just as I was about to ask him what type of knife he used, I realized: Indonesians pronounce "k" and "c" like "ch," so Ali naturally was pronouncing "ch" as if it were "k." It's much easier to cut a chicken's throat than a kitchen's.

We descended the same way we came up, slipping, and sliding, down hardened lava from the 1988 eruption. Now and then I had to grab the branch of a nutmeg tree as a belay—another use for this versatile spice?—to keep from falling down. By the time I reached bottom, I felt I'd been participating in an illusion. True, Fire Mountain was only 2,100 feet tall, less than half the height of Denver, Colorado. Yet it had become incomparably large, even momentous under my feet, as if it'd been touched by geological sleight of hand.

After my assault on Fire Mountain, I decided to spend a restful day exploring Bandanese waters in a *prahu*. A prahu is a dugout canoe made from the hollowed-out trunk of a tropical almond tree. With their narrow girths and unusually low-slung gunwales, prahus are better suited to the delicate Bandanese frame than the more cumbersome Western one. Or so the Bandanese man from whom I rented my prahu delicately put it. He also said I'd look funny. But that didn't bother me. Westerners are supposed to look funny in Indonesia. They talk funny, walk funny, and dress funny, too. Such has been our lot ever since the first European crept onto these sultry shores wearing garments that would not have been out of place in Greenland.

Right then and there I tried to launch my craft. "Slowly, slowly," the owner told me, lest I capsize the prahu even before I got into it. Somehow I did manage to get into it (to balance yourself in a prahu, I'm convinced, requires heavenly intervention), and was soon paddling, after a fashion, in the general direction of Lontar. Fishermen stared at me from their prahus. Small children stared at me from theirs. And I stared right back at them as if I knew exactly what I was doing. I didn't, of course. Despite some familiarity with canoes, I wasn't prepared for this lighter-than-air craft, which the daintiest of starboard strokes would send rushing off toward Irian Jaya. Or with an equally dainty port stroke, it'd rush off toward Singapore.

Finally I found the solution to my problems: a constant use of the J stroke. This kept me from zigzagging furiously, traveling in a circle, or making my landfall in the wrong country. As I paddled around Neira's southern tip, I thought I was doing quite well. Then I noticed a grizzled old woman shoot right past me in her prahu. My self-esteem vanished. But here I ought to mention that women, especially elderly women, are known as the best paddlers in Banda and always seem to be in considerable demand as seagoing chauffeurs.

Before long, I was approaching Lontar's southern coast. Never mind that I'd been aiming for Salomon Beach on its northern coast. At least I'd kept myself away from Singapore. Now I began to wonder what the good people of Lontar would think when I fetched up on their island in one of their own eminently capsizable crafts. I found out soon enough. For after the prahu struck bottom, I made what I thought was an elegant leap ashore and landed facedown in Lontar's rich volcanic sand. Well, partially sand and partially mud. The welcoming committee of children and young adults burst into riotous laughter. Funny Westerner! They slapped their knees and rolled in the mud, too.

Then a man in a fez stepped forward and invited me to his home for a cup of tea. I assumed he just wanted a private performance of my comic routine. Actually, this man had no such interest at all. He was the local schoolteacher and he'd been looking for someone on whom to practice his English for quite some time. Whatever my defects in canoemanship, I seemed to be that person. So we went back to his house, a small bungalow with a slatted driftwood floor and sago-thatch roof. Here lived his entire family, including his seven children, all of whom slept in the same room. Apparently the parents slept in this not very spacious room, too.

Very crowded, I remarked. Oh, not crowded at all, the man replied. And then with a tolerant smile (naive Westerner!), he said: "Banda people like to sleep this way. It is very good to sleep this way. For if a person sleeps alone and he has a nightmare, who would comfort him?"

Whereas Neira, Lontar, and Gunung Api hunch together like three old comrades in an attitude of reminiscence, the islands of Ai, Hatta, and Rhun are distant and farflung, less like comrades than mortal enemies. Rhun, the least comradely, most farflung of the three, is a nutmeg jungle fringed by a tracery of palm trees. Under the 1667 Treaty of Breda, the English gave the Dutch this tidbit of real estate— the only Banda they still clung to—in exchange for the then equally obscure island of Manhattan, in the Americas. A somewhat lopsided trade at that time: Manhattan's nutmeg was nonexistent.

For several days I'd wanted to visit Rhun, but the vagrant winds of the western monsoon kept interfering with my plans. At last there came a day of almost celestial calm, and off I went with a couple of Australian divers. They wanted to look at Rhun from under the water; I wanted to see the island's terrestrial realm and compare it with

Manhattan's. The two-and-a-half-hour boat journey passed without incident until one of the Australians started trolling and a sea-eagle swooped down dramatically from the sky and snatched his artificial lure. Suddenly, he had an eagle at the end of his hook.

We landed on a deserted beach. The very next moment this same beach was swarming with a boisterous mass of people eager to see the Westerners. On Manhattan, they mug you; on Rhun, they mob you as if you were equal parts visiting dignitary, prize orchid, and two-headed calf. Our mob followed us through the village to the house of the *orang besar* (headman), piling in until the room where we were received by this cordial gentleman came to resemble the famous stateroom scene in the Marx Brothers' *A Night at the Opera*.

"How many people live on your island?" one of the Australians asked the orang besar.

"Forty-nine grandfathers," he answered proudly.

After the Australians left, the orang besar told me about an old English fort, El Dorado, which was the one possible tourist site on Rhun. He drew me up a map, and I headed back through the village with a parade of barefoot children running ahead of, alongside, and behind me. A bit slower, but also barefoot, was one of Rhun's forty-nine grandfathers; he was in a *sopi* (palm wine) haze and wondered if I'd come here to reclaim his island for the English . . .

"English!" shrieked one of the kids. And as if this were his cue, he began the ubiquitous practice of English on me. "What your name, mister?" "You have wife, mister?" "Where you from, mister?" Along with other Indonesians, the Bandanese call all Westerners, including women, "mister"—a survival from colonial times when they were obliged to call Dutchmen "Mynheer."

"I'm from America," I told the kid.

"Is it a big or a little island?"

"A big, big island . . ."

Now I paused to rest from the heat. I sat down and opened my copy of Somerset Maugham's *The Narrow Corner*, a novel set in a fictionalized Banda. My escorts paused to rest, too. They sat down inches from my book and stared at it as if it were the world's greatest curiosity. When I turned it upside down, they continued to stare at it, but also stared back at me. Ah, he reads upside down, maybe they were telling themselves: Another insight into the baffling ways of Westerners.

And then I was following a path through the aromatic bush. I passed gay, flitting butterflies with seven-inch wingspans, brilliant orange spiders, and a marsupial cuscus asleep in a nutmeg tree. Finally I reached El Dorado. The fort turned out to be little more than a heap of crumbling stones, even worse off than the planters' houses on Neira. So much for Rhun's entry into the Taj Mahal or Parthenon sweepstakes. But it's the journey, not the destination, that matters most. And I did happen to notice a lovely polka-dotted butterfly resting its wings on one of the crumbling stones.

Back on Neira I got into a chat with Des Alwi, a son of Banda who'd made good as a diplomat, filmmaker, and local hotelier. If the Dutch hadn't traded Manhattan for Rhun, Alwi told me with a sly grin, the whole course of American history might have been different. Perhaps I might have been different, too—a devotee of Queen Beatrix and wooden shoes instead of apple pie.

Where was I? Bent over the side of a small boat just off the north shore of Neira. It was a placid, star-filled night, and I was scouring the water for a very special fish. I'd already seen plenty of other fish on this trip—electric-blue, jade-green, and baby-pink fish, a teeming kaleidoscope of color. I'd also seen fish with spikes sticking out of their heads, fish that seemed to be dressed in tuxedos, and fish whose poison glands were fully capable of delivering me to an early grave. But these were all fish that could be found in any well-stocked reef in Asia or the Pacific. My fish was a Banda fish, occurring nowhere else but in the prodigal waters off Banda itself.

I refer to the laweri (*Photoblepheron bandanensis*), locally known as "the flashlight fish." The laweri has an organ just below the eyes which enables it to light up its own field of vision. This organ goes on shining even after the fish itself is dead, so the Bandanese often take a couple of laweris, stick them in a jar, and they've got an instant night-light. Or if they're fishing in deep water, they might put a laweri at the end of a line and it'll illuminate the bait for fish not quite so remarkably endowed in the ocular department.

Suddenly the boatman gave a shout. He pointed to a small pool of light, at once ghostly and radiant, moving in the water. Several small pools of light. Laweris! These must have been five-watt laweris, since their light was a trifle weak. Then, off in the distance, I saw a group of much larger pools, definitely the twenty-watt variety, swimming briskly as a single unit. As they approached us, the entire sea came alive, shimmered, and gleamed with their presence.

And then they were gone. Once again the water was black as pitch. The only light in all the world came from flickering stars and the boatman's cigarette. But this encounter, so haunting, so altogether unusual, stayed with me long after I hopped that series of increasingly larger planes home. It stays with me even now, as I sit at my desk and write these words, illuminated by an ordinary, slightly boring lightbulb.

Yap Magic

couldn't have been anywhere else in the wide Pacific but in Yap. Behind me is a village meeting house whose thatched gable soars dramatically skywards. Arrayed around me are giant moss-flecked aragonite disks—the time-honored local currency. A young woman swishes by in a voluminous grass skirt that looks instantly combustible. Directly in front of me is a stone path worn smooth by centuries of bare feet and stained a picturesque crimson by beteljuice expectorations.

Traveling here from Guam, Micronesia's most westernized island (the K-Mart of the Pacific, a waggish friend calls it), can feel a bit like traveling to a distant planet, although perhaps not at first.

None of Yap's four closely-bunched islands, Maap, Tomil-Gagil, Rumung, and Yap itself, is particularly scenic, at least not in the standard palm-clad, beach-girt, tropically seductive manner. There's dry pandamus scrub everywhere; the architecturally jumbled capital

Colonia looks as if it had been modeled on an industrial park; and whole villages seem to be constructed out of aluminum siding—their architectural model would appear to be a Greyhound bus.

But look more closely. In that admittedly drab pandamus, you might see a medicine man or woman gathering plants for a magic elixir. One of those aluminum houses might boast a rope strung with stingray stingers, the ultimate in Yapese home beautication. That same house may be resting on a stone dais that predates the invention of aluminum by hundreds of years.

Even Colonia has surprises. One day in a grocery store I saw a bare-breasted woman (in Yap, a bikini is licentious; bare breasts are not) who'd strapped a brassiere around her waist and was using its pockets to carry betel nuts.

The betel nut, in fact, is a perfect emblem for Yap. The green "nut," the seed of the areca palm, is as unassuming as an acorn on the outside. But when it's bitten open, mixed with air-slaked lime, and wrapped in a betel pepper leaf, it produces a pleasurable high, along with a mouth condition that resembles terminal gingivitis. Everybody chews; there's a belief that if you don't, your teeth will be pecked out by blackbirds.

So, too, Yap's true character lurks beneath the surface. There'll be a sudden storm, typical enough for the tropics, but then your guide will say, Oh, so-and-so called it up in a fit of pique. Or you'll notice someone gently ushering a hermit crab across a path—simply a kind-hearted gesture to a lesser creature, you might think. But then you'll be told that these perambulating crustaceans are ancestral spirits, and to step on one would be very disrespectful.

Or you'll see a man wearing a cap that advertises the Santa Monica Yacht Club, only to learn that he's a paramount chief and you must bow low in his presence.

Time in such a setting loses all its compulsion. Early in my visit, I got a bad scrape on some coral, so I went to the local hospital and asked the Yapese receptionist how soon I could see a doctor. "Right away," she told me.

Two hours later I was still waiting . . . and fuming. "You said it'd be right away," I complained.

"Yes," she replied, "but when we say right away on Yap, we don't mean right away."

"What *do* you mean, then?" I sputtered.

"Oh, four, five hours, maybe tomorrow," she said blithely.

An hour later a man showed up with a fish-spear stuck in his thigh. Extensive tattooing, varnished to bring out its blue tracery of bird and flower, gave his upper body the look of ornamental fretwork; he was wearing a *thu* (loincloth) so spartan that it would have put a missionary to headlong rout. Right then and there I reckoned my wait within the context of centuries, not hours. Whereupon it did not seem long at all.

Behind me, the high-gabled meeting house; squatting down next to me, an old *mach-mach* (shaman); a glimpse of the wind-ruffled sea through the feathered tops of palm trees, the sound of tiny lizards clattering in the bush, and the more distant tap-tapping of an adze working a breadfruit log into a canoe.

The mach-mach, a man seemingly bequeathed from the Stone Age to the present age, numbered among his skills the ability to calm a typhoon, cast a spell on an unpleasant neighbor, and cure a toothache. Right now, however, he was performing a palm leaf divination (*pwue*) in order to "read" my future.

Slipping four palm-leaf strips between his fingers, he began tying random knots into each strip, all the while chanting softly to himself. When he was finished, he counted all the knots—each represented a spirit helper who would provide him with some clue as to my future prospects.

The man now fixed me with his ancient gaze and said, in effect, "I'd watch out if I were you."

A Yapese, upon hearing this sort of warning, might take to his sleeping mat (they don't use beds). For a mach-mach's admonition is a serious matter.

But I wasn't Yapese. And besides, I was less worried about my bleak future than the fact that I'd brought the old man the wrong kind of cigarettes, Winston's instead of Benson & Hedges. I made partial amends for my mistake by offering him a handful of brightly colored balloons. Actually, what I really wanted to find out was whether he planned on being buried with his head above the ground, in traditional mach-mach fashion, so he could keep a posthumous eye on things. But I figured it would be somewhat impolite to ask him this.

That same day I began hiking to a place called Alog. Located deep in the bush, Alog is a ghost town. Literally, a ghost town. The Yapese, many of whom refuse to go there, refer to it as The Valley of the Khan (ghosts), a testimony to its weird numen. There was a stream in Alog that flowed uphill, according to my guide Fawgomon, and eels that possessed an inordinate number of heads. And, of course, a profusion of khan.

Our path meandered through clumps of taro planted in plashy hollows before surrendering to the inevitable pandamus. We stepped carefully around the triply fluted, swordlike blades, each of which was edged with rows of fine prickles. Fawgomon pointed out some *chongot* trees, urging me to avoid them, too. He mentioned a friend who'd had a run-in with a chongot that resulted in pieces of his skin falling off.

The chongot (*Semecarpus venosa*) is a tall, respectable-looking hardwood whose bark sweats an acrid white sap that makes poison ivy seem as innocuous as a baby's bottom. So virulent is this sap that you only need to stand near a chongot tree and shout the name of an enemy, and wherever that person is, he'll come down with a chongot rash. Or so the Yapese say.

Not surprisingly, I gave every chongot I saw a wide berth.

After bushwhacking for a mile or so, we crossed a stream and climbed a moderate incline. A short while later Fawgomon announced that we were lost. He blamed this on the khan, who did not appreciate our thrashing through their territory. I blamed it on the absence of a compass and topo map.

But at last we reached Alog. The village belonged to the jungle; its crumbling stone walls and derelict house foundations squinted at us from the dense vegetation. Only the elevated dais on which the local mach-mach's house had rested seemed to be intact. Leaning against this dais, half-buried in the ground, was Alog's stone money, or most of it— one piece had been stolen in 1996, Fawgomon said, whereupon a devastating typhoon struck Yap (stone money=security against typhoons).

There is a beauty to such seemingly unbeautiful places that knocks logic to smithereens. And a large part of Alog's beauty, for me, was its silence; a silence so complete that it brought a palpable whistling in my ears.

All of a sudden the silence was broken by a bird call—*oo-oo-oo-AW, oo-oo-oo-AW, oo-oo-oo-OH*. I asked Fawgomon what this bird was. Could it be a Yap monarch, an indigenous bird I hadn't seen or heard yet?

He frowned. "That's no bird," he said. He also told me that I was standing in a *teliw*, a taboo place, and to get out of it immediately. Only a mach-mach could venture into a teliw without fear of retaliation from the khan who lived there.

Fawgomon was obviously spooked. I was getting a little spooked myself, so I suggested we head back. Easier said than done. We slashed away at the vegetation, thrust aside cables of creeping vines, crossed and recrossed the stream, and succeeded only in getting lost again. We ended up in a clinging, crepuscular thicket out of which I half expected a jabbering Ben Gunn to emerge.

In this situation, Fawgomon did what any Yapese would have done—he stopped for a chew. "There's wisdom in betel nut," he told me, citing a local adage. And sure enough, he noticed a familiar boulder nearby. It had once been a khan who'd made a specialty of harassing children, he said. So now he knew exactly where we were.

Our return hike couldn't have been easier. Soon we found the path that wound through the taro patch. Ten minutes later we were driving back to the welcome jumble of Colonia.

All's well that ends well, or so I thought . . .

Yap is more culturally intact than its Micronesian neighbors, and for good reason—it escaped the world's contagion, the endless tugging and pulling of European powers, until the very end of the last century. The Yapese attribute this to magic—their mach-machs (they say) created contrary winds that blew foreign ships away. The prospect of a chongot-tipped spear in the chest or flank might have been a deterrent, too.

And although in this century Germany, Japan, and the United States have all taken it under their improving wings, Yap has remained splendidly unimproved, either resisting outside influences or making them uniquely its own. There are Yapese who'll proudly tell you that Adam and Eve came from Yap; there are also Yapese who insist that the Christian God is really their trickster deity Iolofath in disguise.

Then, of course, there's the stone money, or *rai*. More than anything else, these herculean disks—they look like millstones, or the discarded tires of an eighteen-wheeler—proclaim Yap's allegiance to its own past.

"Long ago German people come, say only German money good," one Yapese man told me. "Then Japanese come, tell us German money bad and only Japanese yen good. Then Americans come, no more yen, take all away, only dollars good. Then we join FSM [Federated States of Micronesia], still use dollars. Some day maybe dollars no good. But all the time rai very good!"

There are so many of these rai on Yap that they nearly qualify as a geographical feature. I saw them next to private houses, village meeting houses, men's houses, and elementary schools, honoring whatever they rested against—even, in one instance, a sewage treatment plant—with prestige. And after a while, I began to think of them as almost human. I'd be so comforted by their hoary, grandfatherly presence that I'd feel no harm would come to me as long as they were in the vicinity.

There! I was adopting the same mind-set as the Yapese, who use their rai not only as collateral for cash loans but likewise as hedges against calamity and misfortune.

I also felt these disks were obscurely watchful, possibly because the hole in the middle looks so much like a cyclopean eye. Thus I was careful not to breach local custom whenever I found myself in their vigilant company; I avoided all hermit crabs, for example, lest one of these oversized coins totter over and politely reprimand me for crushing someone's ancestor.

Aragonite is not native to Yap, so the disks had to be quarried on Palau and brought back via sailing canoe or bamboo raft. The riskier the journey, the more valuable the disk. A typhoon, a capsize, or an attack by Palauans eager to remove Yapese heads—these would all be financial windfalls. On Tomil, there's a piece of stone money called "Without Tears" because no one died in its quarrying or on the voyage back to Yap; it has comparatively little value.

One day at Leang I saw a disk that looked rough-hewn, even unfinished, and was curious about its story. It was one piece of stone money that I definitely did not feel protected by.

Long ago, the coin's owner told me, there was a very lazy fellow named Marrad. He went to Palau on a quarrying trip, but when he got there, he just sat around chewing betelnut. On the last day, right before the canoes headed back to Yap, Marrad tried to make a rai, and this specimen was the result.

"I guess it doesn't have much value," I said.

"Oh no," the man replied. "Very valuable. No one expects Marrad to do any work ever. He makes this rai. He makes it bad, yes, but at least he makes it. Very, very valuable rai."

Half facetiously, I asked what I might give him for it. Maybe a hundredweight of betel nut? Or a brand-new Ford pickup?

He shook his head, as if he would not relinquish this ill-made coin for all the treasures in the world.

I may have been wrong about the stone money keeping me out of harm's way. A day or so after my hike to Alog, I began itching what appeared to be a mass of insect bites up and down my legs. Yet Yap's insects are generally so mild-mannered that I couldn't imagine any of them making me itch so fervently or so incessantly. I even itched underwater, snorkeling among manta rays in M'il Channel; and when I saw one of these slow-moving giants repeatedly scratch a pectoral fin against some coral, I felt a rush of fraternal sympathy for it.

Eventually, each of these so-called bites became fluorescent, then vividly pustular. I was not a pretty sight.

One night I showed my legs to a local at O'Keefe's Kanteen, a popular Colonia watering hole, and he immediately identified the source of my problem—chongot. If you walk in a stream into which chongot sap has dripped, he told me, the effect will be more or less like wrapping your legs around the actual tree. And I had walked back and forth in Alog's stream many times. A stream that would have been brimming with chongot sap.

What to do? I wasn't too keen on approaching the old mach-mach for help, since I figured he would wonder why I'd ignored his warning. And I'd already spent too much time at the Yap Hospital, with little more than a philosophic attitude to show for it. So when I heard about a medicine woman who had a practise near Qokaaw village, I decided to visit her.

The woman studied my legs, studied me, and then said:

"You are possessed by a khan."

"Possibly," I replied, "but my main concern is this blasted itching. Maybe you can give me a salve to ease it."

She spat out some betel juice and went on to explain that a female khan had attached herself to me. Female khan attach themselves to men, and vice versa. I'd probably picked up my khan in Alog when I wandered into the teliw. And as long as she was with me, I'd have bad luck. Not just bad luck, but increasingly bad luck. My chongot-related malaise was positively cheery compared to what would happen to me later on.

A sobering diagnosis. But my condition was not incurable, the woman said, and especially not incurable if I gave her a few packs of Marlboro's (addiction to cigarettes would seem to be part of the stock-in-trade of a Yapese medicine person).

Mercifully, her cure did not include the customary broth of bones, lizard skins, and fruit-bat hair. Instead she gave me an herbal potion, and then instructed me in its application: I was to smear it on my body three times a day, always pushing outward in order to push away the khan. It was necessary that I perform this action an even number of times. An odd number, and I might be stuck with my khan forever.

"Will this potion make my itching go away, too?" I asked.

"The itching comes from the khan," she replied. She put a fresh quid of betel nut in her mouth and chewed for a moment, then looked me straight in the eye. The message was clear: taboo places aren't amusement parks, so don't go near one again.

Considerably chastened, I told her that I'd learned my lesson. As, indeed, I had. On Yap, one must respect the rules or else, my own else being the acquisition of supernatural form of contact dermitis.

Back in my hotel room I began smearing myself with the herbal potion, which smelled like a jungly version of pesto. I smeared it on religiously morning, noon, and night, as per the medicine woman's instructions. And on the fourth day, my ghostly hitchhiker departed. Or at least I think she departed, because I was now hardly itching at all. Even my chongot sores, previously so fierce-looking, were now only vague pink splotches.

Yap's magic, it seemed, had worked wonders on my behalf.

My luck picked up as well. For days I'd been trying to get to Fais, one of Yap's outer islands and reputedly among the most traditional places in the western Pacific. Fais's only communication with the rest of the world was a not very reliable radio-telephone—the next best thing, I thought, to no communication at all.

Then I got a call from Peter Reichert, the pilot for Pacific Missionary Aviation. He was flying to Woleai Atoll tomorrow, he said, and could drop me off on Fais en route. I was elated. I promptly dashed down to the Governor's Office in Colonia and got a permission form to visit Fais (you need official clearance for any sort of travel to Yap's outer islands).

The flight took only an hour and a half. Yet when I stepped out of Peter's nine-passenger plane, I entered a century that was distinctly not the twentieth. There were no automotive vehicles on Fais except for one decrepit pickup with a shattered windshield. No one—man, woman, or child—was wearing western clothes; not even the torn, permanently smudged T-shirts other Pacific islanders seem to consider the height of fashion. Nor did I see a single item of furniture anywhere, unless a leaf-woven pandamus mat counts as furniture.

At one point I began smoking my pipe, thus making myself a figure of intense scrutiny for half the island's children. They'd never seen a pipe before, so I passed around this strange smoke-belching object for their inspection. There were "ohs" and "ahs" of amazement, and one little girl tried to eat it.

Fais's crushing heat reminded me that Micronesia has the highest annual insolation of anywhere in the world. After a few hours, I began searching around for some sort of shelter. At last I found an official-looking structure with a thatched roof and small low windows, ideal, I thought, for my purposes. I walked right in and upon hearing a chorus of nervous female giggles, rapidly walked right back out again.

Stupid me! I'd unwittingly blundered into the local menstrual hut. Another taboo place violated, doubtless another medicine person to visit, I told myself ruefully.

As I started looking for a less gender-specific refuge, I heard these words spoken in a pronounced southern accent:

"Thank your lucky stars you're not a local, friend. If you were, you would have been fined heavily—probably your entire taro harvest—for that little boo-boo."

The speaker was a gnarled, bearded figure who looked like the proverbial South Seas beachcomber. In fact, Olney Cleveland Grover ("Just call me O.C.") was a beachcomber of sorts, a Georgian who'd been a Peace Corps agricultural advisor on Fais and had long since gone native.

O.C. talked up a veritable storm, not, I realized, because he was lonely (although he did admit that he hadn't seen a fellow American in years) but because he couldn't say enough about this single square mile of raised limestone. Where else in the world is there an actual taboo on work during the summer? Where else can you find such sweet-spirited people? Where else such utter tranquility? He was living in paradise, he said.

Paradise or not, Fais seemed to me like a happy mingling of the old Pacific with Monty Python's Flying Circus. The only book I saw on the island, a Bible, was being used for cigarette paper. I met a shark fisherman and asked him what his tackle was. "I stick coconut in shark's mouth," he said. Then there was the man who pointed to a particular tree and solemnly informed me that its resident spirit was what caused gonorrhea.

And presently I found myself paying my respects to the local chief, a venerable, elaborately tattooed man whose dignified posture on his mat reminded me of a joss house idol. I joined him on a neighboring mat, making sure to hunch over so that my head was no higher than his.

Through his grandson, who spoke some English, he asked me how I liked Fais. Much on an island of this sort ends up lost in translation, so when I said that I liked it very much, although it was a bit difficult for a *wassola* (foreigner) like me to get accustomed to topless women, the old man looked quite appalled. "But all our women have heads," he declared.

The next day, just before I climbed aboard Peter's plane, an islander clutched at my arm. He was worried, he said. Very worried. It was the current U.S.-Iraqi standoff. If there was a war, what would happen to Fais? "One bomb," he told me uneasily, "and our little island would disappear."

I assured him that even if there was a war, no bomb would ever be dropped on Fais: how could a bomb ever target a place so completely off the map?

As they glide almost imperceptibly through the water, slowly waving their massive fins, manta rays exhibit a zenlike calm compared to which most other marine creatures look delirious.

So it is with the Yapese themselves: all their motions seem governed by a stately languor, a hoarding of energy for some unspecified future time when flailings and wrenchings of bodily parts might be necessary. "Give me winter, give me dogs, and you can have the rest," the Arctic explorer Knud Rasmussen famously said. To which a Yapese might respond: "Give me a mat, give me betel nut, and you can have the rest."

And yet there's often a reason for this apparent languor. Consider the men who always seem to be lounging around *faluws* (men's houses). Their inactivity is actually a survival tactic. For according to Yapese belief, the sea is a woman and a very jealous one at that, and any male who incurs her wrath "won't see home again" (as one of my guides succinctly put it). Thus men submit to a lengthy period of celibacy in a faluw before they go fishing, a gesture designed to throw the sea off the scent of other, less aqueous women.

Although not a fisherman, and still less a subscriber to the belief that the sea has an identifiable gender, I often hung out in these faluws, too. Their mood of transcendent ease made me feel as blissful as a lotus eater. And one afternoon in Bugol village I found myself in the local faluw, pen in hand, jotting down these desultory notes:

3:55 p.m. Just saw a blue morpho butterfly flit by. No other movement in sight. No, I lie: there's a gecko creeping towards an insect, too.

4:13 p.m. The tangy smell of a coconut husk fire—the essence of the South Seas—is caressing my nostrils. Too indolent to get up and find out where it's coming from.

4:19 p.m. Watched the same (?) morpho butterfly alight on a nearby piece of stone money. One of my faluw mates has just fallen asleep while reading a *Superman* comic book.

4:30 p.m. Really feeling indolent now. Humidity so thick I could cut it with a knife. No signs of present or imminent toil anywhere in the world.

5:10 p.m. Awoke. Or have I even been asleep?

The whole scene might have taken place on a particularly slow afternoon in eternity. Indeed, that same evening I had a dinner in Bugol that gave me an excellent foretaste of what dinner will be like in eternity.

The fruit bat hors d'oeuvre took several hours to cook, and then as guest of honor I was given the bat's penis (it tasted like leather soaked in Angostura bitters), and then my host's brother-in-law decided to go out and catch some land crabs, and that took a while, and then there was a betel nut break, and then my host narrated a story about how the god Iolofath generously provided sharks with teeth, and this took a while as well, and then I ate grey matter that turned out to be taro root boiled into submission (it tasted like carpenter's glue).

In lieu of red wine, we drank the blood of a sea turtle whose meat was slowly—*very* slowly—roasting over the fire.

Shortly before midnight, I looked up, and there was the Southern Cross sprinkled across the sky like a giant flourish of sequins. The Little Dipper seemed so close that I felt I could take a drink from it. There were stars twinkling and brilliant, stars that the Yapese use as navigational aids, and stars so indistinct that only someone with a powerful telescope could ever navigate by them.

I also noticed a satellite orbiting across the sky, and I marveled at how distant I was from this swift-moving canister of metal, not only in Space, but in Time, too. Especially in Time.

Island of Lost Souls

O f all the places I've ever visited, the only one where I literally crawled ashore was Marble Island in Hudson Bay. At first I balked at the prospect. I hadn't crawled in forty or so years and wasn't sure I could still do it. Also, I was concerned lest I tear my nylon-lined anorak trousers and thus make myself vulnerable to invasions by Arctic weather.

According to my guide, Bill Gawor, I *had* to crawl. At least I had to crawl if I valued my life. To illustrate his point, he told me the following story:

Once upon a time the island was an enormous iceberg. An old Inuit woman, useless to her people, was left to die on its frigid shores. She asked Sedna, goddess of the sea, to let her die on solid ground, however desolate, and not on an even more desolate chunk of ice. Sedna granted her wish, and upon her death, the iceberg turned into Marble Island and the old woman herself became its guardian spirit.

Whoever fetches up here must placate her by crawling ashore or he will suffer his own death within a year.

As I hoped to spend at least another forty years among the living, I assumed the time-honored posture of an infant and crawled from the edge of the water to the high tide mark.

James Knight, presumably, did *not* crawl ashore. With his two ships, the *Albany* and the *Discovery*, he left England in 1719 to search for the Northwest Passage. Having reached Hudson Bay, he decided to over-winter on Marble Island. And neither he or forty men were ever seen again. Nor have their remains been found—clay pipes, a chess pawn, and leather boots, yes, but no actual human remains.

Were Knight and his men killed by the Inuit? Assimilated by them? Did they suffer some mishap with thin ice? Were they the victims of scurvy or some even more virulent disease? The mystery, which persists right down to the present day, makes the better-known disappearance of the Franklin Expedition seem like a mystery even Inspector Clouseau could solve.

Bill and I pitched our tent in a wind-protected hollow not far from Captain Knight's house site, then began our search for Knight-related artifacts. White in all its lineaments, the island had the eerie pallor of a geology that seemed to suffer from a defect in melanin production. Huge upright slabs of quartzite stood like gravestones over the demise of smaller, supine slabs of quartzite. Old Inuit tent rings were almost impossible to distinguish from the glacial rubble that pock-marked the island's landscape from one end to the other.

Our solitude was complete. I turned on my shortwave radio and heard only a distant crackling noise. Either Marble Island was too isolated for radio waves or it inhabited a fourth dimension, a zone where radio waves don't exist. I felt more removed from the rest of humanity than an astronaut, who at least would have contact with mission controls in Houston.

Bill warned me to watch out for polar bears, since their white fur tends to blend in perfectly with the island's own whiteness. You may think you're stepping on quartzite, he observed, but then that

quartzite will rise up and smite you. Forewarned is forearmed. Forearmed is also forearmed, so I carried a rifle with me at all times.

Fortunately, I didn't step on any bears during my stay on Marble
Island. But I did see a peregrine falcon—a bird considerably more
aggressive than the average bear—swoop down on an unsuspecting
golden plover and carry it off to its lair. I also saw a pair of sandhill
cranes, who, upon seeing me, uttered a series of astonished chortles,
as if they'd never encountered a member of my species before.

It was early August, but the temperature seldom rose above
freezing. At one point I lost one of my gloves. "The Old Woman's got
it," Bill said, only half in jest. Afterwards, I took to wearing woolen
socks in triplicate on the gloveless hand.

In a crevasse, we found a stanchion of stout English oak that may
(or may not) have come from one of Knight's ships. But that was the
only thing we found which might have had some connection with
the missing expedition. It was also the only wood we saw on the
island . . . unless a few dwarf willows groveling on the ground count
as wood.

On the Biblical seventh day, a foot of snow fell, putting an end to
our search.

Back on the mainland I decided to query Inuit elders about
Knight's disappearance. Only ten generations had passed since his
fateful overwintering—a mere flyspeck of time in Inuit oral tradition.
Even so, I didn't get much information beyond the usual caveats
about the Old Woman and the dire things that happen to those who
don't pay her the proper respect.

At last, in the village of Kangiqsliniq, I met a tall, dignified *inumarit*
(tradition bearer) named Oli Ittinuar who seemed to have an inside
track on the Knight story. Here's a précis of what Oli told me, which is
what he himself heard from the previous generation of elders:

A big boat came to Marble Island in the spring. The people in this
boat didn't like Knight or his men. Shots were fired. Several of Knight's
men died. Then the rest were forced aboard the boat, though whose
boat this was or to where it sailed Oli didn't know.

I thought of the hostilities between France and England over fur-trading rights in the Canadian North. Suppose a French vessel had put in at Marble Island in the spring of 1720 and found Captain Knight, a long-time nemesis, camped there. The scenario might have been very similar to the one Oli described to me.

Yet where would that that "big boat" have gone after it picked up Knight and his men? With so many new mouths to feed, it wouldn't have gone back to France or probably not even to French Canada. And not to any of the English-held forts on Hudson Bay, either. Maybe it didn't go anywhere at all. Maybe the French hadn't known about the Old Woman, and she disposed of them—along with Captain Knight and his men—just as efficiently as she'd disposed of my glove.

Amid such a plethora of question marks, there was only one certainty: that I was damn glad I'd crawled ashore myself.

A Vintage Encounter

I was camped on a small island in Hudson Bay, helping my Cree guide make a moose stew when I heard the telltale sound of a airplane overheard.

Jack, my guide, looked up at the sky. So did I. Here, thirty miles west of Peawanuck, Ontario, there were no scheduled flights. No unscheduled ones, either. Indeed, the southwestern part of Hudson Bay is an area as removed from normal flyaways as anywhere in the world.

The plane began to circle our camp. Uh-oh, I thought, here comes trouble. This was a guilt reflex, of course. The same guilt reflex a person might have at the unexpected appearance of a policeman.

All at once the plane banked. The next thing I knew, its pontoons were ploughing through the water a hundred or so feet from our island. Then four men dressed rather incongruously in suits, ties, and hip waders jumped out and splashed toward shore. One of them walked up to us and bowed slightly. "May we join you?" he inquired.

I was so far from civilization that such civility struck me as highly suspect.

Travel is a realm of improbable encounters. And the more remote the setting, the more improbable those encounters seem to be. My first thought was that our visitors were representatives of Canada's lengthy legal arm; they'd seen us from the air, and probably thought we were violating some fish or game law. In fact, they turned out to be a group of Italian aristocrats. One was a count, another a duke, and the gentleman in immaculate tweeds was a duke, too—he owned a big estate outside Verona.

"And you?" I asked the man who'd made the introductions, evidently the only member of the group who spoke English.

"I am a king," he smiled. "The 'elevator king' of northern Italy. I manufacture elevators for large office buildings."

Each year, the elevator king told us, the four of them chartered a plane in a different part of the world. Last year they'd hopped around Kamchatka. The year before, Madagascar. And this year it was the Canadian North. What interested them most was meeting Native people and seeing how they lived. So whenever they saw a Native camp, they would drop down out of the sky and visit it. As they were doing right now.

Jack was silent through all of this. I could not imagine what he thought about our visitors. As for me, I felt like I was meeting the cast of a Fellini movie.

Now the elevator king pointed to our stew pot. "You are cooking some sort of animal, yes?"

"Moose," I told him.

One of them said something in rapid Italian, of which I could catch only one word: *vino*. The elevator king nodded.

"What kind of wine are you drinking with it?" he asked.

He looked stunned when I said that there was no wine in our camp. And when he translated this for the others, they looked stunned, too. As if such a thing was not possible.

Even as we spoke, their pilot (a Canadian from Toronto) was bringing ashore some bottles of wine, along with a pot, a cookstove, and a checkered tablecloth. Then the two dukes began cooking up a large quantity of pasta.

"What's that?" whispered Jack.

"Pasta," I said.

"Is it something like spaghetti?"

"The same . . ."

While we were eating our respective suppers, the elevator king began plying us with questions. First, he wondered why we were camping on such a barren little island.

"To escape from the mosquitoes," I told him. "On the mainland, they would eat us alive."

And where did the local Cree spend most of their time? he asked. On relatively mosquito-less islands like this one? In traditional camps? Perhaps in villages? Here I deferred to Jack, who, after all, was a local Cree.

"Actually, we spend much of our time in bush camps on the mainland," Jack said, "but we all have houses in Peawanuck."

"Do your houses have running water and electricity?"

"Yes. Some of us even have TVs and computers."

The elevator king translated this for the others. They didn't seem too surprised by the TVs and computers. At least not as surprised as they were by the conspicuous absence of wine in our camp. They even dipped into their provisions and offered us a veritable wine cellar to remedy our bereft state.

Knowing that they would be most concerned for our welfare if we refused, I accepted a few bottles of valpolicella. In return, I offered them some of our moose. And perhaps thinking we would be insulted if they refused, they accepted that, too.

After dinner our visitors shook hands with us, donned their waders, and splashed back to the plane. With props whirling in a haze of oily fumes, the twin-engine Cessna roared across the water again and then lifted off into the slate-grey northern sky, higher and higher, until it disappeared.

If travel is a realm of improbable encounters, this one seemed to me even more improbable than most. Later, in fact, I found myself wondering if I'd imagined the whole thing. But then I noticed a few thin strands of pasta lying on the island's glacial till. In this boreal setting, they were artifacts as extraordinary as any an archaeologist ever dreamed of.

By the Waters of Walden

Early one Fall morning, I happened to be walking along the shore of Walden Pond. Everything seemed right with the world. The light was canted in such a way as to turn the pond and the trees around it into a clear, crisp etching; a great blue heron swept by with a primordial whoosh of its wings; an old man with a fishing line was frozen in a Norman Rockwell pose. Then I noticed a pair of buttocks floating in the water. They belonged to a woman who, as nearly as I could tell, was naked. A minute or two passed, and the woman remained in exactly the same position, facedown.

My first thought was to approach the old man and find out whether he knew something that I didn't—maybe the woman was a swimmer practicing for some kind of event, or maybe she had a mouthpiece that I couldn't see from where I was standing. But he was lost in a fisherman's reverie, and besides, the woman didn't seem to be moving. So I quickly threw off my shoes and began splashing into the water. It wasn't long before I realized that I was splashing not toward an actual person, living or dead, but toward an inflatable sex doll.

You can imagine my relief. You can also imagine my surprise. Thanks to Henry David Thoreau, Walden is not just a ten-acre kettle pond in eastern Massachusetts; it's also a symbol of liquid Nature, a holy spot for conservationists and literary pilgrims. Even the ordinary citizens who take their leisure in and around this celebrated body of water seem to observe a Yankee caution about profaning it. In other words, it's not the kind of place where you'd expect to find a sex doll.

Thoreau himself might have thought of Tammi (for Tammi, I'm convinced, was the doll's name) as a habitat similar to a floating log and inspected her underside to see if any stone fly larvae or mollusks had taken up residence there. Or, being a practical sort of fellow, he might have used her as a gate hinge. For me, however, she was litter, albeit somewhat unusual litter, so I removed her from the water and deflated her, or at least deflated as much of her as I could—she seemed to have a faulty valve, so not all of the air escaped.

"Crazy kids," the old man observed, and then went back to staring at his line. I assumed this was an oblique reference to some sort of revelry which he, seemingly a fixture here, had witnessed. A high school party, drunken locals, a horny youth—the possibilities were myriad.

The only trash receptacles at Walden are in the vicinity of the bathhouse. And here I was, almost a mile from these receptacles and with a half-crumpled sex doll flung over my shoulder. Tammi's mouth, while not exactly lifelike, gaped open in a more or less provocative manner; her legs drooped down my back in an attitude of acquiescence. As I walked toward the bathhouse, a jogger in lycra regarded me with disbelief, and a man with a clerical collar shot me a look that stopped just short of contempt.

"She isn't heavy, Father," I should have told the cleric, "she's only made of air and synthetic rubber."

Still, I was beginning to feel a bit self-conscious, especially when a little girl asked her mother why an apparently grown man was carrying around a doll, and also why the doll in question seemed to be dead. The mother turned her daughter's head dramatically away from me. More dramatically, I dare say, than she would have turned it in Central Park or Boston Common, both settings where perverts like me are known to prosper.

A few minutes later a poodle manicured like a topiary and so obviously pedigreed that it could have been a candidate for *Burke's Peerage* stretched its leash in my direction and, upon seeing Tammi, burst into a series of indignant yaps, as if to say, How vulgar, how perfectly vulgar . . .

I was trying to decide whether or not to dropkick this rarefied canine into the pond when a park ranger on horseback appeared on the path. Still holding Tammi, I braced myself for a reprimand. *Sir, I expected to hear the ranger say, This is a State Reservation and it is strictly forbidden to bring items like that here. You say you found it in the lake? Oh, yeah?* But he only gave me a lascivious wink—one naughty male greets another?—and continued on his rounds.

By now I was on my final approach to the bathhouse, and while not flaunting Tammi, neither was I trying to hide her.

"Hey, man," a teenage kid shouted at me. "Why don't you blow it all the way up?"

"Bizarre!" one of his friends exclaimed. As a manifestation of Nature's bounty, this was better, a whole lot better, than a great horned owl or a loon striking evensong.

An infant pointed toward me and gurgled happily.

A distinguished-looking gentleman with a hardback copy of *Walden* grimaced as if in pain when he caught sight of what I was carrying.

I did my environmental duty and deposited Tammi in the nearest trash bin. Even so, I couldn't help but think that I was depriving future visitors of a sight considerably more exotic than the grey squirrels and chipmunks they would usually see around here. That Tammi did not consist of flesh and blood, or fur and blood, hardly mattered; she was a magnet for the eye, an astonishment, a provocation, a balm for the curious. Also, when I stowed her in the trash, I confess I felt a little sad. For we had been through a lot together, she and I.

In the Country of the Tinkers

(from *Our Like Will Not Be There Again*)

A n untenanted lot beside a foundry in Sligo town: rusted scraps of iron, giant fernery, a few wadded pages from the *Sligo Champion*, empty bottles of stout and "100 Pipers" Scotch Whiskey, an empty box of Jeyes Mansize Tissues, the defunct body of an Austin Minor, scattered orange peels, several tins depleted of their Batchelor's Peas long ago, a sweep's brush battered beyond repair, broken glass, and a discarded billboard advertising Player's Cigarettes, which are said to please; the whey-headed girl-child of eleven or twelve, a bottle of Guinness resting between her hands, is seated on an old motor-car muffler listening to the ramblings of her elders. Eight or ten men and women have improvised a campfire amid this refuse. The scene is enough to draw a prolonged keen from the dedicated social worker; and a prolonged exegesis from the sociologist.

"Sure, we still have the 'reelies' now," one woman, bound by a nest of faded shawls, remarks of this fugitive gathering. At her feet is a muddy infant, gently asleep. She takes a draught from her bottle of Guinness, and her eyes close with a shudder of ecstacy.

I ask this woman where she got the Scottish word "reelies," and she replies, "Oh, I been travelin' the most of me life. Yer picks up things when yer travelin'."

"At night, when the poor farmer is sleepin', that's when she picks them up," a man roars, and there is a burst of laughter that seems to unite this motley crowd.

I have sat down with these "tinkers" because I happened to be passing on the street when I heard a few words cradled in an antique brogue.

"Yer a great storyteller, Winnie, bugger the rest."

"Bugger the King of Englind, now."

"She's a Queen now, in Englind."

"Well, bugger her, an' all her lords, dukes, an' earls."

"Aye."

"Sewage, filthy scum, filthy riffraff," exclaimed a man in a western tourist office when I inquired where in his town I could find some of these traveling folk. He was not, I gathered, referring to the tourists. Later, when I asked a local tinker about this man's hostility, he shrugged and shook his head and said, not without a touch of irony, "Why, in me grandfather's time, that fellow's people sold their women to the British soldiers in the army garrison here."

Yet to some extent, they are dirty, in the way that people without adequate domestic facilities often are; and to the extent that an office worker is civilized, tinkers are indeed primitive. But it is each generation's presumption to think of itself as less primitive than the one that preceded it, to consider itself more advanced because it is possessed of bigger cities and thicker jungles of man-eating technology. "I woulda gone t'work in London, an I coulda gone," an old Galway tinker told me, "but I heard that it was a wild an' savage place." In certain barren locales, the old orders and rituals of cohesiveness have been swallowed up by mass culture; at least that's what I take it this tinker meant, himself a part of a fiercely communal group, when he called London "a savage place." Very big creatures have a way of not keeping the various sections of their bodies straight. There was never anything especially intelligent about the brontosaurus; it just had an insatiable appetite and a plodding yet inexorable manner.

In 1974, a member of Ballina's Urban Council suggested that all the traveling people be sterilized and then sent to the Aran Islands to live out their lives. This good councillor must have forgotten that the Arans have become a centerpiece for tourism in the West, attracting a thousand day-trippers from Galway of a summer's day. A sterilized tinker does not begin to evoke the same appeal for these tourists as a cart ride with an Aran jarvey around the island, past smiling children who charge just a few shillings to be photographed in their natural setting.

Hatred of the tinker, I think, is hatred of the past. The more violent it is, the greater the need to blot out past images, to lie about origins, to sever the connections between history and one's own person. To be anonymous. For tinkers are like survivals from past generations of rural Ireland, tattered and sustained by drinking, deposited on the self-regarding present by the warp of time and their traveling. Constant movement suspended their growth, and isolated them from the centers of money and knowledge; the endless road taught them perseverance. Owning very little, they clung to their natural customs as other people do to their possessions. And after a time, they came to be considered the people of another country (for the past is another country). An unearthly region where there are hexes and fortune telling, and a few men making things out of tin. A mysterious region: tinkers are somehow supposed to remain healthy by eating soot.

People walk up to them on the streets now, and ask to have their fortunes told, and the tinkers are only too glad to comply, for a few pence. "Yes, yer baby will be a boy." Yet such predictions are set pieces, offered impassively and from a distance—for the tinker looks upon the settled Irishman as a foreigner, too.

The name "tinker" did not give offense until quite recently. It derives from the sounds the tinsmith made at work, and a hammer striking metal was not an indecent sound for the longest time. But when the trade of tinsmithing floundered after the last war, the term started to be used against the remaining practitioners of it, to suggest that perhaps they had outlived their usefulness. And now, with the trade nearly dead, "tinker" can be an insult, a sort of equivalent to "nigger," especially when it falls from the lips of a shopkeeper or publican. There is a young traveling man in Dublin who regularly takes the offending party to the courts if the word "tinker" ever so much as crosses his hearing. The 1963 *Report of the Commission on Itinerancy,* official concern written all through its pages, invented the more neutral words "itinerant" and "traveler" to attach to these people, and since then, those two words have become public domain, rallying cries that knit liberal brows. Yet when an older traveling man calls one of his comrades a "tinker," that is very nearly a term of endearment. For then it has a life-giving effect, as though thirty years of moribundity had been shattered with the tinkling of a word.

The generation sitting at this fire, mostly people in their forties and fifties, prefer "tinker" because of its familiarity. They do not exactly *like* the word, but it is what they've always been called. So it will suffice. Concerning the two recent substitutes for it, one man chortles, "Some shit will never flush." Though he is more pleased with that image than anything else, "itinerant" does exude a counterfeit elegance to him. "We used t'be called 'tinkers.' 'Course some of them is gettin' a bit genteel now and they likes the bigger words, like 'itin'runt.' " And I think "traveler" must conjure up an image for him of an English tourist sniffing the countryside for a Bed and Breakfast. Plainer words suit him better; unpaved roads, too, were once more appropriate to his movements.

Right now, released into drink, these people are hardly interested in pondering the question of nomenclature. They are sitting in this place of discards, discards themselves, and the exuberance of their talk tells me that they are happy. Slowly, I catch the story—first one man telling it, then another elaborating on what he's just said—of how this disheveled version of the outdoors got to be their drinking establishment.

For some time, the appearance of one or more of them in the bar of Kelleher's Hotel had put the fear of God in the management there. The wind was starting to flow between them and the bar's other patrons. "Us folks" were the barbarians at the gates, calling for their porter. Civilized people were starting to stay away; even the uncivilized ones were looking askance at this flotsam of the road. Finally, these "lawless vagabonds" (as the newspapers often call them, apparently confusing them with Robin Hood's men) were refused service at the bar; yet, no harm, they could still buy drink to take away, which is what they do several times a week, consuming it here. They do not tend to think of this treatment as objectionable, except in the rain.

"'Tis baycause we're a right drunken curse of God crowd," arghs Winnie O'Brien. She would often make off with the sample cases of commercial travelers who'd stop in Kelleher's for a bit of sustenance between sales.

Then, Anne O'Brien, Winnie's daughter, would often go inside to beg with her baby swathed in rags, cajoling likely strangers with "Misther, could y' gimme somethin' for the wee wan t'asn't et in t'ree days?" When refused her half crown, she'd deposit the baby in the victim's lap, saying, "Here, y'take care of him, then."

With pints on him, Michael McCarthy would use the opportunity to punch one of his comrades. He insists that he has never "laid me fisht" to anyone other than another traveling person.

Biddie Ward would try to sell used clothing "t'the gentry that would gather inside."

"Big John" Lawrence, a barge of a man, once threatened one of the Wards with what the local newspaper identified as "a touch of Kung-fu—two batonlike sticks joined by a short chain," but threw this instrument of torture to the floor as the two of them "struck each other with their fists and got into grips with one another."

Anthony Lawrence once crashed an empty bottle of Guinness against the jukebox when the publican told him he already had "too much drink taken." "I only let me own people tell me that," he says.

Anthony's wife Teresa would mix drink and strong language in a fashion unacceptable to delicate ears.

Packy Ward would never participate in any of these rows, but he was not beneath removing odd items of furniture from the premises while a row was in progress. But for this technique, his house would be mostly bare.

Patsy Flynn, the loser in this arrangement, was guilty by association. "The boozin' " had never affected him one way or the other. If it did not drive him, as it did the others, to acts of an antisocial nature, neither did it impel him to that overripe sociability that often hastens a brawl. "I stop at eight pints, that's me limit."

It is in such acts of cunning and violence that these people, the oddments of perhaps the very old aristocracy of Ireland, respond to the present moment. And in telling jokes at the expense both of themselves and "the buffers" (the settled population), they turn away the time that crowds them into the vacant lots beyond respectability. Into those scraps of abandonment that fairly describe the public attitude toward them. Nowadays they are at one with nature only in places where nature has been written off as a loss.

This campfire itself helps point to something essential for them. Though the afternoon air presses the skin with a warmth that makes fires redundant, it is the ritual of assemblage, not the heat, that matters. The fire, with the force of a magnet over steel filings, draws them here as to some remote, pleasing memory. It creates a community dissolving all loss of community beyond the space of its heat.

But a campfire represents a relapse, of a sort. In the contemporary past, ten years ago and more, it would have rewarded a day's efforts with a "budget" pack wherein a man attempted to barter a few antiquated skills for a little money, or a cabbage and some spuds. Today, in the middle of a town the size of Sligo, it is a positive eccentricity. Because the O'Briens, the Wards, the Lawrences, and the McCarthys are no longer "on the road," except for occasional scrap-dealing forays, and "the road," in any event, is no longer "open" like it once was, with wide margins where a tent could be pitched and horses could wander. On a narrow road, the motorcar will assassinate a tinker's cart. So the County Council has put them into cramped *tigíns*, pseudo-houses that are a step toward legitimate settlement; if they respond decently to these dwellings, if they do not attempt to make them conform more to nature through small acts of house destruction, then they become eligible for tenement flats, which are a step toward oblivion. The Lawrences inhabit a flat near Kelleher's Hotel. The rest of them are still at the *tigín* stage, and their houses have been dispersed to the four corners of Sligo in an effort to dismantle the clannishness that this fire, temporarily, is restoring to them.

Drink, too, gives them a united front, and it also drives them apart, but when it does that, it solidifies them in their respective clans, and then, woe to the McCarthy from whom a Ward has purchased an imperfect horse on good faith. Duplicity like that usually results in a man defending the blood of his clan with his own flesh, fighting from one stupor until he's bashed into another. Brawling is a very old virtue from pre-industrial times; it brings into hand-to-hand contact people who would otherwise have been ciphers to each other. In the old hero tales, it has the desirability of love.

Only drink can make them heroic nowadays. Only the imbibing of what "Big John" Lawrence calls "God in a bottle" can sponge away the dusty burden of being alive at the wrong time. Yet, as "Big John" says, it is very traditional with them to improve their minds with great amounts of drink: "Not long ago, when there wasn't houses for us in it at all, there was nothin' you could spend yer money on but drink. You wouldn't buy chairs or beds or this sort of thing, baycause you hadn't the house t'put them in. Drink would give you anythin' you wanted, in yer mind, like. Even wit' houses now, they still stick t'the old custom of spendin' all their money on drink. I think meself that a good pint is better than anything you could put in a house, don't you?" For him, drink is a rapid transit to the interior life; the interior furnishings of a house are, well, not connected with the interior life. The tedium of possessions: the tinkers get tired of their things quickly, and trade them away and then trade what they get for them away. "Big John" owns three wristwatches; he got them for a concertina, which he had gotten for a bicycle, for which he had traded a new set of chimney-sweeping brushes. "I figured the day of the sweep, it would soon be over."

Lacking property, these people lack the acquisitor's proper respect for it. To cast a stone through a shop's window is no different from casting it into a field after a rabbit: farmers don't claim the rabbits that undermine their fields as their own possessions.

And God created objects to turn them into fire. For example:

A rotted fence encloses these grounds, and Teresa Lawrence has just kicked a grey slat from it, the one on which is imprinted PRI-VATE PROPERTY. She whacks it against a large stone, throwing the slivered pieces into the campfire. She can't read, but since the written word to her mind exists only to tell her what she cannot do, where she can't drink or put up a "temporary dwelling," it doesn't matter.

The rest of the group have a good laugh at Teresa's decision to place this fence at the disposal of their fire. But they don't seem to realize the precise beauty of burning PRIVATE PROPERTY. Sitting by himself, Patsy Flynn merely smiles. He can read. Still, some years ago he couldn't read either "good, bad, or indiff'runt," and he mentions that he once tethered his horse to a NO PARKING sign outside the town of Tuam. "I thought that the sign said you could tie yer horse there, see," he says. The syntax of his face barely moves: his education came too late to prevent him from being here.

Anthony Lawrence's two little girls are ripping fiercely at each other's frocks. In a fit of jealousy, the younger one has just kicked over the older girl's bottle of cider because their father had spiked it with whiskey, ignoring her own, and now she is defending herself against a physical assault. "You little tinker bitch," she screams at her sister after her right side has been laid bare to the waist. Anthony, ignoring his fighting daughters, begins to talk with disgust of a certain local shop-keeper who has a mastiff on the premises to keep the tinkers away. This dog recently bit one of his daughters when she entered the shop for a stick of candy.

Suddenly, Winnie O'Brien wonders what has become of Packy Ward. He is supposed to be delivering additional Guinness from Kelleher's, and he has been gone far too long. "He'd be a good messenger t'send for death," she comments. Several pairs of eyes look with approval on her: she has just hatched a bon mot.

In her late fifties, Winnie looks at least twenty years older. On her face is compressed the cumulative weight of having to bear "sixteen childher, an' only eight of them still in it." The honey of peace is not to be found in her eyes. Her features are so wind-whipped and striated, Jacob Epstein would have needed to add nothing to them: in these features, one sees the contours of a rural geography, roads and winding rivers and hillocky rises. Such skin as she does possess, stretched to its papery limits, is more than a man can envy.

Winnie remains the constant delight of this group. They are enter-tained by her resourcefulness and general waggishness. They defer to her when she starts to speak, and they watch her when she starts to move. Her body may look frail, but there is still a defiant crispness in her use of it.

A "dudeen," a small clay pipe, is tucked behind her ear, beneath the hair. She tells me that she hates smoking it, but she'll do it anyway if she thinks someone in the streets will be charmed enough by this hearkening back to the "Ould Oireland." In begging, she is just as cal-culating. She reels off stories so patently absurd that she is often rewarded for her performance more than her sorrowful bearing: "Will y'gimme a half crown, misther, for t'send me four stupid sons t'be eddicated at Trinity College?" These appeals, which she knows no one believes, give her the opportunity to match wits with the settled pop-ulation. She aims straight for their ideal of upward mobility. Her own sense of mobility takes a different direction, leading on a level from one place to the next, going nowhere.

"Tell us a story, tell us a story, Winnie," chant two of the children, who have been throwing empty bottles into the fire.

She accommodates them immediately, launching into a boozy monologue, the principal topic of which is indeed the recent peregrinations of her own boozy cunning. Ending with:

". . . a man is a man, anyway, an' this last fellow gave me a drink for nothin'. 'Twas just this Friday last. He was a big man wit' a big saloon car, a lovely car. 'Hello,' he said t'me. 'How y'doin', misther,' says I. ' 'Tis a great day.' 'Tis a great day,' says I. 'Yer a great talker,' he says. 'Not so bad at all, but come here,' says I t'im, an' I says, 'Do you know what you can do for me?' An' he dasn't, bless him, he dasn't know! So I says, 'For the love of God, sir, will y'gimme ten bob for a coupla bottles of stout, an' I'll say a prayer for yer!' 'If yer as good a singer as a talker, I'll give it t'yer.' 'I'm a singer the likes of which y'ave never sane before,' says I. So we wint t'Michael Henry's, no, James Henry's pub, an' I says t'im, I says, 'I'll stand outside the door, 'cause if yer ashamed wit' me t'gwin, I'll stand outside.' 'Not at all,' he says. 'Gwin.' So he left down half dozen of stout an' I said, 'That's very nice an' thanks an' God bless.' 'Oh for God's sakes, sing,' says he. 'Well, gimme a whiskey an' I'll sing anythin' you want,' says I. 'A whiskey, then,' he says. 'Gwon, drink up that then an' sing,' says he. 'Gwon.' 'Well, I never sang in me whole life,' I says t'im, an' up an' walked out."

"With the stout," reminds one of the children. The gist of the story is in the public domain.

"Wit' the stout," Winnie says in triumph.

"Y'd want t'be middlin' cute for that make of man," says her daughter Anne.

"Y'd want fine wits in yer head, all right," she says. Drink has saturated her Muse irreparably, but she still has conferred on this mere "crack" some of the measured sanctity of the wonder tale. She cannot help it; she is a Grand Dame infused with Guinness, and experience comes to her begging to be parlayed into an anecdote.

In the Country of the Tinkers

This is the last recourse of storytelling in Winnie's generation: to skewer the "buffers." Their plots all focus on that. The story possibilities are limited, but they at least clarify this late urban world, locating identities that would otherwise be lost to slum housing. In the retelling of such incidents, they disavow the covering of city cement, the most stifling of all underbrush. Let it be banal, the theft of a roll of toilet tissue, and all the better, it will be turned into a pitched battle between themselves and the "buffers." The results will be a story which makes them seem like Finn McCool's men toying with a militia of mongoloids. Real life is just as merciless; there, however, they themselves are the victims and they drizzle from street to street in the winter of their ruin, ignoring words because they cannot read them.

At last Packy Ward returns with the extra supply of stout.

"Do y'like t'let the grass grow under yer feet, then?" someone asks him.

Packy scowls, and his hair, which naturally sticks out like a thistle, seems to stick out all the more. As it turns out, he has been followed by one of the guards, Guard Kearney, they all know him, a terrible man for harassment. To divert him from their unauthorized assembly, he, Packy, has had to trek over half of Sligo with the stout in his hands.

None of them is sure that he hasn't instead supped a few inaugural drinks with some of the McDonoughs just arrived from Galway and pulled up in their caravan on the Ballina road. But they quickly take the bottles he offers them.

Anthony Lawrence and Michael McCarthy begin to reflect upon the recent death in Loughrea of "King" Ward, "the king of the tinkers" and the pride of the Ward clan, a man of vast generosity who would never have kept his comrades waiting for a drink. These two men were at the king's funeral, along "wit' ev'ry son of a tinker in this country," the news of his death having spread faithfully from family to family (none of whom own telephones). They puzzle themselves with the thought of names, other than those of the old and infirm, which were conspicuous by their absence. Finally, Michael mentions

289

a Ballina man he hadn't seen there, but "he's becomin' a reg'lar nuisance, wit' money in the bank an' all."

There is accord between them: the media publicity given the king contributed in some obscure fashion to his downfall. Michael says that the tinkers no more require a king than do the Irish people at large. This idea of a king was the invention of "the eejots wit' the newspapers" who thought it would be "cute" if the tinkers had a king. As if they really didn't obey any laws but their own. Then, Michael says, having built him up, the newspapers proceeded to tear him down again. "They showed a picture of him in front of his little house in Loughrea. He was comin' out in the morning after bein' drunk the most of the night, it looked like. They said 'This is the King of the Tinkers in his castle.' Flashed him with the camera all boozed up, poor fellow."

I read his meaning: the king died of exposure.

"But he was a fine lad of a man, anyway!" Anthony exclaims.

"An' he wasted what time he was given, rest him," Michael says. "They say that when a man of his sort dies, he will turn inta an old mule an' carry the Orangeman inta Hell."

Then the two of them fall into a heated debate on the virtues and flaws of going up to Belfast in order to purchase furnishings from bomb-damaged pubs and sell them as antiques in the Republic. Their feelings are not much affected by the "troubles" in the North; they have their own troubles.

These traveling people, their travels at an end, inhabit two worlds, the one buried and the other perpetually unborn. The twisted geometries of scrap objects must suffice for their countryside; and their campfires are clandestine now. At their age, with their skills, they are hardly assimilable. The only hope is for their children, who still have the chance to grow up and be like everyone else.

Like the Irish-speaking pockets of the West, the traveling people are a small nation cloaked by a larger one. This nation includes approximately fourteen hundred families, with an indeterminate number of children, who are not always registered, the assumption being that if simple baptism was good enough for their parents, it should be good enough for them. These families are larger now than they ever were before, as though they're arming themselves through youthful reinforcement against a possible purge. Still, the increase of his tribe has always been a matter of considerable importance to the traveling person. Perpetuating his own name, a man attains himself in all his power and glory. The craving for progeny—it has very little to do with sexual self-esteem—reflects an almost holy attitude toward clan and heredity. It goes back to the time when the country was just a collection of warring clans and a chieftain's family and his soldiery were one and the same. Even today, onto the lives of the few tinkers who remain unmarried is inscribed a stigma something like excommunication.

The clan is money in stressful times, when an errant stone has shattered a confectioner's window, and it is mutual aid, when a mountain of scrap needs collecting. Clans *feud*, they don't compete; and feuding clansmen have a closer relation to each other than they do to people on the outside with whom they are on remote good terms. In this world, the urge toward competition has never dictated behavior; family groups will tarmac a road together or they will battle each other over a humiliated girl or a stolen horse, but they will never, never go into business against each other. Private enterprise is not their bag of oats. They are more accustomed, even in the staging of a brawl, to the spirit of cooperation. This is why many of them suffer unusual withdrawal symptoms trying to adjust to urban "society," which is competitive rather than social in the way that their own lives have always been.

On the pre-industrial lifeways of the West, these people themselves are like a window. Despite its apparent fragility, the window has managed to stay intact, if somewhat smudged, and through it, there is the blurred prospect of the old self-contained life of the country, the communal ethic, the tolerance of eccentricity, vital words. Their work habits, on those occasions when work they can perform is offered them, remain pre-industrial with a vengeance; they prefer piecework to wages and they would no more think of laboring for a deferred reward than of operating guesthouses. About the closest they ever come to capitalism is in the shabby stalls they sometimes set up on the outskirts of a town in order to hawk umbrellas, religious icons, and used clothing. But this is just a more sophisticated version of "tinkering."

Not having Irish, the tinkers cannot get the language grants received by denizens of the Gaeltacht. However, the older ones among them still have *Shelta*, or "cant" in the vernacular, a concoction of seventeenth century sham Latin, Romani (the gypsy tongue), English, and old Irish. "Big John" Lawrence: "There was a tinkerman who said t'Cromwell, 'Your gris to the mídil.' When Cromwell asked him t'translate it, your man wouldn't, so he said, 'I can't,' and that's why it's called 'cant' today. What did he mane by those words? 'Your soul to the Devil.' " This "cant" is like a back slang. The tinkers use it mostly in the presence of a "straight" person to communicate troublesome information to each other. Like "The glócates are suni'n for you." (The police are looking for you). For obvious reasons, the Irish government chooses not to reward this sort of thing with stipends.

The daily language of the tinkers is the countryman's English of perhaps a hundred years ago. Up until now, their journeyings have insulated them against the standardized English taught in the national schools; they could hardly know that talk is supposed to be pale and wan. Literacy, which can paralyze speech with propriety, was never needed in their lives. On the road it would not refine the making of tinware, nor would it pitch a wattle tent or help put the canvas over that tent's hooped branches. But now, for the first time in the history of their world, to read and write is to enter life; the older ones have chosen settlement on account of their children, who they rightly perceive would be at a greater disadvantage without education than they themselves could ever be. At the end of the road, there is no place to go but the schoolhouse.

A few of them even regret not being able to read or write themselves.

"If I was eddicated," says Winnie O'Brien, "I'd write meself a big book on the origins of the travelin' people. I heard a good many stories about that from me mother, who got them from her mother, that it'd be an awful shame that they'd be lost for the rest of time."

Yet Winnie is preliterate, not illiterate: her mind's frame of reference pays no heed to the recent invention of the printing press. She goes back to the time of talking.

Acknowledgments

"Death on Ice" and "Looking for Henry Hudson" first appeared, albeit in somewhat different form, in *Smithsonian*; "A Visit to the Zoo" and "A Gigantic Mythopoeic Literary Volcano" in The *Atlantic Monthly*; "Beauty and the Beast," "Island of Lost Souls," "In the Land of the White Rajahs," "Yap Magic," "Daughter of the Wind," "A Vintage Encounter," and "Murder Will Out" in *Islands*; "Mountains of Sulfur" in *Summit*; "Feeding My Demon" in *Stitches*; and "By the Waters of Walden" in *Penthouse*. (Copyright © 2001 by General Media Communications. Used by permission.) "An Arctic Cave Man" and "Wanderer" were written as introductions to, respectively, Malcolm Waldron's *Snow Man: John Hornby in the Ravaged Lands* (Kodansha, 1997) and Hassoldt Davis' *The Jungle and the Damned* (University of Nebraska Press, 2000). "A Walk on the Wild Side" and "Dog Day Revolutionary" are excerpted from *Last Places: A Journey in the North* (Mariner Books, 2000); "Tundra" from *Northern Latitudes* (New Rivers Press, 2000); "In the Country of the Tinkers" and "The Last of the Wandering Bards" from *Our Like Will Not Be There Again: Notes from the West of Ireland* (Reprinted by permission of Ruminator Books, 2001); "Our Man in Everest," "In Banda," and "Getting My Goat" from *An Evening Among Headhunters & Other Reports of Roads Less Traveled* (Reprinted by permission of Brookline Books, a Division of Lumen Editions, 1998); "The Dream People" and the accompanying folktales from *Wolverine Creates the World* (Capra Press, 1993); "The Preserved Woman" from *The Wrong-Handed Man* (University of Missouri Press, 1987); and "The Great Winter" from *Parliament of Ravens* (Loon Books, 1986).